The
EXECUTIONER'S
SON

JOHN H. SCHMITZ

PAGE PUBLISHING, INC.
New York, NY

First originally published by Page Publishing, Inc. 2016

ISBN 978-1-68409-447-9 (Paperback)
ISBN 978-1-68348-461-5 (Digital)

Printed in the United States of America

ACKNOWLEDGEMENTS AND THANKS

I T WOULD BE EASY TO think that thanking God is being too cliché, but that would not be right; I owe everything that I am to Him.

This book had a strange beginning. My son John D. Schmitz (Jack) wrote a short story called "Honest Men and Loyal Officers" that seemed an ideal jumping off point for a novel. I encouraged Jack to write another chapter and eventually wrote chapter two in an attempt to shame him into it. The rewritten story became chapter one of this book as the tables turned and my son encouraged me to keep the story going. There would be no book if not for my son's imagination and penchant for writing. He gave me the most food for thought as the book was written.

Others who read Jack's story also encouraged its continuation. I especially want to thank Sam Arafat whom I worked with in Indianapolis for his "you can do this" encouragement. My friend Ken Black was a faithful reader and gentle critic of the work. Jeff Jones was another consistent source of feedback as the story was written. Gary and Darene Weatherlow helped with editing and most importantly convinced me to rewrite Jack's story in my style as the first chapter.

I want to express my appreciation to my sisters, Sonja and Chris. Both of them encouraged me to put aside the "this is crazy, you're not an author" type doubts that plagued my efforts. Beyond that, they did that knowing me and my eccentricities well; it is a true gift to have siblings that unconditionally accept and love you.

My high school buddy, Pete Kerzel provided editing. Pete was an editor of our high school newspaper and has had a career in journalism. He ripped so many articles I wrote back in the day that when he said the manuscript was clean I trusted that he wasn't just being nice.

Finally, nobody put up with more disruptions to normal life than my girlfriend Lynne Rowe. She listened to me talk about the book on dates, and dealt with me giving up time with her in order to write. Thanks so much for being patient, Lynne!

CONTENTS

The Birth of a Dragon

T HE TWO HEAVILY ARMORED SOLDIERS struggled along a path marked by stones through the King's forest preserve. They were determined to accomplish nothing short of vengeance for a death that had occurred but a few hours before.

"Maybe this isn't their path." Stated the younger of the two. Aside from his own arms, he carried a large and heavy steel shield on his back.

"We're in the King's forest, in which only the King and his friends are allowed to hunt. The only people who would leave markings are the King's company or exceptionally stupid poachers." Said the older of the two.

The two had left their home city a mere two hours prior, and a mere two hours before that they had been present when Duke Heimsteady, the King's best friend, and his loyal servant had returned looking badly beaten from what was supposed to have been a simple hunting trip with the King; only the King was not with them. They claimed that the King had been slain by a dragon, which seemed to have taken up residence in the preserve.

Rumors had been circulating for months about strange fires and gigantic foot prints, but most in the city chocked it up to be tall tales made by the sheriff to discourage poachers from going into the forest. Nonetheless, the two hunters were insistent that this beast had claimed their King in a blaze of hellfire.

Sir Malpolem, the older of the two soldiers seeking vengeance, had been in the King's court when the hunters had staggered in and told the urgent news to all present. The queen had instantly fallen into tears, but for the young heir, only eleven years old, the news didn't seem to register. He greeted it with disbelief and shock.

Sir Malpolem had announced before the court that he would track down and avenge his King, bringing back a trophy of the dragon to hang over the throne for all to see. The hunters had urged him to reconsider, or at the very least delay, but one glimpse at the young heir's wide eyes, told him that he would never forget this deed when he came of an age to understand what had happened.

Taking his page, the executioner's orphan who had been in his service for a bit more than a year, he went into the armory and picked the tallest sword, appropriately named Dragon Slayer, with a staggering five-foot blade. Next, he went to his rooms and retrieved his armor, and finally took on credit from the smith a four-foot-tall iron shield, which he hoped would deflect the searing blaze projected from the dragon's maw.

The page was named Jon. He had been the Royal Executioner's son and had lived with his father until about a year ago when he was entirely orphaned. His mother had died giving birth to him and then his father had succumbed to a plague. Being too young to take up his father's trade, his future looked bleak until Sir Malpolem, one of the executioner's few friends, had taken him into service.

"Have you caught your breath yet?" Asked the Knight striking what he thought was a noble pose.

With a grunt, Jon lifted his hands from his knees under the weight of his heavy pack. With the same haste that had taken their breaths over the two-hour hike thus far, they left the road and found that the markers were abundant, leading them deeper into the woods.

Sir Malpolem was a tall, thin, young man who had attained knighthood at a young age for heroically boarding up and defending the monastery library and its treasures from pagan invaders.

"Why were you in there?" Jon had once asked, "Weren't you a weaver's son?"

"Truth be told, I had snuck in." He had said, "My elder brother became a monk and taught me to read Latin when we were younger, but a weaver's son had no place in the library so I was never allowed in there with him. With his help, before he left for pilgrimage, we found ways to sneak in, and he told me the areas the monks rarely went.

"Lucky the monks never found you, they likely would have imagined you a thief."

"Indeed. On the day the castle was attacked, however, they were struck with fear, and rather than turn their attention to actually defending themselves and the library, the fools huddled up and started praying, doing nothing more than turning a rusty iron lock on the front door. While they were praying, I hauled a bookshelf in front of the oak doorway, which only opened inward. It wasn't long before the invaders started banging at it, and presumably sent for a ram to get inside. While they were at the entrance I left by my secret passage, went around to the front, and started throwing rocks at them to get their attention off of the door. It worked, and they chased me back around to a little hole where there once was a latrine up against the building. Once inside, I pushed over a bookshelf to block the hole."

"So you were just buying time, then?" Asked the page.

The knight had nodded in response and continued his story. "The library was quite a large place, and had multiple gaps in the walls that had only half-heartedly been patched up, so I ran around to another one and did more of the same, throwing rocks, and ducking back inside. I was able to keep this up for around twenty minutes or so, which was just enough time for the guards to fight their way towards us from the gate."

"Maybe the monks' prayers were answered?" Suggested Jon.

"That's what they thought, and they took me to be the answer." Said the knight. "When the battle was over they took me before the King and had me tell of my actions. I might've embellished them a bit, but I was afraid not to embellish for fear of losing whatever reward I was to be given."

"So the King knighted you for defending the library?" The page had asked.

"Do you know what the name Malpolem means?" Asked the knight.

"No, I've never heard of a family name like Malpolem."

"In the King's apparently rudimentary understanding of Latin and Greek, he said he wanted me to be the one good thing to come of this bad war, or Mal Polem. After hearing my story, and presumably after having lost a dozen knights that day, he decreed that my name be 'Sir Malpolem'."

It was in his service to the King that the knight came to be friends with the unlikely acquaintance of the royal executioner, Jon's father, two years before he passed. He was the man who piled wood for the stake burnings and dropped the torch into the dry grass, or held aloft the heavy axe waiting for the King to order it to fall. Because of his position, the folk of the castle avoided him as though his trade were infectious. He wore a hood when ending a life, but his role was hardly secret given his quarters in the castle and lack of any other income.

This stigma blighted his son as well. Sir Malpolem, who often had duties patrolling for the King's guard, allowed Jon to accompany him and over the years taught him to read and told him the stories of dragons and adventurers, that now gripped his soul.

As they progressed, they found that the piles of stones became gradually more hastily placed. They became smaller and sometimes contained less stone and more twigs, suggesting either that the group had become more thorough and attentive as they returned to the road, or that the markers were placed by a group travelling in the opposite direction.

They lapsed into a silence that was only interrupted by the sounds of the forest and their own heavy breathing. Before long the scent of cooked meat came to their nostrils in tantalizing waves. They knew what that scent meant, and they stopped in their tracks.

"Poachers." said Sir Malpolem quietly drawing a dagger as they followed their noses.

They came upon a campsite, or at least what had once been one. It had been completely torn apart in apparent haste; there were definitely signs of both fire and combat. In the center of the camp were the remains of a human being.

"Lord above..." Said Sir Malpolem.

"This is..." Jon started, but words failed him. The body was horribly burnt and blackened, and what was left bore only the shape of a person. To Jon, this was not an unfamiliar sight, though the setting was far removed from the "civilized" burnings of heretics that some clergy had a fondness for.

"What happened here?" asked Sir Malpolem, dumbfounded by his surroundings.

"A burning, apparently." said Jon, almost automatically, his attention directed entirely at the scene before him.

"Well obviously, but how?" Asked the knight. "This is not at all what I expected to find."

Jon walked forward toward a nearly dead fire, carefully stepping into the ring and onto the outermost layer of ash. He gasped, and jumped back quickly, Sir Malpolem responding by lifting his dagger reflexively. "What is it?" He asked.

"A sword!" said Jon, "Hot as hell, nearly burnt my heel."

"Let me see it." Sir Malpolem stepped forward, and with a gloved hand grabbed the blade, wrapped in a charred leather sheath. He stripped away the burnt leather, revealing a shockingly well-polished blade, and at its base an elaborate hilt with a ruby in the center. "This is the King's blade." He said, mouth agape.

"Then is that-" Jon asked, but a glimmer on the hand of the charred corpse answered his question for him: it was a ring. In particular, it was a gold ring wrought with an arrangement of beautiful gemstones of all varieties. A precious heirloom of the King's lineage, passed down for seven generations. There was no doubt that this was the body of their King. "This seems like an awfully calm fire to have been lit by a dragon."

"Don't you see?" Asked Sir Malpolem, "There is no dragon; they killed the King themselves and left his body here to burn, using the dragon as a cover-up."

"Why would they do that?" Asked Jon. "They left at least two priceless artifacts, so it couldn't have been money. They didn't stay to make sure the body was burnt completely, so it doesn't seem planned."

"I don't know. I don't know." Sir Malpolem dropped the sword back into the ashes, a small cloud arising where the hilt hit the ground. He staggered backwards and came to lean against a tree, rubbing his forehead. "What the hell is going on?" he asked, quickly approaching rage.

"Well, let's look some more." Jon suggested, not wanting to anger the knight. "It couldn't hurt. It really doesn't look like an assassination or anything."

Sir Malpolem slumped to the ground and covered his eyes. "That smell, that smell! Why would a man make such a smell?" He said breathing through his mouth as he desperately tried to block out the disgustingly appealing smell of roasting meat. Quickly, however, his hastened breaths began to resemble sobs, and as his left hand fell to the ground he broke into weeping.

"Sire?" asked Jon astounded.

Sir Malpolem was supposed to be teaching him the fundamentals of being a knight, yet here he was weeping before his very eyes. Desperate to find relief from that sight, he turned his attention to the somehow less unpleasant corpse. It was far from the first corpse he had seen. Even peddlers were often unwilling to help dispose of remains after an execution, so often his father had employed Jon in that unpleasant task. In doing so, however, he had seen his share of anatomy. When a man's head fell from his shoulders, he knew where tendons would hang, and what bones would be displaced by the axe. As a butcher knew the bodies of the chicken, cow and pig, he knew the body of man.

He first looked at the hands, completely lacking skin, and having much of the cartilage and fat burned away. He could see clear to the bone in many places, but judging by his experience seeing hands and arms chopped off as minor punishments, he saw nothing out of the ordinary.

He then turned his attention to the King's head. The hair had been burnt off, and the skin on the skull was patchy and bone was showing. The King's mouth was gaping open, frozen as though a final scream still gripped his departed soul. His teeth were blackened from the fire, still held in place by rigid gums. Peering into the mouth, however, Jon saw something very out of place. The King's head was slumped forward; his back was being propped up on the charred stump of a log. To Jon's horror, the inside of the King's mouth had hardly been touched by the fire, and the throat was seemingly still unscathed, which meant that nothing should have been showing, yet there at the back of his throat protruded a small bone. "Sire, look!" He exclaimed.

Sir Malpolem, having stopped weeping was now blankly staring in the direction of the pyre, casually watching Jon in his investigation. He got up, and feebly attempted to regain his composure. "Jon, I don't know what I'm looking at." He said.

"There in his mouth; that bone, do you see it?" Said Jon.

"Yes, I think I do, the one with bits of meat dangling off of it?" Replied the now curious knight. "I don't think that's a human bone." Unexpectedly, Sir Malpolem reached a glove hand into the King's mouth, widening his jaw significantly until it was far beyond what a living human could manage. When he removed his hand, it brought with it the bone in question. "Is that...a rib?" He asked.

"I think it is." Said Jon. "So that explains things: the King must have choked to death on his supper." Both of them stood in silence for a few awkward moments taking in the implications of their discovery. It explained the lack of slashing or stabbing wounds on the corpse, as well as the lack of restraints. They would not have been necessary if the King had been burned *after* his death. The King had not been killed by a dragon, but rather by his supper!

"But what about the hunters?" Jon asked, "They came back covered in ash and blood!"

"They must have been trying to protect the King's pride." Replied Sir Malpolem, "The story wouldn't allow them to bring back his belongings so they sought to burn them with him, and plan to return later to destroy the campsite. They probably weren't counting on my heroism, and why should they have? I'm a damned coward and everyone in the court could see it except the King."

"Sire?" Asked the startled page.

"Do you remember when I told you of how I claimed my knighthood, Jon?" Asked Sir Malpolem.

Jon simply looked at him with a puzzled expression.

"Do you remember when I said I had embellished my story?" Continued the saddened knight. "Well, that was true, but much of the rest of my tale was not." He dropped the rib, which he had been staring at in his gloved palm since he had taken it from the King's throat and sat down as Jon took a seat next to him. "I told you I had defended the library and several monks from invading barbarians. In a way, I did, that is true. But not nearly as heroically as I had implied. I had been hiding in the library, and one of the monks found me right as the invasion reached the doorstep of the library. The monks were unaware of the invaders at that point, and quickly threw me out of the front door. The invaders were running up the hill at that time, and the monk who expelled me saw them, and in his haste slammed the door shut and locked it with me outside."

"How merciless!" Said the shocked page.

"Mercy was the one thing on my mind as I saw the blood thirsty invaders running at me brandishing their spears and knives. I was terrified; I couldn't force my legs to run. With nothing to defend myself, I was panicked." The knight paused, his voice cracking. "I wet myself right in front of them. I was humiliated; faced with death, an educated young man like myself, stood with a great yellow streak running down his leg. The barbarians dropped their spears and laughed hysterically."

"Well what happened? They obviously didn't kill you." Said Jon.

"No, but they beat me within an inch of my life. They thrashed me for what seemed like an eternity, until finally one drew his dagger to finally end my life. Just then an arrow struck him in the chest. They were having so much fun tearing me apart, that the King's guard had made their way to the library with the time I had bought them. After the fight, no one had seen just what happened. The guard charged right past me without a thought, and the monks finally opened the door. Feeling repentant, they brought me in to make sure I didn't get trampled by the soldiers charging out of the castle."

"And since no one saw what really happened..." Began the page.

"I told them I had fought to keep them from damaging the library." Said the knight finishing the sentence. His hand went again to cover his eyes. "I've been a good knight haven't I? I left the castle sincerely intending to avenge my King or die trying."

"Yes sir, if you hadn't earned your knighthood before, you would have now." Replied Jon.

Just then, Sir Malpolem gave a gasp and a stream of blood began to flow from his throat. A dagger had lodged firmly in its base. Jon's eyes widened and he got up to flee, but as soon as he turned he collided with a large man clad in the leather of a hunter. It was the Duke who had been hunting with the King. "Don't fear, I'm not in the mood to spill more blood today." He said as his assassin crept out from behind a tree. "I've heard much of what you said, you two."

"Then what do you want?" Asked Jon.

"I imagine you've seen this body, and recognized who it is?" The Duke responded.

"Yes, the King." Answered Jon, eliciting a groan from the Duke who was probably hoping that the two had not been so keen. "We also know how he died." Continued the now frightened young man pointing to the rib that had fallen among the outer ashes.

"That is good, then. I do not have to try to convince you of our innocence." Said the Duke in a commanding voice.

"Innocence?" Exclaimed Jon as anger began to mix with his fear. "How can you speak of innocence when my master lies dead at your assassin's hands?"

"Nobody was more shocked than I was when, as we sat at the fire laughing the night away, the King suddenly stiffened like a board and started grabbing at his throat." Said the Duke. "I got up to see what was the matter, but there was no saving him. He passed before our eyes, anticlimactically, and appallingly." He walked towards the corpse and reached down to remove the ring from the King's hand. Walking back to the edge of the fire pit he picked up the sword as well. "After we had calmed down, I had to decide what to do. If we went back without the King and his belongings saying that he had choked to death on his meal, we would have been accused of murder."

"But why did you kill Sir Malpolem?" Asked Jon.

The Duke was irritated, having his tale interrupted, and nearly struck Jon for the disrespect, but he restrained himself, and his fists quickly unclenched. "Sir Malpolem was a do-gooder as long as I knew him." He said. "I had always suspected that he had lied his way to knighthood, but until now I had no evidence. All that talk of 'earning his knighthood'; he would've gone back and told the entire truth, and in doing so would have destroyed the honor of our King, and the integrity of his closest allies."

"And what's wrong with the truth?" Said the recklessly emboldened listener.

The Duke was growing more and more impatient. This boy had been given all of the details but still did not see. "The truth would be the death of everyone involved in this affair, and in the long run of the entire Kingdom." Remarked the Duke pointedly. "If I were found to be lying about how the King died, there would be no trial; I would be executed as a usurper, since it is myself and my peers who will manage the Kingdom until the heir comes of age. Without my advice he would be forced to turn to the clergy, who have no knowledge of how to defend the Kingdom. I have no desire to end your life, but if you cannot see just how delicate of a matter this is, I fear I will have to silence you." He reached for his dagger, clearly showing what he meant.

"Fine." Jon said, staring at the remains of his mentor. "I can see that the worth of one man is less than that of a Kingdom. Sir

Malpolem came here to avenge his King, but he is dead. It may not be the way he imagined, but if his memory can contribute to the welfare of the Kingdom, I think he might rest easy." The words weighed heavily on Jon, but he knew that his own death would contribute nothing to the memory of Sir Malpolem. "I will not challenge your testimony, but how does your story cover what's happened now?"

"Simple." Duke Heimsteady said, smiling at Jon's conversion. "Sir Malpolem and his page came out to avenge their King, as everyone at the castle knows." He went over to the remains of the King. "Our poor King, and poor Sir Malpolem, both claimed by dragon fire. By the time we arrived, the dragon had departed. We found a singed field, two flame-bitten corpses, and an unconscious page thrown against a tree by the dragon's tail.

"We recovered the belongings of both the King and Sir Malpolem. They had been abandoned by the dragon, far from a stupid beast, likely knowing that so long as it held onto those things knights would seek it out. And so our story ends; we found you unconscious against a tree, gathered the King's and Sir Malpolem's possessions, and returned to the castle. Sir Malpolem is given a hero's death, as is our King, and you, having faced a dragon, will likely be invited into the King's guard. One day you may even see knighthood yourself."

The assassin handed a shovels to the Duke and Jon. They were to bury the remains of the King and Sir Malpolem, and then burn the area to the ground.

"So that's it then?" Said Jon as they finished. "We make such a grand story to cover up an embarrassing death, and it costs the life of another good man?"

"Well," The Duke said, his eyes narrowing, "I can't say I believed Sir Malpolem's second story either."

Sir Malpolem was buried under a meager two feet of dirt, with no coffin. Two urns that the Duke had provided were filled with ashes from the camp, and were passed as the remains of the two dragon victims. They would be given a proper burial back at the castle. Their headstones read: "A Profound Warrior of God", and "Avenger of the King."

By torchlight the three men returned to the castle. Jon carried the urns said to be holding the ashes of the King and Sir Malpolem, but in truth they held only the legacy of a campsite. Despite knowing this, Jon felt the full weight of two men.

2

Brave or Stupid

JON WAS NERVOUS. IT HAD been five days since the death of the King and Sir Malpolem, and the Kingdom had been in a hectic tide of activity, first memorializing the King, and now preparing for the coronation of a new King. Jon had been largely ignored living in Sir Malpolem's old quarters in the castle, but had been evicted this very morning as the room would be needed for the coming guests.

Jon had spent his time waiting for word from the Duke that he was to join the guard, but no word had come. He had thought about how he would react if he were in the Duke's position and his conclusion alarmed him: Jon knew too much and if he were in the Duke's shoes he would almost certainly have himself removed, or even killed. The more he thought about it the less he understood why the Duke had let him live in the first place.

Having been booted out of his place to live, and having concluded that the Duke would probably want him dead, Jon next received word that the Duke expected him at his residence post haste, so, not knowing what else he could do, Jon set out on the path to the

Duke's manor. It had been a rough day so far, but it had all the promise of getting worse. In fact, this could be his last day on earth, but Jon felt he was doing what he needed to do and resolutely progressed the four miles or so that stood between him and his future.

The fact that Jon carried all of his worldly possessions with him did not burden him on his journey. He wore a rough tunic over some breeches and carried three soft apples and half a loaf of stale, coarse rye bread that he had scavenged from what was left of Sir Malpolem's supplies. He also carried his prized possession, a short sword that had been his weapon in his former life as a page. Unlike most of those around him his feet were clothed as well. Jon had found an old and worn pair of soft leather boots that were only a little too large for his feet. It may not seem like much, but it was more than he had ever personally owned in his life, still it certainly was not enough to weigh him down as he pursued his destiny.

As he came closer to the manor the first thing he noticed was a low earthen wall that surrounded the main compound. It did not seem that it would be very useful as a defense, but within the wall stood the manor itself, a sort of fortified house. It was mostly built of stone but also had some wooden parts, mainly on certain windows and the roof. Additionally, it had slight openings in the stone work where archers could stand in defense against attackers. It was a formidable building, but somehow it maintained a certain charm and warmth; it was somehow both a fort and a home. Surrounding it were much meaner dwellings where servants and peasants lived, except for a large and substantial wooden barn that housed horses and a few milk cows. To Jon the manor seemed like a dreamy place to live; it smelled less like the town, was far less crowded, and the people here seemed to have a sense of purpose as they moved about. Where the town had shadows, the manor had sunshine and light. Where the city offered views of filth and mud, the manor had pastures and open space. Involuntarily he set himself a goal of someday living in the courts of a manor like this.

As he walked through the crude wooden gate in the wall he and the Duke's assassin simultaneously spotted each other and the assassin immediately strode towards him. "I see that you answered the Duke's summons." He said. "Well, you're either very brave or very stupid; I guess time will tell which. Follow me and we'll see if the Duke has time for us right now."

Jon grunted in reply, but the remark unsettled him. The slight joy he had felt by observing the manor scene was immediately dispelled and replaced by a more intense version of the dread he had felt in setting out on this journey. Jon did not feel brave, but he did not like the alternative that had been presented to him.

The assassin escorted Jon to a door off to the side of the main door to the manor house and into a room filled with people of seemingly poor circumstance. Jon followed him as he crossed the small crowded room and approached an attendant standing by another door.

"Please tell the Duke I am here with the guest he sent for." The assassin said to the attendant. This man gave a disdaining glance at Jon and turned to go in the door.

Jon glanced around the room. It was filled with dirty people for the most part; old women, younger women with children and a few nervous looking men.

"Who are these people?" asked Jon.

"They are here to seek justice from the Duke." Responded the assassin. "The Duke is very busy. They will have a long wait before their cases are heard."

In a few minutes the attendant returned and the assassin and Jon were escorted through the door into the room beyond. It was not an overly large room, but seemed spacious after the crowded waiting area. This spaciousness was helped by the fact that there was little furniture consisting only of a large chair near the center of one wall and a nearby desk occupied by what Jon took to be a scribe. On the other side of the chair was another door. The attendant went back to the waiting room and Jon stood uncomfortably and waited in the center of this imposing and nearly empty room.

As they stood waiting Jon wondered about what sort of justice he could expect in this room. Indeed, he wondered what sort of justice he deserved, and he felt fear welling up inside of him. As he stood waiting he wondered what justice even was. Was it what was best for the Duke, or was there a higher ideal of justice? If it was the Duke's purposes that were to be served, then he would likely expect to be killed. If it was a higher justice that the Duke served, he felt innocent of any wrong doing; at least there was none who could justifiably accuse him.

Jon felt strongly that he was a good person, and he had some faith that the Duke was a good person, but then again he had seen Sir Malpolem fall dead by the Duke's order; how good a person was he? He stood there waiting, and brooding, and the more time that passed the more frightened he became. Why had he not run away? Was he stupid?

At last the door next to the chair opened and Duke Heimsteady walked in. He looked at Jon, and then the assassin and nodding said "Boady." Apparently that was the assassin's name.

The Duke turned to the scribe and said "You are not needed right now. Go and have something to eat." The scribe gathered his parchments and immediately left by the door to the waiting room.

The Duke sat down and turned to Boady saying: "Insure that we are alone." The assassin looked about the room, and then went to the door by which the Duke had entered and listened. He nodded and stayed by that door.

Duke Heimsteady turned his attention to Jon and said in a low voice: "I am somewhat surprised to see you. You hold a very dangerous secret, and I am unsure why I originally decided to let you live. Nevertheless, you are now a part of a shared lie, and I cannot simply let you run around town. If you were in my shoes, what would you do?"

Jon gulped as he heard these words. Was he really now a part of the lie that had been told to protect the King's honor? If so, was he also guilty of a part in Sir Malpolem's death? As to the direct question that he had been asked, he had considered the answer and did not like it.

Jon looked the Duke in his eyes. He was not sure what gave him the boldness to do so, but he spoke in a strong voice despite his weak knees. "I can recognize that my life would seem to be an inconvenience to you presently, and perhaps I might not be a noble man and have me killed for convenience sake, but I have faith in you my Lord. I pray that I may be of some service to you." As Jon thought about what he had said he felt the words had come from somewhere else. Had he really just told the Duke that were the situations reversed he might have him killed?

The Duke was also taken aback by the answer, but somehow the words "I have faith in you" had stirred a sense of honor and nobility in his heart. After a long pause the Duke spoke: "Boady, I want Jon to live with you for the present. Keep him close and let him prove his trustworthiness. If he proves untrustworthy I expect you to kill him." He then turned to John. "Do you understand what I have said?"

Jon nodded.

"You are alive by my grace and a sentence of death hangs over you. Your executioner stands nearby and is ready to perform his duty."

The Duke paused to let his words sink in.

Next he asked Jon another question: "How did you and Malpolem find the camp?"

"We followed a path marked with piles of stones." Replied Jon.

"Hmm, I thought so. Boady, you and Jon are to erase that path, and while you are in the hunting preserve look for peasants who might be searching for the dragon's hoard. If you find anyone in the preserve you are instructed to issue justice immediately. Do you understand?"

"Yes my Lord." Replied Boady.

"Very well then, off with you now. You may leave by the main door." The Duke got up and left by the other door leaving Boady and Jon alone.

Jon stood rooted in place, his knees now visibly shaking. Finally, Boady spoke: "Well, you're not stupid. You did well to appeal to the Duke's honor. But you don't seem brave either; in fact, you look like you might piss yourself at any moment. C'mon, let's go to the kitchen and get you some meat to eat."

As Jon walked absent mindedly behind Boady, the assassin continued: "I'm not looking forward to killing you, but I hope you understand that I will if need be."

Somehow those words were comforting to Jon. At least Boady did not want to kill him. As he left the room Jon realized that things had not turned out badly at all. He had a place to live and a job to do, and indeed he would be living in the manor's courts. Somehow, despite himself, he had accomplished that goal.

3

Doing One's Duty

"Eh, Kris! The lad and I need some supper!" Shouted Boady as he and Jon walked into the manor kitchen.

A befuddled and busy man in an apron looked up with a start and said: "Boady, you're not the laird of this manor, but gimme a sec and I will see what I can find fer ye. Who's yer friend?"

"Nobody important yet," replied Boady, "but the Duke has taken him into service today and he and I need to get going on a job. He doesn't look like he's been eating well lately, so I suspect he will be one of the few who actually enjoys your cooking."

The cook eyed Jon appraisingly and said "Are ye hungry lad?"

"I've eaten a bit, but yes, I would be most grateful for some real food." Replied Jon.

"Better make it something we can carry." added Boady. "We need to head out and get to work."

"Well, that's easy then. Here's some dried meat and a piece of cheese. Sorry, but the bread is not done yet." Said the cook.

"Ach! Well, it'll have to do." said Boady. "Thanks my friend. By the way, you remember Doogy from our youth? This is his son Jon."

On hearing this Kris looked more carefully at Jon. "The executioner's son? Yes, I see the resemblance. Well boy, welcome to the manor. Your Da', Boady and I were fast chums when we were your age, but I wouldn't talk too much about 'im. There are a few here who lost loved ones to your father's axe."

Jon involuntarily blushed and looked down. Boady grabbed him by the arm and took him out through the door. "Thanks Kris. See ya soon." He shouted as they left.

The two walked through the gate and a few hundred yards down the main path. Suddenly, Boady pulled up short by some rocks and took a seat. Jon just stared at him.

"Well boy, it's time to eat!" Said Boady. "It'd be a better meal with some bread and something sweet, but I'm sure the cheese is good and I bet it's been a while since you've had meat."

It had been a week since Jon had had any meat, but that was not an unusual length of time. He sat next to Boady as the rations were cut. Jon reached into his satchel and pulled out his half loaf of rye bread and two apples. Boady looked shocked.

"Here I thought you were starving!" he said.

"I've not had cheese in a while, but Sir Malpolem kept the larder provisioned. I have been eating every day. This is what I have left." Replied Jon.

"Saints be praised! We'll have a fine meal after all!" replied Boady "And don't worry. As long as you live with me you'll be able to eat." They both got down to the business at hand: eating their supper.

After a minute or two Boady said: "You know what Kris said about your dad is true. There are many who will dislike you for what your father did."

Jon felt defensive. "My father carried out justice. If he was the one holding the axe, he was not the one who passed sentence. My father killed the guilty."

There was silence for a few moments and then Boady replied: "I have a girl who lives with me named Lil. She would not welcome hearing what you just said. Her Dad was accused of stealing bread, and for all I know he did it to feed his family. Your Dad cut off his hand in court ordered punishment. The hand never healed. Puss oozed out of it and eventually he died a painful death. Her mother was grief stricken and she died suddenly a few weeks later. Lil had nobody left, and I knew her family, so she is now like a daughter to me. I am not sure how she would react knowing I brought the son of the man who cut off her father's hand to join us in our home. Understand that whether your father acted justly or not, I think I can understand why Lil might dislike you if she knew who you were. There are several around here like her. You need to keep who you are, maybe who you were, quiet."

Jon did understand and a tear began to form in his eye. "I do understand." he said. Then an anger flared up inside of him. It was not he who had cut off Lil's father's hand. His father was an honorable man following an honorable profession. Who were Lil or Boady or anyone else to judge him; they did not know him or his father.

Jon took a moment to compose himself and said: "How was my father's work different than your work? I saw you kill an innocent Sir Malpolem. How many other innocent lives have you taken?"

Now Boady was angry, but Boady was older and had been looked down upon by both better and worse men than Jon. He took a moment before speaking:

"You know what Kris said about your dad and me being chums was also true. And Lil's mum was also a friend of ours. I liked your Dad to the end; I did not judge him, but I can understand how others do. It is good that we have this conversation now since the only way you get to live is if I agree to watch you. If we are going to live together we need some rules. Your father's work was painful to him, but he did his duty. My work is sometimes painful to me, but I do my duty. I will not have you judging me to justify what your father did. You are not my judge, and as long as you do your duty I will not have to judge you. You need to understand your place in my household. I am the master there and you will do as I say. As for me killing innocent people, you will come to learn that there are no innocent people; including you. Even so, it is still not your place to judge. Is that understood?"

The words pierced Jon. He now felt shame for what he had said even if he was defending his father. Obviously there was more to Boady than he had ever imagined. "I'm sorry." He said. "My dad meant a lot to me. He too said that I was not in a position to judge. I have never made a habit of bragging about being the son of the executioner, so I have no intention of spreading it around. But I am who I am and people will realize it eventually. I will do my best to do my duty by you. I will listen, and I will learn. I'm really sorry, Master."

Boady chuckled. "You can call me Boady. It is a rare thing for a man to admit that he was wrong. I accept your apology. Let's never forget this talk, but let's move on from it; we have work to do together."

The two gathered what was left of their supper and headed off to the hunting preserve. They walked in silence for most of an hour, but as they neared their destination Boady spoke:

"We are going to be looking for people who do not belong in there as well as destroying the path markers. If we find trespassers we will have to guess how much they may know, and if they could know more than they should we will..." he paused, "act."

Jon absorbed what had been said and replied: "You mean kill them."

"Quite possibly; probably, even likely; can you do your duty?" asked Boady.

Jon was not sure he could. He had never killed anyone, although he had seen his father execute some. On the other hand, if he told Boady that he was not ready to do his duty, would Boady kill him? After a pause he replied: "I have never killed anyone, but you are in charge and I trust you. I will do my best."

"That's a fine answer boy. Had you been more certain I'd have known you were either lying or a fool. You're a brave lad and I trust you too. Do your best not to let me down. How good are you with that sword?"

"Sir Malpolem and I practiced a bit, but I have never used it against an actual foe. I know how to hold it and some basic strokes; it's mainly for stabbing. Honestly, I never thought of using it against someone else. It mainly made me feel special to be armed. I will do my best, but I really do not know how I will do."

"Let's hope you don't have to use it, but prepare yourself in case you do. I'll watch out for you as best I can."

Once they got into the preserve there was little conversation, and what few words were passed were spoken directly into each other's ears in low whispered voices. Boady insisted that the rocks be flung in different directions and Jon soon found his arm tiring. He began to wonder if he would even be able to hold his weapon at this rate. He tried to throw left handed but the results were awkward so he soon tossed the rocks underhanded.

As they approached each pile Boady signaled Jon to stay still as he looked around and listened carefully. Then they would begin to throw. After not too long a while Boady signaled Jon to sit and wait as he stood listening. Jon's arm was grateful for the rest. This journey into the preserve had been far easier than the previous one where Jon had to carry Sir Malpolem's shield, but the day had advanced a great many hours and Jon had been through a lot. He was getting tired.

As he sat in silence Jon began to hear a rustling off to the side. Boady was already focused in that direction and signaled Jon to follow him quietly. As they snuck through the brush they spied a little boy looking puzzled as he observed a snare that held a small rabbit.

Boady drew a dagger and Jon thought "Oh God! Don't kill him!" Yet he said nothing.

After a few moments Boady suddenly got up and started walking toward the child saying: "Timmy. You know you are not supposed to be here."

The boy looked very much afraid as Boady bore down on him holding the dagger. He walked past the boy to the rabbit and slit its throat.

"Mr. Boady! My mum and I were hungry so I thought I would see if some of my Dad's old snares might hold something to eat. When I found this one with a rabbit I didn't know how to get it home." The boy blurted out as Boady glared at him holding the bloody rabbit.

"Jon, come join us." Said Boady.

Jon was afraid that this boy would be his first kill but he reluctantly came to stand next to Boady. Unknowingly he prayed that killing this boy would not be his duty.

"Timmy you know this is the King's preserve and you are not allowed to hunt here. You know this quite well as your father was hung for having been caught once too many times in here. Do you want to be hung?" said Boady.

Tears were welling up in the boy's eyes. "We are so hungry." He protested. "Since Dad's gone we don't get no regular food, and mum's sick. Please don't hang me Mr. Boady!"

"I'm not going to hang you Timmy. Did your mum send you here?" replied Boady.

"No sir. She'd be quite mad if she knew where I was. I figured I'd tell her I caught the rabbit near our house." Said the boy.

"Timmy, it's not just the King's men you have to be afraid of, there's a dragon loose in here. Both Jon and I have seen it. I'm sure a dragon would love to feast on a tender morsel like you. If your mother lost you she would die from grief. Your not listening to her could not only kill you, but it could kill your mother as well. You take this rabbit strait home and tell her I gave it to you when we met on the path. If you get that hungry again, you take a long walk to the Duke's manor and you find my house. Me or my girl Lil will give you some food. Do not come back here. Is that understood?" Boady held out the rabbit.

Timmy took it and started back towards the edge of the preserve. "Yes, Mr. Boady. And thank you. I won't come back and I will try not to ask you for much food." He said as he departed.

Boady and Jon watched him go. Then Boady said: "His dad was one of the 'guilty' people your dad may have hung in his duty. Duty is not always pleasant. We are not near the graves and I doubt he will ever speak to anyone of this adventure. Let's get on with it."

As they wandered away Jon wondered whether Boady would have killed the boy had they been close to the graves. He hoped not, but Boady seemed very intent on doing his duty.

The sun began to set and it became clear that they would be spending the night in the preserve. Jon knew that Boady still had some of his bread and some dried meat, but he thought most of the cheese was gone. Jon remembered that he still had an apple in his satchel. As they approached the hunting party's old camp site Jon's arm was sore and he was more tired than hungry. It had been a long day.

Suddenly they heard voices and Boady motioned for Jon to stop and wait. Boady then went off into the brush to see who was about. He came back shortly and whispered into Jon's ear: "There's three of them. A rough looking bunch camped where we had the boar roast with the King. We have a duty to perform. I'll get one with a thrown dagger while they're unaware. If we're lucky I can get the other two in the confusion after they see their mate's dead. When you hear the commotion you come running." Boady paused and looked Jon in the eye. "Your duty is to make sure nobody escapes. If one of 'em runs, you need to stop him somehow."

Jon nodded, but Boady continued looking at him for some time. Finally, Boady turned to head into the brush. Jon was sweating with nervous anticipation as he pulled out his sword.

While it was only a minute or two, the intervening time seemed to last forever. Suddenly Jon heard a surprised "What!" followed by two voices yelling "Who's there."

Jon moved forward without thought rushing towards the camp while being as quiet as he could. Apparently the men heard him and as Jon got near the camp an arrow flew towards him. It missed by a good bit mainly because a second of Boady's daggers was embedded in the archer's left shoulder.

The men saw both of them as Boady jumped up to attack the wounded man who was larger and clearly angry. He held a cleaver as Boady attacked, but Jon saw the other man, a younger man probably only a few years older than Jon, running away.

Jon moved to cut him off, but in the dusk he soon lost sight of him in the thick foliage. Jon stopped to listen and heard the runner off to his left. As he turned that way the man suddenly sprang out of the brush while looking behind him and almost ran into Jon. Reflexively Jon's sword found the man's belly as he practically ran onto it.

Their eyes met and Jon saw the shock in the other's expression. The man fell to the ground bleeding profusely and staring at Jon. The sword had opened a large wound across his abdomen. As Jon stood staring the other man's eyes became dull. He laid there at Jon's feet, dead, but still looking at his killer.

Boady came through the brush and saw what had happened. Jon just stared at the body. Slowly Boady approached and put his hand on Jon's shoulder. As soon as he was touched Jon turned and vomited.

4

Interview with the Duke

T HE SUN HAD NOW SET, but Jon continued to stare at his vomit. He could hear Boady working after the body had been taken away, but Jon was dazed and confused. The man's eyes and silent expression of shock were still visible to him as if they had been etched onto his eye balls. Finally, he went in search of Boady.

When Boady saw Jon coming he was gentle in his tone: "We need to gather wood. Can you do that? I am piling it a bit south of the camp site." Boady pointed to a star. "See that one? That's the north star. If you go to the camp site and walk away from the star, you'll find the piles. Try to gather wood Jon, it will help take your mind off of it."

Jon grunted and went off in search of wood. There was plenty to be found. When he had as much as he could carry he looked up at the stars. They looked oblivious to his plight, but he saw the one Boady had pointed out to guided him to the wood piles. Boady had made three and Jon took his wood to the smallest.

Jon was about to gather more when Boady approached him and said: "That should be enough. Are you alright?"

Jon mumbled "I guess so." He stood awaiting further instructions while Boady stared at him. He felt awkward under Boady's gaze, but appreciated that Boady was going easy on him.

"You go back to the camp and make us a smaller fire to cook some supper on and give us a little warmth tonight. I'll be by with the flint when I am done here." Said Boady.

Jon turned to leave and suddenly saw the three bodies laid out in a row. The one Jon had killed grabbed his attention with its still open eyes and the shocked expression on its face. Somehow, however, it had changed. It no longer seemed human, but just a slab of cold flesh; it was now just another one of the many dead bodies he had seen throughout most of his life. He did not linger, but he was struck by how different a living body was from a dead one.

Jon gathered wood as he went and built a small camp fire that only needed a spark to ignite it. The smoldering remains of the other men's fire caught his eyes and he used some of the coals to light this new fire. Then Jon sat and thought some more. He was starting to feel better, to return to his senses. He was tired, and he was hungry.

Apparently Boady had lit the fires as Jon smelled smoke drifting over from the south. Jon remembered the apple he had, but as he took it out he felt it would be selfish to not share it with his companion. He decided to cut it with his sword which had hung unnoticed by his side this whole time. As he pulled out the blade he saw the blood; the blood of his victim. He stared at the blade for a few minutes partly wanting to throw it away, but partly fascinated by the fact that this sword had given him the power to take away a life. He gathered some leaves and began to wipe away the blood. The more he wiped the less particular this blood seemed; it was only the blood from another dead body. When he was done, he still could not bring himself to use the sword to cut his apple.

Jon smelled cooking meat in the air and it made him even more hungry. Then he realized what he was smelling and felt ashamed. How could he think of food at a time like this? Still, he was very hungry.

Boady came to the camp and looked at Jon with concern. Jon tried to smile and said: "I lit the fire from the left over coals. I have an apple we can share if you'd like to cut it."

"Thanks." Boady replied with a look of relief. Somehow he produced a small iron pot. "Do you think you can get us some water from the stream a bit North of here? I'll get dinner started."

Jon took the pot and headed towards the stream. When he got there the first thing he did was wash his sword. Next he washed himself as best he could. The water felt cool and refreshing; it felt as if it were washing away what had happened. He then filled the pot and returned to the camp.

Boady took a drink from the pot and put the cut up remainder of the dried meat into the remaining water. Then he added some sliced carrots, potatoes, and Jon's apple. "They must have been farm peasants as they had these in their supplies." He said.

When the stew was warm the two ate it from the pot taking turns.

"Are you sure you're ok? You want to tell me what happened?" asked Boady.

"I'm ok." Replied Jon. He thought of embellishing his story, but he suddenly thought of Sir Malpolem and decided against it. "He ran and I chased after him just like you told me to, but I lost him. As I stopped to hear where he might be he came crashing through the brush right at me but looking the other way. He practically ran onto my sword."

Boady looked at Jon for a moment. "You're an uncommonly honest man, Jon. You did your duty. Try not to let it bother you too much. Try not to think about it."

Both men were tired after the meal, but Boady said he would clean the pot as he wanted to get a drink. Jon lay down with his head against a log and fell asleep, but he did not sleep soundly. The eyes of the man he had killed continued to haunt him, and Sir Malpolem, his father, and others he had known who had passed also visited him that night. When he awoke it was already day light and he felt sore and groggy.

Boady was cooking some more vegetables for breakfast and said: "Well, you seem to have had a good long sleep!"

Jon did not feel like arguing. Boady handed him the pot and told him to finish what was in it and then wash it while he went to check on some things. The smell of smoke still hung heavy in the air.

When Jon got back from cleaning the pot Boady was still not back so Jon went looking for him where he had delivered the wood the previous night. Boady was there smashing to ashes the pieces of wood that still had shape. The bodies of the men were mostly burned but they lay in unusual positions all facing the same direction. By one body lay a cleaver as if it had been held when the body burned. The body of another looked like it had also been holding something when it burned. As Jon walked up to it he saw a knife laying on the ground a few feet in front of it.

"I posed 'em to look like they'd been fighting something; maybe a dragon?" said Boady when he saw Jon. "You ready to head out?"

Jon nodded and the two headed back to camp where they gathered their supplies including a few more potatoes and carrots. They then headed out of the preserve.

"Those men weren't hunters." Said Boady. "They were well armed with two bows, a cleaver, and one had a knife bound to a stick that he could use as a spear. They didn't come here for food; they came here for treasure. Their greed is what killed them."

"I guess." Replied Jon.

"Oh lad. There are no innocents; remember that. You did your duty. You can take pride in that." Said Boady.

Jon wasn't sure. He no longer felt innocent, but he also did not feel guilty. He felt somewhere in between. "I don't think I want to talk about it right now." He said.

"Fair enough." Said Boady. "When we get back we have to report to the Duke. We will first tell him that the dragon killed again, then when it is safe we will tell him something closer to the truth. The main thing is that I want you to say as little as possible. You listen to what I say and you back me up as much as possible. You understand?"

"Yes master." Mumbled Jon, but Boady did not seem to like the reply.

"Look boy, I'm looking out for both of us here, and the Duke and the Kingdom as well. Remember you don't always have to like your duty, but you have to do it anyways." He said.

"I will." Said Jon. "You want to tell me the story on the way?"

Boady did and they spent most of a pleasant morning getting their story together as they walked back to the manor. When they got there Boady went straight to the door they had used yesterday and they were quickly ushered into the room where justice was dispensed, but to Jon it seemed more a room of judgement than justice.

This time the Duke was hearing a complaint. One lady claimed that a neighbor's boy was stealing her eggs. The boy denied this and the Duke could not tell who was in the wrong.

"Give the boy five lashes with a switch on his arse." Ruled the Duke.

All things considered it was a light sentence, but the accusing lady seemed to feel justified. The boy looked scared and dismayed.

The room was now empty except for the Duke, the scribe, Boady, and Jon.

"Well?" said the Duke.

"We came across the remains of three men in the preserve, sire. They were badly burned and the fire was still smoldering. We came here to report as soon as we could." Said Boady.

The scribe was writing now, apparently recording what Boady had said.

The Duke stood up and said: "So the dragon has killed again. Did you see it?"

"No sire." Replied Boady.

"Damn." Said the Duke. Turning to the scribe he said: "See that word is sent to the castle. And see that I am not disturbed."

The scribe gathered his parchments and headed out the door. Soon the sounds of a commotion could be heard outside. The Duke signaled for Boady to check the doors. He did and soon approached the chair.

"Join us." The Duke commanded Jon. When he did the Duke said in a low voice: "What really happened?"

Boady replied: "Three men armed with spears and bows were camped where we roasted the boar. Jon and I dispatched them. We dragged them some ways off from there and burned them last night. I'm sure others saw the flames or smelled the fire. If they investigate they should see signs of a battle with an unknown foe and some badly burned remains of men who obviously died fighting."

"Who were they?" asked the Duke.

"I don't know, but the way they were armed they were clearly hunting more than illegal game. I think they were looking for the dragon's lair." Replied Boady.

The Duke looked at Jon, but Jon said nothing. Turning back to Boady the Duke said: "How did your young companion do?"

"He did his duty." Replied Boady. "He killed one of them."

The Duke looked skeptical. "Did he now?"

"He did." said Boady. "One of them ran and Jon chased after him. When I went looking for them I found the man dead with Jon's sword in his belly. I would not lie to you sire."

"You just lied to me about a dragon." Snickered the Duke. "So, you killed a man? Was he your first?"

"Yes sire." Stammered Jon not liking the way the Duke was looking at him.

The Duke came up close to him. "Would you like to do it again?" he said.

"I did my duty. I did not enjoy it, but I am learning that duty is not always enjoyable." Replied Jon.

The Duke paced a few steps and said "Can we trust him Boady?"

"He's done quite well, my Lord. I am beginning to trust him." Replied Boady

The Duke smiled at Jon and said "Very well. I'm sure you both could use some rest. It is rare that I thank my men for simply doing their duty, but you have my thanks today. Go get some rest. I will send for you." He then tossed a silver piece to Boady and walked out the second door.

A piece of silver was more money than Jon had ever seen. Half of it could buy a cow and all of it might get one an old steed to ride.

Boady put it in his pocket, smiled and said "You have an uncanny knack for saying the right thing to the Duke. Some of this is yours, but I'll hold it for both of us if you don't mind."

Jon imagined how much good he could do and how he could atone for the death he had caused with half a silver piece, but he trusted Boady so he did not object. "That's more money than I've ever seen! You hold onto it until I need it." He said.

Boady smiled and said "C'mon, let's see if Kris has some bread for us today, then I'll show you my home."

5

Good People and Bad People

WALKING OUT OF THE MANOR Jon and Boady passed the scene where the young man who had been accused of stealing eggs was being switched. Perhaps somewhat surprisingly there was not much of a crowd gathered to watch, and it appeared that that had taken some of the enthusiasm out of the Reeve as he administered the punishment. Instead there were many glances at the two as they walked toward the kitchen, and the word "dragon" could be overheard in several conversations.

When they were almost to the kitchen a man approached: "Is it true? Did the dragon kill again? Who was it? Did you see it happen?"

Boady replied for both of them: "It appears so. We came across the burned remains of at least three men who clearly were fighting something. I have no idea who they were and I doubt anyone could recognize them as they were badly burned, but I'm not anxious to go back and investigate more."

"Saints preserve us!" replied the man who then walked off to share what he had heard with awaiting onlookers. Jon looked at Boady and shrugged his shoulders.

"Kris?" shouted Boady as he walked into the kitchen.

The cook came out of a nearby closet and said "Praise God it was not you two who were taken by the dragon! Was it you who found them? Who was it?"

"Aye, Jon and I came across the scene, but we couldn't tell who they were from what was left of 'em." Replied Boady. "Meanwhile, the Duke's given us some free time for today so I am taking Jon to his new home in my house."

"Oh master Jon," replied Kris, "what a terrible way to begin your service to the Duke."

Kris stared at Jon waiting for a reply. After an awkward moment the young man said: "They weren't the first dead bodies I've ever seen, but it was a sad sight to behold."

Kris smiled and put a hand on his shoulder. "You are right son, and it won't be the last sad sight you see I'm sure. You're a brave lad. Now, if you're going home I should pack you some provisions!"

Kris pulled out a large sack and began filling it with way more food than three people could eat in even a week. First came potatoes, then beans, peas, and other greens, followed by some fresh and salted meat, cheese, and lastly three large loaves of bread.

"That should do ya." Said Kris with a sly look as he handed the bag to Boady.

"Thanks Kris. I'll make sure a lot of people appreciate this and that none knows where it came from. You're a kind man my friend." Said Boady as he handed the heavy bag to Jon.

Then, turning to Jon he said: "Let me go out first and take all of the dragon attention. You skirt along just out back of the manor heading west and we'll join back up when it's safe."

Jon had a smirk on his face when he said: "I'll do my duty."

Boady smiled and walked out the door. This time he seemed to encourage people to gather around him. Kris and Jon watched him leave standing at the door. Finally, Kris said: "Circle around behind the kitchen and go over the wall. Then skirt the woods heading west and Boady will catch up to you soon enough."

Jon nodded and headed out the door. The sack was somewhat heavy, but also awkward to carry. Although lighter than the shield that he had carried for Sir Malpolem it was actually more of a burden. The wall was not much of an obstacle as he just walked up the earthen rampart and down the other side. Staying close to the woods he saw no one and soon was a bit off and he hid himself just inside the woods and waited to catch sight of Boady.

As he waited he thought of what a strange man Boady was. When he had first seen him Boady had just killed his friend and former master Sir Malpolem in cold blood. On the other hand, he had spared and even helped Timmy whom he had found trespassing in the preserve. Next he had convicted and killed two other unknown men that he had found in the same preserve and burned their bodies. Yes, it had been his duty, but it could be said that it had also been his duty to kill Timmy. Nevertheless, Jon liked Boady and had even begun to trust him. Was Boady a good man or a bad man?

The question made Jon think of himself. He had also killed someone he did not know. Was he a murderer? Jon did not think so. He and others, like Boady, called him honest. Jon felt he was a good man, but he had killed someone while hardly knowing if he had deserved to die. Well, it had practically been an accident, and it had been his duty as well.

Boady was clearly good, but Jon had little doubt that he had probably committed terrible things; especially killings. Were all men a mix of good and bad? Was he a mix of good and bad? Jon felt that he was good, but he knew that he had told lies, fibs he called them, and now he had also killed a man that he did not know. Perhaps Jon was good and bad as well.

As he was lost in his thoughts he saw Boady walking in the clearer land beyond the woods. Jon got up to join him, but Boady deftly waived him off and kept walking. Jon understood that he should follow Boady from a distance, so he stayed in the woods while keeping an eye on his companion.

Soon they came to a thatch house right on the edge of the wood and Boady motioned for Jon to join him. As Jon walked up a girl with red curly hair came running out of the house and immediately threw her arms around Boady's waist.

"I knew you'd come back, but I was still worried!" she exclaimed.

She then saw Jon approaching and released her grip on Boady.

"This is my girl Lil." Said Boady. "Lil, this is Jon, He will be staying with us for a good while as the Duke has assigned him to me. I think the two of you will get along."

Lil looked Jon over and then flashed the brightest smile Jon had ever seen. "Welcome Jon. Welcome to our home; I see you did not come empty handed!"

Unknowingly Jon blushed. "Yes mam, the cook, Kris, gave us some food to bring here."

Despite her small size the girl took the bag from Jon with relative ease. And looking at Boady said: "This is wonderful! There are many hungry people about. Why don't the two of you wash up a bit and come inside and tell me what you have been up to."

Washing was not common, and Jon could not remember anyone asking him to wash, much less a young girl. Jon looked at Boady who smiled and shrugged. "C'mon Jon. We've a little stream just back of the house."

Lil took the bag inside while the men went behind the house to wash in the stream.

"Why are we washing?" Asked Jon.

"Lil has her ways, and I don't really believe washing will hurt us. Truth be known, I feel better now that I wash regularly." replied Boady.

Boady took sand from the creek and used it to get dirt off of his hands. Jon decided to do likewise. They both dunked their heads in the water and rubbed their faces.

When they were done Jon said: "I've never seen hair that red. Is Lil a Kell?"

The Kells were the pagans who raided their lands, though truth be told there were also raids going the other way.

43

Boady gave Jon a stern look as he replied. "She's my girl, and a better Christian than you or I will ever be. Her dad was one of us but her mum was at least part Kell. I think she was a captive, but we were all just children then. The bottom line is that Lil is my girl, and it doesn't matter what blood runs through her veins. You best remember that if you know what's good for you, boy."

"I didn't mean anything by it." Jon replied sheepishly. "I've just never seen hair like that. It sets her apart, that's all. She is a very pretty girl."

"Aye, she's my treasure. And despite her age you'll learn that she is the lady of this house. If you know what's best fer ye, you'll treat her with respect." Said Boady in a stern voice, but with a proud smile on his face. "C'mon, let's see what Lil has for us to eat."

Jon had never seen a flash of anger like that in Boady, but it seemed to pass as quickly as it had come on. Clearly Boady loved Lil like a daughter and she really was his treasure.

As they entered the house Jon saw a small table set with three bowls and wooden spoons as well as some bread and cheese. There was a bench on one side of the table and a stump on the other.

"We haven't another bench or chair for you Jon, so for now you will have to use the stump to sit on." Said Lil with a reproving glance at Boady. "Just a bit and I'll bring the stew." She added as she stood by a fire and a pot hanging from a tripod over it.

Boady took a seat on the bench and Jon followed suit on the stump. The table looked formal to Jon and the food smelled delicious. As hunger came to grip him, Jon reached for some bread as Lil said: "I wasn't expecting three, but I think we'll have…" Lil paused as she turned and saw Jon getting the bread. "Master Jon. In this house we say grace before eating."

Jon put the bread back and looked sheepish. Boady was looking down with a smile on his face. Lil put a healthy portion of stew in each of their bowls beginning with Jon's. Knowing that he could not begin eating made this wait torture and Jon soon imagined himself ravenous.

At last Lil sat down next to Boady and the two of them made the sign of the cross. Jon hastened to follow having only done this in church previously. Then Lil prayed:

"Bless us oh Lord, and these gifts, which we gratefully receive, through thy bounty and grace in Christ our Lord; amen."

Jon and Boady simultaneously said "Amen." Boady reached for the bread and Jon took this as a sign that he could finally eat. Jon had not been particularly hungry when he had walked into the house, but he had a strong appetite now.

After each had eaten some of their meal Lil asked: "Where were you last night, Boady?"

Boady looked sideways and said: "The Duke gave us a job to do in the King's preserve. It took longer than we thought, so we stayed the night."

"In the preserve? Why does anyone have to go there? It's dangerous with a dragon on the loose!" replied Lil.

Boady and Jon looked at each other and Boady replied with a sigh. "You're going to hear about it sooner or later; the dragon has killed again. Jon and I came across the scene."

"Oh dear me! But you're safe, praise be to God. How terrible a thing for you to see Jon." Said Lil excitedly.

Jon looked up from his stew but did not know what to say. Finally, he said: "It was not pleasant."

"I can see neither of you wants to discuss this. I'm just so thankful that you're safe. So, what will Jon be doing with us?" asked Lil.

"He's to learn to be a warden like me." Replied Boady. "He will help me care for the Duke's forest."

This was news to Jon, but it made sense. It was nice to know he had a profession lined up and that he would not be following in his father's line of work. Jon was pleased.

"And what did you do before you joined us. Jon?" asked the apparently inquisitive Lil.

"I was a page to a knight." Replied Jon evasively. He had almost blurted out the whole truth but thought at the last second that he should not.

Boady quickly interjected. "This is a fine stew my girl, but I am glad Jon is here to help us eat it as it would have been way too much for just us. How did you know we would be here for supper?"

"Thankyou Boady, but you always say that about my cooking. I didn't so much know that you would be home as much as I hoped so, and I figured if you were you would be hungry. Besides, it is never difficult to find someone in want of a meal." Said the effervescent girl.

"Are you about finished?" said Boady to Jon. "I think it's time I showed you what our responsibilities are."

Jon would have loved to linger, but he was afraid of Lil's questions. "You're the master!" he replied enthusiastically.

"You men be about your work and I'll clean up." Said Lil. "While you're out there you can gather some rushes so we can make Jon a bed."

Jon followed Boady out of the door.

"Being the Duke's warden is really not that hard a job, at least not the wardening itself." Said Boady. "Nobody poaches since they know they can get some food from me if they need to. I think the Duke knows, but we've never discussed it. For your first lesson we'll find a dead tree and chop it into fire wood. We can never have too much of that, and I think you need to build a bit more muscle."

Jon nodded and they began to walk towards a low shed adjacent to the house. As they got there they saw a young boy running towards them from the manor. As he drew closer they recognized that it was Timmy whom they had met in the preserve yesterday.

When he came up to them he exclaimed: "I'm so glad you're alright! I heard about the dragon!"

"We're fine Timmy." Said Boady. "It's a good thing you got out when you did or you might have become a crispy dragon meal. How's your mum?"

"She's better, and she said to thank you for the rabbit." He replied. "The food perked her up. She is not strong, but she yelled at me this morning and then sent me here so I think she is feeling better."

"Good." Replied Boady. "Do you need some more food?"

"Well, we never have exactly enough." Said the boy with a shy demeanor.

"Let me introduce you to Lil. She will give you some food to take back." Said Boady and he started back to the house.

Suddenly he stopped and turned to Jon. "I think it's best you get the axe. Wait for me."

Jon understood that the situation was rife for more questions from Lil, so he gladly returned to the shed. As he waited he thought about what Boady had been saying. While none of it had been a lie, because of the dragon, almost none of it had been the full truth either. Could he trust what Boady said? He understood that the truth could cause a great deal of harm, and he had a general trust of Boady and his intentions, but how could he really know if Boady was a good man or a bad man? Clearly he cared for people as he fed those in need, but he was also a killer. Were there two sides to Boady? Where does one draw the line between good and bad men?

Jon's thoughts turned to himself. He was also a killer now. He shared in the lies that Boady told. Was he a bad man? Jon could not accept that judgement. He had done his duty; that's all.

Boady and Timmy came out of the house and Timmy took off for home carrying a small sack presumably full of food. "Let's chop some wood." Said Boady.

The two went into the woods and Boady showed Jon much about holding an axe, swinging an axe, and the angles to take when felling a tree. Jon's arms got very sore, but the work took his mind off of things and he found himself enjoying his time with Boady who was a patient teacher.

When Jon felt his arms might fall off from swinging the axe Boady called a halt and they gathered some rushes to make Jon's bed. There was a small room adjacent to the kitchen and living area, where all three were to sleep.

As the sun began to set, Jon enjoyed a meal of bread and cheese while Boady directed the conversation to the local gossip that Lil had heard: babies to be born, people who were sick, and rumors of impending raids by the Kells. After supper all three cleaned up and it was time for bed. As Jon lay down on the new rushes he felt somewhat satisfied with himself. His new situation as a warden's apprentice had the promise of a pleasant life.

6

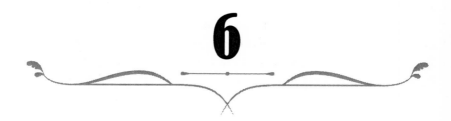

An Invitation

J ON'S BED OF RUSHES WAS comfortable; not as comfortable as the bed he had when he lived with Sir Malpolem, but far better than the cold ground. He had even been given a blanket to use, but he still did not sleep as soundly as he should have. The eyes and expression of the man he had killed haunted his dreams.

In town and around the manor most people were occupied getting ready for the coronation ceremony in the big church in town on Sunday. The Duke and other high nobles would be invited to the feast afterward, but the common folk would also be given presents from their new King. That was in town, but Boady, Jon, and Lil had all that they needed at the manor, so they did not plan to attend. They would let their betters celebrate the special day while they celebrated this day.

"This is the day that the Lord has made; let us rejoice and be glad in it." Lil liked to say. She was a joy to be around. She always had something kind to say or an interesting observation to share. There was something about her smile and manner that seemed to radiate kindness and happiness. Jon understood why Boady valued her so much.

Since their first meal Lil had not asked about Jon's past. Perhaps Boady had said something to her or maybe she just sensed that Jon did not want to talk about it. People often came by the house and one might assume it was to be given food, but Jon suspected some came by just to be cheered by Lil's presence.

That first day after his arrival was somewhat uneventful. Boady and Jon finished chopping wood, brought water to the house, and for a brief time Boady took Jon for a walk in the woods telling him about different plants and trees. Jon thought he would like it here.

That night he still dreamt of the man's expression, but he slept a bit better. He woke before the others, and, not knowing what else to do, surprised himself by going to the stream to wash. The cold water finished the waking up process, and it felt good to be rid of some of the dirt that the past had left on him.

When he returned to the house Lil was up and stoking the fire. "There you are!" she said in a somewhat hushed voice so as not to wake Boady.

"I went out to wash." Replied Jon.

"Well, I'm on my way to wash as well." Said Lil. "Will you stoke the fire while I go?"

"Of course." Said Jon. Lil flashed him a smile that made Jon feel well rewarded for this small effort. Then she went out to wash.

When she returned in a few minutes Lil said: "Would you like to join me for my morning prayer?"

Jon had never said morning prayers, but it would have been impolite to say no.

Lil knelt before a small wooden cross that hung on the wall. Jon knelt beside her. They made the sign of the cross and Lil recited: "Our Father in heaven. Great is your name, your Kingdom come, your will be done on earth as it is in heaven. Thank you for providing for us this day and thank you for the grace that forgives our sins and help us to forgive as we have been forgiven. Protect us from temptation and deliver us from evil. Amen."

"Amen." Repeated Jon. "That's the Pater Noster that we say in church." He added. "I've never heard it in our language."

"Is it?" replied Lil. "My mother taught it to me when I was very little. I find it really expresses how I feel towards God. Do you speak Latin?"

"Sir..." Jon paused. "My former master taught me some and how to read a little bit. The Pater Noster was my first lesson."

"He must have been a good man." Said Lil.

"He was." Said Jon. "I miss him, but I do think I can be happy here."

Boady came out of the other room.

"Am I the last one up? You two make me feel like a sluggard. I'll go and wash up." He said as he went out the door.

Lil looked at Jon like she wanted to continue the conversation, but then she said: "We all have our duty to do, and right now mine is making breakfast. Can you set the table?"

Jon was relieved and gladly went to his task. When Boady came back breakfast was ready and they all sat down, said grace, and began to eat.

As they were eating they heard the sound of two horses approaching.

"What's this then?" said Boady as he rushed outside assuming it was the Duke.

It was not the Duke, but one of his grooms leading a second horse behind him.

"Hello Wren. What brings you here this early?" said Boady.

"The Duke sent me. I have a message for Master Jon. Word came from the castle last night." Replied Wren.

This was a puzzling development. What would the castle want with Jon?

"Well, he's right inside. Do you have time to join us for breakfast?" said Boady leading the way inside.

"As you'll soon hear, I'm to be here for much of the day, so breakfast would be most welcome." Replied Wren.

As they walked in the door, Jon was standing expecting the Duke. Lil had moved to the cooking fire hoping to make herself less noticeable. They were both surprised when Boady entered followed by another man.

"Jon, Lil, this is Wren, one of the Duke's stable grooms. He is here with a message for Jon. Lil, do we have enough to feed a hungry man sent on a journey quite early?" said Boady.

"Of course." Said Lil. "I'll fix you an egg. Help yourself to some bread and cheese."

Jon stood silent and perplexed. What would the Duke want from Jon? Was he to be given another undesirable duty? Jon had a feeling of dread.

"Master Jon." Said Wren. "The Bishop of Witancaester has arrived and the King's coronation mass is set for this Sunday. The Crown Prince has personally requested that you attend the mass and banquet afterwards. You are to accompany the Duke. I have been sent to deliver you some suitable clothing and to teach you to ride and care for the horse that I brought."

This news was greeted with stunned silence all around. While it seemed like quite an honor and privilege was to be granted Jon, he could not shake the feeling of dread that hung around him. Sunday was the day after tomorrow, so there was little time to make whatever preparations Jon had to make.

Boady and Wren sat down on the bench, and Jon absent-mindedly joined them at the table. Lil cooked the egg for Wren and brought it to him. Wren used Lil's spoon and bowl to eat, while Lil stood about trying to keep busy. Oddly, Jon's first thought was that they needed to get a second bench.

"Why would the Prince want me there?" said Jon almost to himself.

Between enthusiastic bites Wren replied: "The messenger didn't say, but I assume he wants to thank you for the service that you and Sir Malpolem provided his father."

Boady looked up with a startled expression. Jon was mortified. Lil was puzzled and just stared at Jon.

"What service?" Jon blurted without thinking.

"I suppose your battle with the dragon." Said Wren.

Jon looked down at his food. The feeling of dread that he had had was now running rampant through his mind and body. "Oh God!" he thought in desperation.

"In any event, I am to teach you to ride today so you can join the Duke, his son, and mother at mass and the feast." Added Wren.

Jon and Boady looked at each other while Lil continued to stare at Jon. Wren didn't notice as he was wholly engrossed in his breakfast. Lil made him a second egg to buy everyone some time to gather their wits.

When Wren had finished eating the men went outside. Boady excused himself and went into the woods and Wren introduced Jon to the horse he had brought.

"This is Mayflower. She's a gentle and forgiving mare with a good temperament." He said. "Have you ever been on a horse before?"

Jon had ridden while in Sir Malpolem's service, but it was rarely to do more than take the horse to the stable where it usually wanted to go in any case. "I've ridden some," he said, "but not much and I am sure I have much to learn."

The answer seemed to please Wren. "Let's see you get into the saddle." He said.

Jon was awkward in his first attempt, and when Wren told him to get down he almost fell. Wren laughed and then encouraged Jon to take several more tries while giving gentle advice. Soon Jon felt comfortable getting on and off.

After finishing this lesson Wren explained how to control the horse both with the reins and his feet. Jon was used to using the reins, but was surprised at how responsive Mayflower was to pressure from his legs and feet. Wren said that they were now ready to take a ride. As they were about to mount, Jon saw Timmy running up. He had a sack hanging from his pants. Timmy saw the horses and seemed awed and a bit afraid.

"Hello Timmy." Said Jon. "This is Wren. He is teaching me to ride a horse."

"Why do you need to know that?" Asked the boy.

Jon looked at him. Why indeed? "Lil is inside if you've come to see her." Jon replied.

"I will see her in a moment," said Timmy, "but I've come with some interesting news. I think we know who the dragon killed."

This was indeed interesting news, but Jon was not sure that he wanted to know.

"Who was it?" said a clearly excited Wren.

"The Schumachers." Said Timmy. "Folks say that they left that very day and were armed with bows and such. They haven't come back and nobody thinks they'd leave their shop this long. Nobody is too sad about it. They weren't a popular bunch. Sold shoes that wouldn't last and then charged us to fix their shoddy work. Of course now we'll have to find some other way to get shoes. The youngest one was OK, though. Wulf would help if he saw you had a problem with your shoes. He stitched mine up once. He was a good one as long as his father and brother weren't around. We'll miss Wulf, but not the rest of 'em."

Jon felt sick. He now knew whom he had killed. Apparently he had killed the "good one." And he had a name: Wulf the Schumacher. The face and especially those eyes came into Jon's vision.

"Hello Timmy." Said Lil as she came out of the house. "It's good to see you. How is your mother."

"She's much better." Said the boy. "I have news! We know who the dragon killed!"

Jon walked up to Mayflower and gently padded her while Timmy excitedly told Lil the news. As he stood there he saw Boady coming out of the woods rolling a large and long stump. He was sweating with the effort as Jon absentmindedly walked towards him.

When he got close he said: "Timmy knows who we killed in the preserve. It was the Schumachers from town."

Boady looked at Jon and then put his hand on Jon's shoulder.

"They weren't a popular bunch." He said. There was an awkward silence and then he added: "Help me get this log up near the house. It's going to become a bench. I'll not have Lil standing during dinner."

Jon just stood there.

"It's your duty." Said Boady in a serious tone.

Jon got behind the log with Boady and together they rolled it up towards the house. Wren, Timmy, and Lil were still talking excitedly as Boady began flattening one side of the log.

After a short while Boady said: "That'll do for now. Let's get it in the house."

As the two of them got the new bench near the house Lil saw them and exclaimed: "Boady! You've made another bench!" She then ran up to Boady and gave him a big hug.

Jon was sure that her smile and hug had made all the work Boady had done that morning worth it. Jon was also sure that there were three other people nearby, including himself, that were envious of the affection Boady had just been shown.

Wren and Timmy watched as Boady and Jon muscled the new bench into the house. They stood at the door while Jon moved the stump so the bench could be placed at the table. Jon was annoyed as the two of them stood there watching.

Then Lil exclaimed: "We can seat five now! Oh Timmy, you must stay for dinner! You four go and wash up. Dinner will be ready soon. I'll set the table and we'll eat!"

Timmy and Wren looked at each other with puzzled expressions. Jon smiled to himself as Boady said "Right this way gentlemen." And the four walked out the door.

The two strangers followed Jon and Boady to the stream and awkwardly began to wash. Timmy was particularly dirty and Jon decided to help him wash his face. Timmy was perplexed by the whole endeavor.

Jon decided to be kind. "If you know what's good for you, you won't start eating until grace has been said."

Timmy and Wren shrugged and followed the men back to the house.

When they got inside Lil said: "Wren and Jon will sit on the new bench. Timmy, you sit on the stump while Boady and I will take our usual seats. Supper is almost ready. Why Timmy! You have such an angels face behind that mask of dirt you usually wear!"

Timmy blushed and took his seat. Jon was genuinely happy to see Lil so excited. He wished he had thought of making the bench.

Why would a simple thing like a bench make a girl so excited? It did not matter. Jon was just glad he had a chance to see Lil even happier than she usually was. She made the room radiant.

Very shortly Lil brought two sausages to the table which already had potatoes, greens, bread and cheese. Timmy was unsure he had ever seen such a feast except on Christmas or Easter. Lil made the sign of the cross and the other four followed suit. When she finished grace all joined in a solemn "Amen."

Timmy and Wren started grabbing for the food.

"Gentlemen!" said Lil. "There's plenty for us all. Let's be kind to one another."

With sheepish looks Timmy and Wren started passing the food around. Jon and Boady simply smiled to themselves. How could a nine-year-old girl have such a commanding presence?

After supper Jon and Wren went for their ride while Timmy stayed behind to help Lil clean up. Boady decided to finish the bench inside the house rather than drag the dead weight back outside. Jon enjoyed riding Mayflower. She was gentle and obedient and seemed to work as hard as Jon to keep him in the saddle. Jon learned to trot, which was bumpy, but after a while he got the hang of it. After a couple of hours, he and Wren returned to the house.

Wren said "I think you won't embarrass yourself too much. Do you want to come back to the stable with me and learn how to care for the horses?"

"I have chores to do here." Replied Jon. "I took care of Sir Malpolem's horse, so I think I can handle that."

Wren looked disappointed but understood and soon rode off after thanking Lil for her cooking. It had been a fine day with the unexpected invitation and the chance to "do one's duty" by riding a horse. Then Jon remembered Wulf Schumacher and a shadow crept over his otherwise pleasant mood.

Lil was especially happy as they all sat down for their evening meal. It was truly amazing how much a bench that she didn't even use meant to her. Jon was somber and Boady seemed deep in thought as he nodded and smiled while Lil sang the praises of his handy work. At last Boady said "Be careful Jon."

Jon looked at him.

"I know you're careful in your speech, but you need to be careful in your acts as well." He continued. "The King's court is full of lies and intrigue. You don't need to get caught up any more than you already are. If you are to be rewarded, many will be jealous. If you are to be disappointed, many will try to turn you to their cause. The court is a complicated and treacherous place. I think they look to give and take offense there. With a child King, God only knows what's afoot."

Jon nodded and grunted.

Lil was not to be turned from her excitement: "But you'll get to go to the big church! And the clothes! There's a linen shirt and woolen breeches! You will be dressed like a gentleman! I wish I were a lady going to a party like that."

Lil got up from the table and promenaded about the room holding her skirt in one hand and making oddly exaggerated gestures with her other. At last she curtsied before the table; Jon and Boady could only laugh.

"So you were Sir Malpolem's page. It is a shame that he had to die. He was well spoken of as a kind and noble knight." She said taking her seat again.

This time it was Boady who stirred uncomfortably while Jon replied. "Yes, he was a good man. He always sought to earn his knighthood every day. He saw it as an undeserved gift that he had to use for good and truth."

This did not make Boady feel any better, but Lil loved what Jon had said.

"Isn't that just how we should all live our lives? God gives the gift of being alive and almost from the start we try to act as if we deserve that gift. But God gives life for a reason. We should use our lives to make life better for others and so to glorify God. Sir Malpolem had it right. I'm sure he is in heaven." She exclaimed.

Jon was not so sure, but he felt what Lil said made some sense out of life; gave it more purpose than merely existing. He also recognized that Lil, and even Boady who had killed Sir Malpolem, lived their lives that way: feeding the hungry and comforting the sick.

In Boady's case it was a shame that doing his duty often took him away from serving that nobler cause. Duty was not always pleasant; it could be very hard indeed.

"Yes, he was a noble knight. I hope he is enjoying peace and happiness now." Said Jon, but he did not believe what he said.

As they rose from the table to go to bed Boady looked at Jon and said: "Be very careful. I know you have been in court before, but as an invited guest rather than a servant people may pay attention to you. The King's court is a far more dangerous place than the preserve. Be very careful."

Jon understood what Boady was saying. "Still," he thought, "I bet Wulf Schumacher would rather have gone to the King's court than into the preserve."

Jon spent another restless night staring into the shocked expression of the man he had killed. While it was not pleasant, something had changed. The face seemed more human than demonic or ghostly. Jon so wanted that face to forgive him for what he had done.

7

A Prayer

J ON WOKE EARLY THE NEXT morning, but Lil was already awake. As he went into the main room he saw her kneeling in prayer. She turned and saw him and said: "Would you join me?"

Jon knelt beside her and made the sign of the cross. Lil whispered to him: "Why don't you pray?"

Jon had been at prayers often, but he had never really prayed himself so he said the first thing that popped into his head:

> "*Pater noster, qui es in cœlis; sanctificatur nomen tuum: Adveniat regnum tuum; fiat voluntas tua, sicut in cœlo, et in terra. Panem nostrum cotidianum da nobis hodie: Et dimitte nobis debita nostra, sicut et nos dimittimus debitoribus nostris: et ne nos inducas in tentationem: sed libera nos a malo. Amen.*"

"Amen." Repeated Lil. "That was nice Jon, but somehow I think it means more in our language. I know that Latin is the language of the Church and God, but I feel God understands our language better than we understand his. But still, it was a nice prayer. I just hope you speak to him in your words as well."

Jon smiled at her. She was right, of course. Jon got very little out of going to church because he understood so little of what went on; and he was lucky, he spoke some Latin. "I think you're right Lil. I guess I never thought much about actually wanting to speak to God. Why would he want to speak with me?"

"My mother always said that love comes from God." Replied Lil. "I suppose he would want to speak with you because he loves you."

"Maybe." Said Jon. "I'll stoke the fire if you want to wash up."

Lil smiled at Jon as she walked out the door. "Goodness that girl has a nice smile!" thought Jon.

As he stoked the fire and blew on the coals Jon's thoughts turned back to God. "What's going on?" he thought. "Do you have a plan for me or are you just toying with my insignificant life?" On thinking this Jon recoiled from his thoughts. God had been good to him. While he had lost both his mother and father, that was not unusual in this time, and he had landed well first with Sir Malpolem and now with Boady and Lil. "Forgive me God. Thank you for the blessings that I have." He prayed in his mind.

Although he had not made the sign of the cross, or said "Amen" Jon felt like he had had an actual prayer time where he had felt God's presence. He determined that he would do it again; silently in his own mind. He would think of God and pour out his heart. Perhaps God could be more personal than the man with the gray beard sitting on high judging everything we did.

Lil returned and Jon flashed her a smile. She smiled back and Jon went out to wash. Boady soon joined him.

"You look like you awoke in a pleasant mood." He said.

"I guess." Said Jon. "What shall we do today?"

"I'm not sure. I'm quite worried about your visit to the castle tomorrow. I think Lil and I will make ready to go and see the coronation as well." Replied Boady.

Jon appreciated the thought although he was unsure what they could do to help him if he needed it. "Thanks," he said, "It will be comforting to know that there will be some friends around somewhere, although I guess the Duke should be a friendly face."

"Don't count on the Duke." Said Boady sternly. "He's a good enough man, but the high born only have use for us if we are useful to them. I'm sure he will be better than most you meet, but I doubt that you really mean much to him; the secret you hold is dangerous to him, so guard it well."

Jon knew Boady was right. He felt that Sir Malpolem had genuinely cared for him, but everyone else he had met at court had their own agenda; even his fellow pages. Jon had never been that excited about going, but now he saw that it was another unpleasant duty that he owed his master: Duke Heimsteady. Jon longed to be free, but he knew no one who was actually in that position, not even the Duke himself.

After breakfast it was decided that Jon would go to the manor and get some bread if Kris had any. While he was there he thought to inquire about the plan for travel into town on Sunday morning. His first stop was the stable where he hoped to find Wren.

When he entered the stable he found Wren speaking with, or rather being spoken to, by a young man about Jon's age.

"There better not be any mistakes! Do you understand?" said the young man.

"Yes Master Aethelstan." Replied Wren. "Thunder will look his finest, I promise."

With that the man turned and seemed startled by the presence of Jon. "Who are you?" he demanded.

"I am known as Jon," Said Jon, "May I ask the same of you?"

"Ah, the Crown Prince's invited guest. You will accompany my father and me to the coronation. I am Aethelstan. After tomorrow you may call me Sir Aethelstan. Until then, I have little time to spare for you. Good day." Said Aethelstan as he marched out of the barn.

"Well, isn't he a pleasant fellow?" said Jon to Wren after Aethelstan had left.

"He is the Duke's son and feels that he will be knighted by the new King on the morrow. I think he is nervous and was here to insure that his steed, Thunder, is looking his best. Thunder will look fine, as will the Duke's horse, Beast. Are you here to look after Mayflower?" replied Wren.

"I hadn't thought of it, but I guess I should give her a brushing and maybe a carrot if I can wheedle one out of Kris. Do you know what the plan is for tomorrow? When do we depart?" answered Jon.

"I'm told that the horses are to be saddled before day break, but I suspect you should ask the Duke's Reeve of the exact plan. Perhaps you can take Mayflower with you tonight." Said Wren.

"A good idea." Said Jon cheerfully. The good mood he had developed at morning prayers seemed to be staying with him. "Where can I find the Reeve?"

"He should be in the room where those petitioning the Duke for justice wait. He'll be guarding the door to the Duke's court." Replied Wren.

"Thanks Wren," said Jon, "I'll see you and Mayflower again soon."

Jon went to the side door where he and Boady had both gone before. As he approached the Reeve the man greeted him: "Master Jon! My Lord the Duke just bade me send you a message. He wishes to speak with you. Please wait and I will let him know that you have already arrived."

With that the Reeve went into the Duke's court. Jon surveyed the room he was in. There were fewer people than on previous occasions but they all had alternately concerned or resolute looks on their faces as they waited for justice. The Reeve returned:

"The Duke bids you wait in the court until he has a chance to speak with you. Please be silent until spoken to."

With that the Reeve ushered Jon into the room he had visited twice before under momentous circumstances. Jon took a place by the wall and tried to be inconspicuous. The Duke was speaking:

"You will apologize for looking at your neighbor's wife, and you," he said turning to the other party, "will keep peace and harmony between you and your neighbor. It is good that you value your wife as a man values his treasure, but we shall have peace in my domain. You are not to make scandalous accusations based on the fact that you saw a man seeing your wife. Is that clear?"

"Yes my Lord." Said the plaintiff.

"Indeed my Lord." Said the accused who then turned to his antagonist and said: "I did not mean to offend you by greeting your wife. Please forgive my offense."

The offended party seemed hard put to accept the apology until the Duke glared at him and grunted.

"Apology accepted." He said through clenched teeth, then added, "For the sake of peace, stay away from my wife."

The Duke cut them off. "Wise advice." He stated. "Let neighbors live in peace."

The Reeve then escorted them out. As they left the Duke turned to Jon and said:

"There'll be trouble there. A man has already lost his wife when jealousy becomes that petty. In any event, I wanted to make sure you are ready for tomorrow. I know you have been in court before, and that you do guard your words, but what will you call the King should he call on you?"

"Your Majesty." Replied Jon.

"Very good. And the Bishop?"

"Your Grace, or your Eminence." Answered Jon.

"Good. You're better schooled than my son! Just remember that the goal is for you to say none of those things. The less you are noticed, the better for everyone. The Crown Prince has invited you for a reason that he is keeping from me. That is not good. You are my man, and I feel that I have been a good Lord to you in the short time you have been in my service. You showed yourself trustworthy in the matter I assigned to you. I demand your loyalty and have every confidence that you will give it to me." The Duke looked at Jon directly.

"Yes, my Lord. You have indeed been most gracious to me and have my loyalty." Replied Jon.

"You are a silver tongued fox!" exclaimed the Duke. "You always seem to know just what to say to me. It actually makes me a bit nervous. On the other hand, I also know that that you share Sir Malpolem's curse for honesty. I doubt that you could convincingly tell a lie; so keep your mouth shut. Is there anything you need from me?" finished the Duke.

"I need only know what the plan is for tomorrow. When shall we depart?" said Jon.

"We depart at sun rise. My wife will ride in a carriage while Aethelstan, yourself and I will ride with a few men to escort us on foot." Replied the Duke.

"If I may be so bold my Lord," said Jon, "may I take Mayflower with me to Boady's to save time in the morning?"

"Indeed." Replied the Duke. "But see to it that both you and the horse are fit for a coronation tomorrow. You seem cleaner than most around here, but bathe fully tonight."

"Thank you my Lord." Said Jon.

"You are dismissed." Said the Duke.

Jon left and headed towards the kitchen. The Duke had been kind to him, even indulgent; it also made Jon nervous. Boady had told him that his superiors only had care for him as long as he was of use to them, but what use did the Duke have planned? Jon said a prayer: "Father in Heaven, guide me." Somehow it gave him confidence.

"Hello Jon." Said Kris as Jon walked into the kitchen. "I hear you'll be attending the coronation. My what high company you keep! What brings you to my humble kitchen?"

Jon smiled. "Kris, my father's friend, I seek company I can trust, and I pray I will always find that in your kitchen."

"My, if you haven't a way with words!" chuckled Kris. "Aye, you'll have that here."

"Boady asked me to see if you have any bread." Said Jon. "Also, if I could have a carrot or two to make friends with my horse it would be much appreciated."

"You'll have both my boy! Ach, if Doogy could see you now he'd be so proud of ye." Said the cook as he handed Jon three small carrots and put four loaves of bread in a sack.

"Thanks Kris." Said Jon. Without thinking he added: "I hope you can come by some time and share stories of you and Boady and my Dad when you were little ones. I'd love to hear them."

"Thanks for the invite, I'd enjoy the telling." Replied Kris. "But I think you're getting ahead of yourself. 'Tis Boady's house you're inviting me to. None the less, I hope we get the chance to do it."

With that Jon headed out the door and back to the barn.

"Hey Wren!" called Jon as he entered the barn. Two other grooms looked up as Wren came out of Thunder's stall.

"Hello Jon. What's the plan?" said Wren holding a brush he had been using on Aethelstan's horse.

"I'll be taking Mayflower with me tonight and meeting the group at sun up. Can you give me a brush I can use on her?" Asked Jon.

"Sure." Said Wren.

Just then Aethelstan walked into the barn. "Wren! I specifically told you to prepare my horse! Why are you ignoring me to speak with this man?"

Before Wren could answer, Aethelstan approached his horse and the horse became nervous. "Thunder!" shouted Aethelstan and the horse became quite animated in its stall. The closer Aethelstan got the angrier the horse became. It kicked once and moved to the side pinning Aethelstan to the wall of the stall. As grooms approached the horse became more agitated.

"Do something!" demanded Aethelstan, but the grooms were afraid to approach lest the horse become even more upset.

"Without thinking, in reaction to a strange impulse within him, Jon approached the stall.

"Thunder." He said in a low calm voice. "What's the matter boy?" he continued. He stroked the horse on its flank and continued to speak in a low soothing voice. The grooms stared while Aethelstan had the good sense to stay quiet.

Jon worked his way to the front of the horse continuing to speak in low soothing tones. When he got to the horse's bridle he reached in his pocket and pulled out a carrot. "There you go boy." He said in the same calm voice.

Aethelstan worked his way out of the stall. "That horse better be ready." He said pointing at Wren and walking out of the barn.

Jon came to his senses. What had made him approach an angry stallion on behalf of somebody who did not seem very likeable? Jon had been around horses, but he was no groomsman. The horse nudged Jon, and Jon broke one of the two carrots remaining in his pocket. He gave the half carrot to Thunder and then said: "That's a good boy." And worked his way back out of the stall.

Wren looked at him wide eyed. "That was quite a feat Master Jon. That horse has a mean temperament. I guess you're more of a horseman than I gave you credit for."

Jon smiled and again wondered why he had done it, and even why it had worked; then he remembered his prayer: "Father in Heaven, guide me." Jon felt he had been guided. He began to have some confidence in the power of prayer.

"Thanks Wren." He said. "I'll take the brush with me and return it in the morning?"

Wren turned to another of the grooms who nodded. "Of course, but be sure to bring it back. We are held accountable for the Master's property." He said.

Jon thanked Wren and the other groom and got to work saddling Mayflower. After leading her out of the barn he gave her the half carrot he still had in his pocket, grabbed the sack of bread, and mounted up. They proceeded back to Boady's house at a slow pace.

Boady was chopping wood when they arrived. "You keeping her for the night?" he asked as Jon rode up.

"Aye." Replied Jon. "We leave at dawn tomorrow, and the Duke says I'm to take a full bath beforehand. I met Aethelstan. Not the most pleasant of fellows. Says he'll be Sir Aethelstan after tomorrow."

"He's a spoiled whelp and his mommy's boy. I'm not sure even the Duke likes him. Better stay clear of him as best you can." Said Boady.

Lil came out of the house. "Welcome back Jon. Ooh, you brought Mayflower! Will she be spending the night?"

"Indeed." Replied Jon dismounting the horse and handing Lil the sack of bread.

"Can I have a ride on her?" pleaded Lil with a smile on her face.

Jon looked at Boady who merely shrugged. How could Jon say "no" to that expectant smile? "Of course, right after dinner." He replied.

"Then you two hurry in." she exclaimed. "Dinner is almost ready!"

Jon and Boady went down to the stream to wash up, leading Mayflower who Jon decided would enjoy a drink. The horse drank deeply while the men washed. Soon the three headed back to the house. Jon tethered Mayflower in a grassy patch near the house and the men went in.

They sat down, Lil said grace, and they began to eat.

To make conversation Jon said: "Aethelstan's horse, Thunder, got upset and threatened to crush him. I'm not sure why I was able to calm the horse, but I think it may have been because of the way Lil taught me to pray this morning."

Lil looked up at Jon. "Did you pray a personal prayer Jon? How wonderful! What did you pray?"

"I just prayed that God would guide me." Jon replied. "When the horse got upset something came over me and I was able to calm it down and give it a carrot."

"How wonderful!" exclaimed Lil.

"Good for you Lad." Said Boady. "That Thunder can be a mean horse. His temperament matches his master's. You best be careful around both. Be thankful you had the carrot."

Perhaps Boady was right. Maybe Jon had succeeded only because he had the carrots. Then again, perhaps Lil was right; Jon had felt supernaturally calm as he unthinkingly handled the situation. Whichever the case, Jon was glad that he had prayed.

After they had finished their meal Lil began clearing the table. "Can Mayflower be as mean as Thunder? Will she like me?" she said.

"Mayflower is much calmer than Thunder." Replied Jon. "If you really want her to like you, give her this carrot." Replied Jon pulling his last carrot out of his pocket.

As they walked outside, Lil held the carrot in front of her saying: "Hello Mayflower. See what I have for you?"

The horse turned its attention toward Lil, and especially towards the carrot. This made Lil nervous, but Jon assured her there was little to fear. When they got close enough for the horse to reach the carrot it snatched it out of Lil's hand. She screeched and laughed as the carrot came to be with the horse, jumping back lest Mayflower decide to confuse her for a carrot.

"She sure is a big horse!" said Lil full of nervous excitement.

Perhaps Mayflower was big for a saddle mare, but she was small when compared to Thunder or Beast, the Duke's horse. They were war horses; as much a weapon as the lance or sword normally carried by their rider. "C'mon Lil. Hold my hand and we'll pet her." Said Jon.

Boady stood aside and watched the proceedings. When Jon had grabbed the bridal and Lil had begun petting Mayflower on her neck he approached.

"Lil, ladies ride side saddle, so let me lift you up while Jon holds the reigns." He said.

With Lil in the saddle Jon began walking the horse. Boady stayed near by making sure that Lil did not fall. Lil loved the experience.

"What a wonderful way to travel!" she exclaimed.

If Lil had had her way, Jon would have spent the rest of the afternoon walking the horse around the house. After a good long walk Jon explained that he had to brush the horse, take off its saddle and settle her for the night. He then needed to take a full bath and have both the horse and himself ready to accompany the Duke into town at sun rise. Lil reluctantly got down, and then ran to the garden where she pulled out another small carrot for the horse. This time she fed her with confidence. Jon doubted that Mayflower had ever had so many carrots in a single day.

Jon felt good about the brushing he gave Mayflower. As the sun moved nearer to the horizon Jon saw a reddish sky which gave him confidence that it would not rain and undo his work. He then went to the stream and took as thorough a bath as he could. He came out feeling clean and refreshed.

"My, don't you look like a dandy gentleman." Said Boady walking up while Jon dressed.

When they went into the house Lil had the table set and Jon saw that she had laid his clothes out on the new bench. Somehow she had made them smoother by holding them over some boiling water. Jon was very grateful for her efforts.

Jon's place was set at the stump, and before Lil finished grace she added: "Father protect Jon tomorrow. Guide him in your will and use him to your glory."

Before she could say "Amen" Jon added: "Thank you God for your protection and blessings. Please let us feel your presence with us tomorrow and keep Boady and Lil safe as well."

The three looked at each other and simultaneously said "Amen."

After dinner Jon checked on Mayflower one last time and they all went to bed.

8

The Coronation

J ON SLEPT LIGHTLY THAT NIGHT before the coronation. While he normally awoke before dawn, he could absolutely not afford to over sleep this day. After many restless hours he walked outside to check the moon; it was beginning to set in the west. To the east there was a slight brightening on the horizon. It was time.

Mayflower stood right where Jon had left her the previous night. Jon decided to go back inside and kneel by Lil's cross. He prayed silently:

> "Father in Heaven, great is your name. Let your will be done in my life this day. Forgive my short comings and guide me as you did yesterday. Deliver me from the evil and temptation I may face. For you are great, Father, and my hope is in you. Amen."

Just as he finished praying Lil walked in. She put her hand on his shoulder and then knelt beside him. After making the sign of the cross she also prayed silently except when she said "Amen" at the end. She then smiled at Jon and said:

"I have some bread and cheese ready for your journey. I suppose you will saddle Mayflower before you get dressed." She paused and looked at him. "God will be with you this day Jon."

Jon looked at her and was struck by the confidence with which she said those words. It gave him both anxiety and courage all at once. "Thanks Lil. I better get Mayflower ready." Was all he could say.

He saddled the horse and brushed her just a bit. Then he put the brush on the saddle so that he would not forget it. He washed himself before going back inside where Lil had the fire going.

"I'll cook an egg for you before you go, but be careful to keep your clothes clean." She said.

Jon smiled and said: "Thanks." He then went to change his clothes trying hard not to wake Boady. He needn't have bothered.

"Watch yourself Jon. And be sure to remember as much as you can of what you hear in small talk. Something is up, and somehow you're to play a part in it. Be careful." He said.

Jon paused, then replied: "Well, good morning to you as well!"

Boady chuckled and answered: "You'll be alright, I guess." He then got up and went out to wash up.

After getting dressed, Jon joined Lil where she gave him an egg and some bread for breakfast. Boady had joined them as he rose from the table to prepare to say goodbye.

"Well, I guess I'm off then. Try to enjoy yourselves in town and don't spend the whole time worrying about me. I've been in court before. I'm looking forward to seeing you both again tonight." Said Jon.

Lil began to fuss a bit with his clothes as Boady put a hand on his shoulder and said: "Take care. May God be with ye."

Lil added: "He is with you. And you look quite the part of a well-bred gentleman. Do us all proud."

Jon suddenly realized that he had never done anything that merited as good friends as these. He smiled and said: "I'll see you both tonight. Thanks for everything. I hope I can prove myself worthy of the kindness you give me." Then he walked out the door, mounted Mayflower, and went off towards the manor.

It was still dark when he arrived, but Wren and several other grooms were holding Beast and Thunder, fully saddled, and doing some last minute brushing. Jon dismounted and walked up to Wren.

"Good morning." He said. "Thanks for the use of the brush." He added as he handed it back to him.

"Good day Master Jon." Replied Wren. "My, don't you and Mayflower look good! Don't mind us, we're all in nervous anticipation of my Lord and his son's arrival."

The grooms continued brushing and it seemed they were trying hard to look busy when the horses' riders would come out. Beast and Thunder looked superb: each wore clothing with the Duke's colors and crest. They were far better dressed than the grooms who cared for them. There was also a single horse wagon suitable for the Duchess to ride in, and a well-dressed groom at the ready to drive it and care for the horses once they were in town.

After a few minutes the Duke came out. "Good morning." He said in a loud and enthusiastic voice. "The horses look fine. Good work men. Hello Jon, you look good as well."

Everyone, almost in unison, replied: "Good morning my Lord." Jon added a smile and nod as well.

"The Duchess and Aethelstan should be here momentarily. Someone help me up on my horse." Said the Duke.

Most of the grooms gathered around the Duke and Beast to assist in this mounting. Beast was a huge horse; he had to be if he was carrying the Duke in full armor. After mounting, the Duke came over to where Jon sat mounted on Mayflower. Jon felt small next to the Duke.

"What will you say when we get there?" asked the Duke.

"As little as possible." Replied Jon.

The Duke looked down on him and smiled. "You always have the right answer! Would that my son knew his place so well; then again, he is in a different place I suppose." Replied the Duke.

Just then Aethelstan came out accompanied by his mother who was fussing over his clothes. As much as Jon was impressed by the clothes that he was wearing, Aethelstan's clothing made him look positively shabby. Like his father, Aethelstan wore a tabard with the family crest, but his breeches were a bright blue, and his shirt was so white that it seemed to glow as the sun began to rise above the horizon.

He walked his mother to the carriage where he and some grooms helped her to get situated in her rather fancy but impractical gown. He then strode towards Thunder. The horse fidgeted.

"Hold him still!" bellowed Athelstan. Then turning to Wren he said: "I told you the horse was to look perfect. Do you call him perfect?" He then slapped Wren with the back of his hand, knocking him to the ground.

As Wren got up he looked down and said: "I'm sorry my Lord. We have done our best."

At this Aethelstan seemed ready to fly into a rage when his father intervened.

"Aethelstan!" he shouted. "The horse looks fine. Mount up and control your passions."

Aethelstan glared at his father but said nothing. Then, with the help of two grooms he mounted the horse who instantly became skittish. Jon heard the Duke sigh, and then gave the signal to head out.

Jon guided Mayflower behind the Duke's horse since they were standing together. Shortly Aethelstan came riding up and sneered: "Get back peasant! I ride behind my father and none else."

Jon held Mayflower back and allowed Thunder to take his place in the line, saying nothing.

After a short time on the road, the Duke urged Aethelstan to ride next to him. Even Thunder looked small next to Beast. Jon held back but could hear some of the conversation:

"What will you say when we get there?" asked the Duke.

"I will greet his majesty, compliment his clothing, and tell him that God is surely smiling on his coronation by giving us such fine weather." Replied the son.

The Duke paused for a few steps, and then said: "There is nothing particularly wrong with your answer, but what did I tell you to say?"

"You did not tell me what to say father." Replied Aethelstan.

The Duke sighed and beckoned Jon to ride with them.

"Jon, what will you say when you meet the Crown Prince?" asked the Duke.

Without hesitation Jon replied: "As little as possible, my Lord."

Turning to Aethelstan the Duke said: "Do you remember me telling you that as recently as last night?"

Aethelstan glared at Jon but replied in an even voice: "Yes, father, but I must make an impression. Even you said that there is nothing particularly wrong with how I intend to greet our soon to be King."

"Jon, do you know exactly what you plan to say to our Prince?" said the Duke.

"I suppose I will simply say 'Your Majesty.' And move on." Replied Jon.

"Don't you wish to make an impression on the Prince?" said the Duke.

Jon had not really thought about that, but he replied: "I suppose that I do my Lord, but there will be many waiting to greet our sovereign, and I hardly think a greeting line is the place to make much of an impression."

"Well said." Replied the Duke. "Aethelstan, this celebration is not about you. You will say as little as possible. Is that understood?"

The Duke then turned to Jon and said "Thank you." Jon took this as a dismissal and fell back.

"Father. Why don't you trust me?" said Aethelstan in a pleading voice.

"Did you hear what Jon said? He said both that the receiving line was not the time and place to make an impression, and also that there were others to consider. You do not consider others. If you wish to lead you MUST think of others, particularly the men you lead. Who are you to a King? Nothing! You are there to witness a coronation, the Crown Prince is there to become the King, none of this is about you." Was the Duke's answer.

"But I am to become a knight today." Said Aethelstan.

"Are you? What makes you think so? Even if you are, this celebration is still not about you; it is about the King." Replied the Duke.

Aethelstan once again glared at his father. The Duke shook his head sideways and Aethelstan fell back in line. Little else was said during the ride, but there was a palpable tension in the air.

Arriving in town, the small procession went straight to the castle where the grooms helped the Duke and Aethelstan dismount. Jon got off of Mayflower on his own and handed her reigns to a sheepish looking groom who had been tasked with helping him. Jon smiled, and the groom looked relieved.

Meanwhile, Aethelstan was directing other servants in helping his mother out of the carriage; apparently there was nothing that they could do right in the task without his guidance. The Duke sighed and motioned for Jon to join him and his family as they walked into the church where a long line was greeting the Crown Prince.

He was a small boy of about eleven years of age named Aerdwolf. He smiled as he accepted the many well-wishers' greetings. The Duke's party was lead to the front of the line to greet the soon to be King. The Duke arranged it so that Jon would be first, followed by Aethelstan, the Duchess, and himself.

As Jon approached the Prince he lowered his eyes and simply said: "Your Majesty."

"Welcome Jon." Said the Prince although the two had never been introduced. Jon returned his smile and moved on.

Aethelstan approached and said: "Good day My Lord Aerdwulf. God is certainly smiling on your coronation; what lovely weather we have!"

The Prince replied: "Good day Heimsteady." He then smiled, but not very warmly, and Aethelstan moved on.

The Duke and Duchess were referred to as Uncle and Aunt, and made their greetings brief. The four were then lead to a pew near the front of the church where they waited for the mass to begin.

After about half an hour a monk, who looked vaguely familiar to Jon, went up to the altar, genuflected and then took a seat off to the side. As the monk gazed out at the church he looked directly at Jon and a shiver went down Jon's back. The monk bore a startling resemblance to Jon's old master, Sir Malpolem. He was thinner, a bit older, and probably a bit taller as well. After a while, the monk smiled and went on to look at others in the gathered congregation.

After Jon relaxed his concentration on the monk, he noticed the Duke looking at him. Jon returned his gaze.

"Brother Johan." Said the Duke. "He has returned from the Holy Land just yesterday. My guess is he will want to speak to you about his brother. I am sure you know what to say and more importantly what not to say."

"Indeed, My lord." Was Jon's reply. "I will especially say as little as possible."

The Duke smiled, while Aethelstan looked somewhat puzzled.

At last the mass started. A choir of young boys sang as a procession headed by the Arch Bishop holding aloft the town's most valuable possession: A Latin Bible illustrated and copied by monks over-seas. Incense was burned and scented Holy water was sprinkled as the procession, including the young Prince made their way to the alter. The incense and water made the crowded church smell much better than it would have otherwise.

As the church went through the Litany of the Mass the congregation responded to the Latin words in the Latin language, while most had little idea of what they were saying. Jon was luckier than most as he had learned some Latin from Sir Malpolem. The reading of the Bible was from the Book of Romans and dealt with God's ordination of authority on earth. Many looked on in awe as the miracle of the Mass was performed and the bread and wine were turned into the actual body and blood of Jesus. Few people took communion, most likely because they had been too busy to give Confession of their sins to a priest the day before. Jon did not take communion, nor did any of the Heimsteadys.

After communion the Bishop gave a sermon on the passage in Romans and stressed to the crowd the reverence that they owed their King as God's chosen leader. To disobey the King was the same as disobeying God and Christ himself.

Then came the actual coronation. Aerdwulf was anointed with holy oil, pledged to lead his people to serve God and the Church, and then the Bishop placed the crown on his head. The Bishop did not actually let go of the crown for the young King's head was too small to hold it, but by the grace of God Aerdwulf was now King. A cheer arose from the congregation, and as it died down Jon could hear cheers coming from outside the church as well.

The King rose to speak to his people accompanied by the Arch Bishop as well as the King's chaplain and former tutor.

"My people," he began, "It is with great solametie (solemnity) that I accept this responsibility from God."

The King paused while his tutor whispered in his ear.

"I will strive to lead and serve you well." He continued as the priest whispered in his ear. "It is customary on this day that I create knights to serve me, but due to my young age I do not personally know many deserving of this honor. As a result, I, I mean we, wish to only knight one man. While those with my father at the time of his death chose to flee as he faced the fearsome dragon by himself, we cannot reward them for their actions. There is only one man who has fought this dragon and lived. We call forth Jon, Sir Malpolem's page, to be the first knight to swear allegiance to our royal personage."

Jon sat stunned in the pew as all eyes turned to him. After a bit the Duke leaned over and said with a certain sternness in his voice: "I think you better go up there. It is not good to keep the King waiting."

In a daze Jon rose from the pew and slowly walked towards the altar. Hardly knowing what he was doing Jon found himself kneeling before the King. Looking up he saw Sir Malpolem's old sword being brought to the King.

The Bishop then said in a strong clear voice: "Jon. Do you swear by the Holy Bible, in the name of Jesus Christ, and by your faith in God to serve King Aerdwulf as your lord and master; to give him homage and fealty and to serve him as your first lord save God and His church?"

Jon hardly knew what he was saying. He had only the vaguest sense of what fealty and homage were. Nevertheless, he looked up at the Bishop and said: "I do."

The Bishop anointed Jon with oil and then the King stepped forward and said: "I dub thee Sir Jon of the Dragon and give thee a quest to rid our land of the beast that continues to kill in our preserve." He then tapped Jon three times on the shoulders and said: "Arise Sir Jon of the Dragon and accept this sword."

Sir Jon looked up at the King and saw a young boy smiling at him. He felt that his duty to protect and serve this boy/King was a duty he could willingly accept. As he rose, the church began to cheer. As Jon turned to face the congregation he looked at the pew he had only recently been in. The Duke looked serious, but calm. The Duchess looked flustered and bewildered. There was anger and hatred in Aethelstan's gaze.

After the cheering died down the Bishop whispered in Jon's ear: "You should return to your seat." Jon returned to the pew. For the next hour or so all of the Kingdom's nobility came forward to swear loyalty, fealty, and homage to the new King. The Duke was one of the first, but Aethelstan was not called forward; he sat in the pew as anger festered in his soul.

Finally, processional music began to play as the Bishop, with the King next to him, led the group of priests and altar servants out of the church. While they were walking out a cheer began: "God Bless the King!" Soon the cheer was taken up outside and the whole town was shouting "God Bless the King."

Suddenly Jon found Brother Johan standing by him. "I am to escort you to the banquet. You will sit at a special table with me and others who are the King's personal guests."

Jon looked at the Duke who merely shrugged, but did not look pleased.

The crowds were already gathered around the church when Boady and Lil arrived, so there was little chance of getting close, and even if they had, they would not have been able to hear the proceedings inside. They stood among the huddled masses as word of mouth spread regarding what was happening inside. It was really like a game of "rumor" as one person told the next what had happened so that by the time the news got to Boady and Lil it was difficult to tell what was really true. Had they really carried the Prince in on a chair? Why?

Eventually news came that the Prince was now King and cheering erupted on all sides. This was at least believable. Then came news that the King would knight everyone in the church save one man; but this was quickly contradicted with the news that only one man was to be knighted. Apparently the one to be knighted was known around town as the executioner's son. Why would the King knight the executioner's son?

To Lil this all made little sense, she only hoped that Jon was alright. Boady felt a sense of foreboding at the news. Next they heard that the new knight was Sir Jon of the Dragon, and Boady smiled at Lil but felt very ill at ease. Had only one man been newly knighted, and was that one knight their Jon? Good for Jon, but what of Aethelstan?

Another rumor spread that the King had spoken ill of the men who had accompanied his father and fled while the former King had fought the dragon. Boady knew that he and the Duke had been those men, and suddenly it made sense; Jon had been knighted because he had fought the dragon and lived.

Lil realized that Jon had been the one knighted at almost the same moment: "It's Jon!" she shouted to Boady throwing her arms around him. "Jon is a knight in the King's service!"

Boady smiled at her and tried to look pleased.

"Oh no!" exclaimed Lil. "Does this mean Jon will no longer live with us?"

Boady did not know what all of this meant, but the anxiety he had felt upon waking that morning was now felt as a ringing in his ears. Somehow he knew that this was not good news. How could it be good news? Boady knew that Jon had never fought or even seen a dragon.

Rumors swirled for a good bit more, but eventually a cheer arose. Everyone was shouting: "God Bless the King!" as the King and his court came out of the church and paraded to the castle. Boady and Lil were too far away to actually see the King, but they heard that he was young, and handsome, and clean shaven with a dazzling smile.

"I thought he was a boy about my age?" said Lil.

"He is." Said Boady. "You can't believe everything you hear."

9

More Favors

ROTHER JOHAN ESCORTED JON FROM the church to the castle, or Keep, where the King made his residence and con-
ducted the affairs of the Kingdom. As they worked their way
through the crowd there was little chance to speak, but the good
Brother seemed to have an amiable and polite disposition; much like
his brother Sir Malpolem had had. Jon was nervous in his company,
but Johan's easy demeanor somewhat offset his nerves by making the
monk so likable. Brother Johan was not a frightening person; he did
not put on airs as to his importance or the great knowledge that a
world traveler must have acquired.

When they got to the banquet hall, Brother Johan took Jon to
one of the tables near the front of the room in front of the King's
own table. There were several tables for the high nobility, but most
knights and other assorted guests were expected to sit in the open
spaces at the hall. At present, they were the only two people who had
taken seats, but the hall was beginning to fill up.

"So," said Brother Johan, "My brother became a knight and you were his page. What can you tell me about him as a knight? How did he become one, and what sort of a knight was he?"

Jon found these better questions than the one he feared that he would be asked. "Well, he became a knight by defending the monastery against the pagan invaders. He held them at bay until the guard arrived. I think I can tell you the whole story, but it is somewhat private and I would not like to tell it here; your brother told it to me in confidence. As for what sort of knight he was, he was noble, kind, generous and always did his best to justify his nobility. He taught me some Latin as well as how to use a sword, and he took me in when my father died. He was the most honest and noble man that I have ever known, and I miss him."

"That's the brother that I remember." Said Johan.

"He would not have been a knight if you had not shown him how to sneak into the library, but that is part of the longer tale." Replied Jon.

Brother Johan seemed satisfied with Jon's answer for now. The hall was beginning to fill up. Jon saw the Duke and his family take a seat at their table, and the King's tutor and advisor came to sit at the table with Jon and Johan.

Johan was the first to speak: "Father Leonis, I believe you know Sir Jon from this morning."

"Indeed." Replied Father Leonis. "Congratulations on your knighthood Sir Jon. I hope you will take your duties, and especially your quest quite seriously."

"Thank you Reverend Father." Replied Jon. "I am dumb struck by the honor that God and the King have bestowed upon me. I will certainly try to live up to its calling." Jon realized that once again he was saying words that he meant but that had never occurred to him. This time he noted that it must be God speaking for him; another answered prayer.

Father Leonis smiled at the answer and said: "Johan and I are friends from childhood, so when we are speaking privately with us you may drop the title. Of course, if others are around I am absolutely your 'most Reverend Father.' Johan, has Jon answered your questions about your brother?"

"He's told me the same story about getting his knighthood defending the Monastery, but like you he has indicated there is more to the story. Unlike you, he does not have the confessional to shelter him from my prying questions, so my hope is that we can speak more privately soon." Said Johan.

"Well, he is to be housed with the guard while he undergoes training, so there should be ample opportunity for that." Said Leonis.

While not entirely surprising, this news shocked Jon. He had not yet realized that his knighthood would take him away from Boady and Lil, nor from the Duke. He knew the Duke would not like that at all.

"Thank you for telling me this." Said Jon. "I would wonder if it was not too early to ask a favor, but I feel compelled to ask none the less. I am currently situated with Duke Heimsteady and living with his forest warden Boady and his daughter. I am learning much about tracking, and the forest, and also use of the bow, axe, and dagger. While my first loyalty is unquestionably to the King, I wonder if I might not continue my residence at the Duke's if he is willing to train me in the martial arts?"

"My, you are bold." Replied Leonis. "I suspect that if the Duke is willing this can be arranged. I will see to it that you get a chance to ask the King tonight, and I will encourage him to accept your proposal. The King is well taken with you. You are the only man who has survived a fight with this dragon, and I see other reasons for him to accept it. I will speak on your behalf, but you must ask him yourself, and you must tell Johan about his brother's knighthood and death."

Jon wondered what those "other reasons" might be, but he was glad he might have a chance to stay with Boady. As food began to be served, Leonis became a very popular man and many people approached him to talk. Jon began to realize that he was seated at the table with the King's most trusted advisor; another unexpected honor. After a while, Jon noticed the Duke looking at him so Jon decided to escape the small but important conversations around him and go see the Duke.

"Shall I go with you?" asked Brother Johan. "I'd like to meet the Duke."

"Let me speak alone to him first." Answered Jon. "I will signal you to join us shortly."

Brother Johan smiled and nodded and Jon walked over to the Duke who pulled him aside and spoke to him in low tones for as much privacy as possible. "Well?" he said.

"The King intends for me to be trained with the guard, but Father Leonis will see if the King will allow me to stay with Boady at your manor. He says that you will have to be willing to train me and I am to remain the King's knight," said Jon.

"Not even a knight for a day and you are already asking favors that the King will grant?" said the Duke in astonishment.

"Well, Father Leonis will speak to him on my behalf." Replied Jon.

"If Leonis wants it, the King will give it to you." Said the Duke. "Of course I will agree to train you. You are being treated exceptionally well: A prime seat with Leonis and a favor being granted already. I wonder why?"

"Since I seem to be getting a lot of favors today," said Jon, "Brother Johan would like me to introduce him to you. May I call him over?"

"Of course." Said the Duke with a smile. "I would like to meet Sir Malpolem's brother as well."

Jon signaled that Johan should join them. "Duke Heimsteady, this is Brother Johan." He said.

"A pleasure to meet the famed world traveler returned from the Holy Land!" said the Duke enthusiastically. "I bet you have a tale or two to tell."

"It is a pleasure to meet you as well, my Lord. Indeed, I did see many strange things and animals on my travels." Replied Johan.

"You must come and share a meal with my family and regale us with tales of your travels. Will you remain in the Kingdom long?" said the Duke.

"I am uncertain what my plans are, but I will certainly stay a while, and I would be most honored to pay you and your family a visit. I assume Sir Jon has received your approval for remaining in your demesne, and I am also looking forward to discussing my brother with him." Replied Johan.

"Very well, then we will arrange for you to visit both of us in the near future." Said the Duke. "If you will pardon me, it seems the Duchess requires my attention. Jon, we will be leaving to return home soon, assuming you have the King's permission. It was nice to meet you Brother Johan. I look forward to us meeting again."

With that the Duke went to his wife with whom he passed a few words and then wandered off into the crowd. Aethelstan sat at the table with his mother looking angry as usual.

"I hope he will wait until you can speak with the King." Said Johan.

"I am sure he will." Said Jon. "We do not have too long a journey and I suspect he wants to win the King's favor. He was close to the King's father, but he seems less comfortable with the son."

"I am sure he is." Replied Johan. "After what the King said about the men who were with his father on the day he was killed, I bet the Duke is indeed anxious to make a good impression. Be careful Jon; he will try to use you."

Jon did not like this comment. "And will you and Leonis try to use me?" he asked.

Johan looked at Jon with a warm smile on his face and said: "I can see that you are wiser than your age and innocent appearance leads one to believe at first. Yes, everyone at court will try to use you Jon. Just remember who your true Lord is."

At that point a well-dressed man and women approached Brother Johan and began asking him questions about the Holy Land and his travels. Jon found himself effectively edged out of the conversation, so he returned to the table and listened to the talk around him. There was talk of an imminent invasion by the barbarians against the child King, and it was said that they already had spies in the preserve scouting out weaknesses. Jon was unsure of what weaknesses they would find in the preserve, but he listened any way.

Then he began to ponder what Johan had said: "Just remember who your true Lord is." Jon suddenly realized how many people he owed allegiance to. Of course there were the King, and the Duke, but also Boady, Leonis if he delivered the favor he had asked, and even Brother Johan as the closest relative of his first mentor Sir Malpolem. In fact, Jon even owed allegiance to Sir Malpolem's memory. Again Jon longed for freedom from all of these "lords" in his life.

After a while Father Leonis left the table to speak with the King. As soon as he did, the conversations around Jon became more hushed and were about Leonis himself. It was clear that there was a new regime in the Kingdom and people were uncertain of where they stood in it. These influential people felt insecure about their place, and Jon suspected the few who made small talk with him were trying to ingratiate themselves in case Jon was or would become someone important. Indeed, everyone at court was going to try to use everyone else to further their interests.

After a while, a page who Jon knew came to inform Jon that the King wished to see him. It was odd to hear someone who had recently been a peer now call him "Sir Jon", and show him respect and deference. When Jon looked to the King's table he saw that the King was no longer there. The page led him to a private chamber.

In the room was only the King, Leonis, and two members of the King's guard. When the page had introduced him, Jon dropped to one knee before the King and waited for him to speak.

"My dear Father Leonis, I do believe that Sir Jon is the only man who sees me more as a King and less as a boy." Said the King. "You may rise Sir Jon. The Father tells me you do not wish to serve in our guard. Why would that be?"

"Your Highness," replied Jon, "It is not that I have no wish to serve in your guard. I will serve you in any way that you ask. I feel that I am learning much in my current situation and feel that the knowledge I am gaining will make me better fit to serve you. Nevertheless, you have already given me more than I deserve or could hope for and I am so much in your debt that I am ashamed to ask for this favor. I will love you no less if I am denied. My desire is to serve you as best I can."

The King sat silently for a moment. Then, turning towards Leonis he said: "You are right my trusted advisor. The kind words that Sir Jon speaks do seem sincerer than the flattery everyone else gives us. He even tells me I can deny him easily. Of course I already know this, still no one else has even considered me denying them; they all seem to feel entitled to my good graces. Sir Jon, do you remember the quest you were given with your knighthood?"

"I do my Lord. At present I have no idea how to slay the dragon, but it will be slain." Replied Jon.

Jon really did not have any idea how a beast that does not exist could be slain. But the idea that this lie would live on and kill more people seemed unacceptable to him. The dragon would have to die somehow.

"And will you be better prepared to slay it by staying with the Duke?" said the King.

"My Lord, I am sure that the training with the guard would be of great service in preparing me to fight, but a dragon cannot be slain by brute force alone. Living with The Duke's forester may give me the skills I need." Said Jon.

"You like the Duke do you Sir Jon? You are loyal to him?" said the King.

"I do like the Duke, your Majesty. I have some loyalty towards him because he has been kind to me and is kind and just to his peasants. I also know he loved your father and he has told me that you are our best hope to save the Kingdom. I pray my Lord that you will find him as good and reliable a man as I perceive him to be. Nevertheless, I have sworn my oath to you. I owe you everything that I am. My first loyalty is to your person. I can accept being separated from the Duke." Said Jon to his own astonishment.

The King seemed quite taken aback.

"You did hear what I said about those present at my father's death, did you not?" he said.

"I did, my Lord. And I know how I felt when I lost my father to the plague. I wanted someone to blame, and you have people to blame in your father's death. Still, your Majesty, blaming them will not bring back your father and our former King. Give them a chance to be redeemed. Duke Heimsteady has defended this Kingdom from the pagans many times at the side of your father. Your father trusted him enough to go on a hunt with him. Duke Heimsteady did not kill your father; the dragon did." Said Jon, then adding: "Forgive me your Highness, I speak too much."

The King looked moved. It actually looked like he was going to cry. "You may leave us." He said. "You shall have our decision shortly."

Jon backed out of the room feeling nervous, but Sir Bendris, the Captain of the Guard, nodded to him as if he approved of what Jon had said.

Back in the room there was silence, but tears were now visible on the Kings cheek.

"I am so angry at Heimsteady and the other." Said the boy. "Yet, you have been trying to say the same thing to me since my father's death, only not as clearly. He is the only person that I have spoken to who had something good to say about the Duke, yet his words seem more honest and less self-seeking than any I have heard. What say you my teacher?"

Leonis moved before the King, knelt on one knee and took his hand. "Aerdwulf, no one can blame you for being angry, but the Duke is your strongest noble and the one most fit to protect you and the Kingdom. If you cannot forgive him, you must at least give him a chance to redeem himself. Sir Jon spoke as he did because he is honest and not sophisticated enough to know that he should never contradict you. I sense he can be trusted to at least tell you the truth as he knows it. Even if you do not wish to trust the Duke, you need to trust someone and those worthy of your trust are in short supply. Trust Jon that he will watch the Duke for you, and then give the Duke a chance to redeem himself and earn your confidence."

Aerdwulf sat in his chair more as a boy and less as the King. Leonis took a cloth from his pocket and wiped away tears.

Finally, the King returned and turned to the guards saying: "Send someone to bring us Duke Heimsteady."

As soon as Jon left the King's chamber the Duke came to him.

"What did he say?" said the Duke.

"He does not seem to like you my Lord." Replied Jon. "He did not give me an answer as to whether I can stay with you."

"That is hardly news after what he said in the church. Damn!" said the Duke. "He hasn't even spoken to me; his strongest and leading noble! I bet Leonis is poisoning his mind."

"I don't think so." Said Jon. "I suppose it could be, but I think Leonis would understand that the King needs you. I just don't know. I've been at court before, but I've never dealt with anything like this."

Aethelstan walked over. "So, Sir Jon, can we leave now?" he said in a sarcastic voice.

The Duke raised his hand to strike him, but Jon stopped him by saying: "That won't help my Lord." Then turning to Aethelstan he said: "No Aethelstan, we may not leave yet. I am sure your father will let you know when we can."

Now Aethelstan looked like he was ready to hit somebody: Jon. There was deep hatred in his eyes as they glared into Jon's eyes, but Jon did not blink. Finally, Aethelstan walked away.

The Duke chuckled. "There must be something to that anointing. You seem a changed man Sir Jon. You handled that well." He said.

Just then a page came up and informed the Duke that the King wished to see him.

"Wish me luck." He said as he departed.

"God be with you." Thought Jon as he watched them go.

As they walked into the King's chamber the page announced: "Duke Heimsteady, your Majesty." The Duke fell to one knee and kept his head down. The King was silent until the page had left.

"Rise good Duke." Said the King and the Duke rose to his feet.

"You are no doubt aware that we are quite displeased with your actions in regard to having let our father be killed. Nevertheless, you seem the only man that others are willing to speak well of on this day. Mind you, plenty speak ill of you as well, but I trust our good Father Leonis and my new knight, Sir Jon. What have you to say?" said the King.

"Your Majesty. I was your father's closest friend, and I wish I could have found a way to preserve his life." Answered the Duke.

"His death is without question the greatest failure in my life. We were all so happy before it happened. I miss my King and more importantly my friend as well. What can I say? I did what I could? There was nothing I could do. I grieve with you my Lord."

At this point a tear formed in the Duke's eye. The King saw it. Soon there were tears in his eyes as well. Leonis was uncomfortable watching the scene. At last the King took his hand and wiped away his tears and said:

"I am told that I need you good Duke. I am told I must forgive you. Seeing tears in your eyes makes that easier to do, but you must earn our trust. I ask you to take Sir Jon and train him for me; remember always that he is my man, not yours. Further, you are to assist him in his quest; it is our hope that this will help you restore some of the honor that you have lost. Finally, I want you to clear our preserve of any pagans and spies that may be there. Give Sir Jon a leading role when this is done. Is that understood?"

"Yes your Majesty." Replied the Duke. "I will try to serve you better than I did your father. I pray that I will earn your trust."

"Thank you good Duke." Said the King. "We pray for the Kingdom's sake that you will. It has been good to see you again, Uncle."

The Duke stood perplexed for a moment, but came to understand that he had been dismissed and backed out of the room. He was in a bit of a stupor as he entered the banquet hall. Jon spotted the Duke and approached him.

"Are you alright my Lord?" he said.

The Duke looked at him and replied: "Yes, it went far better than I feared it might. I am to train you and tomorrow I have a mission for you and Boady. It is the King's mission, as it was stressed to me that you are his knight and not mine." The Duke had a smile on his face as he said this. He then placed a hand on Jon's shoulder and said: "Thank you for whatever it was that you and Leonis said to the King about me."

"I spoke the truth." Was Jon's only reply.

The Duke gathered his family and they, with Jon, headed for the stable to make their way back to the manor.

The day was not as eventful for Boady and Lil. After the banquet started some servants, escorted by members of the guard, came outside and began distributing small sweet breads to the gathered crowd. Most people grasped at them with greed and desperation and eventually the servants and the guard began throwing the bread into the crowd. Lil and Boady each got one and ate the treat, but they were not as hungry or greedy as most people seemed to be. Boady tried to get Lil off to the side lest she be injured in the mad rush.

As they stood watching an older lady with an armful of the small loaves approached them and said: "Master Boady. Did you and Lil get some bread? You have given me food when I was hungry and I certainly can return the favor."

"We each got one Esmerelda." Replied Boady. "You keep what you have and feed your family a treat."

She smiled and went on her way. After a while Boady saw little reason to remain. Lil had watched a puppet show and seen a man on stilts, but they still had to walk back to their home. Realizing that there was little chance to help Jon even if he needed them, they left.

10

A new Identity and a New Mission

THAT NIGHT THE RIDE HOME to the manor was mostly pleasant. The Duke was in a good mood even if Aethelstan and the Duchess were less so. Jon, also felt a sense of accomplishment as they rode. They dropped the horses at the stable right at dusk and Jon began the short walk back to Boady's house. As he walked alone a sense of pride began to build in him. He was now a knight, he had spoken to the King and seemingly influenced his decision, and he had even put Aethelstan, that stuck up prig, in his place, which was for the time being definitively below him. He had even made a point of placing his horse behind the Duke's as they returned and Aethelstan had not challenged him. For one of the few times in his life, Jon felt like someone important.

Arriving at Boady's he was greeted with congratulations and sincere joy for the new knighthood that he had received. He was a bit embarrassed by Lil's question about why some of the town's people referred to him as "the executioner's son", but Boady had quickly changed the subject by asking whether he would still be living with them.

"The King granted me a favor and allowed that I could stay here if I wished." He had replied, making it sound like the King had simply granted his wish. Boady became suspicious of this and asked Jon to accompany him to the woods before they went to bed.

As they stood side by side urinating on a tree Boady said: "I find it difficult to believe that the King simply granted a wish that his new knight could stay at the manor of a man he singled out for embarrassment."

Jon paused before answering. "It is true he was not initially fond of the idea, but his closest advisor, Father Leonis, spoke well of both myself and the Duke to convince him. I think I am supposed to keep my eye on the Duke."

"That's still an amazing level of trust being put in a new knight who neither of them know well." Said Boady. "Be careful Jon. No one can serve two masters."

Perhaps he was tired, but this comment caused a flash of anger to run through Jon. "Are you saying you do not want me here?" he snapped back.

Boady replied in a low, measured, and authoritative tone: "You know that is not the truth. You mean a lot to Lil and me. You are of peasant stock, and you have suddenly been risen high for a deed you did not do. Are you worthy of it? Yes. Did you earn it? No. Guard yourself against yourself as well as against those who would use you."

At first these words made Jon even more angry, but he soon realized that Boady was telling him the truth because he cared, and because Jon had momentarily come to believe that he had earned his knighthood. He had not. He was now trapped just as Sir Malpolem had been trapped by his knighthood.

He calmed himself and said: "You're right Boady. I had almost forgotten. I need to earn this knighthood that I have been unjustly given. I asked to stay with you and Lil because I trust both of you, and that means I need to listen when you reign me in. As a knight,

I am going to give you a difficult order: protect me from myself. Remind me of who I really am. No, I cannot order you to do that, but as a trusted friend and mentor, can you do it all the same?"

Boady put his arm on Jon's shoulder and said: "I will try. Rising so high so fast will be a challenge for you. Pray that God will help you to see when you are being foolish because He knows your heart, and I do not. But I will try."

Jon felt like the evening had suddenly been deflated. He now felt a bit foolish, but he replied: "Thanks my friend. Sincerely, thank you."

That night Jon did not sleep well. The face of the man he had killed kept recurring in his dreams, along with the King telling him that he must kill the dragon. When he awoke both Boady and Lil were already up as Jon quickly dressed in his usual clothes. He then fairly stumbled into the other room.

"Good morning Sir Jon!" said Lil enthusiastically.

Jon gave her a strained smile and left to go and wash up without saying a word. The sun was just above the horizon indicating that Jon had definitely slept later than usual. He mechanically washed his face and thought of what he needed to do this day. He recalled that the Duke had told him that he and Boady had a mission to do so he determined that they would go to see the Duke as soon as breakfast was done.

Returning to the house, Jon took his seat and waited for Lil and Boady to join him for breakfast.

When they had been seated Lil said: "Jon, would you like to say grace, or did you say your prayers outside?"

Jon did not want to say grace and he was tempted to lie about having said his prayers, but it struck him that this was the first morning in several that he had not awakened eager to spend time with God. It also stuck him that he had more to be thankful for than in any previous morning. What was happening to him?

Jon relented and bowed his head as Boady and Lil made the sign of the cross. He quickly imitated them and said: "Thank you Father for the blessings that you have given us, and especially me. Thank you for Boady, and Lil who remind me that it is You who are great, and not me. Guide me Father as I need you more now than I ever have. Amen."

"Amen." Repeated Lil and Boady.

Lil thought it an odd grace. Jon had not even mentioned the food, but Boady looked up and said: "A wise prayer Jon. Ask for His guidance, and listen to it."

It was then that Jon realized that he had not really thought the prayer he had said. Yes, he meant the words, but he was going to simply recite Lil's "Bless us oh Lord" grace. It comforted him.

As they began to eat Jon said: "The Duke has an assignment for us this day, Boady. We need to pay him a visit after we eat."

Boady looked at Jon and replied: "Yes, my Lord."

Jon felt embarrassed, and said: "Let me rephrase that. I think we ought to visit him after breakfast. What do you think?"

"Sounds like it Jon." Replied Boady. "It's hard for me too. Pardon me; I know you better than that."

"You know me well enough my friend." Said Jon. "Lil, Boady, I am a guest in your home. I think we need a rule that this place should be the one place I can go and not be a knight. You are both like family to me."

Boady smiled while Lil said with a giggle: "My brother the knight!"

Jon smiled and felt better. After breakfast Boady and Jon walked to the manor.

"What kind of a mission does the Duke have for us?" asked Boady.

"I'm not sure." Replied Jon. "It's something the King told him to have me do."

Boady and Jon walked in through the side door that they had used before. There were few people there as yet, and the Reeve had apparently just taken up position.

This time, instead of speaking to Boady the Reeve said to Jon: "How can I be of service, Sir Jon?"

Jon was a bit taken aback by this new found respect and stood a bit taller as he said: "Please tell my Lord, the Duke, that Master Boady and I are here to see him."

"Yes my Lord." Said the Reeve and he went through the door in search of the Duke.

As they waited, more people came into the room. Jon could see several of them looking at him and whispering to each other. He did not feel particularly comfortable with his new found celebrity. It seemed to Jon that they waited an uncomfortably long time.

At last the Reeve reappeared: "My Lord. The Duke bids you wait in his court and asks me to tell you that you may now seek him out at the front door. There is no need to unnecessarily expose yourself to the common folk."

Jon gave the Reeve a puzzled look but simply replied: "Thank you."

Even this simple courtesy seemed to catch the Reeve off guard.

The room was empty and Boady began to chuckle.

"My, you have come a long way in a short time!" he said in a mirthful tone. "I hope you are alright spending time with this commoner!"

Jon looked serious and said: "This is going to take some getting used to. I still feel like the same man I was yesterday, but I guess others don't see me that way. I am beginning to think that being a knight is not all that it is cracked up to be."

"Nevertheless, it's your duty now." Said Boady sympathetically.

After a short wait the scribe walked into the room and greeted Jon while ignoring Boady. A short while later the Duke joined them.

"Good morning my Lord." Said all three men simultaneously.

Looking at Jon the Duke said: "You hardly look like a knight Sir Jon. Where are the clothes that I gave you?"

Jon felt a bit embarrassed and said: "I did not realize that they were mine to keep my Lord. I was going to wash them and return them to you."

"Nonsense my boy!" said the Duke. "They are yours to keep and more. I am giving you Mayflower, her saddle, and her bridle. You did me a huge favor yesterday. I feel that I am in your debt."

Jon was flabbergasted; more favors? To this he replied: "Thank you, my Lord, but it is I who feel in your debt. I owe you my life."

Boady and the Duke stirred uncomfortably and Jon realized that he had made a mistake by saying this with the scribe writing what was being said. He quickly added: "It was you who found me after my battle with the dragon."

The Duke smiled and said: "Whatever debt that you owed me is forgiven. You are the King's man now." Then, turning to Boady he added: "Master Boady. I would like to send some men to your house to build a stable for Sir Jon's horse. While the house is technically mine, I wish to consider your feelings in the matter. What say you?"

"How can I object to such a generous offer my Lord. Thank you for your consideration." He replied.

Turning to the scribe, the Duke dismissed him. After a short pause he indicated to Boady that he should check the doors. Then Jon and Boady approached the chair where the Duke was seated.

Looking at Boady the Duke said: "The King wishes us to check the preserve for the presence of spies or Kells. He instructed me to give Sir Jon a prominent role, so Jon will head the expedition. I want you two to go alone as I think a greater number would attract unnecessary attention." Turning to Jon he added: "You are in charge, but I hope you will rely on Boady as I rely on him. Boady knows what he is doing, and as yet I fear that you may not. Do you understand?"

"I do my Lord." Said Jon earnestly.

"You are a knight, so you will take your horse. She may be a bit of a nuisance, but you will make more of an impression if you are riding. Bring your sword and change your clothes. If you find someone in there you may kill them if they are our people. If that happens, I want you to start a fire to make it look like the dragon did it. If there are just a few Kells and you can kill them, then do the same thing. But be careful, we want to avoid trouble with the Kells if we can. If you can find a peaceful way out with them, that would be better, but make sure that they know that the preserve is still being patrolled. If you find nothing, then just build a fire on your way out to remind the people of the dragon. Any questions?"

Jon looked to Boady who said: "No, my Lord. If we find a lot of Kells we will return here to warn you as quickly as we can. If the Kells are in the preserve, they are either hunting for food or massing for an attack."

"Well said Boady." Replied the Duke. "If you speak with the Kells Jon, do so from horse back. The Kells do not have many horses and seeing a mounted man will lead them to believe there are other men nearby."

"Yes my Lord." Said Jon.

"Very well." Said the Duke. "You be off then. I expect a report by some time tomorrow. If I don't get one, I will assume the worst. God speed to you." The Duke rose to leave but turned before he left the room. "Jon, use the front door. You're a knight now."

"Yes my Lord." Said Jon seriously as the Duke left.

"Where to now my Lord?" said Boady with a smile.

"I guess we get my horse, then return to the house so I can change my clothes, and then we get on with our duty. You know, it troubles me that I am asked to keep the dragon alive while I have been quested to kill it. Serving two masters is certainly difficult." Replied Jon.

Boady nodded in response, and then Jon added: "Which door am I supposed to leave by?"

Boady laughed and said: "I only know one way out, so I guess you will have to chance it!"

As they approached the stable Wren came running up and said: "My Lord, Mayflower is almost ready I shall bring her to you shortly." He then cringed as if waiting to be hit.

Jon put his hand on Wren's shoulder, which made the groom flinch. Looking Wren in the eye he said: "Wren, I am the same man I was yesterday. When others are around you should show me courtesy, but when it is just us you can relax. I will not feel a bigger man if I make you out to be a smaller one."

"Thank you my Lord." Said Wren with a smile. "I'll finish saddling her right quickly."

As Wren turned to leave Jon asked: "Where is everyone Wren?"

"They've gone to get wood for your new stable at Master Boady's house." He replied.

Jon looked at Boady who shrugged and said: "Well, it was nice that he asked."

Shortly, Wren brought out Jon's horse. She seemed happy to see him; do even animals recognize nobility? Wren offered to help Jon mount, but Jon waived him away.

"Shall we go?" he said to Boady who had begun to walk. "Thank you Wren. Good day to you."

"And a good day to you as well, Sir Jon." Said Wren as they departed.

In a very short time Jon felt awkward riding while Boady walked. He dismounted and led Mayflower as he walked by Boady's side. Boady looked over and smiled. Jon was all too aware that he not only served two masters, but he also lived in two different worlds. He couldn't wait to get back to the house where he could stop being a knight if only for a bit.

As they approached the house Lil came running up and Mayflower became noticeably happy. Apparently the horse was less impressed with Jon's new found nobility than with Lil's generous hands.

"Is Mayflower coming to stay with us?" she exclaimed as she came up to them. "Some men came and said that they would be building a stable for her. They went into the forest to gather some wood."

"Yes." Said Jon. "Mayflower is now my horse, but Boady and I have to leave for a bit. We will probably be gone all night. Can you get us some food to take along?"

"Of course." Replied Lil. "And I'll pack some extra apples and carrots for Mayflower as well. Welcome home girl." She added while petting the horse's neck.

Jon changed his clothes and hung his new sword to his belt. Boady gathered his daggers.

"Would you like my short sword Boady?" said Jon on an impulse.

Boady smiled but replied: "I really would not know how to use it, and I think you should take both your swords. Having two swords will make you seem more impressive, and a short sword is actually more useful if you ever have to fight in a shield wall."

Jon shrugged and stuck his other sword into his belt. Then they were ready to leave. After saying good bye to Lil they set off as some men emerged from the forest carrying wood suitable for building. They all greeted Jon formally, but Jon just waived to them. He was eager to get under way on his first mission as a knight.

11

Kells!

S INCE THEY PLANNED TO SPEND the night in the King's Preserve, Jon and Boady were better prepared for this trip than they had been for their last visit. Mayflower carried the provisions as Jon and Boady walked side by side towards whatever awaited them. With every step that they took Jon's feeling of the seriousness of the task he had been given grew. While he and Boady had performed a mission in the preserve before, Jon had simply been along on that one; Boady was responsible. This time, Jon had been tasked with carrying out the task for both the Duke and the King. While in practice little had changed, this mission felt much different to Jon.

"What're you thinking about Jon?" said Boady.

"I guess I am thinking about what all could go wrong on our mission, and about how lucky I was that you were in charge the last time we went in there." Came the reply.

"You know; I have never been able to predict the things that have gone wrong when I am sent. Things always go wrong, and being ready for what could happen is important, but I've always found it far more important to be clear on what the goal is rather than how I am going to deal with what goes wrong." Said Boady.

"I guess I get what you mean." Said Jon, although he really did not.

"What happens if we meet people from town?" asked Boady.

"I guess we have to kill them and make it look like the dragon did it." Said Jon.

"Is that our mission?"

"That's what the Duke told us to do. I would hate to do it, but as you taught me, duty is not always pleasant."

"But, why are we being sent into the preserve?"

"The King wants us to make sure that the Kells are not preparing to attack us."

"Will killing our own people accomplish that? What if there are a dozen of them and we can't be sure we will get them all? What if we meet them right at the beginning, before we have even looked for Kells? The Duke said we can kill them and even said it would be good to remind people that there is a dragon, but he did not say you have to kill them. That's what is different this time. In the past you have been given small tasks without a lot of room for interpretation. Last time I told you not to let one-man escape, and you didn't. This time the Duke has tasked you with using judgement; You need to satisfy both the Duke and the King. I think you need to focus on your first task first; then determine if you can meet the other goals." Said Boady in wise counsel.

"I see what you mean." Replied Jon. "If we meet our people I can decide what needs to be done based on the circumstances, but our main task is to see if there are Kells in the preserve. The better question to ask is what we will do if we meet the Kells."

"Right. So, what will you do if we find Kells in the preserve?"

"If there are a lot of them, armed for war, we will head back immediately and warn the Duke and King. I guess if we see just a few we will need to try to stay hidden and watch to get an idea of what they are doing. If it's just one, we may try to capture him. Again, it all depends on the situation." Said Jon.

"Right." Said Boady. "But we are also tasked with making it clear to the Kells that the preserve is patrolled. Your task is all about deciding what needs to be done. My task is to help you do that."

The two walked in silence for a bit as Jon pondered what Boady had said. The more he tried to think about the situations that they might face, the more he realized that he could not make a specific plan for what they might face. "Lord, help me." He found himself praying over and over in his mind. Jon was afraid that he would do the wrong thing. He was glad that Boady was with him.

As they neared the edge of the preserve, Jon suddenly realized that he was hungry. He was about to tell Boady that they would stop and eat now, when he suddenly had a moment of clarity. Instead he said:

"Are you hungry Boady? Maybe we should eat before we go in; what do you think?"

Boady smiled and said: "I think it's high time you thought about that! An army marches on its stomach, you know."

They stopped near a grassy meadow. Jon took some bread, cheese, and apples from Mayflower's pack and brought it to Boady. Before sitting down, he went back to Mayflower and gave her one of the carrots that Lil had packed for her. Mayflower was also one of his responsibilities. He patted her gently and went back to Boady while Mayflower grazed on the grass.

Boady ate with purpose, so Jon imitated his haste. When he finished his meal he went back to the horse and got a couple of dried pieces of meat. Handing one to Boady he said: "You ready?"

Boady took a bight of the meat, got up and grunted. Jon took Mayflower's reigns and they quietly marched into the preserve.

Boady took the lead while Jon followed as quietly as he could while leading a horse. As before, there were frequent stops while Boady paused to listen, but the preserve seemed very quiet. They came to a stream where all of them took a drink, and then they moved on. For two hours, hardly a word passed between them and nothing seemed to happen.

They were deep into the preserve, possibly even on their way out of it, when Boady stopped and put his finger to his lips. He indicated Jon should hold back and snuck off into the underbrush.

He seemed to be gone a good while, and Jon was worried; what if something happened to Boady? As he was thinking this Boady suddenly reappeared.

"There's three of them, somewhat heavily armed, but seem to be hunting. They're putting a deer they killed on a donkey that they brought." He whispered to Jon.

"What should we do?" asked Jon.

Boady looked him in the eye and replied: "I am supposed to ask you that."

Jon was stunned. He took a moment to think and said: "Can we handle them if there is a fight?"

"I think so, but I think I recognize their leader. He's a man I've met in battle, and he's tough. It won't be an easy fight."

Jon took this in and said: "The Duke said to try to awe them with the horse and to try not to get in a fight. I think I need to ride in on Mayflower while you stay hidden and are ready to help if I need it."

Boady looked skeptical, but finally said: "Well, I really don't have a better idea, but you are REALLY sticking your neck out. They could kill you before I have a chance to do anything."

Briefly, Jon got a frightened look on his face, but suddenly he found himself at peace with the decision that he had made. It was not that he was calm, he was very nervous, but he was determined to do what he had said. He nodded to Boady and walked back to Mayflower. He took the supplies off of her, but absent mindedly put two carrots in a pocket, and mounted. Then he urged her forward.

The Kells were all looking at Jon as he came out of the woods mounted on Mayflower. There were two younger men who had smaller axes at their sides and bows drawn and pointed at the rider. At the donkey was an older man, very stocky and muscular, with a large axe now in his hand as he stepped clear of the donkey.

For a moment they all looked at each other in silence. Jon was not holding his weapons, but they were plainly visible and available.

101

The leader said something to the other two men, and they lowered their bows. They all stood there looking at each other for a moment until Jon said:

"You go?"

The leader looked puzzled and said something close to Saxon: "Fight?"

"No." replied Jon shaking his head. "Peace."

The Kell pointed to the deer on the donkey. In response Jon shrugged his shoulder and waived his hands indicating that he did not care about the deer. To this the Kell reacted by pointing to himself and saying: "Kyp."

Jon took this as an introduction and pointed to himself saying: "Jon."

The Kell smiled and seemed ready to head off. Just then there was a great deal of noise and Aethelstan, mounted on Thunder, came charging at the Kell, sword drawn. The horse did not seem well in control, but Aethelstan seemed intent on killing Kyp.

"No!" shouted Jon, but his word had no effect.

As Aethelstan bore down on him, Kyp had his large axe drawn and seemed calmly and intently in control. Thunder came right at him, but Kyp stepped aside and Aethelstan swung his sword, but missed badly. As the horse went by, Kyp took a swing at Aethelstan, but Thunder was fast and the axe missed the rider and opened a large gash on the horse's flank. The horse reared throwing Aethelstan to the ground right in front of the Kell. Jon quickly dismounted and drew his big sword yelling "No! No! No!"

Kyp knelt on Aethelstan's chest and held his axe over his head. The other two Kells were distracted by Boady who had come out of the woods, and another man, about Aethelstan's age who held a bow very uncertainly.

Kyp and Jon looked at each other. Jon suddenly decided to put his sword back in his belt.

"No." he said in a low pleading voice. "Peace. No fight."

Kyp looked confused. Jon held his hands out and said "Peace. No fight." Tentatively he took a step towards the Kell who did not move. Jon walked right up to him and gave him a sincere look. "No fight." He said.

The Kell was uncertain what to do. Certainly there would be losses if he did fight, and he had no idea how many other Saxons might be around.

Jon held his hands up and put his boot heavily on Aethelstan's neck. Aethelstan began to gurgle. Looking down at Kyp, Jon said "Go."

Kyp hesitated for a moment, but then smiled. "No fight." He said.

"No fight." Replied Jon. "Go."

The Kell got off of Aethelstan's chest and walked to the donkey. Jon kept his foot firmly planted on Aethelstan's neck. Kyp motioned for his other two men to join him and they warily made their way off as Jon, Boady, and the other man watched. As they entered the woods the leader turned back and waved to Jon. Pointing to himself he said "Kyp." Pointing to Jon he said "Jon." Jon smiled and waved back.

As the Kells made their way off one of the younger men said to Kyp: "Now what?"

Kyp responded: "We go back and make our report. Keep ready though as there may be more Saxons about. Clearly they are patrolling this woods that is normally empty, and just as clearly they don't want a war with us right now. I recognized one of the men that came out of the woods. He is one of the Duke's trusted lieutenants. The Duke is not a stupid man. He is their best leader in war. This Jon, is obviously either very brave or very stupid. He put his life on the line to preserve the peace. I'll call him brave until he proves otherwise. Meanwhile, we should thank the gods that we all got out of there alive."

"I think my father would have fought them." Said the younger Kell.

"Then we likely would have been needing a new King." Replied Kyp. "And I think your father would have been quite upset if I had gotten you killed. Let's take what we have and return home. We may need to visit again."

"Let's hope our luck holds until we are well on our way home." Said the young Kell.

Aethelstan grabbed Jon's ankle and threw his foot off. "Get off of me oaf!" he shouted.

Jon took a deep breath, and it was then he noticed the rank odor that rose from Aethelstan. He had befouled himself with both his bladder and bowels.

"You shut up or both of you will die at our hands and we'll blame it on the Kells!" came Jon's retort.

Aethelstan stared up at him as Boady walked over. "You both need to calm down." he said. Looking at Jon he added: "Well, I didn't see that happening. You did well. I'm not sure what I would have done."

Aethelstan got up and said: "I would have killed them all. That's what I would have done."

As the other man joined them Jon said: "You damn near did kill all of us with your stench."

Aethelstan flushed with a mixture of anger and embarrassment.

Turning towards the other man Jon said: "Who are you?"

"Bif, my Lord." Said the other man.

"Bif, go get Aethelstan's horse." Ordered Jon.

Jon pulled Boady aside leaving Aethelstan standing in his filth.

"What do you think?" said Jon.

"Well," replied Boady with a smile, "The Duke gave you instructions on what to do if we found some of our people in the preserve."

"Very funny." Said Jon.

"I think we need to go back and make our report, but listen Jon, that boy will be the Duke someday, if he lives. Try to give him just enough respect. Not too much because he needs to know that you're in charge, but some respect. For better or worse, they're both now part of your party." Said Boady.

"Do you think there are more Kells around?" said Jon.

"I doubt it." said Boady, "But we better be ready any ways."

"How can I respect a stuck up befouled brat who just made my job that much harder?" asked Jon.

"To start with you can let him wash himself before we get back. Secondly, although you seemed to have the situation in hand, I bet

Aethelstan's appearance convinced Kyp that there were more of us around. Think of that." Replied Boady.

"Thanks." Said Jon.

Bif was having trouble getting to Thunder. The horse looked angry and would not let Bif approach.

"Ok, back off Bif." Shouted Jon.

Bif backed away and the horse calmed itself a bit. Jon decided to try himself. Thunder began to stir as Jon approached, so he paused. Putting his hands in his pockets he found the two carrots he had put there when he mounted Mayflower. Pulling one out he showed it to the horse and slowly approached speaking in a low and calm voice. The horse took a step towards him, and soon Jon was close enough to give it the carrot. He stroked Thunder's neck and generally calmed the horse down. Then he led it back towards the assembled group.

Aethelstan approached the horse and it became very agitated.

"Stop." Commanded Jon. "You go and lead Mayflower. I'll take care of Thunder."

Aethelstan looked angry, but did as he was told.

"There may be more Kells around, so we walk as silently as we can." Said Jon. "Is that understood?"

Bif and Aethelstan both nodded and the party left by the route Jon and Boady had come. Boady led the way while Jon, with Thunder, took up the rear. They only paused to gather the supplies that Jon had left behind. They walked in silence.

After a while they came to a creek, and Boady hesitated before crossing, looking to Jon.

"Bif, take Mayflower and give her some water." Said Jon in an authoritative voice. "Aethelstan, move a bit downstream and wash yourself. It's a miracle that the dragon hasn't attacked us out of curiosity about your stench."

As usual, Aethelstan looked angry, but he did as he was told. Jon took Thunder to the creek for a drink next to Mayflower. Boady stood alert and on watch.

When Aethestan finished cleaning himself, and everyone had gotten a drink, the party moved on and left the preserve without further incident.

12

Traitor

I T WAS WELL PASSED SUN down when Jon, Boady, Aethelstan and Bif returned to the manor, but there was a buzz of activity everywhere. The grooms and other servants were relieved to see them, especially Aethelstan, as the Duke was preparing to search for him. The Duke himself came running from the stable and uncharacteristically hugged his son when they met.

"Stan! Where have you been? Your mother was worried to tears and I was greatly vexed." Cried the Duke.

"I'm not a little boy father. I was serving you and our King until these two stopped me." Was Athelstan's reply.

The Duke took his eyes off of Aethelstan and looked at Boady and Jon. "I take it you found him in the preserve. Were you able to complete your mission?" he said.

"We have a report for you, my lord." Said Jon.

"Yes, of course." Said the Duke. Then turning to a servant he commanded: "Have the scribe meet us in the hearing room right away." Then turning back to the party he said, "Let's hear what happened."

The Duke led Jon and the group through the front door of the manor and through the house to the hearing room. They were slightly delayed as the Duchess fell all over Aethelstan, smothering him with kisses and pet childhood names.

This greatly annoyed Aethelstan and he finally said: "Mother, I am not your baby any more. I am a grown man. Please control yourself."

The Duchess seemed hurt at this pronouncement, but finally let go of her son as the party proceeded into the room. The scribe had recently arrived and was setting up his desk as the Duke took his seat in the chair.

Looking at Jon the Duke said: "OK, what happened?"

Before Jon could answer, Aethelstan stepped forward and almost shouted: "Bif and I determined to scout the preserve to see if there were any Kells. We found some and we attacked and would have killed them all except Sir Jon stepped forward and stopped us. He is a traitor, father!"

The Duke raised an eyebrow and glanced at Boady who merely gave an annoyed look.

"Hmm, is that so?" Said the Duke. "Bif, is that what happened?"

Bif stirred uncomfortably but then, with his head down, he said: "Your son would not lie to you my lord."

The Duke then looked at Jon with a slight smile and said: "Well, Sir Jon, you are a traitor?"

Jon was flustered, but he was more angry than he was on guard. He took a brief moment to compose himself and said in a strained voice: "My Lord, Boady and I followed your directions. While it is true that your son attacked the Kells, I brought the situation to a peaceful end while Aethelstan lay on his back with a Kell about to split his skull with an axe. His horse had thrown him and still bears a nasty wound from the same axe that was about to kill your son. If he is challenging my honor, as a knight, I believe I have a right to defend it! At this moment I am eager to exercise that right!"

Jon said the last thing in total frustration and it elicited a sigh from the Duke.

"Sir Jon, your honor is beyond question in my eyes. I ask a boon of you; let these rantings, from a child, pass." Said the Duke looking at his son.

"I'll fight him here and now!" shouted Aethelstan. "He's a traitor and a coward!"

"Silence!" bellowed the Duke. "Boady, take my son to his mother. He and I will speak later. Then return here."

"Yes my Lord." Replied Boady forcefully taking a reluctant Aethelstan by the arm and out the door.

As they exited Aethelstan shouted back: "Why don't you ever believe me! I am your son! I would be a knight now if not for that underserving peasant's interference."

As the door closed the Duke took a moment to compose himself. It was late and he was tired. Finally, turning to Bif he said: "Tell me what happened."

Bif was very nervous but he said: "Aethelstan was very upset that he had not been knighted and felt that he only needed an opportunity to prove himself to the King. Having heard that there were Kells in the preserve he ordered me to accompany him on a mission. We found three Kells with a donkey speaking to Sir Jon who was mounted on his horse. Aethelstan determined that Jon was betraying the Kingdom, drew his sword and charged the Kell. Sir Jon immediately shouted that he should stop, but your son bravely charged on, but missed with his sword. The Kell swung his axe, but Aethelstan was too quick. The axe cut Thunder, who reared and Aethelstan fell to the ground. The Kell was on top of him very quickly, but I have seen Aethelstan escape similar situations in training. Then Sir Jon approached the Kell and somehow convinced him to leave. That in itself is very suspicious my lord. He had put away his sword and walked right up to the Kell, but the Kell listened to him. The Kell even waved good bye as he left!"

The Duke took a moment to take all of this in while Jon stood silently fuming. Boady returned and stood next to Jon. Finally, the Duke said:

"Bif, you are a very loyal friend to my son. Loyalty is an admirable trait, but it can be overwhelmed by stupidity, a most undesirable

108

attribute. My son cannot order you to do anything, yet. Understand that."

Then, turning to Jon he said: "Sir Jon, know that I in no way believe you are a traitor. Those charges are ridiculous. And know that you once again have my gratitude; this time for saving my son's life. Please be patient while I hear from Boady; I am most eager to hear what you have to say. Boady, what happened?"

"My Lord," began Boady, "Sir Jon and I scouted the preserve and it was mostly quiet. As we were nearing the edge closest to the Kell lands I came upon three Kells, two younger men armed with axes and bows and the stocky red headed chieftain that you and I have faced in battle before. Returning to Jon we discussed what should be done. Sir Jon determined that he would listen to your advice and try to awe them by riding out on his horse. I thought this both brave and stupid, but could offer no alternative plan. Sir Jon struggled to communicate with them since they apparently spoke no Saxon, and he none of their Gaelic tongue, but he convinced them that they could leave in peace taking one of the King's deer that they had killed. As they were loading their donkey in preparation to go, your son charged on his horse intending to slay the warrior. His horse threw him to the ground and he was about to be killed when Sir Jon did one of the most incredible things that I have ever seen: he sheathed his sword, held out his hands and approached the Kell asking him to stop. By this time both Bif and I had come out of the woods, and I am sure their chief knew that there would be losses if we fought, I also suspect that he recognized me. He could not know how many other Saxons might be around. Jon put his foot on Aethelstan's throat, and the Kell backed away and the three of them soon departed. Once they were gone we returned here to tell you what had happened. Sir Jon followed your instructions."

"Did the Kell really waive to Jon as he departed?" asked the Duke.

"He did, my lord." Replied Boady. "I think it was a sign of respect. You and I are old warriors, it is rare when young men choose to avoid violence and bloodshed. Sir Jon, if you meet him again, he will likely seek you out. Not because he dislikes you, but because he respects you and considers you a worthy foe."

"That is quite a tale; quite a tale indeed." Said the Duke. "Bif, does that sound true to you?"

Bif stammered, "We did not know that you had sent Sir Jon with instructions, my Lord. Yes, the parts that I saw are all true, but do not underestimate your son. I feared for his life, but I have feared for him before."

"Go home Bif." Said the Duke. "You really are a good friend to my son."

After Bif left the Duke wearily said to Jon: "You have done well. I feel that I should reward you, but what can a man give for the life of an ungrateful son? Do you have anything to add?"

Jon looked at Boady and said: "Honestly, my lord, right now I am questioning whether I did the right thing, but I think I know how my father would have felt if it had been me in peril. Your son probably helped us convince the Kells that the preserve is well patrolled. I suspect that their chief was also protecting someone. If we had fought there would have been losses, but they were as likely to win as we were. That, or perhaps he had instructions to avoid a fight as I did. You say the Kell do not have many horses, do they particularly value donkeys?"

"That was the first un-noble thing that you have said to me, Sir Jon, but I can hardly blame you. You did the right thing, and I am most grateful. Beyond that, your report is that of a much more experienced soldier. I will send word to the castle." Said the Duke.

Suddenly, the Duke remembered the scribe. "I wish to read the report you have written tonight. It may require revisions. Leave it behind, and you are dismissed."

The scribe left everything on his desk and departed. Then the Duke turned to his men and said: "I guess I had better talk to my son. Let me escort you to the door."

The three weary men said their good byes.

Boady and Jon walked to the stable in silence. When they got there, Thunder was very upset and the grooms were having a hard time tending to his wound. Unconsciously, Jon put his hand in his pocket and found the other carrot; why did he always have a carrot for this horse? He approached Thunder and the horse calmed down. Jon did not say a word, but both the horse and Jon were comforted by each other's presence.

Meanwhile Boady got Mayflower and lead her out of the barn. Jon turned to him and said: "See if you can find some more carrots to give to the grooms. They seem to comfort Thunder."

Boady found several and gave them to Wren who came and stood with Jon by Thunder. Reluctantly, Jon turned the horse over to Wren and wearily walked back to Mayflower. The grooms wanted to thank Jon for his help, but he put a finger to his lip in concern that the noise might excite the injured horse. Then he and Boady began to walk back to their house.

Boady handed Jon a piece of dried meat from their supplies. It had been quite a while since they had eaten, but Jon was not really hungry. They walked in silence for a bit, but Boady felt he needed to say something to Jon. "You know, you really did well today; even exceptionally well."

"Then why do I feel like everyone thinks I botched the job?" replied the young knight.

"That's not what I heard everyone saying. There is one jealous boy who is upset that you succeeded, but The Duke and I are quite impressed. I mean it Jon; I don't think I could have done what you did today. Do you feel like a failure?" said Boady.

Jon couldn't argue with the facts. The Duke had genuinely complimented his actions, and Boady had also been nothing but supportive. So, why did he feel like he had not succeeded?

"The truth is that I don't really even know what I did or why I did it. You know how some times when you are shooting an arrow you just know that it will hit the target before you even let it go? Then you try to do it again and you can't. That's what today has been like. I was so confident of everything I did, but I didn't even know why I was doing it. Now as I look back, I wonder if I even did anything at all." He said.

It took Boady a moment to take in what Jon had said. Then he had one of the moments that Jon was speaking of and replied:

"You're the one not giving yourself credit! That's not shameful, that is truly noble! Knowing yourself and your limits is a gift that few people have. Trusting God and acting on his guidance is something too few men are willing to do. Now, take the compliments because you deserve them, but you give God the glory and remember that he did this for you. I wonder if David did not feel the same way when he slew Goliath. Don't be upset that you don't want the credit; be thankful that you can still recognize where the credit belongs. And then, with humility, bask in the reflected glory of God's great deed; done through you."

Jon said: "You're a good friend Boady." In his heart, however, he wanted to believe that he had been heroic. He wanted to be someone special all on his own. He even questioned whether God was real or whether he himself simply had good instincts. Jon wanted to be the hero that his heart told him he was not. Jon wrestled with his pride.

When they got to the house all was dark. They unsaddled Mayflower and put her to bed in a mostly complete new stable. Then they both went in and went to sleep. Some of Jon's dreams were about how heroic he could be, but the face of the man he had killed was always present near his greatest moments of triumph. None of his dreams ended badly, yet they were still not happy dreams.

Meanwhile the Duke went in search of his son. He found him in the pantry eating while his mother doted on him.

"That Sir Jon is an uppity, stuck up little glory hound!" said the Duchess.

"That hound saved your son's life!" Came the sudden angry retort from the Duke.

The Duchess glared back at him in anger while the Duke considered whether she should be there for this conversation. In the end he decided that she needed to hear the truth as well.

"Why son? Why do you pursue greatness when you have been born to it? You will be Duke one day. You need only bide your time and learn what it means to be a Duke. Instead you keep trying to impress everyone with how great you are, and every time you do, you show how small you really are. You would be a dead man now if it were not for Sir Jon. I'm surprised that you didn't crap yourself, you were so close to death. Why can't you just accept the greatness that you were born to?" said the Duke.

Aethelstan was ready to explode at his father's words, but the comment about crapping himself threw him off balance. He actually paused before answering. Very uncharacteristically he bowed his head and replied quietly:

"I am a great man father, but nobody recognizes it. They all seek to pull me down; especially Sir Jon. I should be a knight, not him. God means great things for me. I would have triumphed if that man had not interfered. Why will no one allow me to be great?"

The Duchess immediately put her arms around her son and said: "You are great my boy. The others are just jealous, but I have never seen you lose a fight in training. You are my great big hero, and I am so proud of you!"

"He's not proud of me." Said Aethelstan looking towards his father.

"Of course he is! Tell him how proud you are." Came the Duchess' immediate retort.

The Duke was torn. The truth was that he was not proud of his son, but he wanted to be.

"My dear, our son and I need to have a man to man talk. Please go to bed and I will join you shortly." He said.

The Duchess glared at him but eventually got up and left leaving the Duke and his son alone. After a bit the Duke said:

"My son, I have pride in you, but I cannot be proud of what you did today. Nor can I be proud when I watch you bully the servants and act like all of this is about you. God HAS ordained you to greatness, as the Duke, when I am gone. You do not see the responsibility that comes with it. In order to be brave you have to recognize when you are about to be stupid; as you were today. You have to recognize that the world does not revolve around you. You owe something to God, and even the world. They do not owe anything to you. You can lose what you have been given if you do not grasp it. You can throw it away onto the blade of a Kell axe."

There was a moment of silence before Aethelstan responded.

"Why can't you understand me? I don't want you to give me greatness, I want to claim the greatness that is my right! You won't let me. You just want me to be your son, always living in your shadow and never quite living up to your expectations. I will be a great man, and I will not owe my greatness to you or anyone else!"

He abruptly got up and stormed out of the pantry. The Duke did not have the heart to pursue him. Aethelstan was also wrestling with his pride.

Before going to bed the Duke sent the following dispatch to the castle:

> *Sir Jon and my man Boady went to search the preserve for Kells. They were accompanied by my son Aethelstan and his friend Bif. After searching most of the day they found three Kell poaching your game. One was an experienced warrior that was recognized by my man Boady. They were almost certainly scouting as well as hunting. Sir Jon avoided a battle as he knew that there would be losses, and the Kell also did not seem to want to fight leading us to believe that they were alone. They departed in peace as I had instructed Sir Jon to do if a fight could be avoided. Sir Jon showed himself to be a loyal and trustworthy servant of your majesty, and the Kell likely believe that the preserve is well patrolled. I will send other patrols into the preserve and humbly suggest that you do so as well.*

13

Johan Visits

M UCH OF THE GOVERNMENT OF the Kingdom had fallen on Father Leonis. The queen was available to help, but she was truly distraught over the loss of her husband, and were it not for her son, the King, she likely would have joined a cloister and become a nun. Leonis knew this could not last and was determined to get the dukes, barons, and counts together to form a council, but those who had not been with the King when he died were jealous men with little record for leadership. Brother Johan was a trustworthy aide, but Leonis felt trapped between the King, whom he served, and the various leading men of the Kingdom, who each seemed more interested in advancing themselves, rather than protecting the Kingdom. The King needed strong allies dedicated to his cause, but Leonis did not know whom he could trust.

Leonis was pondering this predicament when he was given the dispatch that Duke Heimsteady had sent the previous night. He read it and thought: "At least he did what he was asked to do and no more.

He is not asking for anything. Perhaps the Duke is the man we need to turn to."

Brother Johan joined him and they began to eat breakfast together.

"A dispatch from Heimsteady." Said Leonis handing the message to Johan.

Johan read the brief message and looked up. "It's rather mundane and to the point. The Duke's suggestions are practical and he makes no unreasonable requests. Would that all of our correspondence was like this." Said Johan in response.

While they ate together a servant approached and handed another message to Father Leonis.

"What's this then?" asked Johan.

Leonis got a disgusted look on his face as he read it and handed the note to Johnan:

> *There are Kell parties in the preserve as I have personally seen. While in the preserve I witnessed Sir Jon conspiring with them and even exchanging signs of friendship. We have a spy in our midst. I humbly offer my service to the King and urge you not to trust this man. He has already fooled my father.*
>
> *Yours in loyalty,*
> *Aethelstan von Heimsteady*

"Well, that's more typical, Leo." Responded Johan. "Somebody accusing a person sent on the King's business of not doing his job. The odd part here is that he also accuses his own father of malfeasance."

"It's absurd. Sir Jon has been a knight for less than three days and he has already betrayed us? Perhaps he became a spy while he served you brother. Oh Lord, is there not one unselfish man in the Kingdom?" vented Leonis.

"Well I guess there is us." Said Johan wryly. "I think we should just ignore it. The accusation is absurd."

"We can't ignore it. Who knows how many other people have read this and now stand ready to use the information, even against us, if we don't at least check it out. How can we check it out?" asked Leonis.

"I want to talk to Jon about my brother anyways." Said Johan. "The Duke invited me to have a meal with his family to tell tales of my travels. Let me go and see what I can discover." Said Johan.

"I guess I can spare you for a day or two. Go today and drop in unannounced. Talk in private to the Duke, Sir Jon, and this Aethelstan if you can, and see if you can put their story together. But hurry back; I need someone around that I can trust and talk to. Tell the Duke that we will send a patrol out tomorrow and ask him to send another later this week. Take a horse if you want, but hurry back." Said a clearly frustrated Leonis.

"You'll be alright, Leo." Said Johan. "Remember that you serve God first, and that all things work for good for those who are called according to His purpose. Don't rush, and don't do it yourself. Trust in God."

"Thank you brother." Was Leonis' reply. "I need you mostly to remind me of that. It is hard to remember in the press of day to day affairs."

Johan had walked much of the way across the known world, so he did not want a horse for the journey to the Duke's demesne. He wore his monk's robe and carried a walking staff. He looked nothing like the most trusted friend of the minister of state. Johan had wrestled with pride and had learned that denial of one's own comfort was useful in the fight. Certainly denial of the trappings of pride are useful in that battle as well.

Jon was surprised at how early he woke that morning, considering how late he had gone to bed, but he had not awakened before Lil. As he came out of the sleeping room he found her kneeling by the cross. He joined her and prayed silently:

"Father, guide me. Thank you for helping me get through yesterday, because I know I could not have done it without you. Guide me Father, because I really do not know what I am doing." He prayed.

After getting up Lil said: "I thanked God for bringing you and Boady back to me last night. You must have been very late as I did not even hear you come in. Did everything go alright?"

"Yes Lil, everything went alright. God was with us just as you said He would be." Said Jon.

Lil flashed her magical smile filling Jon with warmth. "You know, my mother always said it was more important that we be with God; that's the surest way to know that He is with you. It's a strange way to look at it, but I hope that you stay with God in all that you do." She said.

Her remark puzzled Jon, but he liked looking at it that way. It seemed to him that he was always asking God to do things for him instead of asking God to allow him to do things for Him. He liked the thought, but was unsure as to how to put it in practice.

"I'll try, Lil. Have you washed?" he said.

"Not yet." She replied. "I try to make prayers the first thing I do."

"I'll stoke the fire while you go and wash." He replied.

She smiled again and went out the door. Jon heard Mayflower stir and he could well imagine the horse was pleased to see Lil. Then he got to work stoking the fire. Jon felt blessed to be where he was.

Boady came into the main room. "Good morning." He said. "Where's Lil?"

"She's outside washing up. What do you think we should do today?" replied Jon.

"I dunno." Said a clearly tired Boady. "You're the knight; what do you think we should do?"

Jon chuckled and said: "I'm not a knight in here. You think we can take a day off?"

"We can try." Said Boady. "I like the idea of it."

Lil came back in and immediately rushed up to Boady and gave him a hug. "Praise God you're home early; safe and sound." She squealed in genuine joy.

Boady hugged her back. He felt blessed to have her in his life. "Good morning my girl! I couldn't bear to be away from you an extra minute." He said as Lil blushed.

Turning to Jon, Lil said: "Thanks for stoking the fire, Jon. Why don't you two go and wash while I cook us some breakfast."

As Jon and Boady walked out the door Jon realized how hungry he was. It had been most of a day since he had last eaten a real meal. He was looking forward to this new day and putting yesterday behind him. What was Lil always saying? "This is the day that the Lord has made; let us rejoice and be glad in it."

Jon checked on Mayflower, and then joined Boady in washing up. They returned to the house and enjoyed a hearty breakfast along with Lil's bright company. Lil asked them about what had happened the previous day, but neither felt much like talking about it.

"I think Boady and I have a day off today, Lil. Would you like to have a ride on Mayflower?" said Jon.

"Can I?!" exclaimed Lil. Then turning to Boady she said: "Is it OK, Boady?"

Boady smiled and said: "How can I say no to your sweet face?"

Lil blushed again, and Jon said: "OK. I will saddle her after breakfast and you can have a ride after we've cleaned up in here. Sound good?"

There were no objections, only smiles.

After breakfast, Jon saddled Mayflower while Boady and Lil cleaned up. Lil was a whirlwind of nervous excitement. When Jon had just finished saddling the horse men came to finish the stable. They all greeted Sir Jon deferentially, while Jon did his best to not let it go to his head.

As Lil rode side saddle, Boady stood behind her to insure that she did not fall off. Lil asked that they actually take her somewhere and they decided to visit Kris in the kitchen. They had a pleasant visit and felt good about refusing the food he offered them. It was good to just visit for a change. Kris seemed especially pleased to see Lil and got a big hug from her in return. Jon began to wonder why he never got any hugs.

As they were preparing to leave, Lil spotted a lone monk walking up the road. "Look!" she cried. "A man of God. I wonder if he needs some food?"

Jon recognized Brother Johan and brought the horse his way.

"Brother Johan," said Jon, "what brings you our way?"

Brother Johan smiled and said: "Well, thanks to you I have a standing invitation from the Duke, and if I am not mistaken, you have promised me a conversation about my brother. It's a fine day, and I thought there was no better time than the present."

Boady and Jon smiled but felt uneasy. Lil, on the other hand, was excited.

"Will you be joining us for dinner? Our house is nearby." She said with obvious glee.

"It would be rude to turn down such a generous offer from a fair damsel mounted on a steed." Replied Brother Johan. "I would enjoy spending time with you if it is OK with the master of the house; I don't want to be any trouble."

Brother Johan looked at Jon, but he looked to Boady with some embarrassment. Boady forced a smile and said: "Of course Brother Johan. Any friend of Sir Jon's is a friend of ours."

"I'm sorry Brother Johan. Let me make introductions. This is Master Boady, the Duke's forester whom I have told you about, and this little princess is our Lil; the finest Christian you will ever meet in your travels." Said Jon, once again not knowing why he had added the last part.

While Brother Johan's comment made Lil blush a little, Jon's comment turned her bright red with glee and embarrassment. Johan was also taken aback.

The three men walked while Lil rode her 'steed.' In the course of the conversation Lil learned that Brother Johan had been to the Holy Land, and she peppered him with questions about the places where Jesus had walked. This quite impressed Brother Johan as she did not once ask him about strange animals and even stranger men. She only wanted to hear about Jesus, the reason Johan had set out on his journey in the first place. It was refreshing, and he began to believe Jon's introduction.

When they arrived, Lil was helped down from Mayflower and immediately ran to the garden to find a carrot. Since the men were finishing up the stable, Jon led the horse to a grassy spot and picketed her loosely in place. Boady went inside with Lil while Johan stayed with Jon.

"The Duke sent us a report last night, but it was rather sparse on the details of your patrol. Can you fill me in?" asked Johan.

"I guess there is not a lot to tell." said Jon. "Boady and I went through most of the preserve and it was pretty much empty. As we got to the part closest to the Kell lands we came across a hunting party led by a warrior named Kyp. Boady recognized him from previous battles. I did as the Duke instructed me and confronted him on horseback. In broken language I convinced them to take the deer and leave. I suspect they thought there were more of us around, and that they now know that the preserve is being patrolled. We came back and made our report."

"The Duke said that there were four of you." Said Johan.

"Well, yes, sort of." Replied Jon. "The Duke's son Aethelstan and a friend of his named Bif had snuck off on their own. While I was talking to the Kell, Aethelstan came charging out of the woods on his horse and attacked their leader. He missed with his sword and got thrown from his horse. Kyp was about to kill him, but….but he didn't."

"Why didn't he Jon?" asked Johan in an uncharacteristically intense sort of way.

"Listen Brother Johan. I don't know what the Duke told you, but I am not a hero. I didn't even know what I was doing. I just reacted; that's all." Replied Jon.

"Jon, this is important. How did you react?" continued Johan very intensely.

"I put away my sword and held out my hands as I walked toward the Kell on Aethelstan's chest. Boady and Biff were now visible, so it was four on three, but we were about to lose our first man. The Kell let me approach and seemed just as eager as I was not to have a fight. Once I put my foot on Aethelstan's throat, the Kell got up and they all left." Said Jon, quickly adding: "I still don't know why I did it!"

"You're an odd man, Sir Jon. That is quite a tale, and one in which you played a heroic part, but I practically had to drag it out of you. Why?" asked the monk.

"I don't know." Came the reply. "I wasn't thinking 'I know what I'll do!' I just reacted. It wasn't me at all. Then Aethelstan accused me of being a traitor. I guess I have to confess I sort of wish I hadn't saved his life, but I am told that is a most un-noble thought. Is that why you're here? Did the Duke accuse me of being a traitor?"

Johan put his hand on Jon's shoulder. "You know better than that." He said. "I think it would be difficult for anyone to believe that you are a traitor, and I think the Duke values you. You are uncommonly honest and humble, Jon. I hope you are able to stay that way. Let's go inside."

As they walked toward the house Jon said: "Trust me; I'm plenty proud. I just want a day off."

When they entered the house Johan was impressed by the level of refinement he observed. The table was set with a plate and spoon for each guest while he had expected that they would all eat with their hands from a common platter. The food smelled good as well.

"I just need a few more minutes." Said Lil. "Jon, have you and Brother Johan washed?"

Again Brother Johan was surprised. In that day and age nobody washed before eating; at least nobody in the Christian world. People in the Holy Land did wash their hands before eating, but Brother Johan had gotten out of the habit. The three men walked down to the stream.

"This is quite unexpected." Said Brother Johan.

Boady replied: "Lil has some strange ways that she learned from her mother, but none of them are bad ideas."

"Indeed, washing one's hands before eating is actually a custom in the Holy Land." Said Johan.

"I probably don't have to warn you about this, but don't reach for any food before we are all seated and grace has been said. If you do you will likely get a stern rebuke from the little lady of the house." Added Jon.

"She's quite a girl, that one. She's my pride and joy." Said Boady.

As they reentered the house Lil asked the men to be seated. The table was set with roasted potatoes, green beans, some berries, cheese, and bread. Lil was cooking some meat that smelled delicious. Johan did not think he ate this well at the castle!

Lil came to the table with a piece of rabbit meat. "God has blessed us with meat that was given to me just yesterday." Said Lil.

"He must have been expecting you." As she sat down she added: "Would you do us the honor of saying grace, Brother Johan?"

This was not at all what the monk had expected. He expected perhaps some raw vegetables and moldy bread, but instead he was presented with a feast. He began to feel guilty that he was possibly taking the best food out of these people's mouth.

The four of them made the sign of the cross and Johan said: "Bless us oh Lord and these thy gifts, which we receive through thy bounty. And thank you Father for the hospitality that I have found among Your servants in this house. In the name of Christ our Lord, amen."

"Amen." Said the other three around the table.

As the food began to be passed Brother Johan said to Boady: "Sir Jon and I were talking about your mission in the preserve. I'd like to hear what you have to say about it."

Lil giggled a bit, causing Brother Johan to inquire: "What's so funny Lil?"

"Jon says he is not a knight when he walks through our door. You're breaking his rule." Said Lil in a happy tone.

"Lil, you need to be more respectful." Said Boady in a stern voice.

"No." said Brother Johan, "That's actually rather insightful and wise. Jon, it is good to have a place where you can be yourself instead of who the world says you are."

"Thank you." Said Jon sheepishly.

Johan turned back to Boady who said: "Jon and I scouted the preserve and it was mostly quiet. As we were nearing the edge closest to the Kell lands I came upon three Kells, two younger men armed with axes and bows and a stocky red headed chieftain I have faced in battle before. We discussed what should be done. Sir Jon determined that he would try to awe them by riding out on his horse. I could offer no alternative plan. He struggled to communicate with them since they apparently spoke no Saxon, and he none of their Gaelic tongue, but he convinced them that they could leave in peace taking one of the King's deer that they had killed. As they were preparing to go, the Duke's son, Aethelstan, charged on his horse intending to slay the warrior. His horse threw him to the ground and he was about to be killed when Jon did something incredible: he sheathed his sword, held out his hands and approached the Kell asking him to stop. By this time, I had come out of the woods along with a companion of the Duke's son, and I am sure their chief knew that there would be losses if we fought. I also suspect that he recognized me. He could not know how many other Saxons might be around. Jon put his foot on Aethelstan's throat, and the Kell got off of him. The three of them soon departed. Jon is humble, but he was really quite heroic."

Lil interrupted: "Jon! You were with God! You were one of the blessed peace makers that Jesus spoke about. Why didn't you tell me this morning?"

She sprang out of her seat and rushed around the table to give Jon a hug. For the first time since the episode had happened Jon actually felt like a hero. Now it was his turn to blush.

Johan was quite moved by the scene he witnessed. These were people united in a special kind of love. "Thanks Boady." He said. "That is the clearest version of what happened that I have heard yet."

The rest of the meal was spent with Johan asking questions about the people he was now getting to know. He learned about how Lil had come to live with Boady, but was told that Jon had come there because he had nowhere else to go. When the meal was finished, everyone, Brother Johan included, helped to clean up.

Then Johan turned to Jon and said: "Can we take a walk? I'd like to talk to you about my brother."

Jon forced a smile and said: "Of course."

Boady found himself ill at ease, but he knew that he had to trust Jon. Jon had to face this trial alone.

14

Belief and Certainty

A s Jon and Johan walked out of the house, Jon was immediately reminded of his knighthood as one of the men
working on the stable approached him.

"Sir Jon, we believe that we have completed your stable. Would
you like to inspect our work and tell us if there is anything else that
we need to do?" he said.

Sir Jon did not want to inspect their work, and trusted that they
had done a good job, but at least this would put off the inevitable
conversation that he was about to enter into. The men really had
done a fine job. They had built a manger for hay, and the walls were
quite tight and a better shield against the wind and rain than most
people had at their houses. The stable was probably big enough to
hold two horses if it had to. The men were pleased as Sir Jon comple-
mented their work.

"Very fine work. I will be sure to compliment your efforts as I
thank the Duke for sending you." Said the young knight.

As they were about to leave, Lil came out with some bread and cheese for the men. "You must be very hungry after all of the work you've done." She said. "Take a break and have some supper."

The men were hungry and anxious to have some food, but the foreman said: "Lady Lil. You are most kind, but we have finished our work and you have been very good to us. We cannot impose on you again."

Lil looked to Jon who said: "Nonsense. A workman deserves his wages and you men have done us a great service. I beg of you, please do not disappoint the lady of the house. Accept this food as an expression of our gratitude."

It was another eloquent speech that Jon knew did not come from his mind. He only hoped that God would guide him in his conversation with Brother Johan as well. The men sat down to eat as Lil complimented their work far more effusively than Jon had. Brother Johan watched and was amazed. There certainly was something different about the people who lived in this house.

Before leaving them Brother Johan said to the foreman: "If you are returning to the manor, can you let the Duke know that Brother Johan is here on a visit and would be much obliged if he could pay a visit?"

The foreman promised that he would, and the monk and knight left to go on their walk.

"So," began Brother Johan, "Tell me how my brother became a knight."

"Well," said Jon, "There are two stories, but I will tell you the one that I think was the truth. I guess I believe this tale because your brother sort of confessed it to me, and it is not exactly a noble tale. I don't know why he would have told it if it were not true.

Your brother used to sneak into the library to read whatever he could. He had apparently been doing this for some time, but on the day of the Kell raid he got caught. The monks apparently did not know that the city was under attack, but as they threw him out of the library they saw the pagans closing in. They closed the door and bolted it leaving your brother outside. The pagans came upon him with the intent to kill, and he was so afraid that he peed himself. As he put it, he stood there with a great yellow streak running down his leg. The invaders burst into laughter. Then they started to beat him mercilessly. Just as they were about to kill him, the guard arrived and attacked the distracted invaders. The monks, realizing that they were no longer under attack, opened the door and pulled him inside. To hide their shame, they made up the other story. The King knighted him as 'Sir Malpolem' because he wanted your brother to be the one good thing that had come out of the battle that had cost the lives of so many. I think it is too odd a tale not to be true."

Johan was silent for a bit and there was moisture in his eyes. Finally, he asked: "Did my brother walk with God?"

Jon did not know what to make of the question, so he stilled his mind and a question came out of his heart: "Do any of us really walk with God? Your brother, my teacher and mentor, tried to be a good man. Boady tells me that there are no innocent men, but I think your brother was the most innocent man that I ever knew. He used his knighthood to help me. He was a friend to my father who had almost no friends. He went to church regularly and taught me Latin from parts of scripture he was able to get his hands on. I guess I am not sure if any man walks with God, but I think God walked with your brother; but I also know that he had doubts. I know that I have doubts. God will judge whether he earned a place in heaven."

"I think God walks with you too, Jon." Said the misty eyed monk. "Our mother taught us to be good boys, and she encouraged us to love God. I guess neither of us always did, but we did what we were told. Eventually I went off on my journey. I was filled with doubt, but I sought the truth. I know my brother sought the truth as well. It was on this journey that I learned the one thing that almost nobody wants to talk about: the fact that a god who is not personal is no god at all. The Bible says that 'All have sinned and fall short of the glory of God.' On my journey God rescued me time and time again. It wasn't because I always said my prayers, or because I was always kind to those in need; I didn't always do those things. But, God rescued me anyways. He had no reason to, He just did. I hope my brother learned that too."

"I want to know the truth." Said Jon. "Sometimes God just seems like a judge looking down on us to hold us accountable for when we slip up. Your brother seemed to have love and respect for God, but I am not sure even he knew what he believed. I am not sure what I believe. The only person I know who seems to know what she believes is Lil; and she's just a little girl. Your brother had a strong faith in something, but I really cannot say what: maybe the church?"

Johan was silent again. Then he said: "You know Jon, it matters much more what you believe than how hard you believe it. My first prior once told me a story:

'Two men were hunting early in the winter. It was cold and there was ice on the lake. Suddenly it began to snow and the wind began to blow hard and cold. The men knew that they needed to find shelter quickly or they would die. The first man wanted to run across the frozen lake, but the second was afraid that it was too early and the ice would not hold them. The first man pointed out that they would likely die if they stayed out and their only chance was to try to cross the ice. The ice held, and the men were saved. Early in the Spring, the men were out hunting again. There was still ice on the lake, and once again the weather turned bad. The first man thought that they could make it back by going around, but the second man pointed out that the ice had held them before and it would surely hold them again. They set off across the ice, it collapsed and they perished.'

Now, in the first case their faith was weak, but what they put their faith in, the ice, was strong. They survived. In the second case, they had far more faith in the ice, but the ice was weak, and they died. What we put our faith in matters much more than how hard we believe in it. Even the church does not claim it can save sinners. The church says it can show you Jesus, and it is He who can save you. I guess, to be honest, maybe the church forgets that sometimes as well. That's why it is important to believe in a personal God. A God who is always there for you. I hope my brother knew that God."

"You're an odd man of God, Brother Johan." Said Jon. "I think Sir Malpolem was an odd man of God as well. Thank you, Brother Johan."

"For what?" asked the monk.

"For giving me a tiny glimpse of what the truth I seek looks like. Like you, I don't know why, but I think God is trying to have a personal relationship with me." Said Jon.

Brother Johan smiled and looked at Jon saying: "'Behold, I stand at the door and knock. If anyone opens the door I will enter and live with him.' Jesus says that in the Bible. I think you hear him knocking; open the door and let him in."

By now the men had wandered somewhere between the manor and the house, and they became aware of a large horse coming towards them. It was the Duke, mounted on Beast, and he came to a halt towering over the two men on foot.

"Brother Johan!" he exclaimed. "I only just heard that you were here. What a pleasant surprise. What brings you this way?"

"Good day, my Lord." Replied the monk. "The King bade me visit your demesne and speak to you and Sir Jon about the Kells you reported to be in the preserve. As good luck would have it, I met Sir Jon first and we were just having a pleasant walk after a fine supper at your man Boady's house. Your estate is certainly lovely."

"Ach, curse my manners." Said the Duke. "Good day Sir Jon. I trust you are rested after your busy day?"

"Good day, my Lord." Responded Jon. "I slept well, and I wanted to thank you for the excellent work your men did building me a stable for Mayflower. They really did a fine job, and I most certainly remain in your debt for this latest expression of your generosity."

"It was the least I could do, and I am pleased that you like it. Brother Johan, will you be spending the night?" was the Duke's reply. He seemed agitated and nervous.

"If your Lordship is offering his hospitality, I would be most pleased to spend the night." Said Brother Johan. "I have instructions to speak to you about the dispatch you sent last night, but by your leave, I should also like to meet your family. You have a son, do you not?"

The Duke smiled tensely and said: "Yes, yes I do. Perhaps we can all share a meal together after we have spoken about the situation in the preserve. I'm sure we would all enjoy hearing the tales from your pilgrimage to the Holy Land. Sir Jon, would you like to join us this evening?"

It seemed to Jon that the way the Duke asked this question was meant to indicate that he was to decline. Normally, the Duke would have told him to be there, so Jon said: "Regretfully, my Lord, I have accomplished little today and I must get to work. I have a new stable to make ready. Of course, I am at your disposal, but by your leave, I am sure I would add little to the conversation."

The Duke relaxed a bit and smiled. Once again Jon had given the perfect answer. "Of course, Sir Jon, I hope you know that you are always welcome in my home, but you have had several busy days. I understand fully." Said the Duke. "So then, Brother Johan; shall we go?"

Brother Johan turned to Jon and said: "Sir Jon, I have greatly enjoyed my visit and I look forward to continuing our conversation. Thank Master Boady and Mistress Lil for me. You and I both can learn a lot from that little girl. I can see why you wanted to stay with them. Fare well."

"Thank you Brother Johan. I also greatly enjoyed our talk and look forward to seeing you again." Replied Sir Jon.

The men parted ways with Jon heading back to Boady's house and the Duke, with Brother Johan, heading towards the manor barn. They were an odd pair. The proud Duke mounted on his intimidating war horse, and the small monk, humbly dressed, walking beside him. Despite the appearance, it was the humble monk who was in control, while the proud Duke was nervous and defensive.

As the Duke and the monk walked along there was little conversation. Brother Johan was deep in thought, and the Duke was uncharacteristically at a loss for words. When they arrived at the barn several grooms helped the Duke dismount, and he led Brother Johan to the manor.

Entering the house, the Duke said to one of the servants: "Inform the Duchess and my son that we will have Brother Johan as our guest at the evening meal, and have the kitchen prepare something special."

"Yes my Lord." replied the servant.

Unthinkingly the Duke led Brother Johan to his court room. He realized his mistake as he entered, but it was too late. Now it would be he who was to be interrogated. The Duke dismissed the ever present scribe, but asked him to leave the notes from last night's report. This edited version he handed to Brother Johan, and he went to the other door to inform the Reeve that he was not to be disturbed under any circumstances. Brother Johan took note of the Duke's agitation while taking a seat at the scribe's desk and reading the notes.

"My Lord. I am not here to vex you." Said the monk when the two were alone. "Father Leonis and I have confidence in you and hope that you will lead the council of nobles when it is formed. Please, let us deal with this matter in trust and friendship."

While Brother Johan said this in an attempt to calm the Duke, it actually put him even more on guard. The Duke did not really know what 'matter' Johan was there to 'deal' with and was afraid that Sir Jon or someone else had divulged the secret of the dragon. Beyond that, when a member of the King's court told one to relax, it was often wiser to be even more on guard.

"Of course Brother Johan." He said somewhat distractedly. He took his seat while deep in thought.

After he finished reading the notes, Johan said to the Duke: "The castle received a second report on the mission to the preserve. It was delivered this morning."

"Oh?" said the Duke in surprise. "Did Sir Jon send his own report?"

"No, Sir Jon did not send it." Said the monk.

"Ah." Said the Duke in a resigned manner. "Well, neither Boady nor Bif can write, so that only leaves one other person who could have done it."

"I notice there is no testimony from your son in this report." Replied Brother Johan.

The Duke looked weary. "I can get you the unedited version if you would like to see it. His accusations are ridiculous; you recognize that, don't you?"

"Yes, my good Duke, I do recognize that." Said the monk to a relieved Duke. "The problem is that we do not know who else may have seen the report that Aethelstan von Heimsteady sent. I have to look into it. By the way, your son thinks that you have been taken in by Sir Jon. Apparently he feels that your judgement cannot be trusted."

The Duke got red in the face and sprung up from his chair. "That stupid spoiled brat!" he exploded. "He feels that he should have been knighted at the coronation, and now he wants to 'earn' a knighthood from the King by attacking someone else! That boy has no idea what nobility is; clearly I have failed as a father."

This comment made Johan feel sorry for the Duke. He got up from his chair and approached the Duke to speak to him man to man: "My lord, you have led our armies in the successful defense of the Kingdom. You were the first and most trusted advisor of our late King. Even so, raising another person is a far more difficult thing. But you are his father, and you must do your duty. He has almost certainly eliminated any possibility of a knighthood for a good long time. You must teach him how to be noble."

"Thank you, Brother Johan." Said the Duke quietly.

"I don't really want to talk to him, but Father Leonis instructed me to do so." Continued the monk. "Shall I tell him what a fool he has been?"

"I don't know." Said the Duke. "Perhaps he would listen to you better than he listens to me, but I am his father. I don't really think he will listen to anyone who disagrees with him. The bigger question is how do I stop him from causing further trouble?"

"I can see that you are a wise man." Said Brother Johan. "You have identified the challenge before us all. Pray about it, and I will pray for you. Perhaps the Lord will give us an answer. In the meantime, I am instructed to speak to him alone, but I will be flexible if you desire."

"Normally it would be out of the question, but we need to learn to trust each other." Said the Duke. "I will send him in to you shortly, and we will see if we are worthy of each other's trust."

"I think I am going to like you, my lord. You are indeed a wise man." Said the monk.

The Duke left to find his son and returned with him a short time later.

"Brother Johan, this is my son Aethelstan. Aethelstan this is Brother Johan, here on the King's duty." Said the Duke. "I will leave you two gentlemen alone."

"Father, don't you want to hear what I have to say?" said Aethelstan in surprise.

"I am fairly certain that I already know what you are going to say. It would break my heart to hear it again." Replied the Duke as he left.

Aethelstan was surprised, but a representative from the King had come to see him, and he was eager to earn his knight's spurs. Meanwhile, Brother Johan took a seat in the Duke's chair while Aethelstan stood before him.

"I take it you sent a report to the castle concerning Kells in the King's preserve?" Began the monk.

"I did." Said Aethelstan proudly. "I seek to protect our Kingdom, and I fear there are traitors in our midst that could prove to be our downfall."

"Traitors?" replied Brother Johan. "Your report mentioned Sir Jon, who else is a traitor?"

"Master Boady most certainly is in league with Sir Jon. Sir Jon could never have completed his betrayal without help. He is stupid and naïve." Came an enthusiastic reply.

"Master Boady, the longtime forester of your father, a man who has fought and killed more Kells than you have even seen; you accuse him of being a traitor?" said the astounded agent for the King.

"Yes, your eminence." Said Aethelstan. "Certainly he has served the Kingdom in the past, but perhaps he became jealous of his betters, or perhaps he was bought by the Kells. He lives with a Kell, and they seem to have more food than anyone else. The situation is all wrong. Sir Jon must have turned him. But it is not too late. We can stop them before their treachery goes too far. They must be arrested."

"So, you feel that Sir Jon, Boady, and the small girl, Lil, are all spies. Is there anyone else?" asked Brother Johan. "Is your father in league with them?"

"No, good friar, I do not think so. I think he is just blinded by their deceitfulness. He is old and trusting. He means well, but he

133

could use my help; he simply does not recognize that. As to others, anyone who has come in contact with Sir Jon must be suspected. All of the stable hands and the cook seem particularly fond of him. They should be questioned and asked to prove their innocence. If they cannot, they must be put out of harm's way." Said the now embold-ened young man.

"Are you certain of this?" asked the monk. "There are many people you wish me to have apprehended and the only evidence you have given me is that one of them lives with a small, Kellish looking girl."

"I have never been more certain." Said the enraptured young man. "Doesn't it just feel like the truth? Can you recognize it? In the unlikely event that I was wrong, it would not hurt the Kingdom, but if I am right and you ignore me, the Kingdom could fall!"

"I see." Said Brother Johan. "These are serious accusations that you make, but you give me no real evidence. Perhaps the girl only looks like a Kell. There are Saxons who have red hair, and she is very young, and I believe grew up among us. It would seem odd that a corrupting spy would throw herself on the mercy of a man by demanding to be fed and housed. Your story is difficult to accept."

"Your eminence." Replied Aethelstan. "Can the Kingdom really afford the risk? I am a selfless patriot only interested in protecting the Kingdom and our King against a crafty and notorious enemy. If Sir Jon were innocent, why would a Kell prince waive to him in parting in the preserve? Because it was a planned meeting and they were friends. Sir Jon has betrayed God by the very act of speaking with His enemies. He seeks to pollute us with their pagan faith. I will not betray God, nor will I stand by while all that we value is imperiled. The truth is hurtful. I recognize that the truth is not always easy to accept, but we must recognize it when we hear it. Trust me. All I want is to protect the King, our faith, and our way of life. You must help me do it."

"You are certain?" asked the monk.

"I have never been more certain." Replied the young man who had thoroughly convinced himself.

"You have given me much to ponder." Said Brother Johan. "I thank you for your time."

Aethelstan was very pleased with himself as he left the room. Brother Johan was appalled. This boy was dangerous!

15

Much Ado About a Donkey

J ON HAD ENJOYED HIS DAY off. When he had returned to the house he found that Boady had gone off hunting, so he settled Mayflower in the new stable and helped Lil with her chores. He gathered eggs from the chickens, pulled some weeds from the garden, and made several trips to the stream to fill the water barrel. It was mostly mindless work, and having his mind free, Jon's thoughts turned to God and what Brother Johan had said about faith.

It seemed reasonable that faith alone could not bring God into being; he either existed or he did not. As Jon looked around him he thought that existence itself proclaimed the reality of God. How else could everything have come into being?

But if God created everything, did that mean that God also cared about his creation? As Jon gathered eggs he thought that people must be like gods to the chickens; we feed them, we protect them, but we also expect them to do what they do: give us eggs. Is that how God is with people? Jon was not sure.

It seemed to Jon that God had a special purpose for His creation. God had created the chickens to lay eggs, but why had God created people? Maybe He just wanted to watch them, but the stories about God seemed to indicate that He wanted more. Jon felt like God wanted to know him personally; he wanted a relationship with his creation. But how can man relate to God?

"Behold, I stand at the door and knock. If anyone opens the door I will enter and dwell with him." Brother Johan had said that Jesus had said that. As Jon weeded the garden he prayed silently, almost unconsciously: "Come in Lord Jesus. Show me You are real and help my doubts. Let's have a relationship. Be the strong truth that I can anchor my life to."

While he did not say anything to Boady or Lil that evening, both of them noticed that something had changed in Jon. He was happy and seemed more at peace with himself. Jon had no dreams as he slept that night.

Brother Johan's afternoon was not as pleasant. Aethestan's wild accusations were a threat to everyone. The way of life that the Duke's son had said he was protecting would not be worth protecting if every wild accusation had to be proven false rather than true.

As he sat in the Duke's chair he thought about the unedited report the Duke had given him to read. Why had the Kells brought a donkey on a scouting mission? Three men could easily carry their own supplies. And why would they stop to kill a deer; simply to prove that they could take one of the King's deer? The report did not really make sense, but at least three men had told essentially the same story. Brother Johan felt that he needed to get back to Father Leonis and make his report.

As he sat thinking the Duke reentered the room.

"Pardon me my lord." Said Brother Johan as he sprang out of the Duke's chair.

"It's quite alright." Replied the Duke. "Well, what do you think?"

The two men now stood facing each other as they spoke.

"I am afraid that your son is a dangerous person." Said the monk. "He seems to think that the entire Kingdom is about him, and that if he believes something then it must be the truth. How can we shelter the entire realm from the divisive nature of his imagination?"

"Brother Johan," replied the Duke, "don't you think you are exaggerating a bit? Stan is a selfish and self-absorbed child, but as such, who would listen to him?"

"Perhaps people who fear the worst because we have a child on the throne. Perhaps selfish men who wish to make themselves heroes and do not care about the truth. I do not think Aethelstan is the only person ready to believe the worst. And he is the son of a Duke; your heir." Replied Johan.

"Perhaps we could send him away." Said the Duke reluctantly. "Perhaps he could be knighted if he goes off to Gaul and fulfills a quest to protect pilgrims. It would satisfy his immediate ambition, give him a chance to learn something about life, and remove him during this sensitive time."

"It is an interesting idea, my lord. I will discuss it with Father Leonis. I do not want to reward his behavior with a knighthood, but he will inevitably become a knight some time, and it would remove him for a time. But another question has also come to my mind." Replied the monk. "Why would the Kells bring a donkey on a scouting mission, and why would they stop to kill a deer?"

The Duke paused before replying: "You're right. That is odd. You have a military mind Brother; I was so distracted by Aethelstan's rantings that I had missed that."

"I think I should report all of this to Father Leonis as quickly as possible. I'm afraid I will not be able to stay the night."

"Of course; I understand." Replied the Duke. "Perhaps you can visit again under more relaxed circumstances. I mean that sincerely, Brother Johan, I would like to know you better."

"And I you." Said the Monk. "Please excuse me to your family."

"Let me take you to the kitchen and give you some food for your journey. It's the least that I can do. Thank you Brother Johan, it seems that I will have to trust you with my son's future. For some reason, I am comfortable with that." Said the Duke.

The two went to the kitchen where Brother Johan was given apples, bread, cheese and dried meat. They then parted ways as the monk walked back to town.

He arrived at the castle just as the sun was setting and immediately went in search of Father Leonis.

"You're back early." Said the Father warily. "I take it you have something to report. Bad news?"

"I'm really not sure." Responded the Monk. "The Duke's son is delusional and not to be trusted. He seeks to remove those who are in his way and insists they prove that they are innocent of his wild accusations, otherwise it is too dangerous to risk that his suspicions may be right. He presents no credible evidence, but places the burden of proof on the accused. Of course he does all of this to protect the Kingdom, our way of life, and our faith. He is dangerous, but that is not why I returned so quickly."

"Oh, then why have you returned?"

"The Duke gave me detailed accounts of the testimony of all four men in the preserve. Something struck me as odd in those accounts: they all insist that the Kells had a donkey, and they all noted that the Kells had killed a deer. Why? A donkey would be more of a hindrance on a spying mission as three men could easily carry their own supplies. And it seems a needless risk to kill a deer. One might also think that the party would have been larger and more experienced than just one seasoned warrior and two young men." Said Brother Johan.

"Yes, I see what you mean." Replied the chief minister. "What do you think it means?"

"I can't be sure," replied Brother Johan, "but it could be that they were there to kill a deer, or maybe several deer. Could it be that we have been so worried about our weakness that we have merely assumed that the Kells are in a position to attack us?"

"That would indeed be a blessing, but I do not think it can be assumed." Said Leonis. "We need to send someone to verify what is going on in the Kell lands. Someone that we can trust; do you have any suggestions?"

"Yes, I have thought about it a great deal." Replied Johan. "I think we could trust the Duke, but this is not an appropriate mission for him. I also thought about Sir Jon, but he is too inexperienced and perhaps under suspicion. Then it occurred to me that this could be a good test for both Sir Jon and Aethelstan. We send them both with the Captain of the Guard, Sir Bendris, and have him observe the two of them. In my opinion Sir Bendris is entirely above suspicion, and he will be a fair judge between the other two."

"A fine plan Johan. The only hurdle is to convince Sir Bendris to leave the King for a few days. Let's see what he has to say." Father Leonis found a servant and asked him to tell Sir Bendris that he wanted to speak with him. A short time later the captain appeared in the room.

"Father Leonis, Brother Johan, you wish to speak with me?" he said.

"Yes, Sir Bendris. Please have a seat. Please read this report that arrived last night." Said Father Leonis handing the knight the report from the Duke.

"It's rather brief, but the Duke is a wise soldier. It doesn't sound too serious, and I have already ordered a patrol in the morning." Replied the Captain after reading the report. "I don't understand why you needed me to read that."

"Here is a second report that arrived this morning." Said the priest.

After reading the letter from Aethelstan the knight looked grim. "These are the foolish rantings of an untested and vain young man. They can't be taken seriously." Said the knight.

"We are inclined to agree with you, but I sent Brother Johan to the Duke's manor to investigate, and he discovered something that is only hinted at in those reports. Brother Johan, please tell Sir Bendris about your observation." Said Leonis.

"The Duke gave me a transcript of the report that he received." Began the monk. "Three witnesses mentioned the presence of a donkey with the Kells, and the fact that the Kells had killed a deer was also generally agreed upon. I think it odd that Kells scouting for a possible attack would both bring a donkey, which would likely be more of a nuisance than a help, and stop to kill a deer. Sir Bendris, we are not men of war, so what do you make of it?"

"A good observation Brother Johan, perhaps you could be a man of war. I agree, I would not burden my men with either a beast of burden nor with the freedom to hunt and bring back meat if I had sent them on a scouting mission." Said the knight clearly deep in thought. "So, what were they doing? Were they merely hunting? It bears further investigation."

"Our thoughts exactly." Said Father Leonis. "We need to send somebody experienced and whom we trust fully to see what is happening in the Kell lands. We think that you are that man."

"My place is by the King," replied the knight, "but I can send a trustworthy group of men for you."

Brother Johan and Father Leonis looked at each other, and the priest urged the monk to respond:

"We thought you might say that, and it is difficult to argue with it, but we also thought that we might put Aethelstan's allegations to rest by having someone above reproach observe Sir Jon on this mission."

The knight looked dumb founded upon hearing this and said: "Aethelstan's allegations are ridiculous. Why are you giving them any further thought?"

Father Leonis responded: "Because he is the son of a Duke, and we fear that he could stir up fear among the people. You and I, along with his mother, are the people that Wulf relies on most. He will surely miss you for the day or two you may be gone, but you need to make sure that you can honestly tell the King that Aethelstan's charges are nonsense. Actually, we hope that you will take Aethelstan as well; sort of test them both."

"Let me get this right: you want me to abandon my first duty to protect the King, and go on a potentially dangerous mission with an inexperienced knight and the spoiled brat of a Duke. Is that right?" Said Sir Bendris.

The two church men looked despondently at each other. Neither really knew what to say; Sir Bendris' words were accurate.

Finally, the knight filled in the silence that filled in the room:

"I can see that I am right. OK, Father Leonis, I will do it, although I am not sure why. We do need an experienced evaluation of the situation, and I would like to get to know Sir Jon a bit better. I'd rather not take Aethelstan, but somehow my intuition tells me that I should. I'll do it, but we need to leave in the morning, and I want to get back quickly. Do the two of them know we are leaving?"

Both of the church men looked relieved, and Father Leonis replied:

"Not yet, but I will send them word tonight. I will tell them to expect to meet you at the Duke's manor in the morning. Does that sound alright, Ben?"

The knight smiled at being called Ben and replied: "That'll be fine 'Leo'. I hope you are sending me on a fool's mission with those two and that we can all laugh about it for years. Gentlemen, I have to make adjustments to my duty roster and tell the King why I will be gone. Good night to both of you."

As the knight left, the two church men shared a smile. Father Leonis wasted no time in sending a messenger with notes to both the Duke, for Aethelstan, and Sir Jon. Neither note explained what the mission was, but merely stated that the two were to accompany Sir Bendris in the morning, and that he would be meeting them at the manor.

It was quite late when the squire, a page on the cusp of attaining knighthood, that had been sent arrived at the manor. He delivered the note to the Duke first.

The Duke had to be awakened and he met the messenger in his night shirt.

"A mission for Aethelstan?" questioned the Duke upon reading the dispatch. "What's this all about?"

"I am not sure my lord." Replied the squire. "I was merely instructed to give you this message."

"Of course." said the Duke. "Do you need a place to stay tonight? I am sure you could bunk with my stable hands."

"My lord," replied the squire. "I have another message for Sir Jon that I need to deliver."

"Sir Jon?" said a startled Duke. "Is he to go as well?"

"It appears so my Lord. I had best be on my way. May I stable my horse here tonight?" said the tired messenger.

"Of course, my boy, but you could also stable it at Master Boady's house where you will find Sir Jon. That would save you some steps this evening." Said the Duke.

"Thank you my lord." Replied the squire. "I had best be off then."

"Yes, yes." Said the Duke as he turned to leave and deliver the news to his son.

The squire remounted and trotted towards Boady's house. The three occupants were asleep, but both Boady and Jon awoke when they heard the approach of the horse. They met the rider outside. The squire immediately dismounted.

"Sir Jon, a message from the King." He said.

"Hello Wil." Said Sir Jon. "You say you have a message for me?" Jon knew the squire from his time as a page for Sir Malpolem. Wil was known as a serious and trustworthy candidate for knighthood, and like Jon, was one of the few who was not of noble birth. He was Sir Bendris' servant.

"Yes, my lord." Said the somewhat startled squire as he handed Sir Jon the message.

"Thanks. Let's go inside and light a candle so I can read this." Said the knight turning to reenter the house behind Boady.

The squire just stood there dumb founded until Jon paused at the door and said: "Wil, you know me better than most. We can drop the formalities. Come on inside."

The messenger looked pleased and followed Jon into the house. Boady had a candle lit and Jon read the message.

"It says that I am to meet Sir Bendris here tomorrow morning and go on a mission of some sort." He told Boady and the messenger. "Wil, do you know what all of this is about?"

"I'm sorry my lord, but I don't, and I am to accompany you as well. I was told by Father Leonis to deliver this message to you and a similar one to the Duke, then Sir Bendris told me to wait for him. He indicated that someone named Aethelstan would accompany you." Said the page.

143

"Aethelstan!" exclaimed both Boady and Jon in unison.

Getting over his shock Jon addressed the page: "Wil, I have a rule here. When I walk through that door I am no longer a knight. I'm just Jon. Please drop the formalities; it makes me uncomfortable. Do you have a place to stay tonight?"

"The Duke suggested that I stable my horse with yours. It is a pleasant night, so I will sleep in the stable if it is OK with you." Replied the page.

"It is not OK." Said Jon. "Go stable your horse and you can sleep with us in here. By your leave, Master Boady?"

Boady chuckled. "Leave is granted."

The young messenger was a bit perplexed, but went outside to put his horse away.

"Well, what do you think?" asked Jon.

"It seems odd." Replied Boady. "Sir Bendris is a veteran warrior and the Captain of the Guard. You'll be in good hands with him. He is very reliable and military in his ways. It should be a good experience for you. I suspect Aethelstan will have a tougher time. You two make an odd team. It's very strange indeed."

"Oh well, it's in God's hands. I'll go where I am told." Said the remarkably relaxed young knight.

Boady took note of the difference in Jon's attitude but said nothing. When the young messenger returned they all went to bed.

Before he went to sleep, Jon prayed silently: "I trust you Lord. Guide me and let me know that you are there." He then faded off into a restful and dreamless sleep.

Aethelstan did not sleep as well. He had not been told that Jon would be accompanying him. He was excited by the news that the King was sending him on a mission. At last he had a chance to prove himself.

16

Aethelstan as Page

J ON AWOKE EARLY THAT MORNING. There was only the faintest glow on the eastern horizon, yet he felt fresh and energetic. He walked into the other room and knelt by Lil's cross: "Lord, I feel Your presence and it comforts me. Let me serve You this day. Guide me as You always have, even when I did not realize it, but most of all, Jesus, let me know and remember that you are there and that you are real. Yes, Lord, this is the day that you have made; let me rejoice and be glad in it!"

As Jon got up he saw Lil watching him from the doorway of the bed room. "Good morning, Lil!" he said enthusiastically.

"Good morning Jon." Replied Lil. "It's good to see you pray. Has something changed in you?"

Jon walked over to where Lil was standing. "Lil, do you have a personal relationship with God?" he asked.

A big smile broke out on the girl's face. "Yes, Jon, I do. I know that Jesus dwells in me, and I in Him. I set the morning aside to pray to him as a special time between us, but the truth is that I speak with Him all day long. Is that what has changed?"

Jon looked down at Lil and said nothing. He put his arms out and gave her a big hug.

Lil smiled even more brightly and said: "Oh Jon! I guess we really are brother and sister now; in the family of God!"

As they released each other Lil asked: "Who is our guest?"

"That's Wil, Sir Bendris' squire." Replied Jon.

"I see," said Lil, "and why is he here? When did he come?"

Jon explained the late night message that he had received, who Sir Bendris was, and that he would be leaving for a few days on a mission for the King. Lil took all of this in and replied: "So we have two horses in the stable?!"

Jon chuckled and said: "Yes, but not all horses are as nice as Mayflower. Let Wil introduce you to his horse before you go near it."

Lil looked disappointed, but she understood. Jon helped Lil stoke the fire and set the table, and then went out to wash up as Lil said her morning prayers and began to cook breakfast. When he returned both Wil and Boady were awake and it was clear that introductions had already been made. As was usual, Wil was taken aback by the insistence that he "wash up", but he dutifully followed Boady to the stream. They then all sat down to breakfast, and by the time the meal was finished Wil fully understood why Jon might prefer to live in Boady's house rather than the castle.

After the meal, Lil took the dishes to the stream to wash them and herself while the men went to the stable to prepare the horses. While they did this, Jon mentioned to Wil that Lil really liked horses and wanted to "meet" his, whose name was Rags because of the patches of different colored fur that she had. Wil was happy to do this after the fine meal he had been given, and even put her up on the horse and let her ride.

It was during this ride that Sir Bendris arrived. He was bewildered by the sight that he saw.

"Wil!" he said sternly, "What are you doing? Your horse is a weapon of war. We do not allow children to play with our weapons!"

Wil looked very embarrassed and immediately took Lil down from the saddle.

Lil ran to Sir Bendris, who was still mounted and said: "Please sir, don't be angry at Wil. I really like horses and wanted to meet Rags very badly."

Sir Bendris looked stunned at being approached by the little girl with a bright smile, so Jon intervened.

"Sir Bendris," he said. "My sister wanted to meet your squire's horse, and I asked him to allow it. You cannot hold him accountable for granting my request."

The Captain could not argue with the logic behind Jon's answer. Jon was taking responsibility, and this spoke well of him, so he replied: "Very well, Sir Jon. I question your judgement, but at least you are not shirking your responsibility for it."

All eyes were on the new arrival as he dismounted his horse. Seeing Boady, the Captain said: "Master Boady, it is always good to see you. Is Sir Jon someone that I can trust in battle?"

"Captain," replied Boady, "I have performed several tasks with Sir Jon both before and after he was a knight and can say he has my full confidence. I have never seen him actually fight, but contrary to what you just said, I find his judgement very sound, his tactics clever, and he is as brave a man as I have ever served with. He may not have a very military bearing, but I think you will find him a reliable and welcome companion."

Both Jon and Sir Bendris were taken aback by what Boady had said. Jon actually blushed.

"We shall see." Said Sir Bendris. "Mount up men. We have to go and fetch the fourth member of our party."

Jon and Wil mounted their horses, and Boady handed Jon a pack of supplies. Before they could leave, Lil fed Mayflower and Rags a carrot as Sir Bendris looked on in astonishment and Wil shifted uncomfortably in his saddle. She then approached Sir Bendris and said:

"Your horse looks hungry, Sir, may I give him a carrot as well?"

Sir Bendris was speechless, but his horse was straining its neck towards the little girl. "Fine." He said briskly, as Boady had trouble stifling a laugh; the Captain of the Guard had been vanquished by a little girl. Then the three headed off towards the manor. Sir Bendris led, followed by Jon, with Wil bringing up the rear. Not a word was spoken on the short ride.

As they approached the manor, there was commotion by the stable. Thunder was acting up while Aethelstan harangued the grooms. The Duke stood by shaking his head until he noticed the riders at which point he nodded to Sir Bendris. Aethelstan was unaware of the new comers.

Sir Bendris dismounted, and Jon and Wil followed suit. Striding up to the scene the captain shouted: "What in God's name is going on here!" Even the horse seemed to calm himself.

"These incompetent oafs have obviously not done their jobs." Said Aethelstan. "Stand aside and let me get to my horse."

Most of the grooms backed away while Wren remained holding the reigns. As Aethelstan approached, the horse began to act up again. In frustration, Aethelstan pushed Wren to the ground. Freed of the only man constraining him the horse reared up and lashed out at his master.

"Back away!" commanded Sir Bendris and the horse was given room. "Now what?" muttered the captain under his breath.

Jon walked up and said: "Let me try."

Without waiting for a response Jon walked up to the horse and spoke to it calmly. Before grabbing the reigns, he stroked its neck and the horse was calm and docile.

"Alright," said Sir Bendris, "give it to the grooms. We need to have a briefing."

Jon handed the reigns to Wren as Sir Bendris approached the Duke.

"'Tis good to see you again, My Lord." He said.

"Indeed it is, old friend." Replied the Duke. "What's up with this mission, then?"

"We will be scouting for Kells." Replied the Captain.

"That hardly seems a job for the Captain of the Guard." Said the Duke. "Sir Jon handled that job admirably just two days ago. Why are you going, and why the special team?"

The Captain looked down and considered how he would answer. "Because it is the King's wish, my Lord. That, and because we will be going into the Kell lands."

By now the other three members of the team had gathered near and heard this pronouncement. Wil and Jon took the news in stride, but Aethelstan was ecstatic.

"We'll butcher those pagans!" he said. "They don't stand a chance against us!"

Sir Bendris turned towards him and said: "Who gave you permission to speak, soldier?"

Aethelstan first looked towards his father, but found no sympathy there. With visible effort he calmed himself and said: "I beg your pardon, my Lord."

The captain then turned to his three men. "We will not butcher anyone." He said. "This is a scouting mission. We will first see if there are any more Kells in the preserve, and then we will try to find out what is happening in their lands. We will avoid fighting if possible, but of course we will defend ourselves if we must. I would like to gain a captive that we can bring back. The report that was made from Sir Jon's scouting mission raises many questions, and we need answers, not war. Is that understood?"

"Yes Sir!" Responded the three in unison.

"Very good." Responded the captain. "Wil, obviously you will act as my squire. Aethelstan, you will page for Sir Jon. I am in charge, but if something happens to me, Sir Jon will assume command. Sir Jon, I only know you a little, but I believe you know my squire, I expect you to give due consideration to his advice."

"Of course, my Lord. I have trained with Wil and respect his accomplishments and judgement a great deal." Said Jon, then adding: "By your leave, my Lord, and with the Duke's permission, might I ask that Master Boady accompany me instead of Aethelstan?"

"Why do you ask, Sir Jon?" replied the captain.

"Boady has taught me much, and I have as full a level of trust and confidence in him as you do in Wil. I am not as comfortable with Aethelstan." Said Sir Jon in reply.

The captain looked at Aethelstan whose red face indicated that he was seething with rage. Sir Bendris wondered if it was because he had been assigned as Sir Jon's page or because Sir Jon did not want him. He approached the angry young man and looked him in the eyes as he said to Jon:

"You will have to get comfortable with him, Sir Jon. The King wants Aethelstan along and we will not delay to add another to the group. We have work to do." Then addressing Aethelstan he said: "You will gain your master's confidence or I will deal with you myself. Your father will not be there to protect you, and I have fought enough battles alongside your father to say that he will understand if you do not come back from a fight. Is that understood?"

"Yes Sir." Said Aethelstan meekly. The Duke looked on without expression to what had been said. He had fought alongside Sir Bendris often enough that he knew he would not kill one of his own men. He might beat him, or tie him up, but he would not kill him. Aethelstan was not certain of this at all.

"Alright then." Said the captain. "Let's mount up and get going." Turning to the Duke he said: "God willing, I will bring your son back in a couple of days."

Before he could turn to leave the Duke grabbed his arm and whispered: "Bring him back a better man, Ben. I know it's my job, but I am failing at it."

Sir Bendris was very surprised at this, but he gave an understanding nod. As he turned to mount his horse, he saw Wil and Jon mounted while Aethelstan struggled to get near his horse.

"Sir Jon." Said the captain. "Can you ride that horse?"

"I have never tried, but I believe so, my lord." Came the reply.

"Then trade horses with your page. We need to get moving."

Jon dismounted as Aethelstan angrily approached Mayflower. Before going to Thunder, Jon looked in the supply pack and found a carrot. He took this to Thunder, then patted the horse and mounted up. Thunder seemed satisfied with the trade.

With everyone mounted, the Captain laid out his order of the march. "I will lead, followed by Wil, then Aethelstan. Sir Jon, you will guard our rear. Move out."

The riders proceeded in order towards the preserve. They rode in silence until they reached the edge of the preserve, where Sir Bendris called a halt.

"We will relieve ourselves and have a quick meal before we enter." He said. "Wil and Aethelstan, picket the horses."

The four dismounted and Wil grabbed the captain's horse, but Thunder would not allow Aethelstan to approach. Seeing the problem, Sir Jon quickly took charge.

"Aethelstan, take Mayflower and Rags. Wil, you take the captain's and my horse." He said.

The captain shook his head but said nothing. Sir Jon followed the horses and took some bread, cheese, and dried meat out of the supply pack. Wil, got some hard tack from his master's saddle, while Aethelstan brought out a fresh apple, some well cooked meat and a new loaf of bread from his supplies, and all four men sat down to eat.

Jon broke off a piece of bread and some cheese and handed the rest to Wil. Wil smiled, offered Jon some hard tack, and passed Jon's food to Sir Bendris who nodded to Jon in appreciation. Meanwhile, Aethelstan was blissfully enjoying his food.

After a short while, Sir Bendris leaned over to Jon and said: "Ask your page to bring you an apple."

"I have my own apples, sir." Said Jon in reply.

"Nevertheless," replied the captain, "have him bring you an apple."

"Aethelstan," said Sir Jon, "I would like an apple. Bring me one please?"

Aethelstan looked up from his meal and glared at Jon. "Where are they?" he said.

Jon felt a nudge from Sir Bendris. "I suspect they are in your saddle bags." Said the young knight.

"Those are my apples..." began Aethelstan, but Sir Bendris was on him quickly. He grabbed Aethelstan by the throat and lifted him to his feet, spilling Athelstan's food on the ground.

"You are addressing a knight, and your master." He said with controlled fury. "You will address him as 'Sir', and everything that you have is at his disposal." He then threw Aethelstan to the ground.

The two glared at each other until Jon said: "While you're at it, bring Wil and Sir Bendris an apple as well."

"Yes, sir." Said Aethelstan meekly. He got up to fetch the apples and handed one to each of the other men.

As they were finishing the meal Sir Bendris said to Jon in a loud voice: "You know, Sir Jon, your page seems to have some very good provisions. Do you suppose we might all share some of that meat for our evening meal tonight?"

Sir Jon swallowed a bite of apple and replied: "I am sure he would be glad to cook some of it for us, my Lord."

Again, Aethelstan just glared, but Wil seemed quite amused.

"Here's the plan." Said Sir Bendris. "Wil, you will take the lead and scout. Aethelstan will lead his and Wil's horses while Sir Jon and I will lead our own. I doubt there will be any Kells there, but we best be ready. There will be no talking, and we will follow Wil's lead. Understood?"

"Yes sir." Said the three others in unison.

The party packed away the remaining food and headed into the preserve.

For several hours the scouting mission was dull. The party only stopped to water the horses briefly, but the day passed uneventfully. This was not the adventure that Aethelstan had hoped for.

Then, as the sun was just beginning to set, Wil signaled for the others to stop, approached Sir Bendris and whispered into his ear. Sir Bendris gathered Sir Jon and Aethelstan and whispered the following instructions: "There's something happening off to our left. Sir Jon, you and your page need to go check it out."

The two tethered the horses and unburdened themselves of anything extra that they carried. Sir Jon drew his short sword as they snuck off into the brush. Aethelstan had a sheathed long sword by his side.

In a short while they found a peasant setting a trap. He had two rabbits hanging from his belt. Jon strode forward and said: "What do you think you are doing in the King's preserve?"

The peasant was caught off guard and looked at the armed men with fear in his eyes. "I, I, I am feeding my family, my lord." He said.

"You're poaching, you thief!" shouted Aethelstan. "I'll take your hand right now!"

"Stand down." Said Sir Jon tersely. Turning to the poacher he said: "Well, why shouldn't we take your hand? You are caught with illegal game on your belt while setting an illegal trap in the King's preserve."

"Please my Lord. I'm only trying to feed my family." Said the peasant in a pleading voice.

Jon did not believe the man. The man looked reasonably well fed and was carrying more food than a desperate, and hungry man was likely to have. Then again, it would do no good to wound a man while they were on a mission.

"Aethelstan, take his rabbits and destroy his trap. What is your name, peasant? Where do you live?"

"Jimmy." Was the peasant's reply as Aethelstan took the rabbits and began cutting the cords that comprised his trap. "I live on Duke Heimsteady's estate."

"Do you?" replied Jon. "And do you know who I or my page are?"

The peasant shook his head.

"This is Aethelstan, the Duke's son, and I am Sir Jon, who also lives in the Duke's demesne. It is odd that we do not know each other as we are such close neighbors. You are a liar as well as a poacher of the King's game." Said Sir Jon. "What shall we do with you?"

"I'll gut him right now!" said Aethelstan drawing his sword. "He has attempted to disgrace my inheritance!"

"You'll do as you are told." Snapped Sir Jon bringing Aethelstan to a stop. Then addressing the peasant, he said: "You will leave and thank God that you are still alive. If I ever see you again under any suspicious circumstance you will pay dearly. Now, go."

The peasant took off as fast as he could. Jon was briefly puzzled as he noticed the westerly direction the man took, but then Sir Bendris and Wil appeared.

"What happened?" said Sir Bendris.

"My Lord, Sir Jon just allowed a poacher of the King's game to escape." Responded Aethelstan.

Sir Bendris silenced him with an icy stare. "Sir Jon, what happened?" he said.

"It was a Saxon poacher, my Lord. We destroyed his trap and took his game. I did not want to burden us with him, and it did not seem worth it to take his life. I sent him on his way." Replied Jon.

"I know." Said Sir Bendris. "Wil and I were watching. While I am not sure I agree with your letting him go, it is of small importance. We have a bigger mission to accomplish. As for you, Aethelstan, how do you expect to earn Sir Jon's trust if you tattle on him like a small child whenever your small intelligence does not understand what he has done? It is difficult to believe that you are a Duke's son. You act more like the spoiled son of a useless, misbegotten priest. If you cannot learn to follow, you will never learn to lead."

Aethelstan stared back speechless. His big chance to impress the King was not going well.

The party resumed their patrol without further incident. As they camped for the night, Sir Bendris instructed Aethelstan to skin and spit the rabbits for roasting. The Duke's son had always had someone nearby to do these tasks for him, but Wil gave him an instructional hand. Pooling their provisions, the party enjoyed a good evening meal. Afterwards, Wil and Aethelstan took the horses to be watered, and then picketed them with their saddles on. The captain then set a watch schedule and they all bedded down for the night.

As Jon took the third turn on watch he had time to think. It amazed him how little he had thought about God during the course of the day. Sometimes God seemed so real, but other times He seemed so unnecessary.

"Forgive me Father." He prayed. "Thank you for being with me even when I am not with you. Oh, Father, help me to remember that You Are God."

It was very late in the night when Jon woke Sir Bendris to relieve him on his watch. Looking at the position of the moon, Sir Bendris noted that Jon had stood watch longer than he had been required.

"Did you fall asleep Sir Jon?" he asked.

"No, my Lord." Replied Sir Jon. "I was praying for most of the time."

It was not what Sir Bendris had expected to hear, but somehow he believed the explanation.

17

The Kell Lands

SIR BENDRIS WOKE THE PARTY authoritatively, but with surprising gentleness. Aethelstan was assigned to gather wood and enlarge the fire. Jon brought out some more bread and cheese, and Aethelstan surprised everyone by producing some eggs and bacon. Wil cooked a fine breakfast and the party was in good spirits.

"In about an hour we will be in the Kell lands." Said Sir Bendris. "Make sure that your weapons are handy and ready, but do not draw them unless we are confronted by armed foes. Our goal is to assess what is happening in the Kell lands; not to raid, not to start a war, simply to gather information." Looking directly at Aethelstan he added: "Is that understood?"

"Yes Sir." Replied all three.

"We will ride from here in the same order that we road yesterday, but each of us will be extra vigilant. As I will be in the lead, you will need to watch to see if I give any instructions. Wil, if I give a

155

signal, you need to make sure that Sir Jon and Aethelstan also get the message. Any questions?" Added the Captain.

There were no questions. While the gear was being stowed Sir Jon approached Sir Bendris.

"My Lord, may I take a moment to wash and say a quick prayer?" he asked.

Sir Bendris did not looked pleased, but did not really see it as an unreasonable request; strange, but not unreasonable.

"Be quick about it." He briskly replied.

Jon walked to a nearby stream and began to wash himself. His mind wondered why this had become such a ritual for him in such a short time. Then he remembered to pray:

> "Lord, my life is in Your hands, guide me, and keep
> my heart open to your instruction." It was all that he
> could think to say, so he quickly added "Amen."

Looking up he saw three men in peasant garb approaching the preserve from the west. Jon guessed that they were Kells. He tried to be stealthy as he backed away from the stream, but just before he got back into the woods they saw him. They stood still in confusion as Jon returned to camp.

He strode up to Sir Bendris with urgency.

"Three peasants are approaching the preserve from the West, My Lord. I think they saw me, and I got the feeling that they were Kells." He said.

"Peasants?" replied Sir Bendris.

"To all appearances. They did not seem to be armed with much, and wore rough clothing. One had a red beard." Said Sir Jon.

"And you think that they saw you." Said the Captain.

"I can't be sure, but they stopped and looked confused as I turned to return here." Replied the young knight.

"Alright." Said the captain in a louder voice. "Mount up men. There may well be Kells in the area, but they do not appear to be warriors. Nevertheless, be ready for anything."

The party mounted their horses and left the preserve headed towards the Kell lands. Not surprisingly, they saw no sign of the men that Jon had spotted. After about an uneventful hour, the captain stopped and turned to his men.

"We should pretty much be in the Kell lands now." He said. "Be on guard."

The group moved on seeing no one. The land seemed quite deserted. Eventually they saw in the distance a burned out hut surrounded by a burned out field. The four gathered together to discuss.

"Something is going on." Stated Sir Bendris flatly. "Any thoughts?"

The men looked at each other in puzzlement, but nobody had any thoughts until Aethelstan said: "Do you think it could be the dragon? It does not seem to be in the Preserve."

Sir Bendris grunted in reply. It looked like a man-made disaster to him, but he had never seen a dragon-made disaster, so who knew? "Let's take a closer look."

The four riders made their way to the hut, through the burnt out field.

"Sir Jon, check out what is left of that hut." Commanded Sir Bendris.

Jon got off of Thunder and walked into the now roofless and mostly burned house. As he entered several crows or ravens took flight. It appeared to have been a two room dwelling much like the house Jon now lived in. As he entered the back room he came upon two badly burned bodies in an embrace. From what was left of their clothing Jon deduced that they were probably a mother and daughter that had been trapped as their house burned around them. It was a grisly sight, but Jon had seen many dead bodies in his day, including some burned witches.

Coming back out of the house, Jon made his report: "It seems like a typical peasant house. There are two bodies that apparently burned with the house in the back room. There's not much else left. Nothing seems hot anymore, so my guess is that this happened at least several days ago."

Sir Bendris dismounted and the other men followed his lead. "Well, we didn't do it, so who did?" he asked.

This time Aethelstan was quicker to answer. "It had to be the dragon." He said. "No wonder things have been so quiet in our realm. This is good news indeed!"

Jon knew that this assessment could not be right, but he could not deny the existence of the dragon. "Maybe." He added.

Sir Bendris had his doubts. This looked like a purposeful raid on a poorly defended settlement. "We need to look further and find out for sure." He said.

Aethelstan could not contain his excitement. "The land lies open to us! The dragon has fought the battle for us!" he said. "With all due respect, my Lord, I think we should report our initial finding as soon as we can. I will be glad to go back to the castle and tell them what we have found."

While Aethelstan had seemingly made some progress on this trip, Sir Bendris had a low opinion of him. The fact was that he did not trust his temperament and thought it likely that the young man would start a fight. The site was still easily explainable as the result of a raid, yet Sir Bendris saw a way to unburden himself of two added responsibilities that no longer seemed necessary on this mission.

"Sir Jon, I want you and Aethelstan to return to the castle and make a report. Wil and I will continue to scout and see what else we can learn." He said.

Something inside Jon did not like this idea. He did not want to return to the castle and report something that he knew was a lie.

"Sir Bendris, if this was the dragon, I am quested to slay it. Why not let Wil and Aethelstan return, and you and I can continue to scout?" Said the surprisingly resolute young knight.

Sir Bendris was trapped. If it was a dragon, Sir Jon had a duty to hunt it down. If not, then there was no reason to send the two back to the castle. While he preferred to continue with his own squire, Sir Jon had inspired a degree of confidence.

After a pause, Sir Bendris said: "Very well. Wil, you will lead Aethelstan back to the castle and make the report to Father Leonis.

Give us some of your supplies so we can continue the mission. This does not look like a good place to scavenge."

Supplies were shifted and the two riders soon departed. Sir Bendris whispered some special instructions to Wil before they left. When the two knights were alone, the Captain asked Jon: "Why did you really want to stay?"

Jon blushed, but once again words sprung from his mouth: "I feel that I can best serve the King here. Why did you really send them off with such an uncertain report?"

Sir Bendris smiled. "You seem so innocent and naïve, Sir Jon, but clearly there is more to you than meets the eye. Yes, I was trying to rid myself of a distraction. Do your best not to be one."

"I will do my best." Said the confident young knight.

The two mounted their horses and continued through a dreary landscape. While their own country had had a good summer with plentiful food and decent weather, here, only a few miles away, was a different place filled with ruin, and no doubt famine as well. They saw few signs of life: no people, no animals, no crops. The landscape was barren.

They approached a second burned out farm and saw two corpses lying on the ground. They were both men, and neither was burned. They had clearly been beaten and slaughtered. This was not the work of a dragon.

Jon dismounted to observe the corpses while Sir Bendris stayed mounted on his horse in a watchful manner. There was little more to be determined. They had been laying there a day or two, but did not seem to have been scavenged much by the birds. That was odd, so Jon looked around.

Hiding inside the burned out house Jon saw a little girl, she was maybe four or five years old. She did not run, but Jon and she stared at each other for several seconds. Jon slowly walked back to Thunder.

"Anything to report?" asked Sir Bendris.

Jon put a finger up to his lip and reached into the supply satchel pulling out some bread and an apple. He walked back towards the girl showing her the food. Slowly she emerged from hiding. Jon did his best to smile and look friendly, but the girl's obvious hunger is what brought her to him. She snatched the food out of his hands and withdrew, eating in ravenous hurried bites.

Sir Bendris stayed mounted on his horse watching the proceedings. Jon let her eat for a bit, and then tried to talk to her.

"We will not hurt you." He said in a calm soothing voice.

The girl just stared. Jon motioned for her to come towards him, but she shook her head. Jon went back to the horse, pulled out a small wooden cup that he carried and poured some water into it. The girl watched his movements. He offered her the water, and with some hesitation she approached. Jon handed her the cup and she drank while keeping her eyes on him. When she finished drinking she looked at Jon for a bit, and suddenly she began to cry. Jon held out his arms and she fell into them. Jon hugged her as Sir Bendris dismounted.

The girl did not speak Saxon, but they determined that her name was Carm. She was very young, and clearly traumatized. John gave her some more food and left her to eat as he went to speak with Sir Bendris.

"I doubt that Wil or I could have handled that as well as you did, Sir Jon." Said the Captain. "What shall we do with her now? I doubt that she is any use to us as a captive."

"Well, I can't see just leaving her here. Perhaps she can help us make contact with other Kells. She might serve as a sign that we come in peace. In any event, clearly this is not the work of a dragon. Someone has attacked this land, and if it wasn't us, who was it?" Replied the young knight.

"It could be other Saxons, or even Nordic raiders, but I doubt it. I suspect that the Kells are fighting among themselves. This isn't just a raid. Whoever did this is trying to totally conquer or subjugate these people; not just steal from them. We need to be careful that we do not run into the wrong Kells." Said Sir Bendris. "Take the girl on your saddle. We'll find some place to leave her."

When Jon tried to put the girl on his horse she began kicking and screaming. When he put her down she pointed to the bodies.

"Leave her." Said Sir Bendris.

"Let me try something first." Said Sir Jon.

Jon walked over to one of the bodies and picked it up. The smell was horrible, but Jon ignored it and carried the body into what was left of the house. Due to the stiffness of the corpse, it was difficult for Jon to place it by the main table in the main room.

The girl followed Jon and stood at the door silently as Jon went back to get the second body. He also placed this body by the table, so it almost, but not actually, looked like the two corpses had died while sitting down for a meal.

Jon held his hand out to the girl, but instead of grabbing it she ran to one of the corpses and gave it a tearful hug. She then went to the other corpse and said something to it in her native language. There were tears in her eyes as she returned to Jon and took his hand. Jon lifted her up on Thunder, who was surprisingly calm and docile. He then mounted behind her and the riders moved on.

They came to a path and decided followed it. The land was mostly open, with rolling hills, but eerily quiet. Jon thought that they might be watched, but there was really no place for any watchers to hide. The horses gave them confidence as if anyone attacked they could easily out run them.

After a while the riders approached a stand of trees. It was not so much a forest, but it was the most substantial land feature that they had seen. Sir Bendris halted.

"If anyone is about, they'll be in those trees." He said. "We will ride up to them and stop before entering, then we will wait a good bit to see if there are signs of anyone within."

Jon nodded and the riders moved on stopping just short of the trees to listen. Whoever was hiding in there was doing a poor job of it. They heard rustling, and even quiet voices speaking the Kell language.

"We come in peace." Shouted Sir Bendris. "We wish to talk."

In reaction there was far more mumbled noise, but shortly a man in peasant guard came onto the path. Jon instantly recognized the peasant that he had caught poaching in the preserve the day before.

"Dimmy!" yelled the little girl as the men faced each other on the path.

Jon edged closer to Sir Bendris.

"That's the peasant from the preserve yesterday." He said. "He speaks Saxon."

"You speak to him." Replied Sir Bendris.

"So, except for the part about where you lived, you were telling the truth yesterday." Said Sir Jon to the man.

"I was." Said the man. "You can see that things are not going well for us here."

"I do see that." Replied Jon in a serious voice. "What has happened?"

"I think you can see that for yourself. Our tribe has been attacked. The people are hungry and many are dead." Replied Jimmy.

"Who has attacked you? It was not Saxons." Said Jon.

"No, it was not Saxons, nor Norsemen, but our fellow Kells from a neighboring Kingdom. Our King refused to give their King his daughter in marriage so that the Kingdoms could be joined, so I guess that they decided to take the land themselves. We were caught unaware while our men were planning to raid your lands. We mostly fled rather than fought." Said Jimmy with a peasant's blunt honesty. "How did you come to have Carm?"

"We found her at a burned out farm with two corpses. It did not seem right to leave her there." Said Jon.

"You have a surprisingly good heart for a man of war. Can you give her to me?" asked Jimmy.

"Can I trust you if I dismount?" asked Jon in return.

"We do not seek a further fight." Replied Jimmy. "I am not sure that we seek another mouth to feed either, but she is one of us."

Jon dismounted and lifted Carm down from the horse. She did not immediately run to Jimmy, but stood next to Jon alternating looks between the two men. Finally, Jimmy called to her in her own language. She looked up at Jon, gave him a quick hug and walked to where Jimmy stood.

"Thankyou." Said Jimmy. "You clearly treated her well."

Then Jon had another of those moments where words he had not thought came out of his mouth: "Jimmy, can you come back and tell our King what has happened here? We do not seek war. I will give some of our food for your people and I will bring you back."

"You cannot promise that Sir Jon." Said Sir Bendris quietly from his horse.

Jimmy looked undecided. "How can you promise that?" he said.

Jon did not know what to say. He had not thought about the words that he had spoken, but he felt confident that he could fulfill his word.

"Sir Bendris just informed me that I cannot." Replied Jon. "But I have every intention to bring it about."

Jimmy looked uneasy. The young knight had good intentions and a good heart, but he would be trusting him with his life; and the knight was very young.

"I am a Saxon by birth, and I was called by God to bring His Gospel to these people. I cannot trust in you, but I will trust in Him. I feel His calling almost as strongly as I felt the call to come to these people. I will go with you." Said Jimmy.

Jon was pleased to hear that Jimmy was a fellow Christian. Sir Bendris was astounded that the young knight had not only procured a prisoner, but a willing prisoner who spoke their language.

"Save enough food for the three of us to make the journey back." Said Sir Bendris as he looked to judge their stores.

Jimmy began to speak to the others hidden in the trees. Three women came out and together with Jimmy and Carm approached the horses. Jon felt guilty and grateful for how much food they were able to give them. They saved mostly hard tack for themselves and gave their better food to the starving Kells.

As Jimmy said good bye to them, Carm came up and said something to Jon.

"What is she saying?" asked the young knight.

"She is thanking you." Said Jimmy. "She also said that she sees Jesus in you. It is quite a compliment as her family was not Christian."

Jon got down on one knee and looked Carm in the eye. "Thank you." He said. "I think the good Lord brought us together." He then hugged her as Jimmy interpreted his words to her.

Jimmy mounted double with Sir Bendris to start the journey, but the riders switched the load with some frequency to try to keep the horses as fresh as they could. There were few stops on the way, and the hard tack they had left to eat did not encourage them to linger over their meal. They made good time, and made it back to the castle very late that night.

On the ride the knights learned that Jimmy had been raised on the Duke's estate. As a young man he went to seminary, but had left there before he was ordained. On his way back to his home he fell in with the Kells and had remained there. The work was frustrating and there were few converts to show for his efforts, but in the aftermath of the attack he had been thrust into a leadership role among the mostly women and children who had survived.

"I was shocked by what Carm said to you." Said Jimmy. "I had no idea that she or most any of the others even knew who Jesus is. Perhaps the Lord is answering my prayers with all of this."

As they rode back, Jon had a prayer in his mind and a Hymn in his heart. He felt like God had guided him and had used his open heart to fulfill His purposes.

18

News of the Dragon Spreads

WIL DID NOT PARTICULARLY ENJOY the ride back to the castle. Aethelstan spoke incessantly, imagining the grand campaign that could now be led against the Kells. The invaders would gain loot; apparently he did not notice that there seemed little loot available at the farm that they had seen. The dragon had put an easy victory at the Kingdom's finger tips; apparently he had forgotten that the dragon had killed his own King, and that it was no friend of the Kingdom's. Wil had tried to get Aethelstan to see reason, but the Duke's son was full of visions of his own glory.

"I hope Sir Jon does not try to kill the dragon." He declared. "The dragon is our most valuable asset in defeating our historic enemy."

"Let's make a factual report to Father Leonis. We do not have to interpret the facts for him." Replied the Squire.

Wil knew that there was little evidence indeed that the ruin they had witnessed was the work of the dragon, but eventually he gave up countering Aethelstan's wild theories. Wil determined to get back to the castle as quickly as they could and make an honest report to Father Leonis. The King's advisors were not fools; they would make a reasoned decision.

The two riders made it back into town in the late afternoon. Both horses were lathered from the hard ride as they were left at the stable.

"The Kell lands lie open to us!" Aethelstan told the grooms. "The dragon has moved into their land and is bringing them the wrath of God!"

Wil roughly grabbed Aethelstan by the arm, got close up into his face and said sternly: "Shut up! We will make our report to Father Leonis, not to the stable hands."

"Do you know who you are speaking to?" asked an indignant Aethelstan shaking his arm loose from Wil's grip. "I am the son of a Duke. You are someone who aspires to be a knight at best. You will not tell me who to speak to or what to say!"

Wil had had enough. He slapped Aethelstan on the cheek and then grabbed his mouth with his hand.

"You are a silly, irresponsible, spoiled brat. I pray the Duke has another son because you will be the ruin of his estate. You will follow my lead as Sir Bendris instructed. Is that understood?" Wil then gave Aethelstan a rough shove that effectively put him on the ground.

Aethelstan was up in a flash and charged the young squire, tackling him around the waist. The stable hands gathered around to watch the fight. Guards came to break it up, but seeing Wil, one of their own, they held back to watch the proceedings. Soon there was a great deal of commotion and cheering.

Wil had been trained to fight, while Aethelstan had only won fights largely because the other boys at the manor were afraid to beat him. After the young squire had freed himself from the tackler, he stood and surgically punched Aethelstan whenever he approached.

The Duke's son soon had a bloody nose, a black eye, and an uncontrolled rage. Becoming frustrated, Aethelstan drew his sword.

"You don't want to do that." Said Wil in a calm voice while drawing his own sword.

One of the guards stepped forward and said: "That's enough. Put away the weapons."

"You stay out of this, knave." Snarled Aethelstan in a blind rage.

He lunged at Wil, but the squire was quick and stepped aside, swatting Aethelstan on his butt with the flat of his sword. Everyone watching laughed.

"Fine, young man. I'll stay out of it. I guess there are some lessons that have to be learned the hard way." Said the guard in a jolly voice. "Don't kill him Wil. It would be a shame to make the stable hands clean up the mess just before dinner."

Aethelstan approached Wil more warily this time. When he got closer he began to swing his sword in a slashing motion. He had expected Wil to back up, but the squire stood his ground and parried each stroke with calm precision. Each time the swords met the reverberations went back into Aethelstan's hand and arm, and soon his sword arm was aching and weak.

"What is going on here!" Shouted Brother Johan coming upon the scene. "Have we not enough enemies? Must we fight ourselves?"

Aethelstan paused, while Wil calmly stood at the ready.

"Wil, Aethelstan, why are you two back? Where are Sir Bendris and Sir Jon?" demanded the uncharacteristically stern monk.

"We have a report to make." Said Wil. "Master Aethelstan wanted to make it to the stable hands, but I disagreed. He decided to settle the question by force of arms."

"You lying peasant!" shouted Aethelstan. "I will…"

"Enough!" shouted Brother Johan. "Guards, escort Master Aethelstan someplace he can clean up and then bring him to Father Leonis and myself in the council chamber. Wil, you come with me."

As Wil and Brother Johan began to walk away Aethelstan yelled: "This isn't over! I will have justice!"

Wil turned back and calmly said: "I would consider it an honor as well as a pleasure to be the one who gives it to you."

Brother Johan grabbed his arm and led him into the keep. When they were somewhat alone he said: "That's not like you Wil. What was that all about?"

"He is an uncommonly annoying person." Replied Wil. "He began spreading rumors about the dragon attacking the Kells. Something we do not know is true. His lies will be all over town before we even have a chance to discover the truth."

Wil was right. Even as they walked the news was spreading around town.

They entered the council chamber and Brother Johan sent a servant to get Father Leonis who was with the King. While they waited Wil told Brother Johan an important detail that was not for general consumption:

"Sir Bendris wanted to send Jon and Aethelstan back because he did not want to be burdened with them when we were likely in a war zone. Sir Jon insisted on staying. Aethelstan is convinced that the dragon has brought ruin to the Kells, but the rest of us are far from convinced. I am to report what we saw and let you draw your own conclusions. It is likely Sir Bendris will be back tomorrow." He said.

Brother Johan took this pronouncement in a puzzled way. "Do you have anything to report?" he asked.

"Yes. But it is a preliminary report. Sir Bendris urges that you wait for his return before making any decisions." Said Wil.

Just then Father Leonis and the King entered the room. Both men rose from their chairs.

"Let's sit and hear the news." Said the King. "I hear that the dragon was sighted and my knights are currently trying to slay it! That is good news indeed!"

Wil looked uncomfortable. Had the rumor spread so quickly that the King had already heard an altered version of it? Finally, he replied:

"Your Majesty, that is not quite the news. We entered the Kell lands and it is clear that something or someone has attacked them. Their fields and homes are burned, and it could be by the dragon, but we did not see the dragon and it very well may be that other people attacked them. Sir Bendris and Sir Jon hope to be back tomorrow with a more detailed report."

As Wil finished, Aethelstan was escorted into the room. Father Leonis waived him to the table and Brother Johan pointed to where he should sit.

"Heimsteady? What were you doing on this mission? And what happened to you? Was there a fight?" asked the King.

Aethelstan was about to answer when Brother Johan cut him off. "Your Majesty, the fight occurred only moments ago at the stable. We are still determining what happened with that. Aethelstan was on the mission at Father Leonis' and my request."

The King looked at Father Leonis who said: "By your leave, your majesty, I will tell you about that later. For now, let's hear what happened on the mission."

"Very well." Said the King in an awkward manner. "Tell me Heimsteady, what did you see?"

Aethelstan became animated: "The Kell lands are in ruin, my Lord! Their entire Kingdom lies open to us! Their fields and homes are burned out and there is hardly a person to be found on their lands. The dragon has won the victory for us! We need only seize the advantage that it has given us!"

"Did you see the dragon?" asked the King.

"It was as good as seeing it. The destruction was massive. I cannot imagine what else could have so totally over-whelmed them." Replied Aethelstan.

"And Sir Bendris and Sir Jon are now hunting the dragon?" asked the King.

"Sir Jon refused to come back because he said it was his duty to slay it." Said Aethelstan.

The King sat back in his chair while Father Leonis and Brother Johan exchanged worried looks. Brother Johan interjected himself into the conversation:

"My Lord, Wil tells me that your two trusted knights hope to be back tomorrow with a more detailed report. Sir Bendris asks that we wait for his report before making any further decisions."

The King hardly noticed what Brother Johan had to say. Instead he turned to Father Leonis and said: "It is like my dream. Their lands are ruined and I need to decide what to do, but in the dream somebody comes and tells me a different way to conquer them. How long must I wait?"

Father Leonis turned to the King and held his hands. "Sir Bendris should be back tomorrow." He said. "You need to at least wait until then."

Absent mindedly the King said: "I pray Sir Jon kills that foul beast. How many other children has it now orphaned?" He then regained his composure and looked to Wil who was fidgeting in his seat. "Wil, do you agree with Aethelstan's report?"

"Your Majesty," said Wil, "I am only a squire, but I have seen war. It is not a thrilling and gallant thing. I cannot deny that what we saw could have been caused by a dragon, but I think it more likely that it was done by men. Sir Bendris is continuing the search for the truth."

"Thank you Wil." Said the young King.

"But your Majesty," interjected Aethelstan, "it does not matter how it happened. The fact is that the Kell lands are ours for the taking. We need only march on them and take them. With God's blessing you could nearly double the size of the Kingdom within weeks of having ascended to the throne! Think of it my Lord: Aerdwulf the Conqueror!"

The boy/King looked to Father Leonis and said: "It is not easy being the King." He then got up and left as Father Leonis followed him.

The three remaining men sat in awkward silence. Finally, Brother Johan asked: "Athelstan, what were you and Wil fighting about?"

It did not appear that Aethelstan had thought about what to say. Eventually he responded:

"Wil was disrespectful to me. I was not going to stand idly by while someone of inferior birth and circumstance tried to embarrass me in front of the common folk."

"Wil, were you disrespectful to Aethelstan?" asked Brother Johan.

"Well, I did lose patience with him." Said Wil. "He was spreading half-truths at best, and making a report to the stable hands before our superiors had been briefed. I am not proud of how I reacted, but I cannot say that I am sorry either. I am used to working in a chain of command; Aethelstan seems only interested in himself. I think that he was disrespectful to my command, as well as to the King and Father Leonis to whom we were to report."

"You are not my master!" blurted our Aethelstan. "I owe you no allegiance and can follow my own lead!"

Brother Johan cut him off. "Who did Sir Bendris say was in charge?" he asked.

Aethelstan was silent, so Wil replied: "He put me in charge and gave me the information that I shared with you."

"He put you in charge for the ride back here." Asserted Aethelstan. "Your command ended when we got back to town."

Wil shrugged and Brother Johan took a deep breath.

"Aethelstan, you will never be in a position to lead if you cannot first learn to follow. You will never be in a position to lead others if you do not lead yourself wisely. This fight has caused both of you to lose respect, and it seems both of you played a big role in it. I suggest each of you look to yourself for what you could have done better and forgive the other. We have no control over what others do or think, but that is fortunate as we have enough trouble controlling ourselves." The monk paused and then added: "I will not ask you to apologize to each other, but I will ask you to forgive each other when your passions have cooled. The Kingdom has challenges enough without us fighting among ourselves."

Brother Johan thought he had spoken wisely, but both of the antagonists thought it a bunch of nonsense. This close to the fight there was little forgiveness in their hearts. Their dislike for each other had taken firm root.

"Aethelstan, leave Mayflower here. Why were you riding Sir Jon's horse anyway?" said Brother Johan. "Never mind, the horse needs rest. Tell the grooms I said to lend you another horse and go home and get some rest. Wil, you and I will speak later."

The three men got up and went their separate ways.

Meanwhile, news of the dragon spread through the town and countryside. The story kept growing until it was said that the dragon had fought beside Sir Jon and Sir Bendris as they conquered the Kells. Serious people found this difficult to believe, but many came to have a deep faith in the dragon who had been sent by God to make the Kingdom great.

While few people were about when Sir Bendris, Sir Jon, and Jimmy rode into town, one of these people greeted them.

"Tell me you didn't kill the dragon." He shouted in a drunken slur as they rode past.

Sir Bendris ignored him, but Jon shook his head to say no.

"What dragon?" asked Jimmy who was riding with Jon.

"It's a long story." replied Jon. "There are rumors of a dragon about. My guess is that the people think that it attacked you."

"It's a wonder the things that people believe and do not believe. They will put their trust in a dragon that they have never seen, but doubt God whose work is all around them. Have you seen the dragon?" asked the missionary.

Jon did not know what to say, so he changed the subject. "We'll be at the stable in just a minute." He said.

They arrived at the stable and woke a groom to care for their horses. The three then wearily made their way into the keep. Sir Bendris found a sleeping servant and told him to give Sir Jon and "our guest" a room. Furthermore, he instructed the servant to tell Father Leonis that they had returned when the priest awoke in the morning. He then said good night to his fellow travelers and went to his room.

Wil sprang out of bed when Sir Bendris entered.

"Captain, you're back!" he said in a surprised voice.

"Yes," replied the tired knight, "Sir Jon got us a native to give a true account of what happened. I'll tell you about it in the morning. How did your return go?"

"I'm sorry, my Lord. I got in a fight with Aethelstan." Said Wil.

Sir Bendris looked at him sympathetically. "Wil, you're like a son to me. I'm sure you had your reasons, but a commander cannot fight with his own men. You can tell me about it in the morning. That spoiled child is truly a challenge, but I had hoped you were up to it."

Wil was pleased by the kind words, but crestfallen that he had disappointed his mentor. "Good night, my Lord. It is certainly a story that can wait." He said.

Meanwhile, the servant had taken Jon and Jimmy to Sir Malpolem's old room. Jon was pleased to be in familiar surroundings.

"Jimmy, you take the big bed. This used to be my room when I was a page, and this bed was always mine." Said the young knight.

"Are you sure?" said Jimmy. "I have only rarely slept in an actual bed. I am sure that the smaller bed would be quite luxurious to me."

"I'm sure." Came the reply. "Before we go to sleep shall we say a prayer?"

Jimmy had gathered that Jon was a man of faith, but he was pleasantly surprised by the request.

"Of course." He said getting down on one knee.

The two men knelt looking at each other until Jimmy began to make the sign of the cross.

"God, you are an awesome God." He prayed. "Who can understand the way you work your will among us? Thank you, Father, for feeding your people and for giving me a chance to serve you in a new and different way. Help me to bring you glory."

Jimmy paused, and Jon came to understand that he should finish the prayer:

"Amen, and amen, Father." He said. "Thank you for being with us today, and for guiding us to your purpose. Thankyou Jesus for making your home in my heart and continue to guide us in the morning. Amen."

"Amen." Repeated Jimmy.

The two looked at each other and exchanged a smile. Jimmy said: "I like the way you pray, brother. You do not ask God to be your servant, but recognize that we are His. Good night, may you experience God's peace in your sleep."

The two then went to bed. Jon was very tired, but before he went to sleep he thought about what Jimmy had said: God is not our servant, we are His. It was a different way of looking at things. He then fell into a deep and peaceful slumber.

19

Faith or Hope

IT WAS A RAINY MORNING the next day when Father Leonis and Brother Johan sat down to breakfast.

"Sir Bendris and Sir Jon returned very late last night." Announced Father Leonis. "They apparently brought someone with them."

"Oh? What news did they bring?" replied the monk.

"I am letting them get some sleep. I am sure if it was important Sir Bendris would have awakened me." Replied the priest. "Such a dreary morning."

"You seem a bit dreary yourself, Leo. What concerns you?" asked Johan.

"The King had a dream. He is convinced that he has to make a decision that will determine the future of the Kingdom. In the dream, a man sent by God advises him, but he is convinced that it is neither you nor me; he seems to be a stranger. The news from Wil and Aethelstan has convinced him that the dream is coming true. He has put the weight of the Kingdom on himself because of a dream. I also fear that he will make the decision about the Kells without us." Said Leonis.

"We need to get a council together. We can't let an eleven-year-old boy decide these things." Said Johan seriously.

"Of course you're right, but how functional will a council be? The Dukes are not united in doing what is best for the Kingdom, they are seeking their own benefit." Said Leonis.

"Then let's add more than the Dukes to the council. You should be on it, and Sir Bendris, and maybe the Queen. That would put the three of you along with the three Dukes; the King would be the deciding vote." Responded Johan.

Leonis stared at his food but said nothing. This proposal had been made several times before, but it worried Leonis as he would lose some of the control that he had. It was not that he clung to power, he just felt a huge responsibility to the King. He wanted to protect Aerdwulf.

"Leo, what has happened to your faith? The fate of the Kingdom is in God's hands, not yours. Either you are called to His purpose or you are not. What does your heart tell you?" said the monk.

"Johan, it is easier to speak of trusting in God when the outcome does not really matter. The decisions that we make can really determine the future of the Kingdom. I wish God would send me a clear message, but all I feel is fear and confusion. I even find it difficult to pray now while I have so many earthly things pressing on me every moment of the day. Where is God in all of this?!" Leonis banged his fist on the table as he said the last bit.

Johan got up from the table and walked behind Leonis' chair. Placing his hands on Leonis' shoulders he said: "Brother, I will pray for you. Listen to what you just said; that is not the Leo that I know and love. You sound as if you are working for your own glory rather than God's. You are different than the Dukes and other self-seeking men in this Kingdom. You are called to guide the King. God is God, and you are not. Remember the anchors of your faith. Remember the personal miracles God has done just for you. Don't walk away from God just when you need Him most."

The two men were silent for a moment. Then Johan said he was going to get Sir Bendris. A tear came to Leonis's eye, and his heart prayed for him: "Father, help me to remember who is in charge. Give me a sign, Lord. Let me know who I can trust. Guide my belief and give me faith."

Leonis was 15 years old when he had asked Jesus to enter into his heart. He was already studying for the priesthood, but prior to that his relationship with God was something that he had done, not lived. He went to church; took the sacraments; tried to be good; but it all felt a bit surreal. It felt like he was putting his faith in the magic beads of his rosary and that he prayed to a cross or a statue. When he asked God to live in his heart he had experienced a lightness of being that he could not describe; suddenly he had felt a sense of purpose. That lightness of being was not there now.

One day not too soon after he had invited God into his heart, as he was walking in the abbey garden, he came to a moment of severe doubt. Had he exchanged one false faith for another? Was there really a God, or did he just want there to be one? Was it all faith, or just hope? As he walked it began to rain. It was not a hard rain, but a steady one. Leonis' heart cried out: "God, show me you are real! Let me walk back to the dorm without getting wet and I will not doubt you."

He was enough of a Bible scholar to know that you should not test God, but God had mercy on him that day. As he entered the dorm he felt dry. He had told Johan about this that same evening, but Johan had pointed out that his hair was long and freshly greased. Surely the rain had rolled off of him because of that. Nevertheless, Leonis knew deep in his heart that God had answered his prayer. Why was his hair freshly greased on the very day he would ask God for a personal sign? Why had it rained just when he was thinking as he was? The world was created by God, so what expectation should he have that an angel might appear to hold an umbrella for him. No, while he might not have witnessed the miracle of creation he no right to deny the miracle of existence around him and that God had touched him personally through it. While that miracle of staying dry might not mean anything to anyone else, it meant everything to him.

God had answered him when he was in doubt; he could not deny it. That small moment with God was an anchor for his faith; and from that foundation of faith came hope.

Leonis remembered that he could trust God. There were dozens of times when he recognized God had acted in his life. How could he deny his faith? God was real; he needed to trust Him. "Praise God." He thought. He felt better. He felt ready to take on whatever God would give him to do. He knew he would not be facing things alone. His doubt had challenged his belief, but it had also strengthened his faith.

Brother Johan met Wil near Sir Bendris' room.

"Good morning Wil." Said the monk. "Is Sir Bendris awake?"

"He is, my Lord, and will be down shortly." Replied the squire. "I am just going to find Sir Jon and the prisoner."

"Prisoner?" asked the monk.

"Well, that or a guest. One of the Kells came back voluntarily. Apparently he is friendly enough." Said Wil.

After inquiring of a servant, the two walked to the room where Jon and Jimmy were staying. They knocked softly and entered. They found Jon and Jimmy kneeling in prayer. "Amen." Said Jon as they entered.

"Pardon us." Said Johan as he noticed what they had interrupted. He then looked again. "Jimmy? Is it really you after all these years?"

"Johan!" cried Jimmy in pleasant surprise. "I certainly did not expect to find you here!"

"Nor I you." Said the smiling monk. Seeing the astonished looks on Wil's and Jon's faces he explained: "Leonis, Jimmy, and I were fast friends at the Abbey where we studied as young men. But you disappeared one day, Jimmy. What happened to you?"

"I gave up." Said Jimmy. "At the time, none of our beliefs made sense to me, so I left. On the way home I was captured by the Kells. I was at my lowest, most desperate point. It was then that I turned to God, or rather He found me, and gave me a calling to bring His Gospel to my captors."

"Leonis is here as well. We will have quite a reunion. When we parted we were friends, but God reached out to all of us. We are brothers in Christ now. Your being here is a miracle, old friend, Leonis needs some encouragement." Said the excited monk.

The two younger men listened in astonishment. It certainly was an odd coincidence that three men who had studied together at an Abbey many years ago had been reunited at this instance in this place.

"Sir Jon, let's go see Father Leonis at once. Are you ready to make your report?" asked Brother Johan.

"I am, Brother Johan. Let's go." Replied the young knight.

They met Sir Bendris near his room on the way back to the council chamber. He was also astonished that the man they had brought back was known by the King's two chief advisors. It looked like it was going to be an interesting day.

As the group entered the council chamber, Leonis was about to leave. "Gentlemen, I will be with you shortly. I am going to get the King." He said.

"Father Leonis, please wait a moment." Interceded Brother Johan. Father Leonis turned to look at him, while Brother Johan just looked back.

"Yes, Brother, what is it?" asked the priest impatiently.

"I thought you might want to meet the guest who arrived with Sir Bendris and Sir Jon last night." Replied Johan holding his hands towards Jimmy.

"Ah, yes, and do you speak Saxon?" asked the priest.

Jimmy smiled and replied in Latin: "I do, and probably better than you do old friend."

Leonis was caught off guard and stared at the new comer for a long moment. "Is it really you? Jimmy? Praise God! I was so busy with my business I failed to notice that God had blessed me!" He took several strides towards Jimmy and gave him a friendly embrace.

Suddenly, Father Leonis remembered who he was: The King's advisor.

"I look forward to renewing our acquaintance." He said formally. "That will have to wait. I must get the King so he can hear the report on what is happening in the Kell lands."

Leonis managed a smile and left to get the King. "I shall return shortly." He said as he departed.

The others looked at each other in puzzlement until Johan indicated that they should sit down. It was several minutes before Leonis returned, accompanied by the King, and his mother. As they entered the room, everyone rose to their feet.

The King looked around the room and then said: "Be seated gentlemen. We have much to discuss." Although only eleven years old, it was clear that Aerdwulf was already growing into his Kingship. Jon noticed that he had a sense of self assurance that was missing on the day Jon had been knighted one week ago.

Turning to Sir Bendris the King said: "It's good to have you back. What have you to report?"

"The Kell lands that we scouted lie in ruins. The fields are burned, many bodies lie about, and the few remaining inhabitants we came across are fearful, hungry, and desperate." Replied the Captain of the Guard.

"It was reported yesterday that this may have been the work of the Dragon. Did you and Sir Jon find it and slay it?" Asked the King in a less than hopeful voice.

"No, your Majesty. We do not believe that it was the dragon. We have brought a Saxon who was living amongst the Kells to explain what happened." Replied Sir Bendris. "Your majesty, this is Jimmy, a man we first encountered in the preserve, and then met again in the Kell lands. He was captured by the Kells some years ago and now seeks to bring them the true faith."

The King turned his attention towards Jimmy. "You are a man of God, then?" he asked.

"I am a child of God's." replied Jimmy. "I once studied for the priesthood, but the Lord had other plans for me."

"That is interesting." Said the King, acting very much like someone older than eleven years. "I should love to hear your story some time, but we are pressed for time. Can you tell me what happened in the Kell lands?"

"Of course, your Majesty." Began the missionary. "The Kell are organized in something like Kingdoms, but they are really more tribal than we are. The lands closest to your Kingdom are led by a King, or Chief, named Arwel. It is not a rich land, so they supplement the food that they farm and scavenge by occasionally raiding your lands. King Arwel has one treasure, a daughter named Anwen. She is a beautiful young maiden, and many other Kell chiefs desire her hand. One chief, Bledyn by name, leads a fierce tribe to the North and West of Arwel's land. Bledyn seeks to unify the Kell under his leadership, but his tribe is not particularly big or powerful, although they are aggressive. Bledyn gave Arwel an ultimatum: give him Anwen as his wife and merge the two lands under his rule, or suffer the consequences. Arwel did not take this too seriously as his fighting men, led by the warrior Kyp, are very capable, and for months nothing happened.

"The Kells recently heard of the death of your father and that a boy had ascended the throne. Arwel determined to gather his forces to make a raid on your lands, ignoring the threat he faced from Bledyn. These men were readying to attack when Bledyn led his men against Arwel. The raid was quick and devastating. While Arwel's men were armed and gathered in the North of the Kingdom, Bledyn came to south burning fields and slaughtering the unarmed inhabitants. The raid has weakened Arwel a great deal, but his army is intact and is likely preparing a raid against Bledyn as we speak. The Kells are fighting amongst themselves, while the people, my flock, starve. It is a sad tale of war, your Majesty."

Everyone around the table was sobered by the tale that they heard, not least the King. It was Leonis who broke the silence:

"Jimmy, you are sure that Arwel has called off his attack on us?" he asked.

"I am not privy to their counsel, Father Leonis, but they seemed to be planning a raid, not a war. Not all of the men had been called to arms. Since the attack Arwel has been gathering food for his full army, and the hatred of the people is against Bledyn, not against the Saxons." Came the reply.

"But they were going to attack my Kingdom." Stated the King. Jimmy did not reply.

"Thank you, good sir." Said the King. "You have given us much to ponder. Sir Bendris, insure that our guest is made comfortable as I am sure we will wish to speak with him again. Since you are a Christian, Jimmy, I invite you to join us at mass this noon. Father Leonis will see to it that you attend. We will reconvene afterwards."

Father Leonis was stunned by the way his pupil was taking charge without consulting him. He almost hesitated to give his advice, but said:

"Your Majesty, we are faced with a very grave question. Shall I send messengers to call the Dukes to give you advice and consent?"

"Of course, good Father. Get them here as soon as you can." Said the King. "Gentlemen, let us prepare to consult with our Lord at mass." He then grabbed his mother's hand and left his counselors in stunned silence.

Privately, Leonis was embarrassed. He had not even realized that it was Sunday, and he was a priest! "Brother Johan, please get Jimmy some new clothes and bring him to church. While you are at it, I think Sir Jon might also use a clean shirt. Sir Bendris, could you walk with me please?" said the King's main advisor.

Leonis and Sir Bendris departed, leaving the others behind. They had not walked far when Leonis grabbed the Captain's arm and said: "Was that our Aerdwulf?"

Bendris looked at Leonis' hand on his arm and the priest let go.

"I was proud of him." Said the Captain. "He was serious and thoughtful. He certainly was different than the boy who was chasing butterflies a little more than two weeks ago. What do you think we should do?"

"Pray?" answered Leonis absent mindedly. "We will discuss it with the Dukes, and form the council. I am not sure what should be done. Our enemy is weak, but I do not like our chances if a boy leads us to war. What are your thoughts?"

"I agree that we are probably not ready for an all-out war. Beyond that, this Bledyn sounds like someone we may want to avoid

181

until we are stronger." Replied the knight. "I think we had better consider our options carefully."

The two men parted. Father Leonis sent messengers to the Dukes to advise them that the King sought their counsel as soon as possible. He gave the messengers no details concerning what the King needed advice about. He then returned to his room to contemplate in silence.

He surprised himself by immediately falling into prayer:

"Father, I do believe. You are more than just a hope, as without you I have nothing to hope for. Holy Spirit, kindle my faith; 'help my unbelief.' Guide me God. Let me act in your will. Help me feel your presence, and let me know what I should be hoping for."

20

Belief, Faith, and Zealotry

D<small>UE TO HIS FATHER'S OCCUPATION</small> and the duties that it entailed, Jon had never attended church regularly growing up, so going two weeks in a row was somewhat unusual. He had attended more regularly as Sir Malpolem's page, but these were treated more as Latin learning exercises than as worship. Jon felt that something had changed in him and that his approach to church should change as well; but it hadn't. He felt like Mass would be more of a waste of time than an experience in spiritual growth, and no matter how hard he tried he could not shake that feeling. Nevertheless, Father Leonis had arranged seats for he and Jimmy, and he was resigned to attending.

After having said morning prayers together, Jon felt a sort of kinship with Jimmy and decided to share his feelings to him: "Jimmy, I have to confess that attending church doesn't excite me as much as the possibility of spending some time discussing our faith and picking your brain about what the Bible says."

Jimmy gave Jon a smile and put a hand on his shoulder. "I couldn't agree more." He said. "Focus on the Bible readings and pray silently. I try not to let all the pageantry distract me from God."

"Wow! I thought I was the only believer who felt that way!" said the surprised young man.

"Jon, I am not saying that church does not have its purpose; how else would the common folk hear about Jesus, and God, and that life really is about something more than mere survival?" Replied the missionary. "Church is where people first begin to believe, but belief is not faith. Coming to faith is something personal, and while church can point the way, a person still has to walk the path to faith on their own."

"Wait, there is a difference between belief and faith?" asked Jon in a startled way.

"Did you believe in God before you came to a relationship with Jesus?" asked Jimmy.

"I guess so." Said Jon. "It doesn't make much sense that anything exists unless God, or something like Him created it all."

"So, you had belief, but God really didn't matter much to you." Replied Jimmy. "God was every bit as real to you as the Pope or Emperor. While you acknowledged His existence, what He did or said really did not make much of a difference in your life. But now you have moved from belief to faith. You find yourself praying without thinking. What you say and do is different. God matters now. That's the difference; you don't just believe, you have faith and trust in God. While you have never seen God, or the Pope, or the Emperor, God makes an actual difference in how you live. You live a life of faith."

"Wow! I guess you sure gave me something to think about during Mass!" Replied Jon.

Jon and Jimmy made their way to the church and were shown to their seats. Brother Johan soon joined them while Sir Bendris and Wil were seated in their usual seats and Father Leonis was near the altar ready to take part in the Mass. The Abbot presided.

Jon focused his mind on prayer, but it was not easy, and he soon practiced his Latin by interpreting what was being said. The first reading was from Joshua at the beginning of the book. (Joshua 1:1-7.) The gist was that God was telling Joshua to take the land that He had promised the Israelites. In light of his conversation with Jimmy, Jon realized that God was calling on Joshua to not just believe his promise, but to act on it in faith. He was being told to put the people at risk because God had promised them that they would take the land.

The New Testament reading was from the letter of St. James. (James 2:14-24.) Four sentences in particular stood out:

"Show me your faith without works, and I will show you my faith by my works. You believe that God is one. You do well; the demons also believe and tremble. But are you willing to recognize, foolish fellow, that faith without works is useless?"

That was the difference between belief and faith: one acts on faith.

The Abbot preached a sermon on acting out one's faith. He put forth that God had promised that His people would triumph in faith. He called on the Kingdom to not live in fear of a dragon or the Kells, but to take up their arms in faith and vanquish God's enemies.

Jon found this sermon odd. Did God really want him to go and kill the Kells in His name? That did not seem to be the God that Jon was coming to know. How did God's desire to dwell in men's hearts jibe with killing those who disagree?

Jon skipped communion because he had not been to confession, but he was surprised when Jimmy, who was not a priest and could not have taken confession, took part. He determined to ask him about it in private. After church, Johan, Jimmy, and Jon left together.

"Well, Jon, how did you do?" asked Jimmy.

Jon looked at Johan, but decided that he trusted him. "I found it hard to concentrate on prayer, but the readings were really quite in line with our conversation." He said. "I am a bit puzzled by where the sermon went. Did God really promise us victory over any non-Christians that we fight?"

Jimmy and Johan looked at each other before Johan responded: "I don't think that was what the Abbot was saying. I think he was saying that we should not live in fear of God's enemies, be they dragon or man."

"Jesus said that His Kingdom was not of this world." Interjected Jimmy. "I heard what you heard, and I think it is wrong. God's Kingdom conquers one heart at a time with love, not force of arms."

Johan seemed uncomfortable with this. "I don't disagree with you Jimmy, but I have watched the fight in the Holy Land, and those heathens will not be conquered by love. It takes swords to defend the faith some times." He said.

"There is a difference between defending and attacking." Replied Jimmy. "War leads to more war; not to Christ."

"Perhaps," said Johan, "but I wonder if the ends don't somehow justify the means sometimes. If we take a land by force of arms and bring the true faith to its people, doesn't that accomplish God's work?"

Jimmy did not like war, but he cared about Brother Johan; he had learned as a missionary that it was not always necessary to win every argument. He determined to end this discussion and said: "'God uses all things for good for those who are called according to His purpose.' This does not mean that all things are good, merely that our great God can use our sinfulness to bring about His good purposes. God deals with us individually, and I think God is dealing with us differently on the subject of war."

"You are right brother," replied Johan with a smile, "and I'm not advocating for war, but sometimes it seems necessary."

Jimmy did not respond, so Jon asked the obvious question: "Do we attack the Kells in God's name?"

Neither of the older men replied until Johan said: "That is not our decision to make. I hope not." He added.

The three were taking a meal in Johan's room when a messenger arrived to tell Jon that the King wanted to see him. Jon immediately left and was taken to the King's chambers.

"Ah, Sir Jon." said the King as Jon was shown in. "The Dukes are not expected to arrive for a couple of hours and I would like to take a ride. I would like you to join me."

"That would be quite an honor, your Majesty." Replied Jon.

"Go to the stable and get your horse ready. I shall meet you there shortly." Said the King with a twinkle in his eye.

This turn of events was stunning. Jon would be taking a private ride with the King? As he walked to the stable Jon realizes that he had two horses there and that he had to decide which horse it was that he wanted to ride. Since Thunder was not really his horse, he decided to saddle Mayflower.

When he arrived at the stable, Jon was surprised at the lack of activity that was going on considering the King was expected soon.

"Going for a ride, my lord?" asked one of the grooms.

Something inside him told Jon not to say anything about the King, so he replied: "Yes, I want to give my horses some exercise. Can you saddle Mayflower while I see to Thunder?"

The groom got to work on Mayflower as Jon was asking himself why he should be saddling two horses. Just as they were finishing, the King caused quite a stir when he entered with only one nervous servant with him. He was dressed in rather plain clothes.

"I knew I could count on you, Sir Jon!" exclaimed the King. Then turning to his servant he said: "You are dismissed. Sir Jon will escort me and you are not to tell anyone where I have gone for a good while. I am the King and will be much displeased if my ride is interrupted."

Jon got an uneasy feeling. Apparently he was about to help the King assert his independence. Then again, he thought, why had he saddled two horses?

"Which horse is mine?" asked the King.

"Your Majesty," replied Jon. "Don't you have a horse? Have you ridden much?"

The King pulled Jon aside while the servant and the groom looked on. "Sir Jon, this is an adventure. I have ridden some, but I want to ride for fun. Please help me with this."

Jon was torn, but eventually he decided that if he was with the King he could not be blamed. "Mayflower is my horse and she is gentle and forgiving." He said. "Let's get you mounted."

The servant continued to look on as Jon and the groom helped the King onto Mayflower. The stirrups were shortened and he fit quite well in the saddle.

"Not a word out of either of you for at least an hour." Commanded the King to the groom and servant. Both men looked nervous but gave their assent.

Jon mounted Thunder and the two rode out into the town. Thankfully few people paid them any attention and they were soon out into the countryside.

"Sir Jon," said the King, "I have one more favor to ask you."

"Of course, my Lord." Replied the young knight.

"While we are on this ride I do not wish to be the King. Please call me Wulf and let's just be two young men on an adventure. I know it can't last, but I want to be a boy for a little while." Said Aerdwulf with sincerity.

"Of course, Wulf." Said Jon awkwardly. "We have a rule where I live that I stop being a knight when I walk through the door. I understand what you are asking. How much trouble can you still get in for what you are doing?"

Wulf chuckled and said: "I don't know. I suspect Mama will be quite upset, but I am the King!"

Jon smiled in return. They decided to ride in some nearby fields where they would be less likely to be seen. The King knew the basics of riding but Jon shared some of the things that he had learned over the last week when he had begun riding regularly. The ride was not particularly thrilling, but the King seemed to enjoy the freedom that he had been given.

After about an hour Jon suggested that they should probably head back. Wulf was disappointed, but agreed that they probably should. As they began a slow ride towards town, Wulf asked Jon a question:

"Are you a man of God, Jon?"

"That's a hard question to answer." Jon said in return. "I think so. I used to believe in God, but now I have faith in Him. I guess that makes me God's man, so I am a man of God. I have a relationship with God through Jesus."

"That's a pretty different answer." Observed the boy/King. "What's the difference between believing in God and having faith in Him?"

"Did you understand the reading from the book of James in church this morning?" asked Jon.

"I find Latin hard." Replied Wulf.

"Well, James wrote that 'the demons believe and tremble,' and that 'faith without works is useless.' I think that 'faith without works' is mere belief. If you have faith, you put your beliefs into action. Faith changes the way you think and act."

"Do you ever doubt?" asked Wulf.

"More than I wish I did." Replied Jon. "A life of faith is really pretty amazing. I guess it's hard not to doubt. But God does little things to prove himself to you, and without doubt I don't think we would even recognize them. I think saddling two horses was one of those little miracles. I had no idea that you had this adventure in mind."

Aerdwulf laughed at that. "I praise God for that miracle!" he said. "Father Leonis says that when you don't doubt you become something called a 'zealot.' He says that people who don't doubt think that their will is God's will. He says that Judas was a zealot."

"I guess I never thought of that." Said Jon in reply. "I do wish that God would make His will clearer sometimes, but I guess if He did we would no longer be us, or it would be hard to know what was of God's will and what was my will. Maybe doubt is one of God's stranger blessings."

"Do you think we should attack the Kells while they're weak?" asked Wulf with certain aura of Kingship returning to him.

"That's not my decision to make." Replied Jon with Johan's words on his mind.

"I'm not asking you to make the decision." Said the King. "I'm asking you what you think. I will make the decision."

Jon was silent for a bit before he replied: "I guess I do not see what we have to gain. From what I saw those people have nothing we want, and once we have taken their land we will just get another enemy. It won't bring peace or make us more secure, we'll just have more of a reason to fight. No, I don't think we should attack the Kells. Why should we attack them?"

Jon said this with more conviction than he felt. He was prepared to do his duty, but something deep inside him made him feel that this war was not right. He was not afraid to go to war, he just wanted to believe in what he was fighting for. If they attacked the Kells, what would they be fighting for?

"I guess we would get more land and I could give you an estate on it." Said Wulf uncertainly.

"I don't want people to die for my gain." Snapped Jon without even a thought. "I mean, your Kingdom is not crowded or in need of more land, and if a lot of us die taking that land it will be even less crowded. I guess if I make this a question of faith, I don't think that God has told us to go and 'smite' them. If He wants us to fight for Him, there are plenty of ways to make that clear to us. He could have let them attack us."

"I like what you said." Replied the serious boy. "A war shouldn't be about what we get out of it. But if we conquer them, they would get to hear the Gospel."

"Maybe." Replied Jon. "I think God could use it to His purposes, but based on our actions would they really get to know the loving God that I have put my faith in?"

"You know, I just offered you an estate in the new lands." Said the King.

"Wulf, I appreciate that." Said Jon. "You have already given me more than I ever thought I would have, and I am already indebted to you. You have all of my loyalty, and you cannot buy any more. Don't go to war to improve my circumstances; I have all I need." After a pause Jon added: "I have a relationship with God. What more can you offer me?"

The King was taken aback by that answer. After a while he said: "I think you really are a man of God. My guess is that anyone else, except maybe Brother Johan or Father Leonis, would have told me it was my duty to fight for them. Thanks Jon. Thanks for going on this ride and speaking plainly with me."

It was then that Jon saw Sir Bendris and Wil riding towards them at a full gallop. "I guess it's time for me to be the King again." Said Wulf.

As Sir Bendris pulled up he exclaimed: "You Majesty! I am responsible for your safety; you cannot simply wander off. The Kingdom rests on your shoulders. Your mother is worried sick!"

"Sir Bendris," replied the King, "I decided to take a ride with one of my most trusted knights. I am the King, and you serve me. I understand your concern, but as you can see nothing is amiss. I will speak with my mother."

The Captain of the Guard was taken aback by this response. Aerdwulf had certainly changed over the past few weeks. "The Dukes are beginning to arrive." He said tensely. "You need to prepare to meet with them, my Lord."

The King nodded and they headed back into town. Sir Bendris seemed grumpy the whole way back, but the King seemed to be enjoying this grumpiness. When they got to the stable several grooms helped him off of Mayflower.

"I greatly enjoyed our ride, Sir Jon. I hope we have a chance to do it again." Said the King.

"As do I, your Majesty. Sometimes it is good to just get away." Replied Sir Jon.

The King walked off towards the keep with Wil at his side. Sir Bendris came up to Jon and grabbed his arm.

"What were you thinking?" he said emphatically.

"I think the King asked me to go on a ride and I happily consented." Said an unflustered Sir Jon.

"He's the King, and just a boy! What if something had happened?" added the clearly vexed Captain of the Guard.

"We didn't do anything dangerous; we just talked." Replied Jon.

"About what?" asked Bendris.

Jon did not know what he should share, so he simply said: "He wanted a chance to just be himself for an hour or so. I know how he feels. We just talked, that's all."

Bendris seemed to be losing some of his anxiety. "Well, his safety means everything to this Kingdom. I hope you appreciate what a huge responsibility you assumed." He said.

"I think I do," said Jon, "but I also know that this responsibility was given me by the King. Whom else do you know that is close enough in age to allow the King to be something of a boy?"

"Alright Sir Jon," replied Sir Bendris, "but you need to know I nearly had a heart attack. That boy's safety is my responsibility."

"I think we both understand that and appreciate it." Replied Jon as the two walked into the Keep.

21

The King and the Council

Upon entering the keep, Jon was immediately accosted by Duke Heimsteady.

"Taking private rides with the King now, are we?" he said with a mischievous smile on his face.

"The King just wanted to be Aerdwulf for a little while." Replied Jon.

"His father and I did the same thing occasionally, and despite the fact that he was older it caused the same uproar around here. Thank God you're all safe." Said the Duke. "So, why am I here? What did you and Bendris find in the Kell lands? Stan tells me the dragon has destroyed them, but I find that difficult to believe."

The slight, guilty joy that Jon had felt regarding his and the King's adventure was dispelled by the Duke's comment. The dragon was not a joking matter to him. He gave the Duke a full report about the destruction that they had seen and the tribe of Kells that Jimmy had said caused it.

"I think you are here to decide whether we are to attack these people while they are weak." Said Jon very seriously.

"And why wouldn't we?" asked the Duke.

"Well, to me, the question is more 'why should we?'" Replied the young knight. "They have a lot of pasture, but we do not seem to lack pasture. Their livestock has been killed off, their fields are burned, and they can hardly feed themselves. What do we have to gain?"

"Wars are rarely fought for practical reasons." Replied the Duke. "We fight for glory. We fight to prove we are strong. The King can make a name for himself by enlarging the Kingdom."

"Perhaps." Said Sir Jon in a less than enthusiastic way.

"What is the King thinking?" asked the Duke.

"I'm not sure." Replied Jon. "He says that it is his decision, and he seems determined to make it. I think, maybe I hope, that he wants to know why we are fighting. He is young, but he thinks big thoughts; I suspect he wonders about whether this war might lead to more wars with the Kells. He does not seem eager to fight, but I don't think that he has made up his mind."

"He thinks that this decision will be made by an eleven-year-old boy?" said the Duke in astonishment.

"Don't underestimate him, my Lord. He is different than the boy you met last week. He is becoming a King. You know that I have loyalty to both you and the King, but out of friendship towards you, I warn you, do not underestimate the King." Said the stern young knight with uncommon sincerity.

"Hmm." Replied the Duke. "Thank you Jon. There are not many who would give such wise counsel to a Duke. I am fond of you as well, and I have come to trust your advice. I will keep your words in mind."

The conversation was interrupted when a large and boisterous man stepped in and enthusiastically greeted Duke Heimsteady. "Duke Heimsteady, my old friend! It is good to see you again!" He said. "And who is your young friend?"

Heimsteady remained subdued and serious. "Hello Duke Coberg, I believe you know who Sir Jon is from last week's coronation." He said.

"Of course!" replied Duke Coberg, "The King's new knight, and I understand riding companion. There's nothing like a little boyish adventure to build a bond, now is there? You have come far very quickly and I am pleased to finally meet you; I hope the feeling is mutual."

"Indeed it is, my Lord." Replied Sir Jon in a somewhat hesitant way.

"So, why are we here?" asked Duke Coberg.

Jon was put on guard by the new Duke's enthusiastic approach, so he looked to Duke Heimsteady.

"Coe, you know as well as I why we are here. We are to decide, or help the King to decide, what is to be done about the Kells." Replied Duke Heimsteady in a serious tone.

"And what will you decide Heimy?" replied Duke Coberg.

"I have not decided." Said Heimsteady. "I would like to get the facts first."

"Really?" Said Duke Coberg. "It has been a while since we have added to our lands, and this sounds like a great opportunity. Why, even Sir Jon may get an estate out of this war."

With this, Duke Coberg looked to Sir Jon clearly expecting support, but Jon had an instinctive mistrust of this man. He reminded Jon of a grown up version of Aethelstan. "The Lord's will be done, my Lord." He replied. "If you will excuse me, I feel the need to clean up a bit after my ride."

Jon's reaction startled and displeased Duke Coberg. As the young knight walked away he said: "What an impertinent young man!"

"Perhaps." Said Duke Heimsteady, but in fact he was quite impressed by the judgement Sir Jon had shown.

The two men stood in awkward silence for a while before Duke Coberg excused himself and went in search of more hospitable company.

These two Dukes, along with Duke Reimold, were each given a suite of rooms in the keep and told that the council would begin soon. Duke Reimold was a thin man with a cunning face and disposition. He looked more like a scribe than a soldier, but his tendency towards privacy left him an enigma to most of the Kingdom. He was respected, but feared; he was neither well liked nor disliked. His family had been given their Dukedom by the King's grandfather, and so, he was considered a newcomer to the ruling class. Neither Heimsteady nor Coberg knew him very well as his estate lay on the far eastern side of the Kingdom. His family was known for meeting their feudal obligations to the King with meticulous precision.

At last the meeting was called, and after some brief formalities they were all seated around the council table. The King spoke first:

"Good Dukes, trusted advisors, and my mother; We have called this council to seek your advice on what should be done regarding the Kells. We will first hear a report from Sir Bendris on the conditions in their land, and then we will ask each of you for your thoughts. We do not expect a decision today. We will consider what you have to say and inform you of our decision when it is made. Are there any questions before we begin?"

This was not what any of the adults in the room were expecting to hear. Was an eleven-year-old boy really telling them that he would be making this decision? Duke Heimsteady was appreciative of the warning that he had been given. Duke Coberg could not contain himself.

"Your Majesty," he began, "if the Kingdom is to go to war, it is the dukes who will lead the army and provide the men to fight it. It is our prerogative to make the decision." He looked around the room for support, but neither Heimsteady nor Reimold gave him any. Both men looked on with blank expressions.

After a pause the King responded: "My loyal Duke, the decision to go to war is a King's decision. By God's ordination it is OUR decision. Your prerogative is to advise us, and I eagerly seek your counsel."

Duke Heimsteady noted that Sir Jon had been right: this certainly was not the boy that he had met last week. He was puzzled and intrigued by the change. Duke Coberg, on the other hand was incensed.

"With all due respect, your Highness, my men will fight where and when I tell them to fight." He declared.

The King looked passive, but Duke Heimsteady sensed he did not know what to say. The Duke saw an opportunity and took it:

"Are you threatening your King!" shouted Heimsteady. "We are sworn to his allegiance! You do not even know what his decision is and you are already prepared to oppose it? I am sworn to my King, so know this, if you seek to commit treason you will not only be facing an eleven-year-old boy, I will stand by the oath I took before God!"

It was a particularly dramatic speech, especially since Duke Coberg had not in any way threatened the King. The King had a slight smile on his face.

"Thank you, Duke Heimsteady." Said the King. "We appreciate your loyalty, but we do not think our Duke Coberg meant to threaten us. Did you good sir?"

"Of course not." Replied Duke Coberg glaring at Heimsteady. "I merely insist that our counsel be taken seriously."

"It will be, good Duke." Replied the King. "That is why we have called you here. Now, Sir Bendris, can you please tell us about your scouting mission in the Kell lands."

Sir Bendris rose to speak and gave a true summary of what they knew. He stressed the devastation that they had witnessed, the burned out fields, and the bodies that were feeding the crows, but he also told what Jimmy had said about the Kell army being intact. It was a more mixed report than what the Dukes had been expecting based on the rumors that they had heard.

At the conclusion, the King immediately spoke:

"Thank you, Sir Bendris. Most of us in this room have not had much time to think about this situation, but you have, what are your thoughts?" he said.

Sir Bendris took his seat before speaking: "There can be no doubt that the Kells are weaker than they have been in a good while. I suspect that they will have a rough winter ahead of them. Nevertheless, what struck me most was the savagery with which they were attacked. The Kells have attacked us in the past, and they have killed and stolen from us, but they have never done what I saw. If we conquer them, we will become neighbors of a far more brutal foe. I think we should let the Kells fight amongst themselves. They are in no position to attack us, so we should use this time to strengthen the Kingdom you already rule."

"Does anyone one else have something to say, or should we adjourn until tomorrow?" asked the King.

Heimsteady and Reimold sat impassively, but Coberg rose to speak:

"What I want to know, Captain, is can we beat them? Our forces are strong and getting stronger every day. If we can conquer these lands the Kingdom will be enlarged and enriched. We might even have a fourth dukedom. If we do the job right, it is these other Kells who will wonder whether they want to fight us. We might even be able to have them fight much of the battle for us and take half of those lands at little cost or effort. The world belongs to the strong; we are strong and they are weak. We should not pass up this opportunity."

Duke Coberg sat down with a satisfied look on his face while the King looked around to see if anyone else wanted to speak. No one seemed eager.

"Well, Sir Bendris," said the King, "can we beat them?"

"Your Majesty," replied Sir Bendris, "if this Kingdom is united we can defeat almost anyone. That said, we do not know much about these other Kells. We do not even know how to contact them."

"Gentlemen, and Lady," interjected Duke Coberg, "God has laid victory at our feet. It is only up to us to seize the moment and enlarge this Kingdom AND God's Kingdom. It would be a betrayal of our faith to let this opportunity pass us by; don't you agree Father Leonis."

All eyes turned to Father Leonis who had been put on the spot.

"I am less certain of God's will in this matter than you are Duke Coberg." Replied the Chief minister. "As you say, there does seem to be an opportunity here, but I am not sure that we would be fighting for God as much as we would be fighting for ourselves. Would you be willing to renounce any claims to the lands we conquer?"

Duke Coberg was stunned by this question. Indeed, Leonis had no idea why he had asked it; it had merely sprung forth from his lips. Now, Duke Coberg had been put on the spot.

After a pause the Duke answered: "As the Bible teaches, 'a workman deserves his wages.'" He replied. "I have a younger son to consider, but I hope you are not suggesting that I am advocating we attack merely for my gain. If my forces share in the trial, we should also share in the spoils."

"Of course, good Duke," replied the King, "I am sure nobody thinks you are doing any more than giving me advice for the good of the Kingdom. Father Leonis, you insisted that Duke Coberg be a member of this council; you could not mean that."

"Absolutely not." Replied Father Leonis with admiration for his student.

"Well, then," said the King, "Let us consider this matter over the evening and reconvene after breakfast. It is my hope that we will all pray and seek God's guidance in this matter."

The men rose to leave as the King spoke to his mother. Duke Heimsteady held back in an effort to be the last to leave, and before he left the King beckoned to him.

"Duke Heimsteady," he said, "may we have a word with you."

The Duke walked over and said: "Yes, my Lord."

"We appreciated your support, even if it was a bit dramatic." Said the King. "It is small measures like that which will earn you our trust."

"Thank you, your Majesty." Replied the Duke. "I wish to share one more thing with you, my lord; your father and I took several rides like the one you took with Sir Jon today. The reaction was much the same. You remind me a lot of your father."

The King blushed while the Queen was mortified. The Duke had a mischievous smile on his face.

"Thank you, Uncle." Said the King and Duke Heimsteady departed.

Upon returning to his chambers, Duke Heimsteady immediately sent a servant to invite Sir Jon and Brother Johan to join him for dinner in his chambers. Brother Johan was unfortunately indisposed, but Sir Jon gladly accepted the invitation and asked if Jimmy could join them. The Duke was glad to invite him along once he learned that Jimmy was the man who had been living with the Kells.

At the appointed time, Jimmy and Jon came to the Duke's chambers and Jon introduced Jimmy.

"It's nice to meet you Jimmy. How did a Saxon come to live among the Kells?" asked the Duke.

"'Tis a long story, my lord." Replied Jimmy. "I actually lived in your demesne prior to that."

"Did you?" said the Duke in surprise. "What did you do among us?"

"I am Father James' son." Replied the missionary in a matter of fact manner.

"Are you?" Said the Duke with some embarrassment as even then priests were not supposed to have sons. "My own chaplain's son. I liked your father, but I was not aware that he had a son. One would think I would be better informed about the goings on at my estate."

"He was a good father to me, but understandably he did not generally make my existence well known." Replied the missionary.

"Yes. So tell me, how did you come to live among the Kells?" asked the Duke in an effort to change the subject.

While Jimmy was telling his story, a servant came and interrupted the discussion. "Pardon me, my Lord." He said. "The King wishes to speak with Sir Jon."

It was not an invitation that could easily be refused, so Jon left the table and was escorted to the King's chambers.

"Ah, Sir Jon!" said the King as Jon was shown into his chambers. "I really enjoyed our ride together. Duke Heimsteady told me that he and my father sometimes did the same thing. Isn't that something!"

"Yes, the Duke told me the same thing when we returned. He said everyone was just as upset then as they were today, My Lord." Replied Jon.

"I want this to be another private conversation, so you can call me Wulf." Said the King. "I want to ask you again if you are a man of God?"

"Well, I have been thinking about that." Replied Jon. "I am not sure whether I can answer that. I am not sure what a man of God is. I am certainly God's man, the same way as I am your man, but am I a man of the King?"

"That's an interesting question." Replied Wulf. "I guess if you were a man of the King you probably would do things the way I would do them. If you are a man of God you would do things God's way."

"Hmm, well I try, but I don't think any man except Jesus has ever done things entirely God's way." Said Jon flatly.

"So, by that way of thinking the only man of God there has ever been is Jesus, right?" said Wulf. "You told me you have a relationship with God through Jesus; what do you mean by that?"

"Not even a week ago Brother Johan told me that the Bible quotes Jesus as saying: 'Behold, I stand at the door and knock. If anyone opens the door I will enter and live with him.' I invited God into my heart, not in a really faithful way, in a really doubtful way, but I asked Him to show me He was real. He has; since then I think differently and act differently. I pray without thinking. I feel God with me, through Jesus." Replied Jon.

"Then why wouldn't you consider yourself a man of God?" asked the King.

"Wulf, why is this so important to you? I hope I am becoming a Godly man, but I am still a sinner; I still doubt. Jesus is the only true man of God."

Wulf looked disturbed. Finally, he said: "I'm going to tell you something, but you better not laugh. Father Leonis and Mama think I am being silly. Before all of this happened I had a dream that I was going to make a REALLY big decision for the Kingdom. In the dream a man of God came to tell me what to do. I guess I am hoping that's you."

"Wulf, that's really amazing!" said Jon. "God speaks to me sometimes, and I just sense the message. I can believe he spoke to you in a dream. The prophet Daniel and the Joseph with the colorful coat both interpreted dreams for their Kings. Maybe dreams are how God talks to Kings. But, I don't know what to tell you."

The eleven-year-old smiled with relief. "Thanks Jon," he said, "I didn't want you to think I was a silly little boy. But, if you're not the man of God, who is?"

"Listen Wulf, there has only been one true man of God. What would he do?" replied Jon.

"You say you have a relationship with Jesus, why don't you tell me what He would do?" replied the King.

"It's a pretty new relationship. I'm not sure I know." Said Jon. "You know; Brother Johan has a relationship with Jesus, why don't we ask him?"

"He'll just tell me I am being silly, like Father Leonis." Replied Wulf.

"Let me ask him questions; then we can figure it out." Said Jon.

"Well, we can try. But don't tell him about the dream." Said Wulf.

"Where do you think we can find him?" asked Jon.

Wulf smiled. "I'm the King; I'll just have somebody get him!"

22

The King makes
a Decision

I T WAS NOT LONG BEFORE Brother Johan was shown into the King's chamber. Upon entering he found the King and Jon sitting in quiet conversation, but it ended in mid-sentence when he arrived.

"Your Highness, Sir Jon, I believe you wished to speak with me your Majesty?" Said the monk in a stiff and formal way.

"Yes, thank you for coming." Said the King. "Jon and I were having a conversation and he felt you could add to it. It is not anything too serious, so let's drop the formalities, shall we?"

"Of course." Replied Johan. "How can I help?"

"Well, Brother Johan, you remember the conversation that we had a few days ago about Jesus knocking at the door and all that? I want to thank you for it and say that I took your advice. I think I have a relationship with God now." Said Jon.

Johan smiled. "I'm really happy for you Jon. But you could have told me that at any time. As happy as I am I must ask why you are telling me now, in front of Wulf?"

"Well, we were talking about what a man of God is, and we sort of decided that only Jesus was ever truly a man of God, so we wanted to ask you some questions about Jesus." Said Jon.

The monk sat down and took a deep breath. He seemed disturbed. Silently he prayed: "Lord, guide my words!"

"You have a relationship with God, and you know Jesus better than I do, and the Bible, we thought you could help." Added Jon in haste.

Johan looked at the King. Suddenly he smiled and said: "Wulf, I know about your dream. Father Leonis told me. If you have decided Jesus is the man of God, you have chosen wisely. We adults sometimes forget that Jesus said 'suffer the little ones to come to me for to such as these belongs the Kingdom of Heaven.' Jesus is THE man of God, and hearing that you want to consult Him makes me think you can be a special King indeed. God talks to us in many ways, and I don't think you are being silly."

Johan was not sure why he had said those things. He had intended to see what the questions were before bringing up the dream that Wulf had had. The result, however, showed that he had done the right thing. At first the King blushed, but then he smiled.

"Thank you, Brother Johan." He said somewhat shyly.

"Great!" Said Jon enthusiastically. "This should make the questions easier. What we are trying to find out is what Jesus would have done if He had the Kells weakened on His border."

"That's a tough question." Responded Johan. "Jesus said that His Kingdom was not of this world, but God told Israel to destroy their enemies on several occasions."

"How did God tell them to attack?" asked the King.

"Sometimes He just told them; other times He sent them angels or prophets. They knew that they had to attack. In other cases, Israel's Kings decided to start wars for their own reasons, and they were badly defeated." Replied Johan.

"What did God want when they fought for Him?" asked the King.

"Well, different things." Replied Johan. "In the reading from Joshua in church today He told them to fight to take possession of the land that He had promised them. Mostly I think He told them to fight for His glory."

"Did Jesus ever have to fight?" asked Jon.

"No, I don't think so. He argued with the Pharisees, He over-turned the money changers' tables in the temple, He even told His disciples to sell their coats and buy swords, but He never really got in an actual fight. When men came to take Him away in the Garden of Gethsemane He told Peter to put his sword away and healed the man who had been injured. I don't think Jesus ever fought for His cause." Said a pensive Johan.

"Why would He tell His disciples to buy swords if not to fight?" asked Wulf.

"Well, let me think." Said Johan. "I think in the book of Luke Jesus is sending out His disciples to spread the word and tells them to sell their cloaks and buy swords. Then, two swords are produced and He says that that is enough. He clearly was not forming an army. I think He was just saying that they should be as prepared as they could be." (Luke 22:35-38)

"So, if Jesus didn't fight for His cause, what did He do?" asked the King.

"Mostly he healed people. On several occasions He fed a lot of people." Johan pause in thought. "I guess He also spread the news that the Kingdom of God was at hand, but mostly he just glorified His father by setting an example for all of us. He also died for our sins, and conquered death by rising from the grave; let's not forget that!"

"So, when should I send our forces to fight for God?" demanded the King.

"I guess, when God makes it clear to you that you should. I guess when you are sure that you are REALLY fighting for God." Said Johan. "Listen, I have been to the Holy Land, and many of our men there really are fighting for God, but some are just there to claim land and riches. We need those men, or I never would have made it there and back. I am not saying never fight, but I am saying that if you do fight, make sure that you are on His side; it makes it easier to be sure that He is on yours."

"So, that's what I should judge:" said the King, "Whether we are really going there to fight for God, or just for ourselves."

Jon had been listening, but a thought occurred to him: "You know Wulf, if you really want to be like Jesus we could feed them. Jesus said that whatever you do to the least of His brothers you do unto Him. Those people need food. That would REALLY be Christ-like!"

"I suspect that would be difficult to persuade the Dukes to do." Replied Brother Johan. "We are supposed to love our enemies, but I have never heard of anyone who has done it. Anyways, Wulf, the hour grows late and you have a big day ahead of you."

"Are you telling your King to go to bed!" said an indignant Wulf, but with a smile on his face. Brother Johan looked uncomfortable. "I'm just kidding." Said the King. "I want to get to sleep and see if God tells me what to do; maybe I will have a dream! I guess I know that you sort of don't have a choice, but I am really grateful that you both came to talk to me tonight."

"Good night Wulf." Said Jon. "Sweet dreams."

Johan waived as he and Jon walked out of the room. Once they got outside Johan stopped and said: "That boy is really becoming a King! He's changing in ways nobody could have taught him. Praise God!"

The King did not have a dream that night; he had a peaceful and refreshing sleep.

As Jon walked to his chambers he was met by Duke Heimsteady.

"Well, aren't we becoming quite the King's favorite!" he said in greeting.

"He wanted to talk, and I quite enjoyed the conversation." Replied Jon.

"What did you talk about?" asked the Duke.

Jon was not sure that this was any of the Duke's business, so, although there was no real reason to hide the subject they had discussed, he decided to be a bit evasive. "We talked about Jesus, and how He would react in certain situations." He said flatly.

"Jon, I can appreciate that you should keep the King's confidences. You and I are friends, are we not? I would appreciate knowing whether you think he is going to choose war or peace." Said the Duke in a more personal way than he had ever addressed Jon before.

Jon looked at the Duke for a moment considering his answer. "He has not made up his mind." Jon said. "I think if we go to war we will all have a clear objective in mind. I think the King will appreciate honesty more than tact. Do you think we should go to war?"

"An interesting question." Said the Duke. "You know; I will take you into my confidence, I have been thinking more about how to impress the King than about what he should do. I think this is one of those decisions that seems bigger than it really is. If we attack, I am confident we will win, but there really is no reason that we have to attack. If we don't attack, we will likely have a year or more of peace. That is not a bad outcome either. The King can get more settled and the Kingdom could use a good dose of peace."

"My Lord, the King is in need of advice, and you are here to show that you are a worthy advisor." Said Jon. "If I may be so bold; I think what you just said would be welcome advice indeed. The one thing I will say to you again is don't underestimate the King; he is young, but he is not stupid. Speak to him as an adult, not as a child."

The Duke clapped Jon on the shoulder and said: "I am once more in your debt, good knight." He paused for a moment, and then said: "Good night!"

Jon smiled and also bid the Duke a good night. He then went to his room and lay down. Almost immediately prayer came to his mind: "Lord, guide our King. Touch Wulf as only you can. Grant him wisdom." As Jon lay there thinking he was pretty sure that there would not be a war.

Jimmy entered the room and said: "Johan was rather upset that the King called him away from Leonis and I this evening, but he came back rather pleased. Has the King made a decision?"

Jon was getting tired, and he was especially tired of people asking him what the King was thinking. He calmed himself and said:

"Jimmy, you know as well as I that if he had made a decision Brother Johan likely would have told you. I will tell you this; the King has decided to seek God's will, and he is determined to find it."

"OK, Jon." Said Jimmy. "I'm sorry; sleep well. That God's will be done is the best any of us could hope for."

Jimmy blew out the candle and the two drifted off to sleep. Jon did not sleep as well as the King; for the first time in several nights the face of the man that he had killed appeared in his dreams.

The next morning Jon joined Jimmy, Father Leonis, and Brother Johan for breakfast. While Jon feared he would get quizzed on the King's feelings, he was pleasantly surprised when he was not. The three men recounted old tales from their youth, some of which were actually quite funny to someone who had not shared in them. Near the end of the meal, Father Leonis asked Jon a question:

"You seem rather quiet this morning Sir Jon. Is everything alright?" He said.

"I'm sorry." Replied Jon. "I did not sleep very well last night."

"Too much excitement the previous day? You took the King for a ride and then were asked to advise him. That is quite a lot for someone who was only a former page not two weeks ago." Said Father Leonis.

"Perhaps." Said Jon. "The truth is that I was bothered by a recurring dream I have. I'm sorry, I have already said too much. I don't think I want to discuss it."

"Well Jon, not all dreams are of God." Replied the priest. "Dreams pass; even recurring ones. Anyway, I believe that I have a council to attend shortly, so I will bid you a good day."

As Leonis departed Jon was left hoping that the priest had been right; that these dreams would pass. Meanwhile, Johan and Jimmy looked on with concern.

Finally, Johan said: "Whatever it is Jon, lay it on the Lord. You have a High Priest in Jesus who died so your sins could be forgiven. Take your problem to God."

This struck Jon as sound advice, but he was not sure how.

Meanwhile, the three Dukes were having breakfast in Duke Coberg's chambers.

"Gentlemen, we cannot leave this momentous decision in the hands of our eleven-year-old King." Said Duke Coberg. "If we present a united front he will be forced to follow our wishes, and we will set a precedent that we will make all of the major decisions until he is ready to rule."

The three men knew each other, but they were not close friends. Neither Heimsteady nor Reimold seemed eager to comment lest their words be used against them. At last Duke Heimsteady broke the awkward silence:

"Coe, why do you feel so left out of the process? The King asked us here to advise him. While he may not be giving us the decision, he is certainly setting a precedent that we will be involved in any major decisions." He said.

"We have a chance to greatly enlarge the Kingdom at little risk or cost!" exclaimed Duke Coberg in frustration. "We cannot let the priests who advise him rob us of this opportunity to increase our holdings."

This was once again met with silence until Duke Heimsteady said: "Duke Reimold, do you agree with Duke Coberg's assessment?"

Reimold did not look like he wanted to answer, but he had been asked a fair question. "My lands do not lie as close to the Kell lands as yours." He said. "We are thus far enjoying a good season at peace, but if war comes to us, it will not be from the Kells; it will come from the Norsemen to the North and East of me. I prefer to discourage that by keeping my forces closer to home. I will ask the King to let me defend the East should he decide that we will go to war."

"Well, if Heimsteady and I do most of the fighting, we will have earned most of the rewards." Said Coberg flatly.

"Of course." Replied Reimold not really believing that the King would choose war.

"That leaves it to you and me, Heimy. Are you with me?" Asked Coberg.

"I'm not sure that I am Coe. I both see this as a tougher decision and a less important one than you. I am actually fine with whatever the King decides, and like Duke Reimold I am enjoying the peace we have had so far." Replied Duke Heimsteady. "Like Duke Reimold, I am not opposed to your position, but I am not exactly for it either. I do not have a second son."

"This Kingdom is sure to suffer if it is led by men as lacking in ambition as you two." Said a disappointed and angry Duke Coberg. "Our former King would certainly have taken advantage of this opportunity."

Duke Heimsteady rose to leave, and seeing this Duke Reimold also rose.

"Coe, I knew our former King far better than you did. He was a dear friend of mine. He may have decided to attack the Kells, but he also knew that there is no such thing as an easy victory. I am sure of this; he would have made his decision without calling you to a council. Whatever decision is made; you have no grievance against the King." Said Duke Heimsteady as he left.

Duke Coberg was quite angry as the two men left. He had been confident that they would see matters his way. In fact, he could not conceive of any other way to see matters.

At the appointed time the council was gathered. The King entered with his mother and Father Leonis started with a prayer, in Latin, that asked for God's guidance in what was to be decided. The King barely listened, but he said his own prayer: "Tell me what to do God. Let us be on Your side."

"We asked all of you to pray and consider the question at hand: do we attack the Kells?" Said the King. "We wish to hear your thoughts; starting with you Father Leonis."

Leonis was caught off guard, but he had considered what to say. "Your Majesty, I am a man of the church, and not a man of war. If we fight, there is the potential that the church will grow among those we conquer, but in my heart I think that God is already reaching out to these people. I am undecided. I am sorry, my Lord." He said.

"We appreciate your usual honesty, my teacher." Said the King. "Why do you think that God is already reaching out to the Kells?"

"Not all of them, your Majesty, but to these Kells. The man Sir Bendris brought back was there to spread the Gospel. As yet he has no converts to show for his efforts, but he feels that they can come to see the light." Replied Leonis.

"I see." Said the King. "But there are no converts as yet?"

Leonis looked down and shook his head. "Thank you Father. Duke Coberg, have you had any further thoughts on this matter?" Asked the King.

The Duke answered eagerly: "This is a great opportunity! We can march to an easy victory and glorify God in accomplishing it! We will share in His glory. If God is on our side we cannot lose, and God WILL be on our side. To pass up this opportunity would be sinful!" said Duke Coberg.

"How do you know that God will be on our side?" asked the King.

"He certainly wouldn't be on their heathen side." Replied the Duke.

The King took a moment to consider this. "I am sure that they feel the same about their gods." He said quietly. "How do we know that God wishes us to pit His might against their false gods?"

"Because He gave us this opportunity. Why would God tempt us to attack if He did not mean for us to succeed? We can conquer them in His name!" Came the confident reply.

The King looked around the table, but could not discern what the others thought of this. "So, it really would be God's war, right?" said the King although he did not know why.

"Of course it would!" replied the Duke with great enthusiasm.

"And He would fight for us?" said the King with a purpose in mind.

"He would, your Highness! We would be doing His will!" answered the Duke.

"Then, as you said last evening, the spoils would belong to Him. We would merely be His servants. We could give the lands to the church and they could serve as a buffer between us and the Kells. Certainly THAT would further God's Kingdom!" Said the King enthusiastically. "That is an idea that I had not considered! Thank you Duke Coberg, I am sure that idea came to you in prayer."

Duke Coberg was deflated, while several of the others around the table worked hard to stifle their mirth. Even Duke Reimold managed a smile.

211

"Now, Duke Reimold, I seek your advicel. What do you think of Duke Coberg's idea?" Asked the King.

Duke Coberg was ready to interrupt, but the eleven-year-old boy managed to silence him with just a look. Duke Heimsteady had never seen anything so regal before. This boy was something special.

"Your Majesty," began Duke Reimold in response, "the Kells are not our only enemy. My lands lie to the East of the Kingdom where our main concern is the Norsemen and Danes. We cannot leave ourselves undefended on that side or the Danes will attack us in the same way that Kells were attacked while they prepared to make war on us. If we go to war for God or ourselves, I ask that you allow me to keep watch on the Norsemen."

"A good point, my Duke." Replied the King. "We had not considered the Danes. But do you think we should gain an easy victory even without your forces?"

"I heard earlier this morning that there is no such thing as an easy victory." Replied Duke Reimold giving a nod towards Duke Heimsteady. "You have my loyalty no matter what you decide. I merely ask that you allow me to protect us from the Danes."

"Thank you good Duke." Replied the King. "We rely on your loyalty and good advice, and are very grateful for it. Now, Sir Bendris, what have you to say?"

"I do not think we should attack." Said Sir Bendris rather plainly.

"You do not think that God will be on our side?" Asked the King.

"Just as Father Leonis is not a man of war, I am not a man of the church." Replied Bendris. "I am a man of war. Duke Reimold is correct in saying that there are no easy victories worth having. The man Sir Jon and I brought back is not a military man, but he says that their army is still intact; that it never got a chance to fight. They are worthy opponents. Based on what I saw; I suspect that the worst raids we have experienced probably came from these other Kells; I certainly can't tell one group of Kells from another. It is also not the size of the army that matters most. While our army gains in skill every day, less than half have ever been to war. As for me, even if you offered to give me their lands I would not want it. They are not rich lands, and we would be constantly fighting to keep them. You know that I will follow whatever decision you make, but I do not think we should fight these Kells at this time."

"Thank you Captain." Said the King. "We do not think you left us much room to misunderstand what you have said."

"Are you afraid?!" interjected Duke Coberg. "What sort of a military leader backs away from a fight?"

"A wise military leader picks his battles carefully, my Lord." Replied the knight. "When and where you fight are every bit as important as how or who you fight."

Duke Coberg stared at him in disbelief. He had thought he could count on a military commander's support with certainty.

"And Duke Heimsteady, what advice have you to give us?" said the King.

"Well," began Duke Heimsteady, "I thought I knew what to say, but Sir Bendris is quite persuasive. I really thought that this was a good decision for you to start your Kingship on, as I thought that you really could not go wrong. If we choose peace, we can strengthen the Kingdom and get ready for what will likely be an inevitable war with these other Kells, but if you chose war, I thought we could win a fairly easy victory and that we would only hasten the coming battle with these new foes. I am now not as certain. I think peace would be a safer choice, and I think that we should learn as much as we can about these new likely enemies."

Duke Coberg looked ready to explode, but said nothing.

"Thank you for your advice Duke Heimsteady." Said the King. "What do you have to say mother?"

"Wulf, your father never included me in these types of decisions." Replied the Queen mother. "He would have asked others, mainly Duke Heimsteady." She said this kindly, but with a resentful look at the Duke. "In the end, he would have made his own decision. I'm sorry, my boy, but I do not know what to tell you."

The King smiled at his mother and said: "Thanks Mama, that is more helpful than you know. We think that there is little enthusiasm for this war other than Duke Coberg's desire to serve God. We choose peace and sense God's approval of our decision."

"I will fight them alone!" Thundered Duke Coberg.

"Then I wish you luck, as you will not be fighting for us or God." Snapped the King in a very adult voice. "If you decide to do that you will commit treason, and lose your lands. You can set up your own Kingdom and I am sure we will fight. Consider this decision carefully my Duke. Make sure you are on God's side."

Duke Coberg looked stunned, but there was nobody there who would support him. The council was over and the participants all went their separate ways.

"Mama, I think I would like to take another ride." Said the King.

23

Wulf Gets to be a Boy

JON WAS THINKING THAT IT was time to go home. It was not that
he was not enjoying himself, but he genuinely missed Lil and
Boady. It was rather incredible that after only a couple of weeks
he already felt like he had a home, and he wanted to get back to it.

While the council was meeting, he went to the stable and started
to saddle Mayflower. He assumed that the Duke would lead Thunder
home, but when he finished with Mayflower he figured that he may
as well saddle the other horse as well. He assumed that he would ride
back with the Duke as there were lots of men about readying other
horses for travel.

When he finished with his horses, he helped others with their
horses. This had a startling effect on the grooms and other men working in the stable; the last thing that they expected was for a knight to
help them with their work. Jon found it helped him forget about the
face he had seen in his drams the night before.

After a while Duke Coberg came to make his departure. He was
in a foul mood and largely ignored Jon except to scowl at him when

he first arrived. The Duke left with an escort of four men at arms, all wearing his livery.

Duke Reimold was next, and when his two men at arms explained who Jon was he came over to introduce himself.

"Sir Jon, I am Duke Reimold." He said. "It is a pleasure to finally meet you."

"The pleasure is all mine, my Lord." Replied Jon.

"I wish you luck on your quest." Said the Duke. "If you are ever in the Eastern part of the Kingdom, know that you are welcome to come for a visit."

It was a brief conversation, but Jon was left with a good impression. The man looked too serious and clever to be trusted, but he had merely exchanged a few pleasantries and had not wanted anything. Jon found this refreshing, and it made him want to know the Duke better if he got the chance.

Finally, Duke Heimsteady appeared, but with the King in his company. When the King saw Jon holding the two horses a big smile broke out on his face.

"Sir Jon! You have anticipated our desire again!" Said the young King. "We were going to ask you to go for a ride later, but since you have the horses ready we may as well go now."

Jon was taken aback. This was not at all in his plans.

"Actually, your Majesty, Thunder here belongs to the Duke, and I had planned to return him, while Mayflower is my horse and I had hoped to ride her back home in the Duke's company."

The King looked disappointed, but then remembered who he was. "Sir Jon, we have so enjoyed your company that we were hoping you would stay longer." He said. "You are our knight, and cannot merely come and go as you wish." He said this in a friendly tone and had a smile on his face, but Jon realized that he was indeed correct.

"As you wish, my Lord." He said rather dejectedly.

"But if Thunder is not your horse, what horse will you ride?" Asked the King. "I REALLY like Mayflower. She is the best horse that I have ridden. She does what I tell her and I fit the saddle quite well."

Jon noticed that the King had dropped the royal 'we' in his speech. He was about to ask a groom to saddle Sir Malpolem's old horse when the Duke interrupted.

"Sir Jon, I wish to make a bargain with you." Said Duke Heimsteady. "You are the only person that I know who can comfortably ride Thunder. Aethelstan can't. I will trade you Thunder with his saddle and bridle for Mayflower."

Both Jon and the King were taken off guard by this proposal. The King was particularly puzzled since the trade threatened to ruin his plans. Sir Jon hoped that it would ruin those plans, but doubted it, and was more concerned about how Lil would react to the departure of Mayflower. Nevertheless, it was too good a deal to pass up. Thunder was a prize worthy horse.

"I guess so my Lord, if you are sure you really want to do that." Said the young knight.

The King looked like an eleven-year-old boy who was watching his plans disappear. He was about to object when the Duke took the initiative.

"Your Majesty, as a gift for your coronation I wish to present you with this horse, saddle and bridle. They are not the finest things, but I hope that they will bring you much pleasure." He said.

Wulf cocked his head and smiled. "Thank you, Uncle!" He said. "It is the best present that I can imagine."

"Now I have another idea." Added the Duke. "Why don't you ask Sir Bendris to ride with us, and you can visit my house and see where Sir Jon lives. Then you, Sir Bendris, and Sir Jon if you desire, can all ride back this evening."

This idea had great appeal to Jon, and he was grateful to the Duke for suggesting it.

The King did not even respond. He turned to a nearby groom and said: "Please have Sir Bendris meet us here as soon as possible." The groom hurried off.

Sir Bendris was not pleased with the idea, but Duke Heimsteady pointed out that it was better if he went along on the King's ride as opposed to searching for him. Finally, the party was ready to depart.

At the King's insistence, he and Jon rode a bit ahead of everyone else so they could talk.

"I guess you heard that we are not going to attack the Kells." Said Wulf as they slowly rode towards the Heimsteady manor.

"I hadn't," said Jon "but I was pretty sure that you would decide that way. There's no sense fighting if you don't know why you are fighting."

"Surprisingly, everyone but Duke Coberg seemed to feel good about the decision." Said the King. "Coberg thought we owed it to God to conquer these people. He said it would enlarge God's Kingdom."

"Not that I am an expert, but Duke Coberg does not strike me as a 'man of God.'" Said Jon. "Did he mean that if a lot of people die God would have more souls in heaven?"

"I think he meant that he would be glad to have his son hold the land for God until Jesus came to claim it." Said Wulf. "Anyways, he got upset when I told him we would give the lands to the church and that they could hold it for God."

"I don't envy you Wulf." Said Jon. "People always want something from you because they think you can give them anything. There's a thin line between being served by people and being used by them."

There was silence for a bit and then the King asked: "And what do you want Jon?"

"You've already given me a lot without my asking." Said Jon. "But right now, I want to go home for a bit. I want to see Lil and Boady. They're family to me; they keep me grounded and remind me of who I am."

"I look forward to meeting them." Said the King a bit stiffly.

"You'll like Lil." Said an enthusiastic Jon not noticing the King's reserved response. "She's about your age, and like you, there is something special about her."

Wulf did not immediately respond. "What's so special about her or me?" he finally asked.

Jon was sort of shocked by the question. How could the King not know that he was special?

"I guess it's that you both are kids who can see the joy in life, but at the same time you have already learned to take things seriously. And both of you seem to care a lot." Replied Jon.

"Why does that make us special? You're not that old, and you care a lot." Said Wulf.

"That's fair." Said Jon. "It's not just that you care, but you both do things about what you care about. You're the King, so you are in a position to do a lot of good if you care to, but Lil is just a girl with a big heart who finds a way to help others. She cares about life in general; not just her own. I'm a little worried about how hurt she'll be when she finds I traded Mayflower."

"So, I'm special because I am King and can therefore make a difference, but Lil is special because she makes a difference when hardly anyone would think she could?" Asked the King.

"Well, sort of." Said Jon. "You HAVE to do things. I am sure it is not easy having everyone expect you to make their lives better. Lil sees opportunities to make life better and just does it. Let me put it another way: if I asked you who you were, what would you say?"

"I would say I am Aerdwulf, the King." Said Wulf.

"I think Lil would not say she was the girl who lives with the Duke's forester and one of the King's knights, I think she would call herself a Christian. She identifies herself that closely with God. God is the essence of her identity. THAT is really special. I hope I can have that someday, but if you asked me, I would probably puff out my chest and say 'I am a knight in the service of Aerdwulf the King.' I am proud to be your knight; I just wish I was more proud of my service to God, like Lil is."

"You have me curious, Jon." Said Wulf. "Let's try not to tell her who I am when I meet her."

"We can try, but you are someone pretty special, it may not work. On the other hand, Lil sees everyone as special, so she may not even realize that you are particularly special." Said Jon.

When they got to the Duke's manor there was a bit of a fuss as Jon and the King insisted on going on to Boady's house alone. Sir Bendris did not want to let his charge out of his sight, but the King was insistent, and the Duke did his best to reassure Bendris that all would be fine. The argument was won when Jon asked if Sir Bendris if he really thought Lil was going to hurt the King. The fact that even Sir Bendris respected Lil was not lost on the King.

Lil saw the two horses approaching and knew that it must be Jon. She ran to the garden and picked some carrots for the horses. She then waited impatiently for the riders to approach. As the horses realized where they were going, they both perked up.

"Wow, what's gotten into Mayflower all of a sudden?" Asked the King. "She's suddenly in a hurry."

"I bet she's excited to see Lil." Replied Jon. "Thunder seems to want to get there as well. Shall we let them trot?"

No answer was required. The two riders raised themselves a bit off of their saddles and the horses immediately assumed a faster gait. Soon they were at Boady's house.

"Sir Jon! You're back!" Said Lil excitedly. "And there's my Mayflower."

The horse seemed genuinely pleased to see Lil, and Lil did not disappoint; giving her a carrot as she craned her neck. Thunder quickly came over to participate in the goings on.

As she fed the horses carrots, Lil finally looked up and said: "Hello, my name is Lil. You must be a friend of Sir Jon's. I hope you will join us for our mid-day meal."

The two men dismounted, but the King answered before Jon could make introductions.

"My name is Wulf." He said. "I live in town and Sir Jon invited me to join him on his trip here." After saying this the King gave Sir Jon a look that clearly said "play along."

Lil ignored the visitor and gave Jon a big hug. "Welcome back." She said. "We've missed you. Why don't you two go and wash up? We can eat as soon as Boady comes back. I will set another two places at the table. I'm so glad you're back; things have seemed dull around here without you!"

Jon gave Wulf the usual explanation about why they were washing in the middle of the day, which amounted to: just do it, it's not a big deal. As they were walking back towards the house they saw Lil was back outside and Boady was emerging from the forest.

"Welcome back Sir Jon!" He called. "I'll wash up and meet you inside in just a moment."

Jon, Wulf, and Lil went inside and Lil told Jon and Wulf to share the new bench. The table was set with venison, a mix of vegetables, some potatoes, bread and cheese. All in all, it was a feast fit for a King.

"Oh, Lil, I have so missed you and your cooking!" said Jon. "I haven't had a meal like this since I left!"

"Boady killed a deer, so we have fresh venison, and the garden is doing very well." Said Lil. "But, surely the King eats better than we do."

Jon and Wulf looked at each other and Wulf shrugged. "I don't think he does, Lil." Said Jon. "And I am sure that he doesn't have as good company either."

When Boady came in he greeted everyone present. "And it is pleasure to meet you, young man." He said to the King.

"Wulf, this is Boady, the master of the house and Duke Heimsteady's forester." Said Jon. "Boady, this is Wulf, he works in the Keep with the King."

Boady looked at Wulf a little suspiciously. Why would Jon bring a random servant of the King's out here, and how does a random servant know how to ride? Boady thought he knew who Wulf really was, but he determined to play along. "It's a pleasure to meet you Wulf." He said. "And how is our King? I hear good things; I hear that he acts much more like a King than one would expect of someone so young."

"He is trying his best, Master Boady. He is trying." Replied Wulf with all too much assurance.

The party sat down to eat, and Wulf did not reach for the food. "Jon, would you like to say grace for us?" asked Lil.

Jon made the sign of the cross and the others followed in his example. "Bless us, oh Lord," he began, "as You do bless us so much. Forgive us our short comings, and help us to know and abide in Your will. Be with the King as he works to rule wisely. Thank you for this food, and thank you for being a God who cares enough to allow us to know Him, through Your son Jesus. Amen."

"Amen." Repeated the other three. Lil and Wulf both gave Jon a smile, but Boady could not get beyond his suspicions. They began to eat.

"Is the King a good man?" Asked Lil to no one in particular.

"He hopes to be." Said Wulf rather distractedly.

"He is as good a man as you will meet." Said Jon resolutely. "As Boady once told me, there are no innocents, but the King is determined to try to do the right thing."

Wulf blushed at this, and Boady noticed. "It's only been a little more than a week," he said, "but he has done alright so far. What is to be done about the Kells? Are you going after the dragon?"

Jon looked at Boady suspiciously before answering. "The King has decided that there is no good reason to fight the Kells, so we will have peace." He said. "The dragon did not attack the Kells, but I will slay this dragon as soon as the Lord grants me how. In any case, it was other Kells who caused the devastation in the lands near us."

"Praise God that the King chose peace!" Said Lil enthusiastically. "It has been a good Summer so far and it would be a shame to see it ruined by fighting just for the sake of fighting."

Suddenly the group heard Timmy's voice calling to Lil, and soon he was at the door.

"Lil, I brought you some apples." He said handing Lil four apples. "I picked them just for you to thank you for helping me and my mum. Hey, did you hear what the King's done? Hello, Sir Jon, hello Boady. Hi there." He directed the last comment at Wulf.

"Come on in Timmy" said Lil taking the apples. "Thank you for these apples, but I insist you take some bread and some venison with you when you leave. Have a seat and join us as we eat."

Timmy sat down on the stump at the end of the table. Lil brought him a plate and asked: "Did you wash?"

"Yes, I even washed the apples before I came up." Said an excited Timmy as he began putting food on his plate.

"I'm Wulf." Said the King. "Tell me, what has the King done?"

Between hungry bites, Timmy answered: "Well, according to Duke Coberg, he has wasted the future of the Kingdom. It seems that there are deserted Kell lands that are ours for the taking, but the

King refuses to allow the Duke to win these lands for him. Dumb, huh? I mean if we had those rich lands all of us would be able to eat without having to work so hard! Sir Jon, you should talk to the King."

Wulf was a bit stunned at this version of events, but Jon had a ready answer:

"Timmy, you need to question some of the things that you hear." He said. "Do you really think the King would pass up free land? I went to those lands with Sir Bendris, the Captain of the Guard, and those lands are neither rich, nor deserted. The lands are burned out, and the Kells will have a hard time feeding themselves, but their army is still together, and they are fighting some really bad men who we will probably have to fight soon enough. You need to respect your Duke, but don't believe everything he says at face value. If Duke Heimsteady and the others felt like Duke Coberg, I am sure the King would have listened to them. In fact, I was with the King last night and I know that he thought and prayed about this decision, I think he decided the right thing."

"Wow! You know the King?" Asked Timmy in awe. "What's he like?"

Jon could not help but smile before answering. "He's alright." He replied. "He is very serious and he blushes when he is complimented, but I like that about him; it makes him human and approachable."

Wulf blushed again, and Boady took particular note. The rest of the conversation was light hearted until Lil asked Jon about the horses.

"Jon, can I have a ride on Mayflower after we eat?" asked Lil excitedly.

Jon paused before answering. "Well, I actually have to tell you something about that. It's a long story as to why, but I sort of traded Mayflower to the Duke for Thunder." He said.

"Oh, no!" exclaimed Lil. "I am sure going to miss her!" Lil almost looked like she might cry.

"I'm sure that the Duke would be OK with her riding Mayflower." Said Wulf trying to be helpful.

"True." Said Jon. "You can ride her, but I guess it will sort of be a goodbye ride. I'm sorry Lil."

Lil looked disappointed, but she responded in her own special way. "Thanks Jon. At least the Lord blessed me with getting to know her." She said. "I sure will miss her."

After eating, Timmy left and everyone else helped Lil clean up; even Wulf. Then they all went outside to give Lil her ride. Wulf was puzzled by the way she sat side saddle on the horse, but Boady corrected him sternly despite his suspicions of who Wulf really was.

"Ladies do not generally ride horses." Said Boady. "And when they do, they are still ladies; they do not ride as men do."

The King took this with equanimity, but he was sure she would have had more fun riding normally.

While Jon and Wulf were giving Lil her ride, Boady spotted two horsemen approaching the house. The Duke was easily recognizable, and soon Boady realized that the other rider was Sir Bendris. They rode up to Boady and dismounted, handing Boady their reigns after greeting him. Jon noticed their arrival but decided to ignore it, while Wulf was so surprisingly enjoying bringing joy to Lil that he did not notice until Sir Bendris walked up.

"Your Majesty, may I have a word with you?" he said.

Wulf and Jon were stunned; their secret was out. Lil nearly jumped out of the saddle.

"Wulf! You're the King?!" She exclaimed. "Oh my! I'm sorry your Majesty." She added making an awkward curtsy.

The King looked a little annoyed. "Yes, Sir Bendris, what is it?" He asked rather pointedly.

"My Lord, the Duke and I were thinking you should head back soon if we are to return tonight." Replied the Captain. "However, the Duke has prepared chambers for us and invited you to dinner if you wish to stay. If that is the case, we must send a message to your mother."

"Thank you, Sir Bendris." Replied the King. "We shall stay the night. Please inform our mother. Meanwhile, Sir Jon will bring us to the Duke's manor later. We wish to be left to our enjoyment presently."

"As you wish, my Lord." Said Bendris backing away. It was rare for the King to speak with him so formally.

The two riders departed and the four others came together.

"It appears that my secret is out." Said Wulf. "Sir Jon has told me that he has a rule that he stops being a knight when he walks into your house; I would like that largely to be true for me as well. I can never really stop being the King, but I have so enjoyed my time just being Wulf that I do not want it to end."

Boady said: "Of course. You must know that we cannot totally forget who you are, but we will try."

Lil just stared at Wulf until he looked her in the eye and said: "Lil?"

Lil suddenly turned on Jon. "You bring the King to our house and you don't even tell us?!" She exclaimed. "Don't you think I would have wanted to clean up? Don't you think I would have wanted to cook a special meal? How could you do this to me?"

Jon gave her a look that said he was sorry, but words failed him.

"Lil, Sir Jon was following my orders." Said the King. "As to the meal I ate, I can assure you that the King has never eaten so well. Nor has he ever been in a more comfortable chamber or been served by a person who positively glows. It is not your clothes, or your cleanliness that make you special, although your clothes are neat and you are certainly cleaner than almost anyone I have met; there is a special glow that comes from you. I am glad that I got the chance to first know you when you weren't trying to impress me. Now let's forget about that and continue your ride."

Lil actually blushed hearing these words, and soon she was back on Mayflower enjoying her ride.

Boady pulled Jon aside. "I had a feeling there was more to him than you were letting on. My, you have come far quickly; confidant of the King! You asked me to watch out for you. Are you handling this OK?"

"Thanks Boady." Replied Jon. "He offered me some of the Kell lands if we attacked and I told him I did not want them. I like him for more than what he can do for me. I think I am OK now, but keep watching."

24

An Awkward Fare Well

BOADY STAYED NEARBY TO MAKE sure that nothing improper was done. Eventually he allowed Jon to hold Lil on Thunder, still side saddle, and the three young people were able to take a bit of a ride. Clearly Wulf and Lil enjoyed each other's company. Eventually, the sun began to settle in the West, and Jon knew it was time to deliver the King to the Duke's house.

"Wulf, I think the time nears when you need to put your crown back on." Said Jon.

"Yes, I guess so." Replied the King. "It's a shame. It has really been a fun day. Think of it, this morning I had to choose between war and peace, but this afternoon I got to just be a boy. I hope I can do this again."

"I really hope you can too." Said Lil. "You're a pretty nice person without being the King. What I mean is, well, I guess I just like you, and I'd like you even if you were just a farmer's son."

Both Lil and Wulf were blushing after this. Jon had to stifle a chuckle, but he quite agreed with Lil. They returned to the house and Boady lifted Lil off of Thunder.

"Thank you for your hospitality, Boady." Said Wulf. "I have really enjoyed myself. I hope I get the chance to do it again some time."

"Well, you're always welcome, of course." Replied Boady. "Understand that we do not often take a day off for fun. We all have work to do; but we look forward to using you as an excuse to skip work if you come again. Work never goes away; it's always there waiting for you."

Wulf appreciated that Boady spoke to him as he might speak to anyone. He was not disrespectful, but he was also not obsequious in what he said. Most of all, Boady did not treat him like a little boy. He noted that while Boady clearly cared a great deal for Lil, he treated her respectfully as well. The King fully understood why Sir Jon had asked to live here.

Lil gave the horses carrots and Sir Jon and the King began a slow ride back to the manor house.

"You have it made, Sir Jon. The King envies you." Said Wulf,

"Life is very nice right now." Said Jon. "Thank you, my Lord."

"You know, this morning I wanted you to stay with me, not realizing what I was asking." Said the King. "Now I realize that I need you to stay with me a while, and it pains me to tell you."

Jon did not immediately respond. He had hoped that he could stay a while. "We all must do our duty, and I am flattered by what you say, but why do you need me?" He replied.

"Because I am just becoming the King." Replied Wulf. "I can talk to you and you actually listen to what I say without trying to use it to your advantage. Help me settle in; I won't make it permanent. Listen to me. The King is pleading that you grant a reasonable request. I don't want to force you, but I really want you to stay with me a while."

"You're right, my Lord." Replied Jon. "It is a reasonable thing to ask, even if you don't have to ask. You have given me so much; I can't refuse you. The fact is I sincerely enjoy talking with you as well. You are special."

The King did not blush. "Thank you." He said. "Would you like to join us for dinner tonight?"

"I think you can understand me not wanting to pass up one of Lil's meals." Said Jon. "The Duke's cook, Kris, is a good man and I am sure he cooks well, but I doubt he can hold a candle to Lil."

"Yes, you are a lucky man." Said the King with a smile. "Make sure that Lil knows I would rather be eating her cooking."

Wren met the riders at the stable and fell to one knee as he greeted the King. Jon spoke highly of Wren as he introduced him to the King, and the King made Wren's day with a simple reply: "It is a pleasure to meet you Master Wren." Stable hands were used to being ignored by their betters.

The Duke came to greet the King and invited Jon to stay, but he respectfully declined and returned to Boady's house. The King had an excellent meal with the Duke, but it was lacking something; the King knew that it was the love and mutual caring that he had experienced earlier in the day. Aethelstan was particularly annoying as he tried to impress the King, not understanding that he had already made a much different impression than he desired.

At Boady's house the subject of discussion was the King's visit. Lil began by chiding Jon for the trick that he and the King had played, but Jon passed on what Wulf had said about wishing he could have had another one of her meals. Lil blushed a deep red.

"Now Lil," said Boady, "don't start getting princess dreams. Wulf is a very nice boy, but he is the King and you are only a nine-year-old peasant girl. Don't let your imagination run away with you."

"Boady!" Cried out Lil blushing even deeper than anyone would have thought possible. Clearly Boady's comments had hit the mark and everyone knew it.

Despite a really pleasant day, the face made several appearances in Jon's dreams that night. As a result, he awoke early the next day, but still did not feel particularly well rested. He ambled into the main room, and after lighting a candle, was confronted by Lil's cross hanging on the wall. It struck him that he had forgotten to pray the night before, and despite his faith he really did not feel like praying now. Nevertheless, he approached the cross and knelt down.

"Good morning God. You know my heart; help it Father. Help my unbelief, let me know that you are there, and let me represent you well today. Amen." He prayed. It was a prayer from the heart, but his heart had not been much in it. As he stood another prayer flashed through his mind: "You have been so good to me; why aren't I more grateful?" While these were not great and admirable thoughts and prayers, Jon's heart was pouring itself out to God.

Jon expected to see Lil watching him as he turned around, but she was still asleep. Wearily he walked down to the stream to wash up. Looking up at the pre-dawn sky he marveled at the wonder and greatness of creation. "I'm so puny in all of this! How can I think that God would care about me?" he thought. It was a depressing way of looking at himself, but then came another thought: "But He does! Not because He needs me, but because I need Him!" This thought, and some cold water on his face lifted Jon's spirit. God had been VERY good to him, and he was excited to see what this day would bring.

When he got back to the house, Boady and Lil were still asleep, so Jon decided to set the table to pass time. When he was just about done, Lil finally appeared.

"Good morning Jon. Have you said your prayers?" She said.

"I have, I've been up for a while." He replied. "Did you sleep well?"

Lil paused before answering. "I guess I did." She said. "I had some pretty pleasant dreams. How about you?"

Jon did not want to answer the question, so he evaded it. "I really do not want to go back to town with the King." He said. "I wish I could stay here with you and Boady for a few days."

"Don't you like Wulf?" Asked Lil.

"I like him a lot, but he has a REALLY big job. Being the King is not as much fun as you might think." Replied Jon.

Lil smiled. "Can you join me for prayers, any ways?" She asked.

The two knelt down by the cross and made the sign of the cross. Lil spoke: "Father in heaven, help me to remember who I am and to be satisfied with that. I am an adopted daughter in Your family, and an adopted daughter in Boady's house. Help me to remember that your blessings are more and better than anything I could imagine on my own. Help me to remember who I am, Father."

Lil looked up at Jon kneeling beside her, and he said: "Amen and amen. Help us both to be satisfied with what we have and to appreciate what we get, as we don't deserve Your love, but You give it to us anyways. Thank You Jesus. Amen."

"Amen." Repeated Lil. She looked at Jon again and smiled. "I miss praying with you." She said. "Try to pray with Wulf."

"I will." Said Jon. "Why don't you go wash while I get the fire going."

Lil looked like she wanted to say more, but after a pause by the door she decided against it and left to go down to the stream. She was greeted by a magnificent Sun rise, and she felt as if the world could be hers for the taking. Then she corrected herself and determined to live God's way to the best of her ability.

Boady was on his way out the door as Lil returned. "Good morning my little princess!" He said in greeting.

Lil smiled. "Good morning, Boady." She replied. "I will make you a breakfast fit for a King."

Rather than frying the eggs, Lil decided to do something different. She mixed in vegetables and some cut up venison with beaten eggs and made what we today would call an omelet. The men were quite impressed.

"That really was special, Lil." Said Boady when they had finished. "But now, we have to make up for the things we did not get done yesterday."

"And I guess I need to saddle Thunder and go meet the King." Said Jon less than enthusiastically.

"I'm going to wrap some of my new creation for Wulf." Said Lil. "You'll give it to him, won't you?"

Both Boady and Jon smiled, and Jon readily agreed to fulfil the task that he had been given. While Jon saddled Thunder, Lil made another omelet, put it on a slice of bread, and wrapped it in some large, fresh leaves, that she kept around for just such an occasion.

It was time for Jon to depart. He gave and got a big hug from Lil, and even Boady was a little more sentimental than usual. "Keep your head on right, Jon. Don't let all of this change who you are inside. People seem to respect you just as you are." He said in parting.

As Jon rode to the manor he praised God in his heart. The gloom he had felt upon waking was being replaced by an appreciation of how good his life really was. Could he really complain about having to spend time with the King?

As he arrived at the stable, the King and Sir Bendris were mounting their horses.

"Sir Jon. I had hoped that we could come and pick you up this morning." Said the King. "For once you did NOT anticipate our wishes." He had a somewhat bashful smile on his face as he said this.

"I beg your pardon, your Majesty." Replied Jon with a smile. "I have always been advised not to keep the King waiting. I bring you a present from Mistress Lil; I hope you did not eat a big breakfast."

"My Lord was in such a hurry that he hardly ate at all." Said Sir Bendris.

The King unwrapped the gift with a smile of anticipation. "What is it?" He asked when he saw it.

"Lil was inspired this morning and made a special creation. It is eggs mixed with venison and vegetables. I quite enjoyed mine this morning." Replied Jon.

Wulf took a bite and smiled in delight. "It is quite delicious." He said. "Sir Bendris, we must go and thank the cook."

Sir Bendris rolled his eyes and said: "Of course, My Lord."

After saying their good byes to the Duke and Aethelstan the three riders made their way to Boady's house. Boady was off in the forest, and Lil was at the stream washing dishes as they came upon her.

"Your Majesty!" Exclaimed Lil, startled. "You do pick the oddest times to pay a visit!" She added as she tried to straighten her hair and dress.

"A thousand pardons, my lady, but we could not depart without thanking you once more for your hospitality and to express our profound appreciation for special breakfast that you sent to us." Said the King feeling a little self-conscious.

"The pleasure was all mine, my Lord." Replied Lil, also a bit self-consciously.

There was an awkward long moment of silence until Jon said: "I'll see you again soon, Lil. Your Majesty, I think it is best we get going."

"Of course." Replied the King. "Fare thee well, mistress, and know that you are in our thoughts."

The horses turned as Lil blushed deeply. The King also was blushing as he had not intended to share his feelings so openly.

They rode in silence for a good while until the King announced: "I want to drop the formalities on this ride, and I have decided something. Sir Bendris, you and Sir Jon will return to the Kells as a delegation. We will bring them some food and assure them that we wish them no harm. You will lead, Sir Bendris, but Sir Jon will speak for me. Jimmy will accompany you as an interpreter."

Sir Bendris was taken aback by the idea, but Jon greeted it enthusiastically. "If I can make a suggestion, a large wagon as a gift for their King would be good, but a smaller wagon with food we can give to the people who are starving would really show that we mean them well."

"I suppose." Replied the King. "Tell the people that they can hunt in my preserve as well, but warn them about the dragon."

"Wulf, I don't disagree with your motives, but don't you think you should discuss this with the council?" Interjected Sir Bendris.

"I guess that I do not see the point. Coberg will be angry, Reimold will be fine as long as he does not have to go along, Heimsteady is as dedicated to peace as I am, mother will have little opinion on the matter, which leaves only you and Father Leonis." Said the King. "I will speak with Father Leonis, but now is your chance to object."

"I worry that you may be strengthening an enemy." Said Sir Bendris.

"Perhaps." Said the King. "But my hope is that they will no longer be enemies for a while if we help them in their fight with these other Kells. I think it is worth the risk. Meanwhile you can continue to train our forces for when we do need to fight. The food we give them will be gone by then."

"It has a fair chance of success." Replied Sir Bendris. "It will be interesting to hear what Father Leonis has to say."

When they returned to the castle the King made it clear that Sir Jon was to be given Sir Malpolem's former chamber as his own. He and Sir Bendris then sent for Father Leonis.

"Your Majesty! I trust you enjoyed your day?" Said Father Leonis as he entered the room.

"I very much did Leonis." Replied the King. "I have also decided to send a delegation to the Kells and I wish to discuss it with you. Sir Bendris and I spoke on the way back."

"It is a sensible decision." Replied the Priest. "Would you like Jimmy and me to go?"

"I had rather thought that Sir Jon and Sir Bendris would go with Jimmy." Said the King. "I also intend to send some food both for the King and for the people on the way, so we will need two wagons and a few men to escort them."

"Exactly what are you trying to tell them, my Lord?" Said Leonis stiffly.

"I want to assure them that we wish to leave them in peace and that they can fight their actual enemies. I will also allow them to hunt in the preserve for the time being, although the dragon may make that a less desirable gift." Replied the King. "Sir Bendris will lead, and Sir Jon will speak for me. We will allow Jimmy to stay if he wishes."

"Wulf, I think the plan makes sense, but perhaps we should consult the council about this." Said Leonis.

"Sir Bendris agrees with you, but we do not see the point. Except for Coberg, the council will agree. There is no need to waste further time." Said the King.

"Very well." Said Leonis. "I will draft a letter to be sent to the Dukes informing them of your decision so they are not caught off guard. We should also meet to discuss what Sir Jon should tell their King."

"Thank you Father. I appreciate your acquiescence to our desire." Said the King. "Please see to it that the wagons are loaded. Sir Bendris we leave it to you to gather the necessary men. Let's meet after dinner to decide what we should say both to the Dukes, and to their King. Please make sure that Sir Jon knows that he should join all of us for dinner."

Father Leonis was uneasy about the way this decision had been made. He did not disagree with what was being done, but the young King had not asked what should be done; he had said what he intended to do. The priest hoped that his pupil was not getting ahead of himself. Yes, he was King, but he was also a boy. Leonis did not envy the messenger who would deliver the news to Duke Coberg. There is more to being King than simply making the right decision, he thought.

After supper, the following message was dispatched to the Dukes:

> *We have decided to send a delegation to our neighboring Kells informing them that we desire peace with them and that they need not fear us as they fight the men who attacked them so viciously. We will send food with the delegation as a gift, and inform them that they may hunt in our preserve, although we will caution them about the dragon. After our previous discussions we felt secure in your support. We thank you for the advice and consent that you have provided us in this matter.*
>
> *Sincerely,*
> *King Aerdwulf*

Duke Reimold was pleased by the news as he had received reports of a long boat in a nearby river. Duke Heimsteady was slightly perturbed by the fact that the decision had been made without him, but he largely agreed with what was being done. The opening of the preserve bothered him slightly, but there was no way to openly communicate the nature of his concerns to the King. He would have to make the best of it.

Duke Coberg was incensed. First the King had failed to listen to his sound reasoning as to why they should go to war, and now he had decided to send "tribute" to the Kells. The Kingdom was sure to suffer if this boy was not reigned in. He determined to find a way to do it. How could Reimold and Heimsteady not see that this boy was preparing to destroy all of their hard work?

A Letter to King Arwel of the Kells, was also drafted to be delivered:

> To Arwel, our neighbor, and King of the Kells,
>
> Aerdwulf, King of Mersya, greets you in friendship.
> We have been informed that your people are suffering for lack of food due to an attack by others. Our trusted advisors have witnessed the devastation themselves. While we could use this opportunity to bring you further harm, we have determined that peace between us would be better, and have sent you a wagon of food as a sign of our good will. Our ambassadors, Sir Bendris, and Sir Jon, can speak on our behalf. We hope that our gift is helpful in your battles with the enemy, and that it can serve as a basis for peace between our Kingdoms for a long time.
> We also will allow your people to hunt in our preserve for this year as they are in hardship. Please know that several of our people have died as the result of a dragon that is sometimes found there.
> We look forward to hearing from you that our feelings are mutual.
>
> Aerdwulf, King of Mersya.

The letter was actually written in Latin, since nobody knew if the Kells even had a written language. It was doubtful that they could read it, but Jimmy could interpret it for them. The entourage was to depart in two days.

Before going to sleep that night, the King asked Jon a question in private.

"Does Lil like me for who I am or just because I am the King?" He said.

"I suppose it is hard to separate the two." Replied Jon.

Do you think she would like me if I wasn't the King?" He asked.

"She said as much, didn't she?" Replied Jon. "You know; Lil is a special girl. She is filled with a love that I think must come from God. She likes almost everyone she meets, but nobody makes her blush the way she does about you. She even asked me to pray with you."

"She did?!" Said Wulf.

"Yes, she did; right after we said our morning prayers." Said Jon.

"What did she pray about?" Asked Wulf.

"Well, I think her prayers are rather private moments, but like me, she prayed God would help her remember who she is: His adopted child." Said Jon. "We prayed that we would be satisfied with what God gives us."

"That's kind of an odd prayer." Said Wulf. After a pause he added: "Alright, let's not disappoint the Lady; can you meet me here for morning prayers before breakfast?"

"It would be a pleasure, my Lord." Said Jon with an exaggerated bow.

The King laughed. "Good night, Jon." He said. "I value our talks."

"I like you as more than just the King." Said Jon. "Sleep well."

Jon slept better that night, but he still had the dream.

25

Treasure

J ON REGULARLY WOKE UP EARLY, but he was uncertain as to how early he could go to say morning prayers with the King. In the early light he looked around the room that he had spent so much time in over the past years, but that was now somehow different; it was his room. He determined that he would change some things; move some furniture and put some personal touches in it. He had to be quiet as Jimmy was still asleep in the main bed, but it felt good to have something concrete that he could do for himself.

Eventually, he decided to go to the King's chamber and at least determine when the King normally ate breakfast. As he approached the room a servant greeted him: "Sir Jon, the King is expecting you."

"Good morning Jon!" Said the King as Jon entered the room.

"Good morning Wulf, you seem in fine spirit this day." Replied Jon.

"I am hopeful that I can start this day off in a good way." Replied the King. "Usually I just get dressed and go to breakfast where Father

Leonis or my mother tell me what I have to do. It will be nice if my first thoughts are about something else. So, how does this work?"

"Well," responded Jon, "I am not sure there is any one way to say morning prayers. Lil has a cross on the wall, and she and I often kneel by it to pray, but when I am not there I usually just find a quiet place to focus my mind on God. Why don't you and I just sit on your bed and see what happens. We will pray silently for a while, and then I will pray out loud and afterwards you can add something if you like."

The two sat down on the bed and Wulf eyed Jon who made the sign of the cross as Wulf followed suit. The prayer that came to Jon's mind was simple and familiar: "Lord, help me to represent you well." It was brief, so he gave Wulf some more time to say his own prayer.

Wulf prayed from his heart: "God, I know you, but I don't really know you. You are a great King, the greatest King, show me how to be a King. Let me know you."

"Father in heaven, you are an awesome and good God." Began Jon out load. "Let your will be done in this Kingdom and in our lives. Thank you for giving us what we need despite the fact that you owe us nothing; help us to be good to those that we meet this day. And protect us, God, deliver us from those who would act against us. We pray from our hearts to you, amen."

There was a moment of silence and then Wulf spoke: "Yes Father, help us to be good to those around us and help us to know those who are not good. Watch over Lil, and my mother, and Father Leonis, and also, God, be with my father, or let him be with You." The King stifled a sob. "Amen."

The King looked up at Jon and there were tears in his eyes.

"It was a nice prayer, Wulf." Said Jon. "It came from your heart. I think that is mostly what God wants to hear; what is in your heart."

"I miss my dad, Jon." Said the King. "I miss him every day, but I haven't been thinking of him very much lately."

"Wulf, I still miss my dad too." Replied Jon. "It is hard, but that is exactly what prayer time is for: pouring out your heart to God. Cry for your dad; it's ok. I think most morning prayers are not with someone else because it should be a very private time. But, it's OK. I am not here as your knight; I am here as your friend."

Jon put an arm around his young friend, and the King cried hard. It was very awkward for both of them, but Jon felt that just being there for Wulf might be the most important thing he would do this day. There was a soft knock on the door.

"We are still in prayers." Replied Jon.

"It's me; Father Leonis." Said the voice on the other side of the door.

Wulf nodded to Jon indicating that it was alright for the priest to enter, so Jon went to the door and let him in.

As Father Leonis took on the scene he was not sure what to do. "Wulf, are you OK?" he asked.

The King ran to Father Leonis and gave him a hug. "I was praying for papa." He said. "I miss him so."

Father Leonis got down on one knee in order to look Wulf in the eyes. "You need to pray for your father, and you need to cry for him. God is the source of joy, but you have to lay your sorrows on Him."

Wulf cried some more, but after a few minutes he suddenly stopped. Wiping the tears from his eyes he looked at Jon and said: "That was not what I expected, but thank you Jon. Let's pray again tonight after supper. Meanwhile, my servant will help me finish getting dressed. Please join us for breakfast."

"Of course." Replied Jon. He and Father Leonis walked out of the room together.

"What did you do?" Asked Father Leonis.

"We just prayed." Responded Jon.

"I have seen Wulf cry tears of anger and resentment, but not tears of sorrow for his father." Said the Priest. "I have tried to say morning prayers with him, but any prayers with him seem less than real. He goes through the motions. Now he wants to pray with you again tonight?"

Jon shrugged. "Last night I told him that Lil hoped that he would pray, so he asked me to come by this morning and we did."

Said Jon. "Lil and I often say prayers together and nothing like this has ever happened."

Father Leonis looked at Jon in a thoughtful way. "You have done your King a great service." He said. "He needs to cry for his father. But tell me, who is Lil?"

"Lil is the nine-year-old girl that lives with Boady and me on the Duke's estate. The King visited with me the day before yesterday and the two of them hit it off pretty well." Replied Jon.

"Brother Johan has mentioned her to me." Said the priest. "She must be an extraordinary little girl; she can impress a monk who has seen much of the world, and convince a King to pray! I must try to meet her some time."

"Yes, there is something very special about her." Said Jon.

Breakfast with the King was not at all what Jon had expected. The King was briefed on what letters were being sent where and of other news like that another long ship had been seen on the river in the eastern part of the Kingdom. He was then given a schedule of activities which included schooling with Father Leonis.

"What do you have planned today, Sir Jon?" Asked the King.

"I will check on the preparations for the journey to the Kells, and I planned to make my chambers feel a bit more like my chambers." Replied Jon guiltily.

The King smiled. "That sounds like a good plan." He said. "I look forward to praying with you tonight."

The King's mother looked puzzled as he said this, but she made no comment as the royal breakfast broke up. Jon headed back to his room, and found that Jimmy was not there. There was not a lot of furniture in the room, but Jon wanted to make changes for the sake of making changes. He shifted the beds around, but found that the wardrobe was too heavy to be moved, even though it was empty.

As he walked to where the main bed had been, he noticed that one of the floor boards moved when he stepped on it. Upon further investigation he found that it was entirely detached from the rest of the floor. He lifted it off.

As he gazed into the hole in the floor he saw a small cloth bag and a scrap of paper, so he pulled them out. The bag contained several coins of copper, silver, and one of gold! It was more money than Jon had ever seen in one place. The paper had Latin writing on it:

> The Kingdom of heaven is like treasure hidden in a field. When a man found it, he hid it again, and then in his joy went and sold all he had and bought that field. Again, the Kingdom of heaven is like a merchant looking for fine pearls. When he found one of great value, he went away and sold everything he had and bought it.

Jon considered what he read. It sounded Biblical, but he was not familiar with it. Perhaps it was referring to the treasure that he had found.

Jon was excited. There was enough money to buy stuff for his room, and something for Lil and Boady! He was rich! What should he do first?

He decided to do as the paper said; he put the money back under the floor and moved the bed back over it. He kept the paper. It puzzled him. He sort of owned the room now. Was it telling him that the money belonged to him as well?

"Good morning Jon." Said Jimmy as he walked into the room. "Are you redecorating?"

"Hello Jimmy." Replied Jon distractedly. "Uh, yes. I thought that since the room is now mine I might change it to sort of make it seem more like mine."

"Would you like me to help you move the bed?" Asked Jimmy. "We could put it against that wall."

"No, thanks. I think I like the bed where it is." Said Jon as non-chalantly as possible. "I found this. It looks kind of Biblical; do you know what it is?" Jon handed the paper to Jimmy.

"Ah, yes." Said Jimmy. "It is a parable from the Gospel of Matthew. (Matt. 13:44-46) It is not very neat writing. It looks like someone just copied it or wrote it from memory. Where did you find it?"

Jon felt a bit trapped by the question. "It was in the wardrobe. When I tried to move it, I found it." He said.

"I wonder if it belonged to Johan's brother." Said Jimmy. "You should show it to him."

"I will." Said Jon. "But tell me, what does it mean? Does it mean that treasure is worth everything?"

Jimmy smiled. "No, it is not actually about treasure at all." He said. "It is about the Kingdom of heaven. Jesus said that a man's heart will be where his treasure is; here he says that the Kingdom of heaven is the most valuable treasure that a man can have. He is basically saying that you should be willing to lose everything in order to have the Kingdom of heaven."

Jon was disappointed by the answer and it showed. "Oh." He said.

"What's the matter Jon?" Asked Jimmy. "You seem to highly value your relationship with God. Isn't it your most valuable treasure?"

Jon paused before answering. "I guess so." He said. "But I also value my knighthood, and my relationship with the King, my home with Boady and Lil. They're all important to me."

"Well, I don't think God is asking you to give any of that up." Replied Jimmy. "But He once asked Abraham to sacrifice his own son for Him. Abraham was ready to do it, but at the last moment God let him not to do it. God tested Abraham's faith by asking for the earthly thing that he valued the most, and he passed the test. God wants to be the greatest treasure in all of our lives. I think that is what Jesus is saying in those parables. We should be willing to sacrifice everything to gain the Kingdom of heaven."

"I see." Said Jon. "Where can we find Brother Johan? I want to show this to him."

"I am supposed to help him supervise the loading of the wagons for the Kells." Replied Jimmy. "Why don't you come with me?"

The two of them went past the stables to a place where two empty wagons stood ready for loading. Brother Johan was telling some workmen to bring food from the store houses for the loading.

"Ah, Jimmy. Good morning Sir Jon." He said as the two approached. "Jimmy, as the workmen bring the food we need to decide whether it goes on the Royal wagon for the Kell King, or on the other wagon for the people. I know it will be tempting, but the best food goes on the royal wagon; understood?"

Jimmy smiled. "Johan, I am just glad the people will be getting something. I have no problem making the official gift be the best of it." He said.

"Can I have a word with you Brother Johan? There is something I need to show you." Said Jon.

"Of course, Sir Jon." Replied the monk. "I am rather busy, but I can certainly give you a minute. What have you got?" Jon handed Johan the paper and a wistful smile came over his face. "Where did you find this?!" He said.

"I found it in the room." Replied Jon. "I take it that it belonged to your brother?"

"I wrote it out to him when I first started learning Latin." Said Brother Johan. "They are parables from the Gospel of Matthew. We used it as his first Latin reading lesson. He kept it all of his life."

"He must have valued it greatly." Said Jon. "I guess you are his heir, so it is yours now." Jon said this with some disappointment in his voice.

"Jon, you and my brother were very close. I suspect that you are his heir every bit as much as I am. I want you to have this." Said Brother Johan.

Jon was caught off guard. It was not the paper that Jon was thinking of when he spoke of inheritance. "Thank you, Brother Johan. I will treasure it." He said with as much excitement as he could muster.

As Jon walked back to his room much of the excitement of find- ing the money or even rearranging the furniture had left him. He was torn. Should he keep the money? Brother Johan had said that they were both equal heirs to Sir Malpolem's estate, so certainly some of the money was his; wasn't it? Jon knew in his heart that this was not what Brother Johan had meant, and in any event, that also meant that some of the money certainly belonged to the monk.

When he got back to the room Jon sat down on his old bed to think. He felt that he deserved a chance to make this room uniquely his. And Boady and Lil, who had given him so much certainly deserved a present. He also knew that he could give some of the money to the poor and it would make a big difference in their lives. Keeping a bit just in case also made perfect sense. God had probably given him this money because He knew that Jon would use it wisely.

Jon laid back on the bed. His own thoughts betrayed a sense of dishonesty. It was not his money, and he knew it; but he could keep the money and nobody would ever know. Somehow, finding treasure was not bringing him any joy.

"God is the source of joy." That's what Father Leonis had told the King just this morning. "But you have to lay your sorrows on Him." Jon decided to pray:

"God, I asked you to protect me today, and You are good. Please let me keep the money and have the joy that it should bring. YOU will always be first in my heart. If You want me to give the money to Brother Johan, at least give me a clear sign that this is what you want. Please God, help me. Amen."

Jon laid back on the bed and thought of the good he could do if he kept the money. As he looked around the room he thought how much better it would look if it had curtains or a rug. He had never wanted curtains or a rug before, but suddenly he felt like they were important to impress people with who he had become. The money would make it possible for him to assume his proper place and gain the respect that he was due. If people respected him more, that would help him to glorify God.

A servant came to the door and informed Jon that Sir Bendris wished to see him in the court yard. Distractedly he wandered down to see what was up. He saw Wil drilling several of the guard under the watchful eye of Sir Bendris.

"Ah, Sir Jon." Said the Captain of the Guard as he saw Jon approach. "I am selecting the men who will accompany us. We will take our best men as we want to make a good impression. The reason I called you here is to tell you to see the court tailor in the keep. He will give you some fine clothes including one of the King's tabards. As I said, we intend to make an impression on our hosts."

This would mean that Jon now had four sets of clothing that he could wear; more than he had ever had before, and this latest set promised to be the finest yet. Nevertheless, Jon took the news in stride. His mind was still on the treasure that he had found.

"Very good, Sir Bendris." He replied. "Thank you for telling me."

"I suggest you also buy yourself some nicer boots. Those old ones will not really fit well with the new clothes." Said Sir Bendris.

Jon was shocked into reality by this request. He had no money for new boots, or did he?

"I'm sorry, Sir Bendris," he replied, "I don't have any money for new boots."

"Sir Jon." Said the Captain in a stern voice. "The King arms you, and in this case dresses you, but you are responsible for your horse, armor, and foot wear. Have you already spent your pay?"

Jon felt slightly embarrassed. "I'm sorry, my lord, I was not aware that I was getting paid."

It was rare for Sir Bendris to smile, especially in front of his men while on duty, but in this case he did.

"Of course you get paid." He said softly. "A knight gets one silver piece a month. See if you can get Father Leonis to arrange it for you. If you have any trouble, I will help you collect it. But spend most of it on new boots."

This was news indeed. One whole silver piece a month! Jon had never imagined that he would earn that much. Then his thoughts returned to the bag of money that he had found. One silver piece was so little in comparison.

Jon excused himself and went in search of Father Leonis. He happened upon him as he was carrying several scrolls near the King's room.

"Father Leonis," he said, "I need just a moment of your time."

"Certainly, Sir Jon." Responded the priest. "I need to give the King a lesson, so I do not have much time."

"Sir Bendris told me to buy some better boots, and he says that I get paid for my service. I have no money so he suggested that I speak with you." The words poured out of Jon's mouth with great speed.

"I am so sorry, Sir Jon." Said Father Leonis. "Of course you get paid. One silver a month. You should have been paid when you were knighted. Forgive the over sight."

Father Leonis stopped a servant who was walking by. "Rufus, please take Sir Jon to Bartleby and tell him that I said to give Sir Jon two month's pay and a bonus of one silver for the special services he has performed. That's three pieces of silver. Do you understand?"

"Yes, your eminence." Replied Rufus. "I will take Sir Jon to Bartleby and tell him that Sir Jon is to get three pieces of silver: two as pay, and one as a bonus."

Rufus looked to Sir Jon, who motioned that he should lead on. As they walked Jon's head was spinning. Before today he had never seen three pieces of silver at once. It was enough money to buy boots, and a rug for his room, and something for Boady and Lil. Still, the little bag contained even more money.

Rufus told Bartleby what Father Leonis had said, and Jon was given the three pieces of silver. The scribe asked Jon to sign his name in a ledger to show that he had been given the money. Jon had never signed his name, but he proudly wrote: "Sir Jon of the Dragon" in a crude Latin script.

He then went into town where he found a shoe maker who actually had a pair of boots that fit him. They were fine brown boots, nicely polished. Jon got a few coppers back from one of his silver pieces. Next Jon went in search of a rug, but he had trouble spending the money it would take to get a really fine one, even though he could afford it. He did not buy a rug, or a tapestry which was even more expensive, or some curtains. He simply could not bear to part with the money.

Before heading back to the keep he stopped at a tavern and spent a copper on a rather large lunch and a tankard of ale. He was quite stuffed as he left. He still had two silver pieces and three coppers as he walked back. On the way he found a leather worker and bought himself a purse to hold his money. This cost him another copper. Then, near the church, he saw a woman with a small girl begging for alms. He felt a tug on his heart and gave them the two coppers.

"Bless you, sir!" Exclaimed the woman. "We can eat for weeks with this!"

Jon had spent a full silver piece on his excursion. It was a full month's pay. True, he had his boots to show for it, and they were what had cost the most, but he could not believe that he had spent so much money so quickly. Apparently, having money might be a hard thing to get used to.

As he hid his new purse under the floor board he thought to himself: "I had planned to spend so much more of the money I found, but I found it harder to spend my own money. How strange?"

It was then that he realized that God had sent him a clear sign. The bag of money was not his.

After hiding his money, Jon went to the tailor for his new clothes. This took longer than he expected since the clothes were actually adjusted to fit him properly. Jon felt proud as he stood in the finished product. He took them back off reluctantly, but he knew that he would be wearing them again soon enough.

26

Instructions for the Embassy

J ON WAS NOT FEELING VERY certain of himself. While he had
determined that the money he had found was not his to keep,
he was still somewhat hesitant about giving it to Brother Johan.
He felt that as long as he did not spend any of it he had not stolen it.
He was holding it for the monk, much as Boady was holding the half
of the silver piece that the Duke had earlier given to the two of them;
certainly Boady had not stolen that from him.

In his uncertain mood he was unsure of whether he was to join
the King for supper or simply meet him afterwards to pray. He determined to try and find out by asking Father Leonis if he could find
him. He cautiously approached the council chamber where the King
often took his meals and saw servants setting the table for supper.

While he stood wondering where Father Leonis might be, Rufus walked in to see how things were going. "Hello Sir Jon." He said respectfully. "Can I help you with something?"

"I was looking for Father Leonis." Said Jon. "Do you know where I might find him?"

"He is currently immersed in the King's business and asked not to be disturbed." Replied the servant.

A frown crossed Jon's face.

"Can't it wait until supper?" Asked Rufus hoping to be helpful.

"Actually, that was my question." Said the young knight. "I am uncertain whether I am to join the King for supper or simply meet with him afterwards."

"We have been asked to set a place for you near the King and his mother." Replied Rufus. "The King expects you in about an hour."

"Thank you, Rufus." Said Jon with relief. "I should have known that while Father Leonis knows everything about the Kingdom's affairs, nobody knows more about the household than you do. I will come back later. Rufus, I really appreciate the help you have given me today; first in getting me some money for boots, and now in clarifying what I am expected to do."

"We are here to serve, Sir Jon." Replied the servant, obviously pleased.

Jon went back to his room. He had not accomplished much in changing it and was not in the mood to move more furniture. He placed his old boots in the wardrobe, and then placed an extra shirt and the new suit of clothes in it as well. This more than anything else made the room feel more fully his.

He sat down on his old bed and a prayer came into his mind: "Lord, give me courage." Jon was not sure where the prayer had come from or what he needed courage for. He would need more tact than courage on his mission to the Kells; how could they refuse food and peace when they were in a desperate battle of their own? He thought about this for a while and guessed it was almost time for supper, so he left for the council chamber.

He was still the first into the council chamber, but he comforted himself in the maxim that he should never keep the King waiting. Rufus greeted him and showed him to his seat.

"Rufus, is there a place I might wash myself before eating?" Asked Jon tentatively.

Rufus gave Jon a rather surprised look. "What an odd question, Sir Jon." He said. "The King actually asked that a bowl of water be provided him so he could wash up before eating. I do not think you should use it, but perhaps you can ask the King. For the future I can see that a bowl of water is provided for your room if you like."

"That would be very nice, Rufus. Thank you." Responded Jon.

After a short while, Father Leonis arrived, and not long after the King and his mother joined them.

When Sir Bendris arrived he said: "Please excuse Brother Johan. He is overseeing the loading of the wagons, but should be along shortly."

"Sir Jon, would you like to wash up with me?" Asked the King.

"Yes, I would." Replied Jon. "Thank you for offering."

The Queen looked on disapprovingly as the two went to the bowl and washed their hands and face. Sir Bendris reacted with a wry smile while Father Leonis merely looked on in puzzlement.

"Wulf, why do you always have to be different?" Said the Queen sternly. "And you, Sir Jon, why do you encourage him?"

The King merely smiled in response, but Jon thought that he was obligated to reply. "It is a habit that I recently started doing, and I quite enjoy it." He said. "Brother Johan says that it is also a custom in the Holy Land. I cannot see the harm in it, my Lady."

The Queen scowled in response. "It is not our way, Sir Jon. We have managed quite well for quite a long time without washing and there is no reason to simply change our way of life. Perhaps it is alright for you, but Wulf is the King and people look to him to set an example. Changes should be considered carefully; not just done as the whim strikes us."

"Father Leonis." Said the King. "Is there something wrong or sinful about washing before a meal?"

Father Leonis felt like he had been put on the spot. "Well, your Majesty," he said, "there is nothing sinful about washing, but the Lord does say one should honor one's mother. Perhaps you should consider why you are doing it and be certain that it is not merely to assert your independence. Perhaps you should pray about it before committing."

"You feel that this decision is serious enough that I should go to God about it?" Asked the King incredulously. "I hardly think that whether I choose to wash before a meal is a decision that will bring ruin to either me or the Kingdom. Mother, I love you, but I AM the King, and if I choose to wash myself I feel that I can do it."

"You'll get sick from it, you'll see." Replied the Queen. "My, isn't the little boy I gave birth to full of himself today!"

The King looked down but could not hide a smile. The others in the room, Jon included, felt awkward witnessing this exchange. The Queen gave Jon a very unfriendly glance.

"Let us say grace." Announced Father Leonis.

They all made the sign of the cross and Father Leonis prayed:

> "Bless us, oh Lord, and these thy gifts, which we receive from Your bounty. Help us to walk in Your way and to remember that there is NOTHING so small that we cannot benefit from Your wisdom in it. In Christ our Lord, amen."

Everyone made the sign of the cross again and then the Queen announced: "Well prayed, Father Leonis." She gave the King a reproving look.

The servants began bringing food to the table and the King was the first to serve himself and then passed dishes to the others.

While this was happening Brother Johan entered. "Pardon my lateness, you Majesty." He said. "The wagons are loaded and the guard has been posted."

"Of course, Brother Johan." Said the King. "Thank you for your service. There is a bowl for washing if you would like to before you eat."

Not knowing what had transpired, Johan said: "That would be most welcome indeed!" He walked over to the bowl and began to wash his hands.

"Brother Johan!" Said the Queen. "Don't tell me you have joined this fad as well!"

Johan was taken aback. Had he done something wrong? Leonis rolled his eyes as the monk looked to him for guidance. "I am merely feeling a bit dirty after having been busy with the loading all day, my Lady." He replied. "I am uncertain what fad you are referring to."

Before the Queen could respond, the King announced: "Now that we are all gathered I believe we have some final instructions for our emissaries."

Father Leonis cleared his throat. "Brother Johan will accompany Sir Bendris and Sir Jon on the journey. If the Kells wish us to leave someone behind he will be the man that stays." Said the Minister of State. "He will learn their language as best he can, and if the two of you return without him we will select someone to replace him as our permanent representative in their court. Sir Bendris, of course, will be in charge of the expedition, but Sir Jon will act as the King's ambassador and speak for the King. You will deliver the letter that you will be given in the morning. Is your Latin good enough that you can read it to them?"

"I believe it is." Replied the young knight. "If I have trouble I will ask Brother Johan for help."

"Excellent." Replied the Priest. "Now, we address this Arwel as the King of the Kells, but of course he is not. He is likely just a petty chieftain. While you are to show him respect, you are to act so as to clearly show our King's supremacy. Aerdwulf is King by God's anointing, while this Arwel is not even a Christian. Be polite, but be clear that he needs our favor, not the reverse. This will be a difficult thing to pull off, Sir Jon, but you have shown a gift for saying the right thing. You will need to use that gift."

Jon nodded in response, but he had never purposefully exercised that gift, so the prospect of it being counted on made him nervous.

"Of course you have Brother Johan and Sir Bendris to advise you." Continued Father Leonis. "Use them well. You have performed great service for your King, but you have never been entrusted with a job this big. You have the King's confidence, but it is still far more responsibility than you have ever been given; take care in accomplishing your task. Understood?"

"Yes, your eminence." Replied Jon.

"Jimmy will act as your interpreter." Added the priest. "He has asked that he be allowed to stay behind when you depart, and as much as we both like him, you are not to consider him one of us. It pains me no small amount to say that despite his being a Christian, he is more one of them than he is one of us. Nevertheless, we have no better interpreter, and I think we can be reasonably sure that he means us no harm. Again, rely on Brother Johan for help in handling him. That is all I have to tell you. Do you have any questions or does anyone else have anything to add?"

Before Jon could even respond the Queen responded. "Sir Jon, you have the confidence of my son, our King." She said. "You will be representing all of us, so I implore you not to embarrass the Kingdom by acting in strange ways that are not our own. Represent us truthfully and well."

"Of course, my Lady." Replied Sir Jon, though he could not believe how much the hand washing thing had affected her.

"Sir Jon." Said Sir Bendris. "You will speak for us, but I am in charge of this expedition. I expect us to work together as well and in the same way we worked together on our last mission. Do I have your agreement on that?"

"You do indeed, Sir Bendris." Replied Sir Jon. "I have much to learn and you have already taught me much. I would not feel as good about our mission if you were not going along."

Sir Bendris seemed satisfied with the answer while Father Leonis smiled and said: "THAT, Sir Jon, is an example of why you have the court's confidence. You REALLY have a gift for saying the right thing."

Everyone around the table smiled, with the exception of the Queen. The rest of the meal continued in somewhat serious conversation on what might be encountered in the Kell lands. The King was in a good mood and occasionally made comments that seemed to be intended to tease his mother. Her mood did not improve as the meal progressed.

When the meal was finished the Queen spoke to her son. "Wulf, I would like to help you prepare for bed." She said. "May I escort you to your room?"

"Of course, Mama." Replied the King although he felt the request showed that she still saw him as her little boy. "Sir Jon, please come see me in about an hour."

Once again the Queen gave Jon a harsh look. Then the two of them left the room.

Father Leonis came over to Jon. "I think you have a problem that may be more difficult to handle than the Kells." He said. "I do not think you have done anything wrong, but you had better watch yourself around the Queen."

"What have I done to displease her?" Asked Jon in alarm.

Father Leonis put a hand on Jon's shoulder and said: "It will work itself out."

As he left both Brother Johan and Sir Bendris also gave Jon a pat on the back and smiled as they left. The proceedings made Jon very nervous.

As Jon prepared to leave he spotted Rufus supervising the cleanup from dinner.

"Rufus, what have I done to displease the Queen?" Asked Jon in a pleading voice.

Rufus eyed Jon warily. "Sir Jon, it is not our duty to intervene in relationships between nobility." He said. "With your leave, however, I will say this to you man to man: None of us know you very well and you have come very far very fast. Clearly you have the King's favor. Treat the King well and you will gain the trust of all of us who watch out for him."

"Thank you, Rufus." Replied Jon. "That is three times today that you have done me great service. I truly hope that I can earn your friendship and return the favor."

Rufus smiled and resumed his duty as Jon returned to his room.

Jimmy was there as Jon walked in. "Hello Jon." He said. "Did you have a good day?"

Jon shrugged in response. "I guess so." He replied.

"Well, I am meeting Johan and Leonis." Said Jimmy. "This is probably our last evening together for a while."

"Enjoy yourself." Replied Jon. "I'll see you tonight."

Jon set an hour glass and watched the sand fall. Having little else to do he took out the piece of paper where Johan had written the Bible verses. He hoped that he valued his relationship with God as much as the verses described, but he had his doubts. When the hour glass was more than half empty he decided to go to the King's chambers. The Queen was leaving as he arrived.

"My Lady." Jon said in awkward greeting.

The Queen eyed him warily. "Sir Jon, mind yourself around my son." She said. "You have already encouraged him to sneak off on secret rides and have taught him strange new habits. I do not approve. You will be held responsible if something goes wrong."

Jon did not know how to respond so he simply lowered his head as she huffily walked out of the room. He knocked on the door and the King welcomed him in.

"Jon! How was your day?" Said the King as he entered.

"It was alright." Said Jon. "I seem to have angered your mother, how was your day?"

"Don't worry about Mama." Said the King. "She just wants to keep me as her little boy and she blames you for my growing up. My day was busy. There is a lot riding on your mission, but I know I can count on you."

"I will do my best." Said Jon.

"So, about this morning," said Wulf, "I'm a little embarrassed, but I do miss my dad."

"I understand, Wulf." Said Jon. "When my father died I was totally lost. I don't know if you know this, but he was the royal executioner. With a job like that we didn't have many friends. I lost my dad, and pretty much my only friend. I didn't know where I was going to go or what I was going to do. Life as I knew it was gone. My guess is you feel a bit like that; like the life you knew is gone."

"Yes, that's sort of how I feel." Said Wulf. "But I know where I am going to live. I AM the King. I still have my mother. I guess what I am angry about is that God allowed this to happen, and that nobody but you and Sir Malpolem fought for my dad. It's like God himself decided to take him from me."

"Wow." Said Jon. "That really is different than me. I lost my mother when I was little. My father executed lots of people's fathers. I look around and I see people dying everywhere. I guess I never thought to ask God why; it just seems to be the way the world is."

"That's not the way the world should be." Said Wulf. "God should be in control. God shouldn't have let a dragon kill my dad!" Wulf was getting REALLY angry.

"I don't have a good answer for you Wulf." Said Jon calmly. "I know that God has been good to me, but my life has had pain as well. I believe that God loves me, but you're right, I am not sure why God allows these terrible things to happen. I think it is a fair question to ask Him."

"I'm too angry to pray now." Said Wulf.

"Indulge me Wulf." Said Jon. "I guess I don't know why, but I think that these are the type of heartfelt questions God wants us to ask him. Now that you have brought it up, I want an answer as well. Let me pray for both of us."

"I'll try." Said Wulf with moisture in his eyes.

Jon took a moment to compose himself and then made the sign of the cross. Wulf followed suit, and Jon began to pray:

> "Father in heaven, you have blessed us, but right now it does not seem enough. We are sad Father. We both want to understand why you allowed our earthly fathers to die. Why do so many fathers and mothers die? Why do so many innocent children die? You can stop it God, why don't you?!"

Jon was getting quite worked up, so he took a moment to collect his thoughts.

"God, I have felt your love. I have seen the beauty of your creation, and I appreciate and value it. It is treasure to me. Why do we also have sadness? You are great and powerful, God, make the world work your way. Help Wulf and me understand. It's not that we don't love or appreciate you, it's just that we don't understand. Jesus, if you are really in my heart, help me! Amen, Father, amen."

Jon looked at Wulf. The King looked back. His eyes were moist but he was not crying. He began to nod his head. "Yes, Jon." He said. "That is my prayer."

Suddenly Jon wondered if Lil ever had thoughts like this. Lil lost her father to the King's justice and her mother to sickness. Was Lil angry?

"You know Wulf, I wonder what Lil would say about all of this. She has lost as much or more than we have. I wonder if she is angry." He said.

"I want to ask her." Said Wulf. "I'm going to ask Father Leonis during lessons tomorrow as well. I need to know why."

Jon nodded in response. "Good night my Lord." He said.

"Good night, Jon." Came the reply. "I appreciate your friendship more than your service. Maybe I will be able to pray tomorrow morning. Please come by."

"I will Wulf." Said Jon. "Until then."

Jon was deep in thought as he went back to his room. He lit a candle and noticed that there was a bowl of water on a small table near the wardrobe. He washed his face and laid down. His mind was racing, but the only real thought that he had was "why?" He laid there restlessly with a question, but no answers came to him. "I wonder what Lil would say?" He thought.

27

The Journey Begins

J ON DID NOT SLEEP WELL that night. If anything his dreams were
even worse. It seemed like the face kept asking: "Why did I have
to die? Why did you kill me?" As much as Jon did not have
an answer for his and the King's questions, he also did not have an
answer for the dead Wulf Schumacher's question. He did know that
it was not God who had killed Wulf Schumacher; he had done that
himself. Could God have stopped him from doing his duty? God is
all powerful; He could do anything.

Jimmy was still asleep when Jon got up and lit a candle. He
walked to the bowl of water and washed himself. That made him feel
a little better, and a little more awake.

He wondered why God had allowed him to kill the Schumacher
boy. While it was true that he had not asked Jesus into his life at that
point, God seemed to already be guiding him in other ways, like in
what he said at times. Couldn't God have protected him from his
own sinful ways? An answer came to him: if God simply stopped
him every time he decided to do something wrong, he would lose all

freedom to be himself and would not even be capable of choosing to have a relationship with God. In order for Jon to make the choice to be good, he had to have the ability to choose to be bad. People had the ability to choose good or evil, if they didn't, they would not be able to come to God of their own volition. God wants people to make the choice to have a relationship with Him; He does not force Himself on others.

This did not answer the entire question that Jon and the King had regarding why bad things happened to innocent people, but it was a step in that direction. He was suddenly eager to share what he knew with the King.

Jon put on his new clothes and boots. He did not have a mirror, so he could not see himself, but he knew that these were the finest clothes that he had ever had, and it gave him a certain pride to wear them. He walked a bit taller as he went to the King.

A servant showed him into the King's room where Wulf was getting dressed.

"Good morning, Jon." Said the King. "Did you sleep well?"

"I really didn't." Replied Jon. "I was bothered by our questions from last night. I think I have a part of an answer, but not the whole answer."

"Great!" Said Wulf as the servant finished buttoning his shirt. "Father Leonis stopped by after you left last night, and he asked to join us this morning. He wants to help us get an answer. I hope you don't mind him joining us for prayers."

"Not at all!" Replied Jon. "We need all the help we can get!"

The King had just finished getting dressed when Father Leonis came into the room. "Good morning, your Highness, Sir Jon." He said.

"Good morning, Father." They both said in unison.

"Sir Jon, Wulf invited me to join you for prayers because I think the questions you are asking are very important and difficult." Said the priest. "I am tempted to simply give you answers that have been passed on to me, but I also feel that it is important for a believer to struggle with these questions. My goal is to help the two of you work through this on your own. As such, I prefer that I not lead this prayer meeting, although I hope that you Majesty and I will continue to pray in Jon's absence."

Jon nodded as Wulf responded: "Thank you Father! Let's begin by setting a rule during this time. I am Wulf, he is Jon; you may be Father Leonis if you like, but I feel a need to be just another of God's children when I come to Him in prayer at this time."

"That is excellent, Wulf!" Replied the priest. "During this time you may both address me as Leo. Wulf, you make me a proud teacher when you say something like that. Some men never learn to come before God in humility."

Wulf and Leo both looked to Jon.

"Well, I was telling Wulf that the question of why God had allowed his father to die made me restless all night." Said Jon. "I don't think I have a full answer, but I did come to this realization: if God stopped us or did not allow us to sin, we would have no choice in what we do. If we don't have any choice in going to God, then we really can't accept him by choice. I think God wants us to want Him of our own choice; He wants us to want to have a relationship with Him. If we can't be bad, then we really can't be good either."

Father Leonis looked eager to speak, but he held back and looked at Wulf instead.

"I guess I never thought of that." Said Wulf. "It sort of explains why there are bad people around, but it doesn't explain why people die of illnesses or why my father was killed by a dragon."

"What do you think of that?" Asked the priest looking at Jon.

"I totally agree!" Said Jon. "It does not explain the main question we are asking, but it changes how I look at it. We all try very hard to be good, and I think we are most of the time. But I know that I have done things that were not good; things that I am ashamed of. Now that I have a relationship with God through Jesus, I wonder if God will ever get so tired of me that he will decide I am not worth the trouble."

Wulf looked shocked at this pronouncement. "Are you saying that maybe God got tired of my father?" He said. "Are you saying my father deserved to die?"

Jon had not looked at it that way and was equally shocked by the questions that he had been asked.

"OK, let me take a stab at this." Said Leo. "I don't think that was what you were saying, was it Jon?" Jon shook his head in reply. "St. Paul wrote that we have all sinned and fall short of the glory of God. That is why we need a savior. That is why Jesus came: because we all deserve death for our sin. Yet Jesus told a parable of the wheat and the weeds. In it He said that God does not pull out the weeds lest He also pull out some wheat. What He meant was that God wants to give everyone a chance to come to Him, and I think that is what Jon was saying."

"Yes, exactly!" Exclaimed Jon.

"So, we all deserve death for our sinfulness, but God wants us to live with Him." Continued Leo. "Yet there is still sickness, and pain, and war, and even the King's justice which may sometimes fall on the innocent. Is God the source of it?"

Leo looked at Wulf, but the King did not have an answer, so he turned to look at Jon.

"I guess that is the other part I am saying." Said Jon. "Not all of that is caused by us, but a lot of it is because we can all be greedy and vengeful; not care about what is really right or wrong, but rather care about what it is that we want. Mankind causes a lot of its own misery; then when we don't want to take responsibility for it, we blame God."

The King was thoughtful, but silent. Father Leonis was smiling in approval.

"Wulf," he said, "why is it cold some times?"

Wulf had a puzzled look, but replied: "I guess because there is no heat."

"Good." Continued the priest. "And Jon, why does it get dark?"

"Because there is no light?" Replied the young knight.

"So, both of you, why is there evil?" Asked Leo.

Jon and Wulf looked at each other. "Because there is no good?" asked the King puzzled.

"Well, right, or at least very close." Replied the priest. "Jon, do you want to give it a try?"

Jon thought it over for a moment. "Because God is not there!" He exclaimed. "We also sin when we forget about God. But are you saying that bad things never happen to those who are with God?"

"No." Said the priest smiling. "I am not saying that. But St. Paul also said that all things work for good for those who are called according to God's purpose. He doesn't say all things are good, merely that God can use bad things for good. Wulf, I don't think we are telling you why God allowed your father to die, but your father's death served a purpose. And I pray every day that your father is now happily in God's presence, but…"

Father Leonis could not finish the sentence. He wanted to say that some good was already coming from Wulf's father's death, but that would not sound right. The death was a tragedy, but Wulf was acknowledging God because of it. Still, Father Leonis did not feel that he knew God's will to the point that he could speak for God in this instance.

"But what?" Demanded the King.

"But I think you are called according to His purposes." Said the priest. "I think that God can use this for good in your life. I am not saying that it was good that your father died; I have faith that God did not want your father to die any more than He wanted Christ to die, but their sacrifices can be used for good. Use it for good, Wulf."

Wulf just looked at Leo. He wasn't angry or confused, but he did not quite know what to make of what had been said.

"The world is a broken place." Continued the priest. "We do not live in the Garden of Eden. God promises that He will fix it eventually, but if He suddenly decided to wipe out evil, I really worry about which side I would be on. I have sin in my life, just like Jon has. I am sure that you do as well, Wulf. We need a savior in order to relate with God. Thank you Jesus."

The three of them sat in silence for a moment until Jon said: "I don't think God has answered our question yet, but I think it is starting to get answered. Let's keep asking, Wulf. Let's pray, and let's ask."

"Why don't you start, Jon." Said the priest. "I'll finish, and Wulf you join in after Jon if you'd like."

The three made the sign of the cross and bowed their heads. Jon took a moment before he began:

"Father, thank you for wanting to have a relationship with me; a sinner. God, I try hard to be good, but so often it just does not end up good. Help me, us, to keep our eyes on you. Be our light so we don't walk in darkness, be our heat so we do not become cold, be with us, God, so we can know that there still is good in the world; because You are here. God, I believe in You. More than that, I have faith in you; but I don't understand. Help me understand why people get sick and die; help us understand why Wulf's father died. Thank you Jesus. Amen."

There was a long moment of silence before Wulf prayed: "God, I am a King, and I want my will to be done, but You are a greater King and yet Your will often does not seem to get done. Help me to remember that if I expect people to follow MY will, then I need to follow YOURS. I try, but I know that I don't always. Thank you that I have forgiveness because of Your son Jesus. Help me to be as patient with others. I pray God, that papa is with you. I pray that he is happy, and that You will make good come from his death. Help mama too. And be with Lil, and with Jon on his journey. And be with me. Amen."

Father Leonis was taken by the depth of the King's prayer. His student was suddenly a different person. He began his prayer: "Father in heaven, there is no name greater than yours. You are the source of all that is good and the bringer of joy to the sad and peace to the restless. Thank you, God, for having mercy on a sinner like me. Thank you for allowing a weed like me to be turned into wheat. Guide us all, Father, I pray in Jesus' name. Amen."

"Amen." Repeated the other two.

Father Leonis put his arm around Wulf. "I am only your teacher." He said. "But I am so proud of how you prayed. You prayed like a Godly King. God IS calling you to His purpose. You will find an answer."

Wulf looked at Leo and smiled.

"I'm hungry!" Said Jon.

They all chuckled and went off to breakfast.

Breakfast was sort of light hearted, but there was an extraordinary politeness about it. The King offered his mother food before he took some, and he thanked the servants. The queen was quite startled by this as she felt that it was less than regal behavior, but she decided to let it pass.

Afterwards, Father Leonis and the King escorted Jon to the stable. Sir Bendris had seen to it that Thunder had been saddled and was rather impatient when Jon finally appeared.

"Good morning your highness, Father Leonis." He said in greeting. "Sir Jon, we have been waiting on you."

Before Jon could answer the King replied: "Forgive me, Sir Bendris." He said. "We had great need of Sir Jon and detained him."

Sir Bendris gave Jon an annoyed look, but said: "Of course, your Majesty. We are now ready to leave if it pleases you."

"By all means, Sir Bendris." Replied the King. "Sir Jon, represent our King and this Kingdom well."

"I will do my best, my Lord." Replied Sir Jon.

Sir Bendris noted that the King had told Jon to represent 'their' King rather than himself. This disturbed him. Who was this other King?

The party was quite impressive to the eye. While the wagons were rather plain, every soldier, ten in all, was dressed in a uniform. They were not as well dressed as Sir Jon and Sir Bendris, but they certainly did not look like some sort of rag tag outfit. Jimmy wore rather plain clothes and rode in one of the wagons, while Brother Johan wore a newer cassock and rode in the other. Slowly the caravan made its way through town and onto the west road that went towards the Kell lands. Sir Bendris and Sir Jon rode in the lead, while Sir Bendris' squire, Wil rode in the back watching the soldiers march beside the wagons. All but Jimmy and Brother Johan were well armed.

Progress was very slow on the dirt roads. The two knights rode in silence until they were a bit out of town.

"It seems you have made quite an impression on the King, Sir Jon." Said the Captain of the Guard.

"He has been very good to me and given me more than I ever thought I would have." Replied Sir Jon. "If I can truly be his friend as well, then at least I can repay him in a small way."

Sir Bendris did not immediately respond. "The safety of the King is my responsibility." He finally said. "I hope that you are as sincere as you seem to be, but I have seen men turned by greed and opportunity. The King is young. I like you, Sir Jon, but I am also watching you."

Jon did not really know how to respond. He trusted Sir Bendris, and there was not really an accusation behind what he had said, but it seemed somehow threatening.

"Thank you, Sir Bendris." Jon eventually replied. "I value your counsel and hope you will tell me if you think I am doing wrong. I can assure you that I do not mean the King harm, and that my feelings are more driven by gratitude than ambition."

Sir Bendris gave Jon a surprised look. He shook his head and said: "You will be a fine ambassador. You somehow always know just what to say." His normally serious face broke into a smile and he clapped Jon on the shoulder.

Jon felt better about the brief conversation, but the older knight's reference to greed reminded Jon of the bag of money he had found and kept. While Jon was not overtly greedy, greed was not a stranger to him either. He determined that he needed to talk to Brother Johan as soon as he could.

After several hours the caravan was beyond Duke Heimsteady's estate and the road had become little more than a path. Progress slowed even more. As they came to a place where there were some rocks, Sir Bendris called a halt for food and rest. Jon determined that his opportunity had come.

"Brother Johan, may I have a word with you in private?" Said Jon nervously but with determination.

"Of course, Sir Jon." Replied the monk, excusing himself from Jimmy's company.

Jon did not really know how to begin the conversation.

"Um, I wanted to thank you for giving me the scripture that you wrote out for your brother." He said.

The placid monk smiled at Sir Jon and said: "You are most welcome. I am flattered that you had such a fond attachment to him."

"Well, there is something else." Continued Jon, but the monk just smiled in return. "I sort of have a confession to make."

"I am not a priest Sir Jon." Replied Johan. "Perhaps you can confess to Father Leonis when we return."

"No, Brother Johan." Said Jon in confusion. "I have sinned against you. I need your forgiveness, and I want to make it right."

The monks smile faded into a look of puzzlement. He could not imagine what Jon could have done to him.

"You see, when I found the paper, that wasn't all I found." Said Jon. "There was a bag of money as well. A lot of money. I guess I just couldn't bear to part with it yesterday, but I am sure it is yours as your brother's heir."

"Really?" Replied Johan. "I am sure the temptation was great, and you have my forgiveness. The truth is that I have learned in my travels that it is easier to not have a lot of money; it keeps your reliance on God. Nevertheless, perhaps you can help me decide what we should do with it once we return. Jon, I have been tempted as well; you did the right thing. Forgive yourself."

"Thank you, Brother." Said Jon. "Listen, there is a loose floor board under the main bed in my chamber. Beneath the board is your bag of money, and my purse with two silver pieces in it. If something happens, take your money and give mine to Boady and Lil, OK?"

The monk eyed Jon with a concerned expression. "Why the morbid thoughts, Jon?" He said purposely dropping the knightly 'Sir'. "We will come out of this fine and we can get the money together."

"I don't know." Replied the knight. "I guess I am just realizing how much I am in God's hands, and if He decides that I won't see tomorrow, then I won't see tomorrow."

The monk gave Jon a soft smile. "That is not a bad way to live your life, Jon." He said. "But know this: God has plans for you; you have work to do. If God were to call you to Him tomorrow you would be in heaven, because you wear Jesus' righteousness. Death would not be sad or scary. But don't be looking to die; serve God with your life. Living your life for God is often harder than dying for Him. In the book of Jeremiah, it says: 'For I know the plans I have for you, declares the Lord, plans for welfare and not for evil, to give you a future and a hope. Then you will call upon me and come and pray to me, and I will hear you. You will seek and find me when you pray to me with all your heart.'" (Jer 29:11-13)

As Jon walked away to eat with Sir Bendris and Will he reflected on the strange conversation that he and Brother Johan had just had. Jon did not approach the monk with morbid thoughts about dying; he merely wanted to tell him about the money. Nevertheless, there was wisdom in what Brother Johan had said.

Soon enough, Sir Bendris got the wagons and men on the move. The journey was painfully slow as the terrain got rougher, so they had only made it to the western boarder of the Kingdom when they called a halt and set up camp for the night. They would be in the Kell lands the next day.

28

Too Good to Believe

J ON JOINED BROTHER JOHAN AND Jimmy for prayers both
that evening and the following morning. While Jon liked and
respected both men, these prayers did not have the same sense of
comradery that his prayers with the King had. Even his own prayers
had a certain formality to them. Nevertheless, God had granted Jon
a good night's sleep; the answer to his personal prayer just before he
closed his eyes.

He did not have to ask Sir Bendris for a chance to wash in the
morning as Sir Bendris made the entire party wash up and neaten
their clothes as best they could. This group was intended to make an
impression, and Sir Bendris' usual commitment to his duty insured
that everything that could help with that was done.

Once inside the Kell lands the party was able to see the people
running away as they approached. Who could blame them? While
the party was dressed to make an impression on the Kell court, it was
armed well enough that an unarmed populous would want to avoid
them. Eventually it was decided that Jimmy should walk a good dis-

tance ahead of the group and call out to the people in their own language promising them food.

Soon enough there were many nervous visitors who were stunned that these foreigners would offer them food for what they saw as no reason. Jimmy did his best to assure them that they were acting on God's behalf but, this sort of generosity towards starving people who had traditionally been enemies and did not acknowledge God, was hard to comprehend. While most were extremely grateful for the food, the people were VERY suspicious.

The second wagon became lighter as they progressed. The people that they met were starving, with many of the children having bloated bellies. Jon's heart went out to them: "Why God? Why do these children have to suffer?" He had an answer to this question; this was a famine that was caused by men. Still, it pained him to witness it.

At one-point Jimmy came running back to the caravan. "There is a party from King Arwel's court that wishes to speak with the leaders." He announced. "They come bearing a branch to signify their peaceful intentions, but they are armed and outnumber us."

It was not an unexpected development, but it still needed to be handled correctly. These people had been enemies for a long time and it was just as likely that they intended to steal the gifts as accept them.

"Tell them that Sir Jon and I will meet two or three of their leaders half way between our two groups." Said Sir Bendris. "You will join us to interpret."

As Jimmy jogged back towards the Kell force, Sir Bendris gave Will instructions: "If they attack, be ready to burn the wagons and make them pay dearly as you retreat. Put our archers on top of the wagons and shoot at anyone armed who approaches unless they are accompanied by us."

Will acknowledge the orders and began to implement them. The force was prepared to fight desperately if need be.

"Well, Sir Jon," said the Captain, "this is what we came here for. Let's ride a bit out front and wait for Jimmy. We will stay on our horses throughout. If it is an ambush, at least we can try to get away."

This was indeed the moment that they had been waiting for, but Jon had never considered that they would be met as anything but friends. The preparations that were being made impressed him with how serious this task was; suddenly he realized that the fears he had expressed to Brother Johan the day before were actually valid. "Help us to go with You, God." He prayed silently.

Soon enough Jimmy rejoined them and the three of them moved forward to a party of three Kells. All three were on foot, but were fierce looking warriors. Jon recognized that Kyp, the Kell he had met in the preserve, was one of them. This made him feel a little better.

"Tell the red bearded one, Kyp, that it is good to see him again." Sir Jon said to Jimmy.

Jimmy looked up at him puzzled. "You know Kyp? He speaks Saxon." He said.

Kyp began to laugh. "Yes, Jon, I speak your language." He said. "Perhaps not as well as my own, but better than you did the last time we met!"

Jon let a sheepish smile cross his face while Sir Bendris looked on perplexed.

"Why have you come?" Demanded Kyp, the smile vanishing from his face.

Jon immediately got serious. "I bring a letter from our King, Aerdwulf von Mersya, to your leader, Arwel. We also bring a gift of a wagon of food for Arwel." He replied.

"Our 'leader' is also a King. You will refer to him as such." Replied Kyp. "Why do you give our people food as you come?"

"We come in hopes that we can depart as friends. King Aerdwulf wants to make this evident to all." Said Jon. "Also, having a desperate and starving rabble on our border can only lead to trouble."

This last part was not something Jon had planned to say; it had come out without a thought. This also gave him confidence that God was guiding his words.

Kyp turned to his fellow warriors and gave them a synopsis of what had been said. He then turned back to Jon. "It is difficult to believe that you allowed a young boy to make such an odd decision.

It is also difficult to believe that your leader would send YOU to speak for him."

Jon did not know what to say. Perhaps it was difficult to believe, but it was true.

"You may believe what you wish." Said Sir Bendris. "I lead this expedition while Sir Jon speaks for the King. We have no obligation to explain ourselves to you. We have done nothing that you could interpret as hostile since we arrived. We offer your King a gift. If he does not want it, we will leave. If you wish to fight us, you may win the battle, but you will lose the war you will have chosen to begin."

Jon nodded in approval of what Sir Bendris had said. Kyp turned to those with him and there were confused murmurs.

"Why do you suddenly want peace with us?" Asked Kyp.

Jon was about to answer when Sir Bendris cut him off with a motion from his hand. "We have come to speak with your King. We are not a large enough force to threaten you. Will you take us to him or not?" He said.

Kyp was not pleased by the answer, but he respected it. He turned to his companions and spoke with them again.

"What are they saying?" Whispered Jon to Jimmy.

"They are discussing whether they should allow you to continue." He whispered back.

"We will place a party of men before you and behind you, but allow some space between. You will follow us to King Arwel's court. You will not distribute any more food to the people." Said Kyp.

Jon looked at Sir Bendris and whispered: "I don't have a problem with that."

Sir Bendris thought for a moment before answering. "It sounds reasonable." He said. "But tell them we will give food to anyone who approaches us but we will not call people to us. We do not have to be too agreeable, and I doubt that anyone will approach."

"The second wagon is a gift to the people." Announced Sir Jon. "Our King wishes that they get it. We will not call to them, but if they approach us we will give them food."

"Nobody will approach you. Why make this more difficult Sir Jon?" Said Kyp with calm disappointment.

Jon calmed his voice as well. "If nobody approaches you will basically have what you want." He replied. "We are not here to take orders from you; simply to offer you peace and food."

Kyp did not consult the others with him. "Very well." He said. "Goronwye will lead ten men behind you while Ioerwurth and I will lead the bulk of our men in front. Gornwye and his men will pass near you as they go behind you, but they will not come too close to your party or the wagons."

"That is acceptable." Replied Sir Bendris.

As Kyp turned to leave Jon called to him: "Kyp, we could give you some food from the second wagon if you like."

Sir Bendris was not pleased by the suggestion but said nothing.

"Let me speak with my companions." Said Kyp.

Kyp spoke to them in Welsh and at first one of them became quite upset.

"They don't want you to give food to the people." Whispered Jimmy.

Then they calmed down and began to show signs of approval.

"We will trust you, Sir Jon." Said Kyp turning towards him. "We will send ten men, unarmed, to take the food. Let us pause for a mid-day meal. I will return to you alone when it becomes time for Gornwye and his men to take up position in the rear. I am putting my life and the lives of our men in your hands because of our previous encounter; you have earned a degree of trust."

"It is agreed." Said Sir Jon.

Thunder began to turn around on his own and Sir Bendris had to act quickly to keep up. They slowly rode back to the wagons.

"Why did you offer them food?" Asked Sir Bendris quietly.

"I'm not sure." Replied Sir Jon. "I think their men are hungry, and perhaps they would be driven to attack because of it. I'm not sure why I did it, but I feel good about it."

"You did well, Sir Jon." Said the Captain. "I don't agree with all of it, but you handled it well. Suddenly walking away was a brilliant sign of our dominance."

Jon chuckled. "I think Thunder decided that!" He said. "Thanks for speaking up when Kyp challenged me. We make a good team, I think."

Sir Bendris merely grunted in reply.

While the three men that Sir Jon and Sir Bendris had met with looked like fierce warriors, the men who came for the food were thin and clearly hungry. All of them ate as they loaded their satchels, and they ate with intent and desperation. Surprisingly they emptied most of the second wagon, filling their arms as well as their satchels. They smiled and nodded as they headed back.

"I begin to think we could win an easy victory over this foe." Commented Sir Bendris.

"That's not why we are here." Snapped Sir Jon with more vehemence than he intended.

Seeing the sad shape of the Kell army made the men feel less uneasy about their situation, but Sir Jon realized just how valuable the gift that they were bringing was. It was really pretty amazing that they hadn't been attacked by the starving people of this land.

As the Saxons began their meal, peasants began to appear looking for food.

"The Kell soldiers told them to come." Said Jimmy after speaking with one that he apparently knew. "They won't share the food that we have given them, but they told the people they had little to fear from us."

Jon had been hungry in his life, but never this hungry. He found it difficult to eat much himself while orphaned children with bloated bellies approached looking for food. The second wagon was soon empty, and people stopped coming after a few had been turned away. Jon was tempted to give some of King Arwel's food away, but that was not what he was supposed to do. Duty is not always pleasant or easy. He began to regret that he had fed the soldiers. "Why God? Why?" He prayed silently, but he knew the answer. This was not God's intent or doing.

Eventually, Kyp came walking up towards the wagons. Jon went out to meet him.

"Gornwye is gathering his men and will be passing by soon." Said Kyp. "I do not expect any trouble as they have just eaten. What made you offer us the food?"

"I don't honestly know." Replied Jon. "It seemed like a good idea at the time."

"By now you know that we have a lean and hungry army." Replied Kyp. "You did the right thing. I am not sure that we could have controlled them if you had not. Why would you be kind to your enemies?"

Jon was tempted to reply as Sir Bendris had in the earlier meeting, but this was not a formal conversation. "Our God is a God of peace more than a God of war." He replied. "Our King wishes to serve God. Not everyone agrees, but there is a chance for us to live side by side in peace; at least for a while."

Kyp looked deeply into Jon's eyes. "You're sincere." He said. "It's not what we would do."

Jon shrugged. "Our God says that we should 'do unto others as you would have them do unto you.'" He replied. "We have faith in our God. We will give His way a chance."

Kyp looked down and shook his head. "It is all rather amazing." He said. "Too good to believe in fact. We are taught that you cannot trust things that are too good to believe. I respect you, Jon, and I sense you have a good heart; It will be interesting to see how you stand up to King Arwel."

"Thanks Kyp." Replied Jon. "If I am with our God, it will be more interesting to see how your King stands up to me."

Kyp smiled and turned to leave. Before he had gone far he turned and said: "You're the first Saxon I was ever glad to meet. When we first met I looked forward to fighting you, but now I am less certain." He then resumed walking back to his forces.

Gorwye and his force of men walked by within sight, but not too close. Some of his men smiled and winked stealthily as they passed. They did not appear to be in a fighting mood.

Jon was relieved, but Sir Bendris was on guard. "This is going too well to believe." He said. "And if something is too good to believe…"

"You shouldn't trust it." Said Jon finishing the sentence. "Kyp just told me the same thing."

Even though one of the wagons was empty, progress was slow over the rough terrain. They were escorted onto a road that was more like a path, which helped, but not a lot. It took most of two hours before they saw their destination.

The 'King's' court was at a sort of village settlement that looked a bit like Duke Heimsteady's estate. It was surrounded by a lower earthen wall and there were three long buildings. The party was led through a gate that spanned a break in the wall. The people inside looked almost as desperate as the ones that they had met along the way. They stared with greedy eyes as the wagon proceeded into the compound.

As they came to a halt, a well fed, indeed rotund, man came out of one of the long buildings and began to yell at Kyp.

"That's King Arwel." Said Jimmy walking up to Sir Jon's horse. "He is asking Kyp why he did not kill us and take the food. He does not want more mouths to feed."

Kyp spoke to Arwel in a hushed tone that could not be heard. Their King scowled in response and motioned that the men on the horses should come into his house.

Jon began to understand what Kyp had been trying to say to him.

29

Princess Anwen

A S THE TWO KNIGHTS DISMOUNTED, Sir Jon pointed to Jimmy to indicate he should accompany them into the King's house. Seeing this, Arwel immediately objected.

"King Arwel says that only you two are invited." Said Kyp.

"Then tell King Arwel that we decline his invitation." Replied Sir Jon. "Jimmy will be our interpreter."

Kyp explained to the King who shrugged in response and continued into the long house. Inside it was dark, with a dirt floor, and the air was fetid. It was not a Kingly abode. Arwel sat himself in the only chair and said something to Kyp.

"Our King wishes to know what you want." Said Kyp.

"Tell him we bring a letter from our King to him." Replied Jon. "We come in peace."

Kyp spoke to the King, who was about to respond when a clamor arose outside. Arwel got up unceremoniously and went back outside as the Saxon party followed.

Will and the armed guard were fending off hungry people, including some soldiers, but were being aided by the men who had escorted them to this place. Arwel bellowed a command and everyone stopped. He said some more and the people backed away from the wagons.

"The King said that if anyone touches his food they will be immediately put to death." Whispered Jimmy.

Arwel turned around and rudely busted through the group of people at the door as he went to retake his seat. Everyone reassembled as before. He then told Kyp to take the letter. Kyp apparently explained that he could not read it which elicited a scowl and more words.

"Our King askes that Jimmy read him the letter." Said Kyp.

Jon handed the letter to Jimmy who proceeded to interpret it as best he could:

Aerdwulf, King of Mersya, greets you in friendship.

We have been informed that your people are suffering for lack of food due to an attack by others. Our trusted advisors have witnessed the devastation themselves. While we could use this opportunity to bring you further harm, we have determined that peace between us would be better, and have sent you a wagon of food as a sign of our good will. Our ambassadors, Sir Bendris, and Sir Jon, can speak on our behalf. We hope that our gift is helpful in your battles with the enemy, and that it can serve as a basis for peace between our Kingdoms for a long time.

We also will allow your people to hunt in our preserve for this year as they are in hardship. Please know that several of our people have died as the result of a dragon that is sometimes found there.

We look forward to hearing from you that our feelings are mutual.

Arwel continued to scowl as he listened, and then paused before responding. The other Kells present in the room murmured enthusiastically in reaction to what they had heard. As Arwel noticed this he said something and the other Kells, excepting two guards and Kyp left the room. As this was happening, the King spoke to Kyp.

When the room had largely emptied, Kyp said: "Our King asks why?"

"We wish you well." Replied Sir Jon. "We feel it would be best for all of us if we live in peace."

This was duly interpreted and Arwel responded.

"We believe that you are afraid of us. He is tempted to kill all of you and attack your Kingdom immediately." Said Kyp.

Sir Bendris tensed noticeably. He was clearly getting angry. Jon looked at him and smiled.

Turning back to the King, Jon drew his sword and immediately threw it at the Kings feet. "Tell him to go ahead." He said with a bold calmness. "We will die, but he will lose his Kingdom, and likely his life as a result. We have seen the state of this land and your army. We could crush you at will with only a small portion of our army. If he wants another war to fight, killing us would be a good way to start one. We grow tired of his rude ways."

Kyp looked shocked, as did Jimmy and Sir Bendris. Arwel apparently asked Kyp what had been said, a look of concern on his face. Kyp dutifully relayed what Jon had said, but Jimmy noted that he left off the part about Arwel's rudeness.

Arwel glared at Jon. Then, suddenly he began to laugh. He got up from his chair and said something directly to Jon. Kyp was about to interpret when Jimmy cut him off.

"He says he likes you." Said the monk in astonishment. "He wishes that his men were as willing to die for him. He wants you to leave the wagon and set up a camp outside the compound and you and Sir Bendris may join him for a dinner tonight."

"Tell him that you will join us as interpreter." Said Jon with a scowl still set on his face. "Tell him that he may unload the wagon, but that it is not a gift and we will be taking it with us when we depart." Jon looked to Sir Bendris who nodded in approval.

Jimmy relayed the information and Arwel smiled and waved them off. Jon did not need an interpreter. He picked up his sword and turned to leave. Kyp followed. Once outside Sir Jon gave Will an order:

"Unhitch the horses from the King's wagon and lead them and the other wagon out of this compound. We don't need them to decide to eat them. Then find a spot where we can make camp." He said this so forcefully that it was hard to believe that the words were actually coming from him.

Will looked to Sir Bendris who nodded in approval.

Kyp tapped Sir Jon on the shoulder. "You did well." He said. "I think he really did want to kill you. Perhaps your God was with you."

Jon looked at Kyp and grunted in reply. "How can you serve him?" He said.

Kyp shrugged indicating that he did not know what to say and turned away. "Duty is not always easy or pleasant." He said over his shoulder.

Camp was set at a pleasant spot along a stream near the compound. In fact, almost any spot was more pleasant than where these people kept court. Sir Bendris busily set up watches and gave instruction for the camp's security. None of them felt safe staying here.

"How did things go?" Asked Brother Johan as he walked up to Jon and Jimmy.

"You won't be staying here." Replied Jon. "Their leader is not a King; he is a brute and a bully. We demean ourselves by dealing with him."

Johan looked at Jimmy who merely shrugged.

"What's next?" Asked Brother Johan.

"Sir Bendris, Jimmy, and I go to a dinner tonight." Said Jon. "God, I hope it isn't in his fetid, stinking house. I wonder if this wasn't a mistake. Maybe we should conquer this place. At least the children might get food then."

"Jon, I think we should pray." Said Brother Johan.

Jimmy grabbed Jon by the arm and the two older men led him out of the camp to a quiet spot near another part of the stream.

"Listen, Jon." Said Brother Johan. "Nothing worth having is ever easy."

"I question whether this is worth having." Said Jon in reply.

Johan grabbed Jon by the shoulders. "Jon, listen to me!" He said. "You have been given a very important task. None of us can afford to have you act like a boy right now. You speak for the King. If this duty is difficult, you need to figure out how to accomplish it. There is no time to feel sorry for yourself."

Jon sighed.

"Perhaps I should have warned you Jon." Said Jimmy softly. "But you handled him far better than anyone I have ever seen or heard of. Most people cringe before him. You showed him you weren't afraid. How did you ever find the courage to say what you said?"

Jon looked up at Jimmy. "I don't know." He replied. "Kyp said he thought my God might have been with me. I guess He was."

"Then we should give thanks." Said Brother Johan. "And you should understand that your King IS with you as long as you are doing His will. God sent you here for a reason. Serve Him."

Without making the sign of the cross, Jimmy began to pray:

> "My God! You are an awesome God! You feed the hungry and humble the proud. You give us strength when we don't even realize how much we need it. Thank you God for delivering us and giving Jon the words that he needed to say. Guide us, Father, in your will. Help us to feel and rejoice in Your presence."

Jimmy fell silent, but Johan began:

> "Lord Jesus, thank you for being in Jon's heart. Help him to remember that he is never alone. Help him to remember as St. Paul said that 'when we are weak, then we are strong' because our reliance is on You."

Johan seemed to want to say more, but he fell silent. After a pause, Jon began to speak:

"Yes, Lord, calm me. Help me to remember that You are my hope and salvation; not me. Guide me Father. Keep me focused on Your will."

Jon stopped and Brother Johan began to make the sign of the cross. Jimmy and Jon followed suit.

"Are you alright Jon?" Asked Brother Johan.

"I think so." He replied. "I thank both of you. Why is it often so hard to pray from the heart when things are going well, yet easy when we are in need?"

Both of the older men smiled. "You are growing in Christ, little brother." Said Jimmy.

It was a fair evening as Kyp came to get the two knights and Jimmy.

"Will we be eating outside?" Asked Jon as they began to walk back to the compound.

"I'm afraid not." Replied Kyp. "Arwel is having a hard time holding on to his food. If he had a feast outside there might be a riot."

"You're being awfully blunt." Commented Jon.

"You can see for yourself that we are not in good shape." Came the reply. "I think you've already won the hearts of the people, if not the King. Seriously, why are you doing this?"

Jon paused before answering. "The King and I prayed about it. He felt this was the right thing to do." He said. "I think the council went along because we prefer you fight these other Kells than have us do it."

"You're rather blunt yourself." Replied Kyp. "I appreciate your honesty. This God you worship is an odd fellow."

Jon shrugged as they walked into the long house. The smell of cooked food could be discerned, but it was overwhelmed by the stink of the place. Jon basically lost his appetite. Arwel was seated in his chair and was being served by two young and filthy girls. They looked hungry. Kyp guided the guests to a spot on the floor near Arwel's chair.

Other girls came and offered food. There was meat that seemed to be rabbit, some potatoes, and very few vegetables. Mead, a sort of beer/wine made from honey was served in large drinking vessels. One girl tried to put the food in Jon's mouth, but Jon held up his hand. On a whim he ripped a piece of meat off of the plate that the girl held and held it up to her lips. She looked startled, but Jon smiled and she ate it. The other girls looked at her in envy.

Arwel suddenly seemed angry and said something to Kyp.

"Our King asks that you not feed his women." Said Kyp.

Jon gave Arwel a disdainful look and shook his head. This did not improve the King's mood.

"Behave yourself." Said Sir Bendris sternly.

Suddenly the sound of music was heard. As the tune began to develop, several people began to clap along. A dancer appeared and began to dance. Unlike those around her, this young woman was clean, and had an easy and unforced smile. She was perhaps fourteen or fifteen years old, but moved with an almost super-natural confidence and ease. Jon was mesmerized by her. She seemed the loveliest thing that he had ever seen.

The girl looked at Jon several times while she danced, and when she finished she looked directly at him and gave him what seemed to be a special smile. "Did she just wink at me?" Jon asked himself. Suddenly the affair did not seem as dismal.

Jon stood and applauded. He noted that he was the only person who did so, but he did not care. He nodded in approval as he sat back down to drink some more mead. Perhaps unwisely he avoided eating more food.

"Who is she?" Jon asked Kyp.

"That is the King's daughter, Anwen." Replied Kyp. "She has already caused us one war, guard against her starting another. Keep in mind whose daughter she is."

Jon looked at the girl and then her father. He was frankly astounded that they could even be related, but as more mead was poured into his vessel, the girl grew more real to him and King Aerdwulf and his mission began to shrink into a more shadow like realm.

The dinner went on, and somehow Anwen's presence made Jon forget about how disappointed he was about having to attend it. At one-point people started dancing with each other and she came up to Jon and pulled him into the dance. While he did not exactly dance well, he enjoyed himself immensely. He thought it was a shame that that they did not speak the same language, but he felt that he read her thoughts well enough. Jon had found an object he felt was worthy of his desire. She was a treasure that he would be willing to sell every-thing for. While he refused to call Arwel a King, somehow Anwen was clearly a princess in his mind.

Kyp escorted Jon to Arwel after the dance.

"Our King wishes to know what this talk of a dragon is all about." Said Kyp. "We do not believe in dragons."

"Tell him that whether he believes or not does not matter." Replied Jon. "What matters is whether there is or is not a dragon in the preserve."

After Kyp told this to Arwel the King laughed. Jon felt good about his answer, perhaps helped by generous servings of mead, which seemed to be the one thing that was in plentiful supply in this Kingdom. He was slightly off balance as he stood.

The hour became late and it was time to leave. Arwel called Jon and Sir Bendris to his chair.

"The King says that he will grant you the peace you have asked him for." Said Kyp.

Jon's head was dizzy from the mead, and while he wanted to impress Anwen's father, this 'granting of peace' struck him as wrong. "Tell him we are pleased to live in peace with our neighbors," said Jon, "but tell him we do not need his offer. It is we who are telling him that we do not intend to attack. We wish him luck against his real enemies."

Kyp did not want to interpret this, but Jon urged him on. When the King heard what Jon had said he laughed and said something back to Kyp, who looked relieved.

"The King says that you have spunk, Sir Jon." Said Kyp. "He looks forward to killing you when all of this is over. It is a compliment."

Jon looked at the King and winked. It was probably the alcohol that he had consumed that made him do it, but it clearly unsettled Arwel. Kyp took Jon and the other Saxons and led them outside.

"That was probably unwise." He said. "You may not respect our King, but he is a dangerous man."

Jon smiled at Kyp in return. "Please tell Princess Anwen that I will see her again." He said.

Kyp looked at Sir Bendris who took Jon and led him back to the encampment and his bed. Jon took a deep breath as he lay down. The stars seemed to be spinning over his head.

"Lord, give her to me." He prayed; then he passed out into a deep and dreamless sleep.

30

Jon Finds a Priceless Pearl

J ON DID NOT WAKE UP early the next morning, and when he awoke he did not feel like moving. His head hurt and his stomach was queasy. The camp was a hive of activity as the men prepared to head back home. Jon knew he needed to eat something, even if he did not feel like it, and he also knew that he needed to saddle Thunder. He stumbled down to the stream to try to wash up, but once there he dunked his whole head in and drank deeply. The cool water was a shock, but it made him feel a bit better.

"Good morning, Jon." Said Brother Johan. "I brought you some bread to eat."

Jon looked up at the monk, his hair dripping, his fine shirt rumpled and wet. "Thank you." He said. "I don't feel well."

Brother Johan squatted down and gave Jon the bread. "I take it you have not drunk mead before?" he said.

Jon slowly shook his head no.

"You will feel better soon," Said Johan, "But you probably won't feel good again until tomorrow. Try to drink a lot of water."

Jon reached into the stream and cupped some water in his hand. "I need to saddle my horse." He said after drinking.

"You need to make a good impression on King Arwel before we leave." Said Johan. "I will see to your horse. Eat some more bread, and try to neaten up."

"Thanks." Said Jon meekly as Johan began to walk away.

Jon got up slowly and began to follow Johan. He had his second best shirt in his saddle bag, along with some food that they had all packed for the ride home. While Johan had not said anything that could be interpreted as accusatory or critical, Jon felt like he had let him, and everyone else, down. He hoped that he had not made too much a fool of himself the night before. Then he remembered Anwen. He really did not care too much what the King of this poor excuse for a Kingdom thought of him, but he wanted to impress Anwen, and maybe her father. Jon was inspired to do his best.

The thought of seeing Anwen, even if only to say goodbye, gave him energy and determination. He forced himself to walk straighter and committed himself to look his confident best. He decided to ignore how badly he felt.

Brother Johan was putting the saddle on Thunder, helped by one of the soldiers. Jon got his shirt out of the saddle bag and ate a bit of bread as he changed.

"You look better already!" Said the Monk.

"I have an impression to make." Replied Jon.

"Make your King proud." Said Johan.

Jon went off in search of Sir Bendris. He found him talking to Jimmy. The party was set to go, but the other wagon had to be retrieved and goodbyes had to be said.

"You look better than I thought you would." Said Sir Bendris as he walked up. "A bit red eyed, but you're walking steady enough."

"Thank you." Replied Jon. "Did I do anything too bad last night?"

Sir Bendris and Jimmy looked at each other before the knight replied: "You got a bit surly." He said. "But Jimmy thinks it may actually work towards our good. Arwel is not used to people who look him in the eye without fear. I'm glad we are not leaving Brother Johan here; I am not sure what he can accomplish. Jimmy is determined to stay."

"This is where the Lord has called me to serve." Said Jimmy. "I've enjoyed my time away, but the Lord can help me make a difference here. I think the food we brought has helped in my task."

Jon nodded slowly and smiled meekly. "I'll miss you Jimmy." He said. "I wish you well and look forward to seeing you again. What do we need to do now?" He said looking at Sir Bendris.

"The three of us go and say our good byes and arrange to get the wagon." Came the reply.

As they walked through the camp towards Arwel's compound Jon saw some of the soldiers giving their personal rations to children who were begging around camp. It made him feel proud to be a Mersyan. He determined to imitate them when the party left.

In the compound, things were only just beginning to get moving. Jimmy asked to see Arwel, but the King was still asleep, so he asked about Kyp who was brought to them.

"Good morning!" Said Kyp in a loud and cheerful voice, looking at Jon.

Jon looked as bright as he could and responded in a like manner. "Isn't it a lovely morning!" He said smiling brightly and looking Kyp in the eyes.

"Still, you look a little red eyed." Said Kyp with a grin.

"Perhaps," countered Jon, "But you look a little red-eyed yourself, and I am awake and in a good mood."

Kyp looked down and shook his head. "Ah, to be young again." He said looking at Sir Bendris.

"Can we take the wagon and prepare to leave?" Asked Sir Bendris.

"I think so." Said Kyp. "But you will need to say good bye to our King."

"Then we'll get it hitched up and back to our camp." Said Sir Bendris. "We'll be back."

As he turned to leave Jon stood still while Jimmy moved to follow. "Are you coming, Sir Jon?" Asked the Captain of the Guard.

"I think I will stay and speak with Kyp a bit more." Said Sir Jon.

"Why don't you stay with him." Said Sir Bendris to Jimmy.

As Sir Bendris walked away Kyp looked at Jon.

"Um, I was wondering if you might aid me in having a conversation with the Lady Anwen." Said Jon.

Kyp looked disappointed. "Sir Jon, I like you." He said. "You have courage, a good heart, and a mostly sharp mind. Yesterday I would have said you were very smart, but this question shows that you are just as stupid as any man. Anwen is a lovely girl, but if you want to be smart you will put her out of your mind. She's trouble. She flirts with any man who visits her father; not just you. That's how we got into the fight we're in. The outside is pretty, but the inside, her heart, is black as coal and as cold as ice. Let her be."

Jon could not imagine that anything God had made so lovely could be bad. He felt that he had discerned her soul just by looking at her. Kyp had to be wrong; if she was rough in some way, it was only because she was forced to live in this rough environment. Jon could rescue her from that. Love conquers all, and if he loved her enough her coal heart would sparkle like a diamond. She would be the jewel of his life; his priceless pearl.

"Jon, Anwen is trouble." Said Jimmy to give support to what Kyp had said. "You can't get to know her if you can't speak to her, and you are leaving shortly any ways. You're young; God willing there will be one that will complete you as a man and as a Christian."

Jon liked and respected both Jimmy and Kyp, but what they were saying was making him angry. How could they know what God had put in his heart? Anwen could complete him, and he could lead her to Christ. Why were they being like this? Were they jealous? In his heart he knew that was not the case, but his desire for her led him to any excuse that could justify his pursuit. He must have that priceless pearl.

"I can promise you both that I do not intend to propose marriage." Said Jon. "She is part of this Kingdom's royal family and as ambassador I feel it is my duty to foster a relationship between her and our people. I do not think I am making an unreasonable request."

Jimmy and Kyp looked at each other. "Wait here." Said Kyp. "I'll see if I can get her."

Kyp hoped that Anwen would refuse the invitation. He was heartened when he found her just waking up and looking somewhat rough.

"Tell him that I will be there shortly." She said when asked.

Kyp walked back feeling silly that he was playing messenger for two teenagers. "Duty is not always pleasant." He thought.

"She says that she will be here shortly." Said Kyp returning to the two waiting Saxons.

The meaning of 'shortly' was stretched as the men waited close to half an hour. By the time Anwen appeared the wagon had been hitched and removed and Sir Bendris was on his way back to the compound. To Jon, the wait was worth it.

When she appeared her hair was brushed and her clothes were neat if not particularly fine. Her eyes sparkled as a result of having spent much of the night dancing rather than drinking. Her genuinely good looks were even more remarkable when set against the dirty and disorganized background of the compound that she lived in.

"Greetings." She said with a smile as Kyp interpreted.

Jon felt justified in his desire. She was remarkable! "Princess Anwen, I wanted to personally tell you how much I enjoyed your dancing last night, and thank you for inviting me to join you." Said Jon. "It was the highlight of my evening."

In Kyp's interpretation this came across as: "He says he likes the way you dance."

Anwen knew that he had to have said more, and the silly smile on Jon's face told her that it had been complimentary.

"You dance almost as well as a Kell." She replied. "I hope our Kingdoms will have a long friendship and that we can see each other again."

Kyp interpreted this as: "She says you're a good dancer too, and she hopes our Kingdoms can be friends."

Jon was thrilled to know that she thought he was a good dancer; he ignored the rest of it. Falling on one knee he grabbed her hand and kissed it. "Until we meet again!" he said.

This was interpreted as: "Good bye."

Anwen rewarded Jon with a bright smile, but she began to laugh to herself as she turned away. Jon stood in awe as she walked away.

Jimmy wanted to laugh at Jon's behavior and at the sparse interpretations that Kyp was providing, but mostly he felt relief that he had not needed to interpret.

Sir Bendris walked up as Jon was rising from his knee and Anwen was walking away. He gave Jimmy a brief look, but only got a shrug in return. "We are ready to depart as soon as we can see King Arwel." He said to Kyp.

"I will see if he is ready." Said Kyp as he went back into the long house. When he came back he was escorted by a young man who somehow seemed familiar to Jon.

"This is Crown Prince Rhys." Said Kyp. "King Arwel has sent him to dispense with the formalities. Sir Jon, you may remember Prince Rhys from our earlier encounter."

The fact that the King was unwilling to say goodbye to the delegation could be interpreted as rude and insulting, but nobody was really looking forward to seeing him again. Everyone, with the possible exception of Jon, was eager to get on their way.

"My father thanks you for your visit." Said Rhys in very broken Saxon. He then turned to Kyp and said something in his native language.

"The King invites you to return, and would welcome more gifts of food." Said Kyp obviously interpreting.

"We have enjoyed our visit and hope it will begin a long friendship between our two peoples." Replied Sir Jon. "If you, the King or anyone else from the court should like to visit our King, you will be assured of a welcome."

Kyp looked to Jimmy to interpret this, and he did. The two Kells stood looking at the three Saxons while nobody knew what to do next. Finally, Sir Jon extended his hand towards Rhys who accepted the hand shake and the two knights turned to walk away while Jimmy shouted a "Fare Well!" after them. As the party began their departure with 5 men riding in each wagon, Jon heard Sir Bendris mutter under his breath: "A man does well to leave a turd behind him." All except Jon were glad to be leaving.

There were beggars along the path most of the way out of the Kell lands, but Jon did not notice them. His mind was on Anwen. He imagined that she must love him as much as he loved her, and pictured the two of them living on an estate, raising children, and generally enjoying the good life that they could give to each other. Jon had not prayed the entire day, and now he was looking to Anwen for his joy, but the wrongness of this approach did not even occur to him.

The party made it into Saxon land as the Sun began to set. Sir Bendris called a halt and camp was set up. Everyone but Jon was short on rations, so he distractedly shared what he had with his fellow travelers. Fortunately, the archers were able to kill a deer before it got too late and the party enjoyed the comradery of an ample meal. Jon was present, but he was not really a part of it.

As he sat lost in his own thoughts, he contrived a plan. He would return to the castle, make his report, and then, after gathering his money and belongings, ride back to the Kell lands. He could help Jimmy in his mission and win Anwen as God intended him to. In fact, Brother Johan really did not want his brother's money, so he could take that as well and have plenty. He could pursue happiness and win a good life. Just as the Bible said, he would sell everything he had to obtain his priceless pearl. It did not make sense, but love rarely does; the fact that the Kingdom of Heaven was hardly in his dream escaped him.

As things wound down for the night, Brother Johan approached Jon. "You haven't been yourself today." He said. "Are you still feeling sick?"

"I'm fine." Jon replied. "I guess I am just thinking about the future."

"God has plans for you." Said Brother Johan putting a hand on Jon's shoulder. "His plans are bigger than anything you can imagine."

"I don't know." Said Jon smiling. "I have a pretty big imagination!"

Johan returned the smile. "I bet you do." He said. "But you are not God. I've found it is better to let Him imagine your future. Have you prayed today?"

It was then that Jon realized that he had not. "Of course." He replied defensively.

"Would you like to join me for evening prayers?" Asked Johan sensing that Jon had not answered truthfully.

"Sure." Said Jon as non-chelantly as he could. As they walked away a thought came to his mind. "Brother Johan, does God ever answer our prayers?"

Johan stopped and looked at Jon in surprise. "Hasn't he ever answered yours?" He asked.

"Well, yes." Replied Jon feeling silly. "But I have never asked for anything just for me, I think. I've asked Him to guide me and such, but I never asked Him to make me a knight, or to give me a horse or clothes. Does he ever answer prayers like that?"

Johan paused before answering. "I think God answers all prayers." He said. "In the Holy land the Arabs imagine a creature called a Djini. When one finds one it is obligated to grant whatever the person wishes. I do not think God is a Djini. He grants what He wills and answers 'no' to that which is not in His will. Most of the Arab stories about the Djini end with people ruining their lives with what they ask. I think it is truly a blessing that God does not grant us everything that we ask for, but yes, God answers our prayers. You've experienced that yourself. Do you trust God?"

"God has been good to me." Replied Jon. "I don't know why, but he has." Jon felt like he should say more, but he really had nothing more to say. He did trust God. He wanted to be a Godly man.

"Let's pray, Jon." Said Brother Johan making the sign of the cross as Jon imitated him. "Father, you are so good to us. You give us blessings we do not ask for and spare us from the desires of our own corrupt hearts. Help us to grow in Your will. Forgive us, Lord Jesus.

We are sheep, easily led astray. Guide us Good Shepard. Help us to recognize the difference between Your will and our own. Let Your will be the priceless pearl for which we surrender all."

Jon was overcome with grief and a tear formed in his eye. Johan's prayer had spoken directly to his true heart. He was so ready to abandon the truly priceless pearl. "Forgive me Lord." He said almost sobbing. "My eyes have wandered far from You. Help me Jesus. If it is in your will, grant me my heart's desire, but if it is not, remove that desire from my heart. It is difficult for me to ask that, God, because I really want it, but let me want You more."

Johan had a suspicion that he knew what Jon was talking about and was pleased and relieved by the prayer Jon had spoken. Silently he begged God to grant Jon peace in His will. "Thank you Jesus." He said and made the sign of the cross.

"Are you OK little brother?" Said Johan once again putting a hand on Jon's shoulder.

"I think so." Replied Jon. "Thank you. Thank you for reminding me of who I am. And thank you for not telling me that I am wrong; for letting me figure it out."

Johan smiled and they returned to camp.

As Jon lay down to sleep he tried to dream of an idyllic life with Anwen, but it just did not come as vividly as it had all day. He did not sleep well because his pleasant dream was replaced by the familiar face asking him "why?"

31

Perception

T HE FOLLOWING MORNING WAS UNEVENTFUL, except that Jon awoke with a heavy heart. He had enjoyed dreaming about the life that he and Anwen could have lived; now his life seemed mundane and boring. He was an executioner's son who had risen to be, first a page, and then a knight and confidant of the King, but his life seemed boring. Anyone could see that this perception of his life was very different than the reality of his life, but to him, perception had become reality.

Sir Bendris led the group into town and to the castle stable early in the afternoon. Brother Johan and Jon went to the kitchen to eat a mid-day meal before making a report to Father Leonis and the King along with Sir Bendris.

"You seem tired Jon." Said Brother Johan as they walked. "Didn't you sleep well?"

"No, not really." Replied the young knight. "I don't know. I just don't feel happy today. I just don't feel excited about my life."

Brother Johan stopped and looked Jon in his eyes. "That's an amazing statement." He said. "I wonder where you are looking to find excitement."

"OK, let me explain it to you." Said Jon, his broken heart wanting sympathy. "Until we spoke last night I was imagining a wonderful life, with a loving woman, and a peaceful home to live in. It was an impractical and unrealistic dream about a woman I hardly know, but it was a beautiful dream. That dream is gone now, and the world does not seem as hopeful as it was before."

"Oh, Jon." Said the monk in the sympathetic tone Jon had been hoping for. "Your dream is not dead. You can still have a wonderful life, and a loving woman, but you need to wait until your time comes. God probably wants that for you, but you need it in His time to fully appreciate it. You need to find joy in Him before you can really appreciate his creation."

"It's my life." Said Jon. "Don't I have to find a way to be happy?"

"Boy, that's an old question." Said Johan. "How much of your life have you been responsible for so far? Did you choose your parents? Would you have chosen the parents that you got? Did you earn becoming a page for my brother, or a knight in the King's court? Did you scheme your way into the friendships that you have?"

"I loved my parents." Said Jon defensively. "I served your brother well. I never asked for a knighthood, but I am doing my best to be worthy of it..."

"So might it be fair to say that you are making the most of the opportunities for happiness that you have been given?" Asked Johan cutting Jon short. "Jon, even the King did not get to choose to be the King. There's only so much that we can control, but God controls everything. You do make choices, but God gives you the opportunities. It's when we confuse our own will with God's that we become dissatisfied."

"So, what am I responsible for?" Asked Jon.

"You need to trust God." Replied Johan. "You need to make good choices with the opportunities you are presented with. Ideally, you look to God in everything you do."

Jon nodded in response. "That's not easy." He said.

"Only Jesus ever did it perfectly." Replied Johan. "In the book of Proverbs it says: 'The mind of man plans his way, but the Lord directs his steps.' (Prov.16:09). It is OK to have dreams and goals, Jon, but let them be Godly dreams and goals. Let God guide your steps. Don't let pleasant dreams make you sad about your life."

Jon saw the sense in what Brother Johan was saying, but he wanted what he wanted; it was not going to be easy to put what God wanted first.

After a quick meal, the two men headed to the council chamber where they met Sir Bendris just entering. The King and Father Leonis were having a discussion of their own as they entered.

"Welcome back, gentlemen!" Said Father Leonis as they came into the room. "We are eager to hear what you have to report, and curious as to Brother Johan's presence, despite our joy at seeing him."

The King sat with an expectant smile as Sir Bendris began the report. "Our journey was largely without incident." He said. "The Kell people are starving and we made a good impression on them by distributing the food in the second wagon."

"That is good to hear." Replied the priest. "Sir Jon, how were your dealings with their King?"

"Their King is hardly worthy of that title." Said Sir Jon in a focused but tired voice. "He is more the chieftain of a gang. He is a brute who has little care for his people and seems to be used to threatening them with harsh punishments or even death in order to enforce his authority. At the outset he felt that we were giving him tribute and wanted him to grant us peace. I insisted the reverse was true and hope that he got the message."

The King and Father Leonis reacted to these words with puzzlement. "So, are you confident that we are at peace with these Kells?" Asked the King.

"I am confident that they do not pose a threat to us." Replied Sir Jon. "Perhaps Sir Bendris would give a better answer."

"I agree with Sir Jon." Said Sir Bendris. "They do not pose a threat to us, but I would not want to be in a position where we had to rely on or trust King Arwel. They are weak and we could conquer them almost as easily as Duke Coberg said we could, so we are not currently in any danger, but Arwel is not somebody I would want either as a friend or an enemy."

The King and Father Leonis looked at each other. It was clear that they had expected different news. Finally, Father Leonis spoke: "Did the visit accomplish anything? Should we muster the peasant leavies and our army for an attack?"

The two knights looked at each other and were uncertain of how to respond. Brother Johan broke the silence: "I am not sure why we should want to attack." He said. "Their population is starving. Their lands do not look like they were particularly good before they were raided, and they have an angry enemy who is forcing them to fight for their existence. I feel good about what we have done, but I think it is best that we stay out of their trouble to the degree that we can."

"And do you gentlemen agree with what Brother Johan has said?" Asked Father Leonis.

"Yes." Replied Sir Bendris succinctly.

"I do." Said Sir Jon. "I think their populous is relieved that they do not have to fear us and grateful that we fed them. I suspect that if things get worse they may even flee to us. I do not believe that we should set ourselves up as their best hope. My prayer is that Jimmy can bring them hope and accomplish something."

"So, if Jimmy is theirs and our best hope for accomplishing something, why isn't Brother Johan staying to help?" Asked the King. "Couldn't you accomplish in their court what Jimmy is accomplishing among their people?"

The three men looked at each other not really knowing what to say. Finally, Jon replied: "Arwel greeted every courtesy we extended to him as a concession or sign of weakness on our part." He said. "He would have seen Brother Johan as a spy and possibly tried to leverage him being there against us. I did not see what he could accomplish. I never discussed it with either of you, but I sensed that you agree."

"I agree fully." Said Sir Bendris. "We should not dignify their so called King with our ambassador."

"I was bit torn." Said Brother Johan. "There was part of me that wanted to accomplish great things, but I was not eager to stay.

I never really met Arwel, but what I saw of his rule disgusted me. I was glad Sir Jon made the decision that he did and did not feel the need to argue it."

Father Leonis looked to the King who shrugged.

"What do we do now?" Asked the priest.

Jon looked to Sir Bendris who gave an answer: "We leave them alone and watch them as best we can." He said. "I am a military man, not a diplomat, but I think we did accomplish some good among their people. They will not be eager to fight us."

Sir Jon felt compelled to add something: "The food that we gave to Arwel may well have been wasted, so if we feel compelled to do anything, I think that we should feed their people. It might even send a message to Arwel that we are strong."

Sir Bendris shrugged. "It might," he said, "but I don't see why we should antagonize him either."

"We have much to think about." Said Father Leonis.

"Gentlemen, we thank you for your service." Said the King. "You all look tired; especially you Sir Jon. Take this opportunity to get some rest. We invite all of you to join us for our evening meal, and look forward to evening prayers with Sir Jon."

The King said all of this in a very regal way. "Thank you, your Majesty." Replied all three men and they proceeded to back out of the door leaving the priest and the King behind.

"This was my first big thing that I tried to do in my reign, but my emissaries do not seem enthused with what they accomplished." Said Aerdwulf after they departed.

"Peace is usually better than war, but it is certainly less exciting." Replied Leonis. "You have prevented a war, and nothing they said makes that seem wrong, but from most perspectives it is hard to consider it an accomplishment. Jesus said 'Blessed are the peace makers,' but he never said that they get victory parades."

"I guess." Replied the King.

Jon asked Brother Johan to accompany him back to his room. When they got there he retrieved the bag of money that he had found and presented it to the monk.

"There's no rush in giving this to me." Said the monk barely looking at what he had been given.

"I find it a hard temptation to bear." Replied Jon. "I want to get rid of it before I become too attached."

"And so the temptation passes to me." Said the monk with little enthusiasm. "At least help me to figure out what I can do with it."

"Finding it was a curse to me because I knew that it really wasn't mine." Said Jon. "But it really is yours. You can take it with a clear conscience. Let it bless you. Get a horse if you have need of it, or some clothes. Buy a book if you can find one. It's a lot of money; you can make your life better with it."

"My life is fine." Said Johan almost sadly. "The Lord has blessed me. Having a degree of wealth is a burden and a responsibility that I fear will bring me more misery than joy. I find that we are often more owned by our things than owners of them."

"I suppose you could give it to poor people or to the church." Said Jon. "Even in a summer of plentiful harvests there are many needy people about."

"Indeed." Said Johan. "Maybe I can get it to Jimmy and he can use it for the Lord's work. I just wonder if having money wouldn't put him in danger."

"It almost sounds like you are as eager to pass on the temptation as I was." Said Jon. "I'm sorry Johan. Hey, you know what might really help Jimmy?"

The monk looked at Jon with expectation. "A Bible!" He said. "Or at least a good bit of scripture. Then he could start a church of sorts. Or at least spread the Gospel from the word of God."

"Exactly what occurred to me!" Exclaimed Jon. "Where do we get one?"

"I guess I can go to the Abbey and see if they have one that they can sell." Said Johan. "Or I can commission one, but that would take a long time. Let's see how much money we have."

Johan spilled the contents of the bag on the small table that Jon had in his room. The gold piece stood out, and there were five silver pieces and a dozen coppers.

"That's a lot of money." Said Johan. "I can see why you were tempted. It will be hard to spend. I don't think it is enough for a whole Bible, but we can get most of one; maybe the Gospels and the Mosaic books. Maybe even some Psalms. We'll have to see what we can find. Want to go with me to the Abbey?"

"Sure." Said Jon.

"Good." Said brother Johan. "Because it would be difficult for me to spend this on my own."

"We'll support each other." Said Jon not knowing what the monk was trying to say.

"Well, in one sense I will need to support you." Said the monk. "You see, while you say the money is mine, in another way it is not. It is mine by right of inheritance, but I took a vow of poverty when I became a monk. Now maybe I am living up to my vow by buying something for the Lord's work with Jimmy, but the Abbey may see it as I am spending THEIR money. Between us, let's consider it God's money, but you will have to spend it. I will assist you in spending it wisely."

Jon was shocked by the revelation. Was Johan sinning by spending money that he had rightly attained? Did his vow of poverty mean that he owed anything he got to the church?

"Well, are you violating your vows?" Asked Jon. "It seems that giving the money to the Abbey would relieve both of us of the temptation."

"Have you ever heard Jesus' parable of the talents?" Asked Johan and Jon shook his head. "Three men were given different amounts of money called talents by their master who was going away for a while. The first got five, the second got two, and the third got one. The first traded with his money and doubled it to ten talents. The second invested and doubled his money as well. The third buried his money to keep it safe. When the master came back he went to the three men to settle accounts. The first two men were rewarded for what they had accomplished with what they were given. The master said that since they were trustworthy with small things they would be given larger things. The third explained that he knew the master was a hard man and 'reaped where he hadn't sown' so he hid the money in order to return to him. The master was very angry and called him a lazy man. He took away the money, gave it to the first man, and cast the servant out. I did not take a vow to give anything I got exclusively to my order. God has entrusted me, us, with this money; we need to use it wisely. I feel like simply dumping it into the Abbey treasury would be the same as burying it. I feel that giving Jimmy some holy writings would be investing it." (Matt. 25:14-30)

"Well, did you tell them that whatever money you got was their money?" Asked Jon.

"No, that was not part of the vow." Replied Johan. "Who would have ever thought I would get that kind of money? But I gave them all of my possessions when I joined, so they may see it as a right to keep anything now. Look, Jon, let's just do it this way; it will save everyone some trouble. You know, the Bible says you should never swear by anything as you have no control of anything. Learn from my mistake and be careful when you make promises." (Matt. 5:33-37)

"I don't have a problem in helping you." Said Jon. "You're not breaking your vow as I see it. You still won't own anything. I guess I just don't see what the problem is."

"The problem is that what I think I promised may not be the same thing as what THEY think I promised." Replied Johan. "It is a matter of perception. If you spend the money the question does not get asked."

"Fair enough." Responded the young knight. "Shall we go today?"

"Let's pray about it and go tomorrow." Replied Johan. "Shall we pray now?"

"Is there ever a bad time?" Replied Jon with a smile.

They both made the sign of the cross and Johan began the prayer:

> "Father in Heaven, great is your name." He began, "You bless us in the most unexpected ways. Help us to live up to the responsibilities that you entrust us with. 'To whom much is given, much is expected.' (Luke 12:48) Help us to understand what is expected.

Guide us in the work you have set out for us. Forgive us when we are wrong. Let Your Spirit fall down upon us Father. I pray in the Holy name of Jesus. Amen."

"Father, forgive me." Said Jon. "I am weak and easily distracted. Help me to keep my eyes focused on You. Give me Your perception so that I may see reality and choose wisely. Thank you Lord Jesus. Amen."

Johan gathered up the money and handed the bag back to Jon. "You keep it until we go." He said. "You've let go of it once, it won't be as hard next time."

Jon smiled and place the bag back under the floor board. "I'll see you at supper." He said.

32

Who is in Control

AFTER JON AND BROTHER JOHAN had parted ways, Jon laid on the main bed to get some rest. He slept a bit, but mainly he thought of the challenges he had been through the last couple of days. While he was determined to do things the right way, it was so easy to get distracted from God's way. First there was the money, then Anwen and his dreams of what he saw as a better life; he had simply set God aside when he really needed Him most. He came to understand that it is easiest to trust God when you are in deep trouble and do not know what to do, but harder to trust Him when things are seemingly going well. "It's when I think I'm in control that I forget about God." He thought.

At last he got up and went to his bowl of water to wash. The coolness helped him feel more awake and fresh. He smoothed his hair as best he could and went to the council chamber for supper.

"Good evening, Sir Jon." Said Rufus as Jon entered the council chamber. "Welcome back. I am sure you will enjoy supper more than the meals you have been having; we're having pheasant tonight."

"Thank you Rufus." Replied Jon. "It is good to be back. The hunger in the Kell lands is amazing to behold. Thank God we have enough to eat."

Rufus smiled in response as Jon took his seat and waited. It was not long before Brother Johan and Father Leonis joined him.

"Hello, Sir Jon." Said the priest. "Did you get some rest?"

"A bit, Father Leonis." Said Jon. "I had a lot on my mind."

"Well, perhaps the embassy did not go as well as you had hoped, but you accomplished what you set out to do." Said Father Leonis. "Even if you do not come back covered in glory, at least we have a reasonable assurance of peace."

"Thank you, Father." Replied Jon realizing that the priest had misread what had occupied his mind.

The King, Queen, and Sir Bendris all arrived together and took their seats. The King immediately went to the bowl of water and washed himself while his mother looked on with annoyed bemusement. When they were all seated the King nodded towards Father Leonis.

"Would you mind saying grace tonight, Sir Jon?" He asked. "The King and I have missed your company at evening prayers and are eager to hear you."

Jon was surprised and annoyed. There were two clergymen at the table and yet he had to lead the prayer? As soon as he thought this he realized that it was a poor and selfish attitude to take. He began to make the sign of the cross and the others followed.

"Bless us Lord, and these gifts of abundance." Prayed Jon aloud. "Help us to remember that we depend on You and that even the air that we breath is a gift to be appreciated. Keep us from temptation and self-reliance, but rather help us to remember You in all that we do. Thank you Jesus for your guidance. Amen."

"Amen." Replied the supper guests and all made the sign of the cross again.

The King and Father Leonis smiled at Jon when he had finished, but the Queen seemed somewhat surprised. "Did you just pray that we be less self-reliant?" She asked. "My boy, it is only through the efforts of self-reliant men, like my late husband, that this Kingdom came into being."

Jon was puzzled by the Queen's insistence that anything he did had to be wrong in some way, but he felt obligated to respond. "I was merely stressing our reliance on God, my Lady." He said. "We mortals certainly have to do our part, but it is important to recognize our reliance on God for our success."

"Sounds like an excuse for not taking responsibility to me." Replied the Queen. "If our late King had simply said 'it's God's will' every time he faced a challenge there would not have been a Kingdom for Wulf to rule. 'God helps those who help themselves.'"

Jon was getting angry. This was not at all what he was saying! He also knew that 'God helps those who help themselves' was from pagan mythology, and not the Bible. He took a moment to collect himself.

"Are you ignoring me, or merely at a loss for words?" Said the Queen. "It is not like you to not have a response ready."

"My Lady, I fear you did not understand my prayer." Said Jon looking up and right at her. "If we do not act as God wants us to act we will pay a penalty. I was merely expressing my humility before God and my desire to be on His side, rather than have Him on mine. I do not shirk a challenge, but I also have learned that things do not go well if I leave God out of what I do."

"Well, you do not seem very humble to me, young man." Said the Queen huffily.

Jon was speechless. The other men around the table were understandably reluctant to come to his aid against the Queen. Wulf, however, had heard enough.

"Mother!" He said. "Sir Jon has been polite, and there was nothing wrong with his prayer. He is MY guest at this meal and as a Knight of the Realm he deserves courtesy."

"Listen to you, my child." Said the Queen almost shrieking. "Whenever he comes around you become a disrespectful little boy. Perhaps you should choose your friends more wisely. Father Leonis, did you hear what your student said to his mother?"

"My Lady…" Began Father Leonis. "Humility before God is a worthwhile goal. It is written that 'God is opposed to the proud, but gives grace to the humble.' (James 4:6) Jon said a nice prayer. Nevertheless, Aerdwulf, though you are now King, you have been your mother's son since birth. You owe her respect. 'Honor your father and your mother' is one of the ten commandments."

Father Leonis had hoped that he had given each of them a bit of what they wanted, but instead he managed to disappoint both the King and his mother.

"Sir Bendris," Interjected Brother Johan trying to change the subject. "Have you thought of anything we should do about our neighbors, the Kells?"

"Well," Replied Sir Bendris quickly, "We have already opened the preserve in order to help them help themselves. Perhaps we can distribute some bread to them as well. It will only make them feel better about us and will keep desperate people from coming to us to steal food."

"An interesting thought." Said Father Leonis. "What do you think Sir… uh, Brother Johan?" The priest had decided to leave Jon out of the discussion as much as he could for fear of inciting the Queen.

"As we camped in their lands, and as we journeyed back home, our men gave of their own rations to feed the hungry." Said the Monk. "It gave me pride to see it; they were feeding 'the least of His brothers.' I think our men saw our former enemies as real people. It could help us both to be kind."

"Well, I can see where my son gets his odd ideas." Said the Queen. "We cannot take responsibility for these people. It will only make them dependent on us. They need to pull themselves up and get themselves out of the trouble that they're in. We have given them an offer of peace; doing more would simply rob them of the opportunity to accomplish something on their own. I think we have done quite enough, if not too much, already."

While the others all looked down, the King was flabbergasted. How could he 'honor' his mother when she had said something so contrary to his own Christian values? These people were not starving because they were unwilling to care for themselves. He began to wish that they would eat the meal in silence.

"Well, we don't have to decide anything right now." He said refusing to give in to the urge to argue. "The pheasant looks excellent. Let's enjoy our meal."

Jon was quite hungry as he had not eaten very much over the past few days, but this conversation had taken away some of his appetite. He too wanted to argue with the Queen, but something held him back. The rest of the meal passed mainly in silence except for a few compliments for the food.

"That was an excellent supper." Said the King rising from the table. "Rufus, please send our compliments to the cook. Sir Jon, and Father Leonis, I would be pleased to see both of you in my chambers in a few moments."

Jon and Leonis gave each other a glance as the King left. 'Good nights' were said and the two proceeded towards their meeting with the King. As they walked, Father Leonis felt the need to say something.

"Jon, you did the best you could." He said. "I am not sure what the Queen has against you."

"It wasn't by my power that I held my tongue!" Said Jon venting his frustration. "I think she was wrong in almost everything she said!"

Leonis merely shrugged as they arrived at the King's chambers and were shown into the King's bed room.

When they were alone, the King blurted out: "How am I supposed to honor her when she says such ridiculous things? These people did not cause their own misery. And she has probably never worked for anything that she has ever gotten! And Jon's prayer was absolutely appropriate. I have to allow her to continue in her wrong-headedness just because she is my mother?"

"Let's sit down and discuss this." Said Father Leonis. "I think your mother was wrong in most of what she said; I wanted to correct her as well, especially when she quoted Hercules as if it were the Bible. I am proud of both of you for the way you reacted."

"Then why did you throw the Ten Commandments at me?" Said the King pointedly.

"Jon just told me that it was not his power that made him hold his tongue." Replied Father Leonis. "I suspect that holds true for you as well Wulf. Wulf, it is important to 'honor your mother' and I am proud of you for holding back. Let's ask why you both wanted to argue with her? Jon?"

"Well, because she was wrong. I had not made a silly prayer that had in any way disrespected what Wulf's father had accomplished."

"And what about you, Wulf?" Asked the priest.

"She was so very wrong." Came Wulf's reply. "She was purposely goading my friend, and then she totally ignored the facts regarding the Kells. She just decided to imagine them as lazy people who do not need our help. She acted like I do not know what I am doing!"

"So," said Father Leonis, "Jon felt accused of being silly, and Wulf wanted to correct her opinion that he did not know what he was doing. It sounds like both of you felt you were right and she had some nerve saying that you were not. Listen, I think she was wrong to, but does that make us right? An argument would have just made her more determined. Jesus said we can expect people to reject the Gospel from our lips, as they rejected it from His. He put it in a rather impolite way: 'Do not cast your pearls before swine lest they trample them underfoot and turn to tear you to pieces.' (Matt. 7:6) There is no sense arguing just to prove that you are right; argue if you can prove that God is right. You both honored her and kept her, and yourselves, from a prideful temptation. You weren't mad because she was wrong; you were angry because she said YOU were wrong. That's not humility or righteousness, it is pride and self-righteousness."

Jon knew that Father Leonis was right. He was not angry that the Queen had been wrong, he was angry that she had attacked him and misunderstood what he had prayed. He was angry that he had been shut out of the conversation. He had taken it all personally.

"Are you calling my mother a swine?" Asked the King with a mischievous smile on his face.

"No I am not!" Said Father Leonis with determination. "I am saying that what is right matters more than our perception of being right. I am saying that there is no point in arguing with someone who is not ready to listen."

The King was almost laughing as Father Leonis defended himself. Jon could not resist joining in.

"So, you're saying that Jesus said she was a swine." He said with feigned seriousness.

"No, I am not saying that Jesus called anyone a swine!" Exclaimed the exasperated priest. It was then that he noticed that both Jon and the King could not restrain their laughter. "Very funny." He said after a moment's pause.

"You were casting your pearls before us swine!" Said the King laughing.

"Maybe." Said Leonis. "You two were twisting what I had said in a dangerous way. If I hadn't replied, you may have thought I was agreeing with you."

"I missed having you around, Jon." Said the King still smiling ear to ear. "It's fun to have someone to share mischief with."

"I'll leave you two to catch up on things." Said Father Leonis. "Just as Wulf missed his friend, I missed my friend Johan. I will come back in a while for evening prayers."

"Thank you, Father Leonis." Said the King. "You are more than a teacher and Minister of State to me; you are my friend as well."

Leonis smiled and left the room.

"So, official business aside, how was your trip?" Asked the King.

"Wulf, it was miserable." Replied Jon. "There is a part of me that wishes you and everyone else could see the horror of what I saw: children starving and parents helpless to feed them. There was so much suffering. Seeing it is different than hearing about it. It helps you realize how lucky you are."

"At least you were able to help them." Said Wulf. "You brought them food and the hope of peace."

"We brought them food and it was very welcome." Replied Jon. "But they are still at war with the other Kells. And their King is a horrible man. You've heard all of this; let me tell you what was really bad. After a very short time I didn't care anymore. The King's daughter, Anwen, is a beautiful woman and once I saw her nothing else mattered. I started to want her more than anything else. I wanted her more than God, more than peace; she seemed to me to be the key

309

to happiness. While our men shared their rations, I forgot as I only thought of her. And I never even spoke with her! I have no idea who she is other than she is very pretty. I was told that she was the cause of the war, and I would have been ready to fight for her as well."

The King smiled in a sympathetic way. "A girl did that to you?" He said. "She must be pretty indeed! You seem to have come to your senses quickly enough."

"Maybe." Said Jon. "My dream, of a perfect life with her was beautiful, and it still haunts me. I want that life. But that life was so unrealistic; there was no you, no Kingdom, just an estate, and me and Anwen. It was everything, and everything was all about me. It made me forget who I am."

"I'll make a confession to you, Jon." Said Wulf. "I dream of a life like that with Lil some times. She likes me for who I am rather than what I am. She is pretty and kind. Sometimes I think that she is just what I need to be happy."

"You're a bit young for a dream like that, aren't you?" Replied Jon.

"As long as I can dream it, I'm not too young." Replied the King. "The problem is that it is just as impossible a dream. I will have to marry royalty; I could never have a girl like Lil. I'll be forced to marry someone to help the Kingdom; maybe even your pretty Anwen."

Jon immediately flashed with envy and jealousy. Anwen was royalty in a very strange way and it occurred to him that he was not. He could not have Anwen when he wanted her, while the King could be forced to take her when he didn't want to. The world's rules are strange.

"You're the King, not a prince." Said Jon. "You will have a say in what happens."

"Maybe." Said the King. "But as you like to say, 'duty is not always pleasant.' You know, speaking of Lil, why don't we go for a visit tomorrow? You could probably use some of her good sense."

"Do you think we could go the day after tomorrow?" Asked Jon reluctantly. "I have to take care of something with Brother Johan tomorrow."

"It must be pretty important for you to deny your King." Said Wulf. "What could be so important?"

"I'll go if you insist." Said Jon. "As you just said, 'duty is not always pleasant.' Just kidding, time with you is usually quite pleasant. Johan and I need to find and purchase some scriptures for Jimmy. It's a long story as to how and why, but the task is a burden on both of us and we really want to get it done."

"That's a pretty expensive task!" Said Wulf. "Where did you get enough money for that?"

Jon was unsure how much he should share with the King, but he had no desire to lie to his friend. "It was Sir Malpolem's money." He said. "Brother Johan and I both feel a burden to invest it wisely."

"Well, OK." Said Wulf. "I will have a message sent to Duke Heimsteady tomorrow, and we will go the day after for a visit. Let me know if you need help accomplishing your task with Brother Johan."

The two continued to talk and make plans for their visit to Boady and Lil until Father Leonis returned for evening prayers.

"Good evening, gentlemen." He said as he entered the room. "Jon, Brother Johan asked me to send a message to the Abbot regarding the purchase you plan to make. Have you shared it with Wulf?"

"I have Father." Replied Jon. "He has most generously delayed our trip to the Heimsteady estate until the day after tomorrow."

Leonis raised an eyebrow in surprise. "Wulf, you do surprise me!" He said. "It is a worthy mission that Jon and Johan are on, although I am not entirely comfortable with all of the details, but I know how much you are looking forward to the trip. It is quite good of the King to delay for the good of others."

"I want to take a day to not be the King." Said Wulf. "It would be strange to make it happen only because I am the King."

"You are wise beyond your years." Said Leonis. "Did you and Jon discuss your question?"

"No we didn't." Replied Wulf. "We got distracted by other matters."

"Wulf and I have been discussing why things like his father's death happen." Said the priest. "We have not come up with good answers; he seems to think Lil may know better. Have you had any thoughts Jon?"

"Well, not really." Replied the young knight. "I saw disease and starvation everywhere I looked in the Kell lands, but it was clear to me that mankind had caused all of it. Is it a punishment because they're pagan? I don't think so; the same happens to Christians. I think we bring most of the misery on ourselves. I found me making myself miserable as well. It's a tough question, but I share Wulf's eagerness to hear what Lil has to say."

"Wulf, can I join you on your trip?" Asked Father Leonis in a pleading voice. "I need to meet this remarkable girl."

"I guess so." Said Wulf unenthusiastically. "Listen, if you come you can't be my teacher while we are there. I want to get away from my overly-organized life. You come, maybe we all have a meal together, then you go see Duke Heimsteady so Lil and I can just be kids for a bit; ok?"

Father Leonis was a little hurt by what the King had said, but he understood it. He determined to show the King a different side of him once they were there. "Fair enough, Wulf." He said. "I will stay out of the way as best I can. I'll send a message to the Duke to expect us."

"Why don't you ask the Duke to send Boady a message to expect us as well." Said Jon. "Neither Lil nor Boady read, so someone will have to talk to them. Let Lil know that the three of us are looking forward to her legendary cooking!"

After this discussion the three said their evening prayers. All of them thanked God for the safe return of the embassy and asked God to guide and protect Jimmy in his efforts to bring the Kells into God's Kingdom. Afterwards, Jon returned to his room exhausted.

It had been a long day with a lot of ups and downs, but Jon felt good as he laid down. He was too tired to dream that night, so he had a restful sleep.

33

Unpleasant Duty

DUKE HEIMSTEADY HAD SUMMONED BOADY, and Boady was apprehensive about what he would be asked to do. This was not usual as he trusted the Duke, but something about this summons made him nervous. He waited impatiently until the Duke arrived.

"Good morning Boady!" Said the Duke in exaggerated good humor. He excused the scribe so they could speak alone.

"Good morning, my Lord." Said Boady apprehensively.

"Our friend Sir Jon has done a marvelous thing by removing the Kells as a threat for the time being." Said the Duke. "Nevertheless, I see a problem."

Boady also saw a problem, and his fear was that he would be asked to prolong it. He merely stood listening as the Duke continued to speak:

"We've told the Kells that there is a dragon in the preserve, and for the good of all of us they need to be convinced of the truth of it. If the dragon simply disappeared, people would doubt that it ever existed. Someone needs to suffer by the dragon, and unfortunately you are the only person I can trust to make that happen."

A rush of anxiety coursed through Boady's entire being; this was the worst case scenario that he had imagined. "What exactly do you want me to do?" He said. "The preserve likely has more people in it now, so it would be difficult to set a fire. Maybe I can just tell someone that the dragon has struck and the rumor will spread?"

"Boady, I realize that I am not asking you to do a small or easy thing." Said the Duke. "You are my most loyal man. We have fought together and faced death. You understand as well as I that someone is going to have to die. You don't have to burn the bodies, but you need to make them look like they died after being attacked by something like a dragon."

Boady looked down. He could not bring himself to say 'no' to his Lord and master, but he also could not bring himself to say 'yes' to another cold blooded murder. He was being asked to kill people merely for trying to feed themselves in a place that held a secret; a secret that these people knew nothing about nor had any interest in.

The Duke was becoming nervous as the silence continued. He had no alternatives if Boady said no. He might even have to have Boady killed to protect the secret. Nervously he reached in his pocket and felt a coin. Pulling it out he saw that it was silver; not something he usually carried around unless he was traveling.

"This is well beyond your usual duty." Said the Duke at last. "I know that you cannot refuse me, but I feel you deserve a reward for doing this. Here is a silver piece, and you will get another when the job is done. I wish there was another way, but this is something that only you can do, and it has to be done."

Boady looked up and took the coin. He said nothing, but nodded and turned to walk out the door in a downtrodden manner. While Boady was his man, it pained the Duke to see how much he had troubled his loyal servant and steadfast companion.

For Boady's part, it was not the silver that had convinced him; it was when the Duke had said 'you cannot refuse me.' Boady had been the Duke's man for most of his life. He had never disobeyed an order or denied a request. The Duke's man was who he was; duty is not always pleasant.

The task weighed heavy on him as he walked back to his house. He had killed people before but he fully understood why he was doing what he did. In war, it was kill or be killed. Sir Malpolem and the Schumachers were directly threatening to uncover the secret of the old King's death, but these people only posed a threat if they were near the graves and if they could understand the significance of what they might find. They were as innocent as one could be in this world of lies and secrets. Still, questions would be raised if people thought there were no dragon, or worse, there never was a dragon.

"Hello Boady." Said Lil as he walked into the house. "Did everything go ok?"

"I have to go on a mission to scout the preserve." Said Boady unenthusiastically. "I need to see if the dragon is still around."

"Oh Boady!" Responded Lil with concern. "I know you are always careful, but be especially careful in this mission. Dragons are not something to trifle with; pray God protects you."

Boady grunted in response and went into the other room to pack some gear. He took a blanket, his small shovel, a canteen, and his daggers. He did this mechanically, with almost no thought. As he went back into the main room it occurred to him that he had best wait until dusk to perform his duty. There was no reason to hurry out. He would leave after the mid-day meal.

"I'm going to fill my canteen." He said as he came back. "I think I will leave after we've eaten. I suspect I will need to spend the night in the preserve."

"The food should be ready in an hour." Said Lil. "I will pack you some food for the trip."

"Thanks." He said absentmindedly as he walked out of the door.

He went to the stream and filled the canteen. He then sat down to think. There had to be another way. Boady had been brought up to always do his duty. The fact that he was even questioning what he had to do was unusual for him. As a result, simply not doing his duty never occurred to him. He would serve his master; he never considered whether there might, or should be, another higher master in his life. Duty was duty, and duty was not always pleasant.

Finally, he got up wand washed himself in the stream. Mechanically he walked back to the house.

"Everything is ready." Said Lil as he entered and sat down. Lil sat down next to him and made the sign of the cross. "Father, be with Boady on his mission." She began in prayer. "Let your purposes be served in what we do. Bless this food and guide us in our actions. We pray in Jesus' name. Amen." Boady said nothing as they both made the sign of the cross to close the prayer.

"You'll be OK, Boady." Said Lil. "Lighten up!"

Boady did not have to respond as there was a sudden knock at the door. It was Timmy arriving with his uncanny sense of when meal time would begin.

"Hello Timmy." Said Lil in greeting. "You look so clean! Would you like to join us for our mid-day meal?"

"Well, I hadn't thought to," he said obviously lying, "but I guess mama wouldn't mind. Thanks. Hello Mr. Boady."

"Hello Timmy." Said Boady looking up from his food. "How is your mother? Do you bring any news?"

"Mama is doing fine." He replied. "She's even growing stuff in a little garden! She always tells me to thank you for your help. The big news is the Kells in the preserve. The dragon seems to be gone. People are starting to wonder if there ever was a dragon. I know there was because you told me so and because the King and the Schumachers got killed by it. How soon people forget."

He said the last thing with a serious, adult like, look on his face and shook his head. For once, Boady was somewhat glad to hear his news. At least it confirmed that the Duke was right about people losing faith in the dragon. At least his mission would actually accomplish something.

As the three finished their meal, Boady got up and said: "I best be going."

"Where are you going Mr. Boady?" Asked Timmy. "Do you need some help? I could come along."

Boady liked Timmy, but the boy also got on his nerves with his habit of showing up at inconvenient times and the way he seemed to make it his purpose in life to spread rumors. For the briefest moment he considered letting him come along and be the needed sacrifice, but it was not a serious thought.

"No, Timmy." He said. "Your mama needs you and I may be gone a while. I need to scout the preserve to see what has happened to the dragon."

"Wow!" Exclaimed the boy. "You sure are brave Mr. Boady. Be careful; it's got to still be there somewhere."

Boady gave a small smile and walked over to Lil. They gave each other a long hug.

"I hope to be back as soon as tomorrow." He said with his arms still around her. "You be a good girl while I'm gone."

"I will." She said handing him a sack of provisions she had packed for him. "I'll pray for you. I hope you can cheer up. Look to the Lord for your joy."

Boady gave her a wry smile and walked out the door and towards the woods. Had he looked back towards the Duke's manor he would have seen a messenger riding up with a dispatch from the castle.

The Duke had just sat down to eat when he was interrupted by a servant. "There is a messenger from the castle here to see you my Lord." He was told. "Well, show him in!" Said the Duke emphatically.

The rider was introduced and he handed the Duke a letter.

My Dear Duke Heimsteady,

The King, Sir Jon, and I wish to visit your estate tomorrow. Specifically, the King wishes to visit Mistress Lil whom I understand lives with your man Boady. The three of us hope to spend the day with them, and then the King wishes that he and I could have supper with his uncle. Please inform Master Boady of our plan and we look forward to seeing you on the morrow.

Father Leonis

The Duke was uncertain of what to say. The timing could not have been much worse.

"Aethelstan, give the man a copper." He said somewhat distractedly. Aethelstan seemed almost offended by the request, but found a coin and flipped it towards the messenger.

"Please tell the King and Father Leonis that we look forward to their visit." Said the Duke. "I will see to it that the rest of the message is delivered."

The messenger bowed and left.

"The King is coming for a visit?" Said Aethelstan in hopeful surprise.

"He's not coming to see you." Said the Duke. "We will be hosting him and Father Leonis for supper tomorrow. Let's make sure we are ready for that. Excuse me, I have something to take care of."

The Duke walked out of the manor and towards the stable. "Wren, saddle my horse and bring it to me at Boady's house." Said the Duke not wanting to wait. He continued to walk towards his forester's home hoping that he was not too late.

When he arrived he fairly burst through the door startling Lil and Timmy who had just finished cleaning up. "Where's Boady?" He demanded.

Lil saw who it was and fell to one knee. Timmy imitated her out of a sense of confusion.

"Welcome, my Lord." Said Lil. "I'm afraid Boady left not half an hour ago on the mission you gave him."

"Then I'm too late." He said dejectedly.

"Too late for what, my Lord." Asked Lil rising to her feet.

"The King is coming to visit you tomorrow, along with Sir Jon." Replied the Duke distractedly.

"The King is coming to see Lil and Boady?!" Exclaimed Timmy not realizing that he had already met the King there once. "Wow! This is news."

The Duke looked at Timmy and asked: "Who are you?"

"I'm Timmy, my Lord." Replied the suddenly sobered boy. "I live on Duke Coberg's estate but I visit Lil and Boady every once in a while to give them news."

"Timmy," said the Duke forcing himself to be calm, "you need to keep this news secret for a few days. Nobody needs to know the King's plans. Can I trust you to do that?"

"Well, I guess so." Said the boy. "That will be a hard secret to keep. Why would the King visit Lil and Boady?"

The Duke was speechless, so Lil tried. "I am going to tell you another little secret." She said looking Timmy in the eye. "Remember that boy who was here visiting with Sir Jon that one time? That was the King. He is sort of a friend. Please Timmy; keep this secret for me. It means an awful lot."

Timmy was stunned. "That was the King?" He said. "Wow, I've eaten with the King!"

"Timmy, you need to keep this secret." Said Lil sternly. "You need to keep it for me. Think of everything we have done together. You need to keep your mouth shut or, or I won't be able to be your friend anymore."

Timmy looked hurt. "You're my best friend Lil." He said. "Of course I'll keep your secret if it means that much to you. If I was the King's friend, I'd brag about it, though."

"Please don't Timmy." Said Lil. "And don't come back tomorrow. I will pack you and your mother some extra food because I would really hate to lose you as a friend. It's a big secret, Timmy, you have to keep it."

The boy nodded and gave Lil a hug, completely forgetting the presence of the Duke.

Just then Wren came in and announced: "I've brought Beast to you my Duke."

"And you're the Duke!" Exclaimed Timmy, his awe reignited.

"Yes Timmy, I am Duke Heimsteady." He said. "You can tell people that you met me, but that is all. I think the less you say the better for the next day or two."

Timmy dropped to one knee. "Your wish is my command, my Lord." He said in all earnestness.

"Alright Lil." Said the Duke. "I've delivered the message myself. Apparently Father Leonis will be along as well. The three of them all plan to have a mid-day meal with you. Let us know if you need anything." The Duke turned to leave but turned back to look at Timmy one last time. "I'm counting on you, young man." He said sternly. "Help me remember the name 'Timmy' for the good you did rather than a failure to do your duty."

"You can count on me, my Lord." Said Timmy in all earnestness as the Duke and Wren left.

Boady got to the preserve somewhat late in the afternoon and headed towards the King and Sir Malpolem's graves. He saw snares set in much of the woods and other signs that people were regularly coming into the preserve. Once or twice he heard voices in the distance, but he did not investigate. He still was not sure what he would do to fulfill his duty.

It was almost dusk when he got near the old camp site. He was being stealthy and he became aware of two female voices nearby. They spoke Kell, so he could not understand what they said, but they seemed unconcerned. He saw that they were picking berries and that the older girl, maybe fifteen years of age, had a dead rabbit with her. The other girl was very young; perhaps five years old.

"Duty is not always pleasant." Boady thought to himself. The girls were packing up to leave. He threw a dagger and it lodged in the older girl's skull. She fell to the ground. The younger girl stood still looking at her companion in shock. As Boady emerged from his cover she looked at him and began to cry and say something. It almost sounded like "Jesus, Jesus." to Boady's ears, but he knew that was unlikely. He walked up to her and coldly slit her throat at one jugular vein. She fell to the ground and bled to death.

Boady stood there and looked at what he had done. It seemed unreal. Suddenly he threw up, collapsed to the ground and began to cry. This had been a most unpleasant duty, and it was not finished yet. He needed to find a way to make it look like a dragon had committed the murder that he had just done.

After he had recovered a bit, he decided to crush the older corpse's skull with a rock figuring that it would look like the dragon had stepped on her. It was gruesome. He did it with tears in his eyes, but truth be told he was gripped by madness. He broke her leg and pelvis as well.

He walked over to the smaller girl's body, lying in a puddle of her own blood. He was about to crush her with the same rock, but he could not bring himself to do it. Boady stared at her in disbelief. Had she really called on Jesus as she died? She couldn't have. He used a dagger to make two more cuts near where he had slit her throat. It looked like a claw mark. Eventually he decided he had to make it look more real. He took the rock and smashed that side of her face. She now looked like she had been horribly mauled by something.

Boady was overcome with grief and guilt. He went and sat down by a tree. He began to cry. He could not do anything. He sat there all night crying and wishing that he could undo what he had done. Even 'duty' could not excuse the crime that he had committed.

34

A Peaceful Day

J ON WOKE EARLY AS USUAL, but this time he felt refreshed. A good night's sleep has amazing power to shape a person's positive view of the world. He loved the fact that he could just walk across the room and wash himself. He awoke with gratitude in his heart; he was counting his blessings. After getting dressed he went to the King's suite for morning prayers.

"Good morning Jon." Said the King when Jon was shown into the room. "I'm wearing good clothes today because I want to dress down a bit tomorrow."

Jon smiled. "Wulf, you know it doesn't matter what you wear." He said. "You are who you are."

"Sometimes it is nice not to stand out." Replied Wulf seriously. "You look well rested. I take it you had a good night's sleep?"

"I did." Replied the young knight. "No dreams; just sleep. The best I've had in a while. How about you?"

The King blushed. "I slept alright." He said. "I am excited about our trip tomorrow. Do you think I should bring Lil some flowers or something?"

"I think Lil will be glad to see you no matter if you do or don't." Said Jon. "On the other hand, I am willing to bet we can watch her turn bright red if you do bring her something!"

"She does blush easily." Said the King not realizing that he suffered from the same trait.

"Good morning Wulf, Jon." Said Father Leonis entering the room. "Before I forget, I just sent a message to the Abbot asking him to cooperate with you in purchasing some scripture. Hopefully that will make things easier for you. And yes, Wulf, I have dispatched a message to Duke Heimsteady to expect us tomorrow. I have not forgotten about the flowers either."

"Thank you, Father." Said Jon as Wulf blushed again.

"Now for an awkward request." Said Leonis. "Jon, I don't think you should join us for breakfast. It's not that you've done anything wrong, but I think it is best we give the Queen some room."

"What?!" Exclaimed the King. "Jon has done absolutely nothing wrong. There is no reason he should be disinvited to breakfast. And by the way, I invited him so you can't uninvite him."

Leonis took a deep breath, but Jon came to his rescue. "Wulf, I know that I haven't done anything wrong." He said. "But your mama REALLY doesn't like me. If I go to breakfast, neither she nor I will enjoy it. She will just like me even less. Let's pray God works this out for us."

"Well, it's not fair." Said the King. "Maybe you're right, but if she speaks badly of you I am going to stand up to her. She's wrong and you're right; she needs to understand that."

"Be careful how you do that." Said Father Leonis. "'Honor your mother.'"

"C'mon Wulf." Added Jon. "This is not the biggest thing facing either of us. We don't have to fight this battle right now."

"If you're OK with it." Said the King disappointedly. "But she's wrong, and you haven't done anything bad. I know that."

"Let's pray, shall we?" Said Father Leonis.

Their prayers were not particularly heartfelt or inspired. Wulf's mind was on getting through this day so that he could enjoy his trip tomorrow. Jon was hurt by the Queen's attitude toward him and spent his time dwelling on how wrong she was. Father Leonis had today's schedule on his mind. The prayers were routine; none of them really gave God much thought.

After prayers, Father Leonis and the King went to the council chamber for breakfast while Jon went to the kitchen to eat. While he was still treated with a great deal of respect, the young knight was getting a reputation as someone who the servants could talk to. As a result, Jon learned that there was a book seller visiting the town, and he determined to seek him out at the tavern as soon as he could find Brother Johan.

When he was done eating, he returned to his room and retrieved the money he had under the floor boards, including his two silver pieces. He then went in search of Brother Johan. Due to the fact that the royal breakfast took longer than Jon's quick meal this took some time. After nearly an hour Jon met Johan near his room.

"The Queen missed you at breakfast this morning." Reported Brother Johan. "For the King's sake she spoke somewhat well of you, but I suspect she wanted a sparring partner."

"I bet she did." Said Jon. "I hear there is a book seller at the tavern. Let's check in with him before we go, shall we?"

"I think the longer we delay the less anxious we will seem to the Abbot." Said Johan. "He is likely to drive a hard bargain."

The two men wandered into town and approached the tavern. There were a few tired looking men eating some breakfast and the tavern keeper pointed out the one who was the book seller.

"Good day." Said Brother Johan as they approached. "We are in search of some books and we understand you may have some for sale; is that correct?"

The man looked up at them with bleary eyes and tried to smile. It looked like he had had a rough night. "Indeed, Gentlemen." He said as cheerfully as he could. "I am Nicholas Scriff, purveyor of parchments, scrolls and books. I have several for sale. And who might you be?"

"I am Brother Johan, in the service of our King, Aerdwulf, and this is Sir Jon of the Dragon, one of the King's most trusted knights." Replied the monk.

"Ah, Sir Jon!" Replied Nicholas. "I have a scroll that I am most sure you would be interested in. I have an instruction on dragon slaying penned by St. George himself and passed on through many generations. It is certainly fortunate that you found me!"

"Really?" Said Sir Jon. "That is interesting. What language is it in?"

"Why Latin, of course." Replied Nicholas. "The only language fit for writing excepting maybe Greek."

Johan smiled and Jon understood the joke. "I am afraid that I am not interested." He said. "I am puzzled, however; I was not aware that St. George spoke Latin or that he wrote at all!"

The book seller looked down in disappointment, but then looked up. "Perhaps it is not by St. George, but it is an instruction on killing dragons." He said. "I am sure you would find it useful in fulfilling your quest."

Surprisingly, despite the fact that Jon knew there was no dragon, he was tempted by this offer. Brother Johan, however, spared him this temptation.

"We seek religious books, scripture mostly." He interjected.

"Well, I have a Plato, much of Augustine's work, and a newly acquired copy of the Sermon on the Mount." Said Nicholas. "Does any of that interest you?"

"Perhaps." Said Johan. "Can we see them?"

"Certainly." Replied the book seller. "Wait here and I will get them."

As he left the table John whispered to Johan: "Do you think I should buy the dragon slaying text?"

"Do you think it will help you?" Replied Johan. "I have my doubts."

Jon had to agree. "Of what he offered, only the Sermon on the Mount was really of interest." He said.

"Agreed." Said Johan. "We can't act too interested, however."

Nicholas returned with a scroll, and three loosely bound books. "This is the scroll on dragon slaying." He said handing it towards

Jon. "This large book is Augustine, and here is Plato, and here is the scripture."

Jon examined the scroll he had been handed. It was barely legible and seemed full of fanciful notions about spells of protection that could be invoked. "It is quite interesting." He lied. "Hard to read, though. How much do you want for it?"

Johan looked at Jon quizzically while Nicholas replied: "It is a quite valuable and ancient text." He said. "I couldn't part with it for less than two silver pieces."

Jon gave the man a hard look, and set the text aside. "I don't think I am interested." He said.

"Come now, Sir Jon." Said the peddler. "This text could be of priceless worth to you. It could save your life. I like you Sir Jon, perhaps I could take less just for you. How much do you have?"

"I thank you for showing it to me Nicholas, but I doubt that it would be useful." Said the young knight. "I rely on God, not magic, to fulfill my quests. I doubt that the author of this ever saw a dragon."

"These young ones think they know everything; eh brother?" Said Nicholas turning toward Johan.

"Sir Jon has already fought a dragon once." Replied the monk. "It is how he earned his knighthood. May I see the Sermon text please?"

Nicholas handed Johan the smallest text that he had brought and he studied it a moment. "Well, it is not the most legible, but it does appear to be a true text." He said. "It looks like it was torn right out of a Bible. Where did you get it?"

"I purchased it in Francia from a Norseman." Replied the seller. "God only knows where he got it."

"May I see it?" Asked Jon and the pages were handed to him. Jon studied the text; there were parts of the pages that seemed faded, but it was legible. Even to his barely literate eye there were mistakes in the grammar, but that could mean that it had been translated from the original Greek. All in all, it would not make a bad start to their collection. "I suppose its's ok." He said.

"How much?" Asked Johan.

"For three silver pieces you can have it and the treatise on dragon slaying." Replied Nicholas. "I've grown fond of you, Sir Jon. I want you to survive your next fight and actually kill the dragon."

"We will consider it." Said Brother Johan rising from the table. "How long will you be staying here?"

"Not long Brother Johan." Said the peddler. "I must go to Witancaister where there is a greater market than here. I may have to leave shortly."

Johan considered this and doubted it was the full truth. Nevertheless, it was a plausible story. "I will give you a copper if you stay one more night." He said on impulse. "If we wish to purchase something from you we will return later today."

Johan looked to Jon who pulled out a copper piece. The merchant grabbed it greedily and Johan noticed the tavern keeper looking on with interest.

"I suppose I could stay one more night." Said Nicholas. "But if someone comes and wants it, I will have to sell."

"Fair enough." Said Brother Johan. "Come Sir Jon. We have an appointment to keep."

"Indeed." Replied Jon as mysteriously as he could. As they rose to leave Brother Johan noticed the tavern keeper approach Nicholas with a look of intent.

When they got outside Brother Johan spoke first. "You did well Jon." He said. "You seemed interested but not too interested. By the way, St. George was a Roman soldier; he almost certainly spoke Latin although I doubt he ever fought a dragon. He was martyred for his faith."

"If he was a good Christian, I doubt he would have relied on magic." Said Jon. "That text is more likely to get me killed than to save my life. Why didn't you buy the Biblical text? It seemed good to me."

"First, I want to see what the Abbot may be willing to sell." Replied Brother Johan. "Secondly, Nicholas seemed a bit desperate. I don't think he has any money to pay the tavern keeper. We will get a better price if we return later."

"Considering you're a monk, you might make a fine merchant." Said Jon with a smile.

"I am the son of a weaver, and travel will teach you some skill in bargaining." Replied Johan. "It will be different with the Abbot. When we get there, speak freely about how impressed you were with Nicholas' wares. Let him know that he has some competition. Say something like four silver pieces is a bargain for the complete works of Augustine. In truth, such a work would probably cost two gold pieces at least!"

Jon looked forward to playing a role in the negotiation. It made the outing seem more like an adventure.

When they arrived, the Abbot had several texts laying out for them. "Brother Johan I have no interest in bargaining with you or Sir Jon." Said the Abbot. "Father Leonis has said that the King approves of what you are doing, and that our cooperation will go far with him if Sir Jon gives a good report. Tell me how much money you have to spend and we will determine which of these texts are fair to give you."

Both Brother Johan and Sir Jon were a bit disappointed in this. They had looked forward to the challenge. On the other hand, the King's influence was clearly working in their favor.

"Of course, your eminence." Said Johan exaggerating the Abbot's title. "Sir Jon, how much do you have to spend?"

Jon was uncertain about whether to lie, but Johan gave him a nod that encouraged him to be honest. He pulled out the bag and dumped it on the table. "I have one gold, five silver, and eleven copper." He announced. "The Lord has put it on my heart to obtain scripture with it."

"That is a lot of money, Sir Jon." Said the Abbot. "How did you come by such a sum?"

Johan and Jon had not anticipated this question. Fortunately, as usual, Jon had a good answer: "It is an inheritance." He said flatly.

"My, I did not realize that executioners could amass such a fortune." Replied the Abbot. "I suppose that many will pay to insure a less painful death." He added with a bit of disdain.

Jon felt a flash of anger but kept his cool. "My father was an honorable man." He said coldly. "We should speak respectfully of the dead."

Suddenly the Abbot remembered that it was Sir Jon that he needed to impress. "I meant no slight, Sir Jon." He said. "Your father was certainly a most honorable man and I will see to it that he is remembered in our prayers to atone for the poor way that I expressed myself."

"Thank you." Said Jon. "So what do we have here?"

"I have much of the Bible here." He replied. "Some of it only recently transcribed. May I make a suggestion?"

"Please do." Replied the young knight.

"Here is a Gospel of Luke, and another of John." Said the Abbot with deep appreciation for the works that he was displaying. "I think that those alone might cost most of what you brought, but I will include some Psalms, the creation story, and this single page of the ten commandments."

Johan was stunned at the offer. It far exceeded anything that he reasonably expected. "That is a very generous offer, Sir Jon." Said the monk in an almost stunned voice.

"I quite agree." Said Jon despite the fact that he had no idea how much he could expect to obtain. The texts were mostly newer and legible. "Will these texts be useful for their purpose?"

"The entire Bible would be better." Replied Johan. "If I had to choose, however, I think these are what I would choose. The Abbot is probably offering you between two and three gold pieces' worth of texts."

"I am stunned by your generosity kind Abbot." Said Jon. "Know that these will be used to grow the Kingdom of God, and that I will certainly thank the King for his support and proclaim your generosity."

"Sir Jon, Father Leonis told me that you intend to pass these on to Jimmy." Said the Abbot kindly. "Father James' son was one of my brightest students, but he has an odd attitude towards the church. Nevertheless, I feel that he has been touched by Jesus. I will appreciate any kind words to the King, but I also wish to support Jimmy. Please pass along my regards."

"I will, Father." Said Jon. "And thank you."

"I shall have the texts bound together for you." Said the Abbot. "When would you like to get them?"

"Brother Johan will take them to Jimmy." Replied the young knight. "Brother, when will you be leaving?"

"I have to wait for Father Leonis to get back." Said Johan. "I suspect it will be on the third day from now."

"They shall be ready the day after tomorrow." Proclaimed the Abbot.

"Thank you Father." Said Johan. "Thank you from the bottom of my heart."

"It is good to see you again, Johan." Said the Abbot softly. "Good luck in your further travels. Don't be a stranger."

"I won't." Said Johan and they were shown out the door.

"Let's go tell the book seller that he is free to leave." Said Johan as they got outside. "The Abbot really surprised me. He was such a tough teacher; I suspected he would be a hard nut to crack. I thought he'd be all about the money. Instead he was quite generous."

"Perhaps God was working on his heart." Said Jon. "I take it we did better than either of us could reasonably expect?"

"We did indeed." Replied Johan as they walked into the tavern.

The book merchant suddenly brightened as they approached. "Gentlemen! Back so soon? How can I help you?"

"Actually," said Johan, "we have obtained what we sought from the Abbey. We wanted to tell you that you could leave if you wish."

The color drained from the man's face and he slumped back to his seat. This raised a feeling of pity in Jon.

"You seem distressed." Said Jon quietly. "Let's not bargain. How much money do you need to pay your bill and get to Witancaister?"

"You were my last hope." He said in a crest fallen manner. "Please do not toy with me."

Johan looked stunned as Jon resolutely walked up to the tavern keeper. He returned shortly thereafter. "You owe fifteen coppers here and you need another five or so to travel." He said. "Your copy of the

Sermon on the Mount is poor Latin and barely readable, but I will give you twenty-five copper for it. I am over paying."

The man looked up with new hope in his eyes. "Bless you, kind sir!" He said. "I will fetch it now."

"I will pay your bill and give you the remaining ten." Said Jon and he approached the tavern keeper. He handed the man a silver piece from his purse and got fifteen coppers in return. He placed five in his wallet and awaited Nicholas' return.

The merchant was very grateful for the ten coppers that he received and offered to give Jon the text on dragon slaying as well. Jon refused it and they were soon on their way out of the door.

"Why did you do that?" Asked Brother Johan.

"I don't know." Replied Jon. "I have never had money before. Perhaps I am not good with it."

"No, Jon." Said the Monk. "You have a good heart, and now you have some scripture of your own!"

The rest of the day passed peacefully. Jon skipped dinner with the King using the excuse that he had to prepare for tomorrow's trip. Evening prayers were lively as Wulf was quite excited about the coming excursion.

It had been a really good day. Jon hoped that Lil and Boady had had just as good a day. Little did he know that his friend was huddled in the woods crying, overcome by grief and guilt.

35

High Hopes

THE KING WAS UP AND dressed when Jon arrived at his room for morning prayers. He was a ball of energy as he made his preparations for travel.

"Good morning Jon!" He exclaimed as Jon entered. "Are you ready to go? I had the stable saddle our horses; They wanted to give me a new saddle, but I like the saddle I have, so I am just getting new stirrups."

"Good morning Wulf." Said Jon. "Did you get any sleep? We still need to eat breakfast, you know. We'll be there soon enough."

The King took a deep breath. "I am so excited!" He said. "You're right, I hardly slept. I need a break from all of this schooling and work for the Kingdom. I deserve it, don't I?"

"I guess so, Wulf." Said Jon softly with a smile. "But be careful; I think that when you get your hopes up too high, when you think you know exactly how things are going to go, that's when you get most disappointed. Let's rely on God for our blessings, not Lil or ourselves."

"You can sound so old sometimes!" Said the King with a chuckle. "You know; I was thinking that we could bring an extra horse for Lil. Then we could all have our own horse when we ride!"

"Slow down, Wulf." Replied Jon. "It's a nice thought, but Boady would never go for it. Lil has not ridden much and she has to ride side saddle. Let's let her ride with us this time. Maybe you can bring a pony or something next time, but we need to ask Boady."

The King looked disappointed. "What good is it being the King if you need to do what everyone says you can all the time." He said looking down.

"Lighten up, Wulf." Said Jon. "You may not have it as good as a lot of people assume you do, but you have a pretty good life. You can even consider bringing your friend a horse or a pony. Most people in this Kingdom would consider a pony winter food if they could consider having one at all!"

Before the King could answer Father Leonis entered the room. "Good morning, gentlemen." He said. "I see everyone is nearly ready to go. Thanks for seeing to the horses, Wulf. Why the extra horse?"

"I thought Lil might want a horse of her own to ride." Replied the King. "Jon does not think it's a good idea. Do we have any ponies?"

Father Leonis was perplexed by the question, but Jon had an answer: "Let it go, Wulf." He said. "She'll turn red enough from the flowers; you don't want to make her faint!"

The King blushed and let out a nervous laugh. "Let's pray and get to breakfast, shall we?" He said.

Father Leonis made the sign of the cross and the others followed suit. "Father in heaven, you are so good to us. We pray your blessing on this day. Guide us in all that we do. I pray in Jesus' name." He prayed.

Jon spoke next after a brief pause: "Yes, Lord, continue to bless us as you always have. Protect us from our own foolishness. Help us to remember to look to you for help and salvation. Let the glory be yours; a reflection of Your light is enough for us. Protect Brother Johan on his journey to Jimmy, Carm and the other Kells. Bring your light into their darkness. Let us all be with you, Lord Jesus, I pray in

Your holy name." The words were spoken without thought. Jon was gratified that he did not know what had prompted that prayer.

"Father, help me to be a King." Prayed Wulf. "But also help me to be a good man. Bless mama, and Lil, and Boady and all of those in need in my Kingdom. And be with Papa; let him know Your joy. In Jesus' name I pray, amen."

All three made the sign of the cross in closing.

"Are you ready to face mama?" Wulf asked Jon.

"God, help me!" Replied Jon as they walked to breakfast.

As they walked into the room, the first thing they noticed was a somewhat large bouquet of fresh flowers in the center of the table.

"Are those Lil's flowers!" Said the King. "They're awesome! She's going to love them."

"You might make her faint after all." Said Jon dryly. "How are we going to carry them?"

"Don't worry." Said Father Leonis. "The gardener has a way to wrap them and we will carry the vase separately. They'll get there."

The King went to his bowl of water and washed up while Jon and Father Leonis took their seats. Shortly, Brother Johan, Sir Bendris, and then the Queen, came in and sat down.

"What lovely flowers!" Exclaimed the Queen. "Did you get those for me my boy? How sweet."

There was a look of sheer terror on the King's face for a moment, but he soon recovered. "Would you like some flowers Mama?" He said. "These are a gift to my host at Duke Heimsteady's estate, but I can certainly get you some."

"That's alright Wulf." Replied the Queen. "I know who they are for. My, you are growing up! Just don't grow up too fast." After she had said this she gave a stern look toward Father Leonis. "Welcome back, Sir Jon. We have missed you these last few meals."

"It is good to be back, my Lady." Replied Jon non-committedly.

"Your Majesty, I feel the need to have Wil accompany you on your visit." Said Sir Bendris. "While I have the highest confidence in Sir Jon I feel the King deserves more than one knight for his security."

The King was about to argue, but he decided there was little point to it. Wil was a reasonable companion and he was likely to lose if he argued anyways; an argument could delay their departure. "If you feel it's necessary, Sir Bendris." He said. "I am sure the Duke will not object to an extra guest."

The quick acquiescence surprised both Father Leonis and Sir Bendris, but they were pleased. After a quick grace by Brother Johan the meal progressed without a significant incident. It became clear in the discussion that Brother Johan planned to depart for the Kell lands as soon as the Abbey had the manuscripts bound and ready, and Father Leonis had returned to oversee the Kingdom's business. He would take a horse and a pack of as much food as he could carry, along with the scriptures that he would deliver. It was clear that he was eager to depart.

After breakfast the group escorted the King to the stable where Wil was mounted and four horses stood ready to depart.

"We do not require the extra horse after all." Said the King as he approached. "Thank the men who saddled it for us. We regret that we created unnecessary work for them."

"Wulf!" Said the Queen sharply. "You are the King. You do not apologize!"

"Yes, mama." Replied the King not wishing to let anything delay their departure.

Soon enough the party was mounted, good-byes had been said and they were on their way. The King set a brisk pace and they arrived sooner than one might have expected. The Duke had set men to watch for their arrival, and when they informed him of the King's coming he immediately mounted Beast. He correctly suspected that the King would go to Boady's house first and he hastened to meet him.

Lil was also anxiously awaiting Wulf's arrival, and when she heard horses she came outside and greeted him with a bright and genuine smile. "Good morning, your Majesty." She said as they rode up, making a brief curtsey. You are early. I am glad you are here."

The King dismounted without saying anything, but Jon thought he noticed a red tinge to his complexion. Wulf pulled out the vase from his saddle bag and handed it to Wil. "Could you bring us some water?" He asked. "It is very good to see you Mistress Lil. I would like to introduce you to my teacher and friend Father Leonis."

"I've heard much about you from both the King and Sir Jon." Said the priest. "It is a pleasure to finally meet you."

Jon got off of his horse, walked up to Lil and gave her a big hug. "I've missed you little sister." He said. "Where's Boady?"

"He left on a mission for the Duke just before your message arrived." Said Lil with her eyes back on the King who stood nearby seeming nervous.

Everyone turned as the Duke and his large horse came thundering up to the house. He awkwardly dismounted as Jon stepped forward to offer assistance. Falling to one knee he said: "Welcome, your Majesty. I trust you had a pleasant ride?"

"We did indeed, Uncle." Replied the King. "When can we expect Boady back?"

"Regretfully I had just sent him to check on the preserve when your message arrived." Replied the Duke. "I hope he will be back soon."

An uneasy feeling came over Jon when he heard the news. He hoped he was wrong about what Boady's real mission might be.

As Will returned with the vase full of water the King replied to the Duke: "I look forward to dining with you this evening Uncle. Sir Bendris insisted that Wil come along for extra protection; I hope the extra guest will not be too much of an inconvenience."

"Of course not, your Majesty." Said the Duke recognizing that his presence was inconvenient to the King's intentions. "I will leave you alone and tell the house to set an extra place for Master Wil tonight." Wil and Jon helped the Duke get back on Beast and the Duke bid a fare well and rode off.

"Father Leonis and Wil," said the King, "We find these titles annoying. Sir Jon began a custom at this house that we dispense with formalities while we are here. Except in obvious situations, you may call me Wulf." He then retrieved the vase, went back to his saddle and got the flowers. Lil looked on curiously as he unwrapped them and place them in the vase. "A gift for you, Lil." He said.

"Oh, Wulf, you shouldn't have!" Exclaimed Lil as she saw them. "They are so beautiful!"

Lil turned so red Jon thought she might actually pass out. Then he looked at Wulf and saw that he was just as red! Father Leonis' and Jon's eyes met and they both had trouble stifling a chuckle. There was an awkward silence as the two looked at each other.

"Maybe we should get these flowers inside." Said Jon at last.

"Oh yes." Replied Lil snapping out of her reverie. "I have to check on the meal I am cooking as well."

"I'll picket the horses around back." Said Wil.

"Oh wait!" Said Lil. "I have some carrots for Mayflower and the others." She dashed inside quicker than anyone would have thought a girl in a dress could move and returned just as quickly. The horses were extremely glad to see her and soon enough Lil, Jon, Wulf, and Father Leonis went into the house while Wil took care of the horses.

The house smelled good as Lil was cooking their meal. "Please have a seat, gentlemen." She said as she checked the food. "Oh, my! The flowers really brighten this place! Thank you so much Wulf. That was very kind."

"This place is bright enough without them." Said Wulf. "I'm glad you like them."

The three men sat down with Wulf taking Boady's seat. After stirring a bit Lil came and sat beside him. "So, how have you been?" She asked as non-chelantly as she could.

"I've been fine." Replied Wulf. "Father Leonis came along to ask you a question we have been struggling with. Jon and I told him you would have an interesting answer."

Lil turned to Father Leonis with an inquisitive look. "I am not well educated." She said. "What could I possibly tell you?"

Father Leonis cleared his throat. "Well, I am told that you have a great relationship with Jesus and that you may have a practical way of looking at a question that we have been thinking about." He said. "Jon, why don't you explain where we are."

Just then Wil walked in and Jon motioned for him to sit down next to him on the bench. "We are sort of asking why God allows bad things to happen to good people." He said. "We understand that if people have a choice in what they do, then they can make bad choices, but we don't really understand why innocent people die of diseases and such."

"Or why God would send a dragon to kill my father." Added Wulf seriously. Everyone looked to Lil.

"Why are you asking me!" Said Lil feeling like she had been put on the spot. "It's not like bad things have never happened to me. My mother died of illness shortly after my father suffered the King's justice. I never thought to question God about it!"

The men around the table were taken aback. They had not meant to upset Lil, but the question surely did. Jon responded:

"We're sorry Lil." He said. "Of all the people I know, you seem the fullest of God's joy. I know that you have not had any easy life, but generally you are about the happiest person I know. I guess it never occurred to me that you had never asked the question."

Wulf took Lil's hand. "I'm sorry Lil." He said.

"Of course I've asked that question." She said looking down. "I asked it all the time when my mother died. Finally, something she used to say came back to me: 'The Lord gives and the Lord takes away; blessed be the name of the Lord.' I think what she meant was that we should trust God. I trust God enough not to question Him. But that doesn't mean that those things don't hurt. They make me very sad. I miss my mother so much." Lil had tears in her eyes when she looked up.

Father Leonis was struck by the wisdom of what she had said. This truly was a remarkable girl. "That's the best answer that I have ever heard." He said suddenly, getting everyone's attention. "Your mother was quoting the book of Job. In it a man suddenly finds his life coming apart. His family gets killed in a storm; his animals die; he gets sickness throughout his body. His friends come and tell him that God must be punishing him but he insists that he has done nothing wrong. At first he says what your mother told you, but eventually he cries out to God and God answers him: 'Where were you when I formed the heavens and the earth?' God asks. In the end God scolds his friends who accused Job of being punished. He makes it clear that they had no right to judge Job. Then God restores Job. Job learns to turn to and trust God, but to never accuse God. He is God, and we are not. It is not always an easy answer to accept."

"Yes." Said Lil wiping her tears away. "My mother told me that story when my father was taken from us. I have made it a point to trust God, and to cry out to Him when I am sad or angry. God loves me; I can trust Him."

"I'm so sorry that we upset you Lil." Said Wulf still holding her hand. "I don't ever want to hurt you."

"It's OK, Wulf." Replied Lil. "I know how much you miss your father. God is the answer to your sorrow, not the cause of it. Turn to Him and He will restore you; just like he restored Job. Don't run from God in your sorrows; run to Him. Trust me, it helps me. The world is broken since Adam and Eve disobeyed God, but God is the only hope we have in it."

Father Leonis was in awe of what she said. He felt that she could hold her own against the greatest minds in the church. How was he to teach Wulf when Lil was available? He was not jealous; he was grateful that he had met her.

Jon's reaction was different. He had not been particularly faithful when he had lost his father and Sir Malpolem. He saw his life not as one of tragedy, but one of many undeserved blessings. Now that he knew Jesus, Lil's answer made total sense. God had used the bad things in his life to draw him into a relationship. Jon was happy in that relationship so he didn't question how God had accomplished it.

The entire conversation puzzled Wil. He saw himself as a self-made man. While God might exist, he did not play a big role in his life, so there was little sense in blaming him or crediting him. Perhaps his attitude could best be summed up in the words of Hercules: "The Gods help those who help themselves."

Wulf didn't know what to think. He could acknowledge the sense in what Lil had said, but he wanted to know why. He trusted God, but he wanted an answer. Perhaps God needed to work more in his heart before the King would accept God's lordship. Mostly he was upset that he had upset Lil. It pained him to think that he may have hurt her. He liked and trusted Lil, so generally, he accepted her answer. Now, he wanted to brighten her day.

Lil herself, was surprised by what she had said. When her mother had died she had no other place to turn but to God. Boady had been a friend of the family's, but she had no idea what a good friend he actually was. She had thanked God for sending a rescuer more than blamed Him for needing to be rescued. Her mother had taught her to ALWAYS trust in God.

"I'm going to check on the food." Said Lil at last. "Jon, can you set the table for everyone?"

Jon got up but the King also got up. "Let me help too." He said sincerely. Jon shrugged and started handing Wulf the plates. The table was quickly set and ready. Leonis marveled at this; the King helping to set the table! Lil had an interesting effect on him.

"Why don't you guys take a slow walk and wash up." Said Lil. "I think things are almost ready."

The four men filed out of the house and went to wash up. They took their time and the meal was ready when they returned. Lil's smile had returned as well. Father Leonis said grace and they all enjoyed Lil's excellent cooking while the King took turns making Lil and himself blush. After the meal everyone helped Lil clean up and they were ready for the ride to begin.

36

Boady

IT WOULD NOT BE ACCURATE to say that Boady awoke the next day; he had not slept. In another sense he was still asleep. Boady was in a deep depression. He needed to do something but did not have the energy or clearness of mind to be motivated to move or to decide what he should do. He sat against a tree unable to move, but not wanting to stay.

As the sun began to rise, birds began to sing, but he did not hear them. Whenever he opened his eyes they immediately came to rest on the two mutilated bodies that lay before him. Deep inside he knew that if he stayed there someone would find him and possibly put together what had happened. His duty was to stop the truth from being discovered; duty is not always pleasant.

Finally, he got up and retrieved his bag of food, but it took all that he had to do it. He first pulled out some bread and ate a few bites, but his mouth and throat were dry. He did not have the energy to go to the stream to wash or get a drink. Reaching back into the bag he found an apple. He grabbed a dagger from his belt to cut it but dropped it before he could; it was covered in blood. After a fit of crying he took another, clean dagger, and cut the apple. His body craved the juice and moisture, but his mind told him he did not deserve it.

Boady was gripped by a madness of contradictions: he wanted to move, but he did not want to do anything; be wanted to complete his mission, but the mission was no longer important to him; he wanted to live, but he was convinced that he deserved and needed to die.

As the sun rose, Boady found himself moving. Thoughtlessly he gathered his belongings and prepared to leave, although he did not know where he was going. He began to walk towards the little girl he had killed. He stood over her as he began to cry again. He wanted to leave all of this behind, but he did not want to leave her.

Again, without thinking he picked up the bloody corpse and began to walk. He walked and walked carrying the corpse like a cross. There was no thought behind this, he only knew that somehow he had to carry the burden of this sin with him wherever he went.

He continued to walk, carrying the little girl, without a sense of destination. Several times he fell from exhaustion. Getting up was hard, but he relished the pain of it as if the punishment could somehow justify him. Each time he picked up the body again and walked.

He was now in more familiar territory, but he did not recognize it. He was approaching Duke Heimsteady's estate.

After their mid-day meal, the four men and Lil went outside to ride the horses. Father Leonis insisted that Lil ride with Jon, but somehow the sheer joy of the previous rides was lost due to Father Leonis' presence in the group. The King's high expectations were not being met.

"Father Leonis?" Said Wulf in exasperation. "I don't know how to say this, but I think there are too many of us riding together. Would you and Wil mind going back to the house? I promise we will stay within sight."

Leonis had to think about what to say. It was hurtful that his student was basically telling him that his presence was spoiling the fun, but he also understood how and why that might be so; it would be hard for Wulf to express himself freely with his priest, his teacher, and his chief minister of state right there. "Alright Wulf," he said, "but do stay in sight. Sir Jon, you are being trusted with a serious responsibility."

Jon smiled. "I have borne that responsibility before." He said in a matter of fact way.

Wil and Leonis turned and rode slowly back to the house. Once they got there, Wil stayed mounted so as to better watch the King while Leonis went to the garden and got a couple of carrots for the horses. Apparently Lil was influencing his behavior as well.

Meanwhile, Lil had decided that it was time for her to ride with Wulf, so an exchange was made. The two adult like children simply enjoyed being together although much of what they said seemed awkward to Jon as he listened, and he was amazed at how often they could take turns blushing. The ride was more relaxed now that it was just the three of them.

At one point Jon looked away from the two younger people to hide an urge to laugh at what had been said. In the distance he saw someone walking as if in a trance and carrying something. He felt compelled to investigate.

"Wulf and Lil, I need to go and check something out." He said. "Why don't you two get off the horse and talk a bit while I go investigate?"

Lil and Wulf were so much enjoying each other's company that they were not even curious about what Jon wanted to investigate. "Good idea." Said Wulf dismounting so he could help Lil off of Mayflower.

Jon turned and waved to the ever watchful Wil. Wil did not understand what he wanted, but he saw the King dismount and he saw Jon begin to move away, so he began a trot towards the King. "I'll be right back." He said to Father Leonis.

The priest climbed onto his own horse to get a better look and saw Jon riding away by himself as Wil headed towards the now riderless Mayflower. Since Jon seemed unhurried in his departure and was riding away, he deduced that the King was OK, but he decided to head down there any ways.

As Jon got closer to the man he had seen walking he recognized that it was Boady. He seemed to be carrying a body. He urged Thunder into a gallop. Boady did not change his walk or give any sign that he was even aware of Jon's presence as the horse was brought to a stop right in front of him.

Jon looked at the scene in front of him. One side of the body's head had been smashed, and Boady had blood all over him. "Boady!" He shouted. "What happened?!"

Boady stopped and looked at him with empty soulless eyes. He fell to his knees, put down the body, and began to cry. Jon's eye was drawn to the body that had been placed on the ground with the uncrushed part of her face upwards. He recognized Carm, the girl he had found with Sir Bendris in the Kell lands; the girl he had prayed for that very morning.

Dismounting he walked up to Boady and put his hand on him. Boady violently shook it off.

"What happened Boady?" Jon said in a soft tone, the shock of what he was seeing being realized.

Boady simply cried, and for a while Jon gave him some distance. After a bit of pacing Jon came back and said firmly, but not harshly: "Boady, you need to tell me what happened."

Perhaps it was the authority in Jon's voice, but this time Boady looked at him and said: "It was the dragon, Sir Jon. It killed two girls. You have to slay it. I can't do my duty anymore."

Jon slumped to the ground in front of Boady. He wished that he did not understand the mad ranting that had come from his friend; but he did. Carm was dead, Boady was a wreak, and the dragon still lived because he had not found a way to kill it. He had not done his duty. Jon felt he shared in the tremendous guilt of this crime. He began to cry with Boady.

After a short time, Jon remembered the others. He needed to get moving. "Boady." He said, but Boady did not move. He simply continued to cry. "Boady." Jon said softly in a plaintive way. "You're like a father to me. I love you like a son. I need you Boady. I need you to help me."

It seemed an odd thing to say, and indeed Jon did not know why he had said it then, although he recognized that it expressed his true feelings. "You take Thunder by the reigns and lead him. I will carry Carm."

Boady looked at him. "Carm?" He said.

"That's her name Boady." Said Jon through his tears. "I'll carry her and we will give her a burial."

"She's my burden." Said Boady. "You can't do my duty. I have to carry her."

"I want to carry her for you." Replied Jon. "You can't carry this burden. You're too weak now. You need to lead Thunder. That's your duty right now."

Only God knows why, but Boady got up and took Thunder's reigns. Jon picked up Carm and began to walk towards the house. Boady followed. Carm was light and there was little blood left in her; still, there was enough to stain Jon's shirt.

Wil looked to see what Jon was up to. "Sir Jon seems to be going back to the house with another man." He said. "They are carrying something. We need to return."

The King was annoyed, but he did not argue. "Help me get Lil back on Mayflower." He said as he himself mounted the horse. Father Leonis handed Lil up to him. When they were all mounted they saw the strange thing the Wil had reported to them. Jon was carrying something while another man followed leading his horse. They began to ride back to the house and arrived before the other two had. It became clear that the man was Boady and that Jon was carrying a body.

When the two men got close enough Lil ran up to them. "Boady, Jon, what happened?" She cried. She saw that both men had been crying, but Boady showed no signs that he even recognized her.

"Take Boady into the house, Lil." Said Jon sternly. "Put him in bed and give him some food and water. We will speak later."

Lil had never seen Jon this serious. She did as she was told. She led Boady like he was a mindless animal. He did not even acknowledge her presence.

"Wil, get Thunder." Ordered Jon. "Father Leonis, you have a burial to perform."

Wil went and took Thunder around to the stable as Jon walked past the King and priest carrying his burden.

"What is this, Jon?" Said Wulf as he walked by.

Jon paused to look at him. "Not now, your Majesty." He said. "Not now. We will speak later."

Jon carried the body near a tree behind the house and then went to the stable to get a shovel. Returning to the tree he began to dig with a purpose.

Leonis and Wulf stood not knowing what they should do. Leonis motioned for Wulf to stay and approached Jon. "What's going on Jon?" He asked. "Who are we burying?"

Jon stopped digging and looked at Leonis. "Her name is Carm." He said. "We prayed for her just this morning."

The two looked at each other until Jon began to dig again. Leonis returned to the King who had been joined by Wil.

"What is going on?" Asked Wulf.

"I'm not sure." Replied Leonis. "Apparently the body is someone named Carm. Jon says we prayed for her this morning. Now we are going to bury her. Wil, why don't you see if you can find a shovel and help Jon dig the grave."

Wil went to help Jon. They dug in silence.

"I'm going inside to check on Lil and Boady." Said Wulf.

Lil was coming out of the sleeping room as Wulf entered. "How's Boady? He asked.

Lil had an extreme look of concern on her face. "Apparently the Dragon has killed again." She said. "He almost doesn't seem to be here. He keeps saying that he can't do his duty; that he let everyone down. He insists that Jon has to kill it. A lot of what he says does not make sense. He's a bloody mess. Something terrible has happened. Oh, Wulf!"

With that she fell onto Wulf and wrapped her arms around him as she started to cry. Slowly Wulf put his arms around her as he had no idea of what else he should do. He held her as she cried. Wulf felt guilty for enjoying the moment.

Suddenly she lifted her head and rushed out of his arms. "Boady needs food and water." She said. "I'm sorry, Wulf, I need to take care of him right now."

"It's alright Lil." He said. "My arms are always open to you. Let me know if I can help."

Lil did not blush as he said this. She was intent on getting Boady something to eat and drink. The King, however, when he realized what he had said, blushed deeply. He went back outside.

"How's Boady?" Asked Father Leonis when he saw Wulf approach.

"Not well." Replied Wulf. "I'm worried about Lil too. Apparently the dragon killed the girl."

"Dear God." Replied the priest. He had had some doubts about the dragon's existence, but now he had seen its work. "Boady must have dragon sickness. He may never recover."

The two walked over to where the grave was being dug.

"I'm going to look at the body." Said Father Leonis. "You stay here. You don't need to see something like this yet."

The body had rigormortis and was permanently in a twisted position. One side of the face had been crushed, but apparently the dragon had not put its full weight on it as the other side was normal except for a few cuts. The neck on the skull's crushed side showed three marks as if a claw had tried to rip open the flesh. Leonis had never seen anything like it; it further convinced him that the dragon had done this, but he was puzzled by the lack of any sign of fire.

Jon and Wil had finished digging the grave. "I need to get Boady and Lil for the ceremony." He said as he gently laid the body in the grave. He jumped out and walked towards the house without a further word.

There was nobody in the main room when he entered, so he went into the sleeping room. He saw Lil helping Boady drink some water. "We're ready to bury her." Said Jon as gently as he could. "Boady, for your own good you need to join us."

Boady gave Jon a startled look, but got up. Once again, Jon was not sure why Boady had to be at the funeral, but he was sure that he

347

had to be there. How could God have anything to do with what was now happening? This entire tragedy was man's doing.

Lil followed Boady after giving Jon a worried look. Boady walked right up to the grave and stood there silently, refusing to see anyone else.

"Jon, you are the only one here who knew her." Said Father Leonis. "Do you have some words you would like to say?"

Jon did not want to speak, but he felt it was his duty; duty is not always pleasant. "I met Carm with Sir Bendris when we first scouted the Kell lands." He said. "Her family had been killed and she was hiding in the ruins of their house. She stayed and protected the bodies. Somehow I was able to convince her to go with us even though she didn't speak our language. Later, Jimmy told me that she had said that she saw Jesus in me. As much as I want that to be true, I don't see how."

"She called on Jesus as she died!" Yelled Boady. "She called on Jesus!"

Father Leonis gathered that Boady had seen the dragon attack and now had the madness that was called dragon sickness. "The Lord giveth, and the Lord taketh away; blessed be the name of the Lord." He said in a loud clear voice. "Father, we commend this soul to you. Although she was a Kell, we trust that she knew You and was part of our family as well. Take her into Your bosom and let her enjoy the peace and joy that only You can bring." He reached down to grab a handful of dirt. "Ashes to ashes, dust to dust, from the dirt we were made and unto it we return." He then tossed the dirt into the grave.

Everyone made the sign of the cross. Jon grabbed a shovel and started refilling the grave. Boady stood there crying until Lil grabbed his arm and led him inside. The others just stood there. Eventually, Wulf grabbed the other shovel and helped Jon. It was the first time he had ever done manual labor. Leonis and Wil looked on in wonder. "He is growing up." Thought the priest.

When Lil got Boady into the house he saw the flowers on the table. "She should have those." He said calmly and walked over to them. He picked them up and headed back to the grave. He arrived just as Wulf and Jon had finished returning the dirt.

Boady placed the vase in the middle of it. He then turned and walked back.

"Those flowers are for you Lil!" Yelled Wulf as she walked away following Boady.

"And they are beautiful." She called back. "I will always think of you when I see flowers, but Boady needs to give these to that girl."

The King was blushing again.

"I'm sorry your Majesty." Said Jon. "I think Lil and I need to take care of Boady. Please tell the Duke that the dragon has killed again. Tell him Boady may well be one of its victims." He said this with a touch of anger in his voice, but the listeners thought it was simply the emotion of seeing someone he cared about buried.

"Of course, Sir Jon." Said the King. "Please tell Lil that I will come see her in the morning. We will pray for all of you."

Jon nodded and looked like he wanted to say more, but finally he walked up to and into the house.

"Wil, can you get Thunder into the stall and then join Father Leonis and me at the Duke's manor?" Said the King.

"Of course, my Lord." Replied Wil.

Leonis and Wulf got on their horses and began a slow ride to the Duke's. Neither felt like talking. This day had certainly not turned out how they had expected it to.

37

Dragon Sickness

WHAT HAD BEGUN AS A happy day had lost its luster. Boady was returned to his bed where he cried again until he finally fell asleep. Exhaustion had accomplished what he did not have the will to do. Lil watched him as he turned restlessly and cried out in his dreams.

She did her best to wash away the blood that covered him, but at times it seemed like Boady did not want to be clean. Jon paced and helped when he could, but how could he really help Boady? Boady kept speaking about his duty and that he was doomed. Lil took them as the ramblings of a mad man, but Jon understood; still he did not know what to do. How could he help Boady?

When Boady had attained a relatively peaceful state, Lil motioned Jon to join her in the other room. As they sat at the table she lowered her head and began to cry. "Poor Boady!" She said through the tears. "What could have happened to him? How do we cure dragon sickness? God help us!"

...

"Of course." Thought Jon. "God has to be the answer. Either He exists or he doesn't; He is our only hope."

"Lil, we need to pray." Said Jon resolutely.

Lil got up and went to kneel by her cross. Jon followed and they both made the sign of the cross, but neither spoke. Finally, Lil broke the silence: "Oh God, You give and You take away. Please don't take Boady. Bring him back, Father; restore him! You are our hope and salvation; bring Your light to the darkness that Boady is in." Having said this, she returned to silence.

"Father save us!" Said Jon. "Save us from our sin; save us from ourselves. Fall down on me and wash me clean. Show me the path Lord! Show me how to kill the dragon! Please God, don't desert us." Jon began to sob. His prayer had made it clear to him just how over his head he was. He needed God to rescue him. He felt alone in his troubles. Lil noticed that he had not mentioned Boady in his prayer.

After several more minutes of silence, Lil said: "Help us Lord Jesus; we pray in Your name. Amen." She then made the sign of the cross and Jon followed suit. Lil got up and started preparing some food.

"I better go check on Thunder." Said Jon and he walked outside. The day was fading, and Jon was glad to see it go. Still, he feared tomorrow.

The Duke was surprised at the early arrival of his guests. "Is everything OK?" He said as they rode up.

"Apparently the dragon has killed again." Replied Father Leonis. "Your man Boady seems to be suffering from dragon sickness; I suspect that he witnessed the attack. He brought a Kell girl's body back."

"Oh my!" Said the Duke, seemingly taking the news hard. "I had better go and check on him. Wren, get me Beast."

"You'll learn nothing right now." Said Father Leonis. "The man is mad with dragon sickness. Sir Jon and Lil are looking after him. It is best to leave them alone. Hopefully he will recover soon."

The Duke waived off Wren with the horse. "He brought a body back?" Asked the Duke. "Why would he do that?"

"I don't know." Replied the priest. "Apparently Sir Jon knew the girl, however. We just buried her. She was a terrible mess."

The Duke almost blanched when he heard that one of the victims was a friend of Sir Jon's. He determined that it would be best to avoid the young knight, even though he desperately wanted to know what had happened.

Just then Aethelstan came out to them. "Your Majesty!" He exclaimed. "Are you done your riding so soon? I would be glad to ride with you if you wish; I have a fine new horse."

"No thank you." Said the King flatly. "Uncle, is there a room where I might have some privacy? I need to collect my thoughts."

"Of course, my Lord." Said the Duke enthusiastically. "Wren, help the King down from his horse. Your room should be all ready for you."

Aethelstan tried to find an opportunity to inject himself into the conversation, but there was little conversation to join. He was largely ignored as his father led the King to his room personally.

"Stan, why don't you see what has happened to Wil while I show Father Leonis to his chamber." Said the Duke.

Aethelstan was not enthused about being told to look after a mere page, but he went to do it hoping to find out what had happened. Meanwhile, the Duke took Father Leonis to his room and determined to learn what he could.

"Father Leonis, what exactly happened?" He asked. "I understand that the dragon has killed again, but what has happened to Boady? Why did he bring a body back?"

Father Leonis sighed and told the Duke what had basically happened. "Boady seems distraught that he did not do his duty." Said the priest. "He says that he can't do his duty and that Sir Jon must kill the dragon. He seems entirely mad."

"I asked Boady to see if there was any sign of the dragon." Said the Duke. "He did his duty and more. What can he possibly mean? Perhaps I should tell him that he did his duty."

"Perhaps." Replied Father Leonis sternly. "But I would wait. Hopefully Boady has fallen asleep. He is in the grip of dragon sickness and I doubt that he would understand a word you say right now."

"You may be right." Said the resigned and distraught Duke. "I will check on him tomorrow. I will leave you now; we will have supper in about two hours."

The Duke left the room and wandered a bit aimlessly until he found himself in front of his chapel. This room was not used very much; in fact, the Duke no longer had a personal chaplain. The local priest was summoned on the rare occasions that he was wanted. Nevertheless, at this moment, the Duke felt like entering.

It was a larger room, but not too large. There were four pews that each could sit about four people, a single stained glass window depicting the virgin mother holding the Christ child, and a simple altar table overlooked by a large crucifix. The candle indicating the presence of Christ in the Eucharist was not lit.

The Duke had an odd relationship with faith. He acknowledged God and the church, took the sacraments, and was content in his opinion that he was a good man. The fact was that he trusted his soul to the church; if he went on most Sundays and the high holidays and took the sacraments, then the church would see to his salvation. Despite this, he did not trust the clergy in general; he viewed them as hucksters who were intent on separating him from the 'evil' influence of his money. He trusted the church but had little use for those in it. He lived by the creed that God helped those who help themselves.

At that moment, the Duke was not sure that he could help himself. He was not even sure what problem he faced. Perhaps Boady was acting; playing his role to the extreme. Certainly Father Leonis seemed very much convinced of the dragon's existence. Still, the situation made him uneasy; it did not feel like he was in control. How could he help himself if he was not in control?

Unconsciously he made the sign of the cross and knelt down. He looked up at the crucifix; he had nothing to say. Finally, his heart poured out what was in it: "This game wearies me. It does not serve a further purpose. Please end it, God." It was the sincerest prayer that he had said in years; he had set the terms of his faith and he was living by them.

Aethelstan found Wil walking out of the barn after having seen to his and the others' horses. "Welcome back Wil." He said by way of greeting. Athelstan was possibly the last person that Wil wanted to see.

"Hello Aethelstan." Replied Wil. "What have you been up to?"

"Not a lot." Replied the Duke's son trying to be friendly. "How about you? What has happened?"

"We have seen evidence that the dragon has indeed attacked." Replied Wil. "There is little doubt about it this time. In fact, Boady apparently witnessed it. It was not a pleasant sight."

"So perhaps we weren't so wrong after all." Replied Aethelstan. "Perhaps the Kells were attacked by men AND a dragon."

Wil looked at Aethelstan not knowing what to say. Apparently the possibility of having been wrong was not something that this person could entertain. "Perhaps." He said quietly. "Do you know where I am to be quartered?"

"My father arranged a room for you near the King's." Replied the Duke's son. "I'll show you where it is."

Lil and Jon had a quiet supper together. While it was obvious why neither of them had much to say, Jon began to suspect that Lil might be angry at him. It would be unfair if she was, but Jon was feeling guilty and felt that he deserved anger; but not from Lil. She had no right to judge him.

"Hey, guess what I got yesterday!" He said trying to break the mood.

"What?" Asked Lil in a tired but not unfriendly way.

"Let me get it." Said Jon getting up and going to his saddle bag. He pulled out the manuscript that he had purchased. "It's the Sermon on the Mount from the Matthew Gospel. I bought it from a book seller yesterday."

Lil reached out her hands to hold the pages. "Wow. Real scripture." She said with a sense of awe. "I've never had the actual word of God in my own hands. Can you read some of it to me? I really need the Word of God right now."

Jon began to read out loud, but Lil seemed fidgety. "Do you know what it means?" She asked.

"I'm sorry Lil." He replied. "Let me try to interpret the Latin."

Jon began again, interpreting phrases as best he could as he went along. It was tedious work, but Lil sat enraptured by what he said. She actually smiled as he went through the Beatitudes. When he got to the Our Father he was tempted to gloss over what it said, but Lil insisted on hearing every word. Right after the Our Father he translated the following:

"If you forgive men their wrongs your heavenly Father will forgive your wrongs. But if you do not forgive others then your Father will not forgive you." (Matt 6:14-15)

Jon paused after saying this. He realized how full of anger he was. He had not been there when Wulf's father had died, but he had been sucked up into the lie about the dragon by Boady and the Duke. He was angry that Boady had killed Carm. He was livid that the Duke had sent him to do it. There was a part of him that wanted to see both men brought to justice. They deserved it.

And yet, that was not at all what he wanted. He wanted Boady back. He wanted the Duke to help the King govern well. He also did not want to be held accountable for killing the Schumacher boy or for the lies that he had helped to spread. He wanted forgiveness for them and himself. He continued to read.

As he read, Jon began to realize that the Sermon on the Mount was a practical guide to living the Christian life. There was a lot in the writing that said you needed to clean up your own life before you could begin to try to tackle other people's sin. It really seemed to be saying that you should let other people deal with their sin.

"How can you say to your brother 'Let me take the speck out of your eye,' when there is a log in your own eye? Hypocrite, first remove the log from your own eye, and then you will see clearly enough to take the speck out of your brother's eye." (Matt 7:4-5)

Jon needed to start sawing at the logs he saw in his own eyes. He realized that he needed forgiveness every bit as much as Boady or the Duke. When he had read the entire manuscript he felt moved by what he had read.

"Wow!" Said Lil. "That was awesome! I wish Boady had heard it."

"We'll let Boady hear it." Said Jon. "We'll read it to him when he wakes up. Lil, I think I want to go outside for a bit and pray." Lil replied with a smile as he got up to leave.

It was dark. The stars looked down on him. "You are an awesome God!" He thought as he walked a bit. He soon found himself at Carm's grave. He knelt beside it.

"For give us Carm." He said. "None of us wanted this to happen. Be with Jesus. Father, take Carm into your Kingdom. Forgive me Carm! Forgive me for ever having gotten mixed up in this lie! Jesus, help me! Help me kill this dragon! Rescue me, Lord!" He began to cry. What had been done could not be undone.

After a while he got up and wiped his tears. It was not that he really felt better, but he did not feel like he was alone with his problems. He knew that Jesus was with him. He also knew that his next step was to forgive Boady and the Duke.

Lil was kneeling by her cross praying when he came back inside. She smiled at him and made the sign of the cross. Then she walked up to him and gave him a hug. They held each other, speechless, for a long time.

"Let's try to get some rest." Said Jon at last. "Boady is going to need us when he wakes up."

Jon felt a stirring inside him as he laid down. Nothing had changed since he had found Boady, but he felt hope. Perhaps it was an irrational hope; but he had hope all the same. Wulf Schumacher visited him in his dreams, but this time Jon asked forgiveness. He admitted that what he had done was something terrible and wrong. He did not make excuses or try to justify what he had done. The face was not angry; it simply faded away.

38

God Works in Mysterious Ways

JON AWOKE EARLY, BUT NOT as early as Lil. Boady was still asleep as he left the room, but he found Lil kneeling by her cross.

"Good morning Jon." She said with red eyes that had clearly been crying and suffered from a lack of sleep. "I've been praying; would you like to join me?"

Jon knelt beside her and made the sign of the cross. "Heavenly Father, show us what we need to do." He prayed. "But help us to look to You, not us, for the answers. Your ways are not our ways. Help us to stay focused on You. Teach us to do things Your way. Amen."

"Amen." Repeated Lil. She looked up at him with a puzzled expression.

"I think Wulf will be coming by this morning." Said Jon as they rose to their feet. "Maybe you should go wash up while I get the fire going. It's going to be OK little sister."

Lil gave Jon a hug and then walked outside. Jon began to stoke the fire. As he placed wood on it he recalled what they had read last night: "You fool! Remove the log from your own eye." He recalled. He decided that he needed to do a better job of remembering God's way in what he did. As he set the table, he determined to clean himself up as much as he could. "Help me, Lord Jesus." He prayed silently.

Lil came in carrying eggs and looking much better. She had washed herself and pulled back her hair. "I'm going to make Wulf my special creation." She said. "I'm so sorry he didn't have a better visit."

"Sit down a second, Lil." Said Jon. They both sat at the table and Lil looked at Jon expectantly. "Do you know who I am?" He asked.

"Of course I do." Said Lil quietly. "You're Sir Jon, a knight of the realm, the Kings friend, ambassador to the Kells, Boady's helper, and most of all, my brother in Christ.

Jon was taken aback by the list of titles she had laid on him. There was something else he wanted to get off of his chest. "Thanks Lil." He said. "I guess I am all of those things, but there is more. Do you know who my father was?"

"I don't need to know Jon." Came the reply. "I know who your Father is."

Jon hesitated. "Listen Lil," he said, "I don't want to hide this anymore. My Father was the King's executioner; he may well have been the man who caused you father's death."

Lil looked at Jon with a blank expression. She seemed to be taking in what he had said. "I knew that Jon." She said. "You are not your father, and if you were, I would have forgiven you. I admit that it was hard when I first came to realize who you were, but now you're my brother; you're a decent and honest man who strives to do right. If you want forgiveness from me you have it, although I don't know what I need to forgive you for. I love you, brother; and I need your strength now. I need you to fulfil your quest and rescue Boady from his dragon sickness. I need you to be strong in the Lord for me. I want you to do what you prayed this morning: keep your eye on Him and do things His way."

Jon leaned over and gave Lil a hug. "Thank you sister." He said. "I will do my best. God willing, I will fulfill my quest."

It had not been what Jon had expected. He had hoped to lighten his burden by ridding himself of one secret, but instead he merely felt his main burden more fully. His sister, the girl who loved him, was counting on him to not only kill a dragon that did not exist, but to also 'rescue' Boady from his madness, and to do it all in 'God's' way. He felt more trapped than ever.

Jon went to the stream to wash as dawn was breaking. Had it not been for the flowers he would have barely noted Carm's grave. Was she counting on him too? He hoped not; it felt like the whole world was resting on his shoulders. How can you kill something that doesn't exist? With the truth? He hoped there was another way. As much as he wanted to do things God's way, the truth might well bring his whole world tumbling down. "Lord, give me a real dragon to slay." He prayed silently as he washed. God works in mysterious ways.

Walking back towards the house he saw the King and Father Leonis making their way from the Duke's manor. "Company," thought Jon, "just what we need." His mood was turning towards the worse.

"Good morning Wulf, Father Leonis." Said Jon as they rode up. "Did you sleep well?"

"Not particularly." Replied Wulf. "You?"

Jon did not answer, but helped them dismount.

"How's Boady?" Asked Father Leonis. "Any change?"

"He's been sleeping. It took a while, but he finally fell asleep." Replied Jon. "He was restless at first, but he is sleeping deeply right now."

"And Lil?" Asked Wulf.

"She's holding up." Said Jon. "She'll be glad to see you. She's making you her special creation for breakfast. She's a strong girl, but she's hurting a lot. I wish I could make it all go away."

"You need to kill that dragon, Jon." Replied Wulf.

Jon grunted and moved to go inside as the other two men followed. "Lil, we have company." Said Jon as he entered.

"Good morning Father Leonis. It's good to see you Wulf." She said turning from her cooking. "Do you need to wash up? Breakfast is almost ready."

"I washed before I got dressed." Said Wulf. "I do that before every meal in honor of you, my Lady."

"I'll head to the stream." Said Father Leonis as Lil blushed.

"Are you alright, Lil?" Said Wulf after the priest had left. "I worried about you all night. I want to help you somehow, but I don't know what to do."

"Thank you Wulf." Said Lil shyly. "Your being here helps. I need you to pray; my hope is in God, not in you or Jon or even myself. God has always been there for me, and He will be there this time as well. Pray, Wulf, pray."

Wulf wanted to hug her, but she was holding a hot pan. He followed her with his eyes as she put an omelet on each plate. She then put down the pan, walked up to him, and gave him a brief, friendly hug. He was gratified, but he had wanted more than that; he had wanted her to fall into his arms like she had yesterday.

Father Leonis returned and they all sat down around the table. As the priest began to make the sign of the cross Wulf interrupted him. "Let me say grace, Father." He said.

The King made the sign of the cross and everyone followed suit. "Bless us Lord, as you always do." He said. "You give, and You take away; blessed is Your name. We don't always understand what You are doing, but we don't have to understand; we need to trust. I trust you God. Bring Your joy back to us. Heal Boady. Heal us, Father. Use all of this to Your glory. In Jesus' name, Father, show us the way. Amen."

"Amen." Repeated the others. Lil just stared at Wulf and he began to feel uncomfortable.

"What Lil?" He asked in a startled way.

"That was beautiful, Wulf." She said quietly. "It was like you were praying from my heart."

Wulf smiled and blushed. "I'm sorry that this visit had so little happiness for us." He said. "Jon told me I needed to keep my expectations under control."

"It's not your fault Wulf." Said Lil still looking at him. "I am so thankful that you were here."

It was an uncomfortable moment for Jon and Father Leonis to witness. Jon cleared his throat. "So, what happened to Wil?" He said to break the mood.

"Wulf was hoping that Boady might join us at the table, so he asked Wil to meet us here later." Replied Father Leonis. The King and Lil continued to look at each other as if they were in a silent conversation. "This is really a fine breakfast, Lil." Continued the priest. "I can see why Wulf was so looking forward to it."

"Thank you, Father." She replied as the spell broke. "I do enjoy cooking."

The meal ended too soon for Wulf and Lil. The time for parting had come.

"My Lady, it has truly been an honor meeting you." Said the priest. "You are everything and more than what I was told. You have a profound faith; I wish I was as confident as you. I hope we are able to see each other again."

Lil smiled and curtsied.

"Sir Jon, are you ready to go?" Continued Father Leonis.

"By your leave, my Lord," said Jon to Wulf, "I wish to stay here a while longer. I want to see if I can speak with Boady and figure out a way to fulfill my quest."

"Of course, Sir Jon." Said the King. "I would have been disappointed if you had not asked."

The King turned to Lil. "I will miss you." He said bluntly. "I will pray, as you asked. I have been praying, and I will pray more. I will trust in God." He clearly wanted to say more, but something inside him made him stop.

A tear came to Lil's eye. Suddenly she fell into his arms just as he had hoped. She held him fast, not in a romantic way, but in a sincere and loving way. "I'll miss you too, Wulf." She said. "Be a great King, and do pray. I will be praying for you."

This time Father Leonis cleared his throat. Slowly the two of them let go of each other and stood side by side, twin shades of red rising in their faces. They held hands as they walked outside.

Wil and the Duke came riding up as they came outside. Wulf let go of Lil's hand and mounted Mayflower as Jon helped Father Leonis onto his horse.

"Just a minute!" Cried Lil dashing around the side of the house. She came back holding several carrots and gave each horse one to eat, including Beast. She then handed another one to Wulf. "Be good to Mayflower." She said with a twinkle in her eye and a smile on her face.

The King laughed. "Good bye Mistress Lil." He said happily. "I look forward to seeing you again. Perhaps when all of this is over you can come and visit me. You can arrange that, can't you Uncle?"

"Of course, my Lord." Replied the Duke somewhat thrown off balance. "It was a pleasure having you visit. I'm sure that you know that you are most welcome any time."

"Sir Jon, we look forward to your return." Said the King turning to Jon. "Meanwhile, I urge you to find a way to fulfill your quest. Kill that dragon!"

"Yes, my Lord." Said Jon solemnly. "God willing I will find a way."

The King turned to leave and his two companions followed suit. He paused, looked back at Lil and winked as he gave her a smile. He then began to leave as Lil once again turned bright red. The two men left behind watched them leave mainly because Lil would not take her eyes off of them.

As they got to be a good distance away, the Duke cleared his throat. "Lil, I need to speak with Sir Jon." He said. "Do you have something to do?"

"Of course, my Lord." Said Lil finally taking her eyes off of the King. She then went inside.

Jon went over to the Duke's horse and helped him dismount.

"They seem quite taken with each other." Said the Duke referring to Lil and the King. "Ah to be young again!"

Jon was not in the mood for small talk. "Why did you send him out again?" He said angrily. "What did you hope to accomplish?"

"You know as well as I that the dragon has to be real or we will all suffer the consequences." Replied the Duke forcefully. "Boady succeeded better than I could have hoped. How is he?"

"He's a wreck." Replied Jon. "You've shattered him. He seems stark raving mad."

"I shattered him?" Asked the Duke. "I did no such thing. What exactly happened?"

"Near as I can tell, Boady found two girls in the preserve and he killed them." Said Jon, still angry. "One of them was only a few years old. She was a girl that I knew. Boady may have used the daggers, but their blood is on your hands."

"You're being rather impertinent." Said the Duke returning Jon's anger. "Don't forget your responsibility in all of this. Your entire life is built on the foundation of the dragon. You should be grateful that I strengthened that foundation."

Jon remembered the 'log' in his own eye, but still, it was not easy to ignore the fact that the Duke had turned both he and Boady into murderers. Now he was acting like Boady's madness was just an unfortunate and unexpected side effect.

"You're right." Said Jon. "I'm not innocent, but why do you insist on feeding this dragon? I need to kill it. How do I kill it?"

"Jon, we are in this together." Said the Duke. "You'll... we'll find a way to kill this dragon. I've brought Boady the rest of his pay. He's certainly earned it. I need to see him."

"No." Said Jon. "He's finally sleeping, and he does not need to see you the first thing when he wakes up. You can pay him later. I don't think you realize what has happened to him. Father Leonis calls it dragon sickness, but Boady has gone quite mad with guilt over his sin. I'll tell him you stopped by, but I need to try to help him back to our world."

The Duke took a few paces to try to get control of his temper. Who was this young man to tell him whom he could and could not see? He had practically made 'Sir Jon.' Still, Jon was a friend of the King's, and he held a secret that could end everything the Duke had accomplished. Perhaps he should have killed him when he first found him, but it was too late now. Their fates were intertwined. The Duke forced a smile onto his face.

"OK, Jon." He said. "I have to trust you. Don't let me down, and tell Boady I wish him well."

With that the Duke climbed onto Beast with surprising ease. Jon stood there glaring at him. The Duke nodded and rode off.

Jon went inside and found Lil feeding Boady in his bed. He looked haggard, but that was better than looking stark raving mad. "Good morning Boady." He said with a smile on his face. "How are you feeling today?"

"Not well. My Lord." Replied Boady. "I'm afraid I won't be able to help you today."

"That's alright, Boady." Said Jon. "You remember that I am not a knight in your house, don't you? I'm just Jon; your friend. Your friend who wants to help you."

Boady just stared at him uncomprehendingly. Lil offered him some more egg. He ate it staring at Jon. "Nobody can help me." He said after swallowing the food. "I'm doomed." He began to cry again.

Lil urged Jon to leave, but Jon came and took the food from her instead. "Lil, trust me, will you?" He said. "Leave the house for a bit. Boady and I need to talk."

"He's not ready, Jon." She protested, but Jon had that feeling; for some reason he knew that the arrow would hit the target.

"Trust me." He said. Lil nodded and left.

Boady looked at Jon suspiciously. Jon offered him more food, but he would not take it. They sat in silence for several minutes.

"Boady, you once told me there were no innocent men; I am not an innocent man." Said Jon without knowing why. "I'm not innocent, in fact I deserve hell, but I am forgiven. You can have that forgiveness too."

Boady began to cry again. "I'm damned Jon." He said through the sobs. "It's a Cardinal sin! Even the church can't forgive a Cardinal sin. I'm damned, and I am afraid. She called on Jesus, and I just cut her down. I'm damned. There can be no forgiveness for what I have done. I beat them both with a rock. I crushed their bones. I'm damned; no just God could possibly forgive me."

Jon reached out his arms and took Boady into them. Boady continued to cry and his tears soaked Jon's shirt. Jon did not know what to say.

"Boady, we're all guilty." Said Jon. "My sin killed Jesus. I am a liar and a murderer. Jesus didn't come to condemn; He came to save. The church can't forgive your sins. Only Jesus can. At best the church can bring you to Jesus. As long as Jesus lives, you have hope. He died for ALL of our sins. Accept His gift. Accept His forgiveness."

Boady let go of Jon. "He can't forgive my sin." He said.

"He can and He will." Insisted Jon. "It's why He came. He is your hope and salvation. You and I have a lot to be forgiven, but Jesus saves. Let Carm's grave remind you of how grateful you are to have a Savior. What we've done can't be undone, but there is hope in Jesus. Let's be grateful and live our lives for Him. Both of us. Don't let yourself be damned. Bring Jesus into your heart."

"I need a Savior." Said Boady. "I need you Jesus!" He cried out.

"Do you want to pray with me?" Asked Jon.

"He can't forgive what I've done." Said Boady slumping back into his bed. "I can't forgive what I've done."

"You're right Boady, you can't forgive what you've done, but Jesus can." Said Jon. "You have to let Him. You can't forget it; you need to remember what Jesus saved you from. You need to remember that Jesus saved you from being damned, because you surely are without Him. I'm damned without Him too. We both need to remember that. Let Him save you Boady; accept salvation. He is your only hope."

"He would do that for me?" Said Boady. "I'm a cold blooded murderer."

"'Forgive them Father for they know not what they do.' Jesus said that as He was being crucified." Said Jon. "He prayed forgiveness for His own murderers. He can forgive you."

"He's my only hope." Said Boady in a stunned voice. "I have hope in Jesus! I have hope in Jesus." He then slumped back in his bed and went to sleep.

"Boady?" Said Jon. "Boady? Do you want to pray?"

Boady was mostly asleep, but he kept repeating: "I have hope in Jesus."

Lil came back in the room. "How is he?" She asked.

"I've got hope in Jesus." Said Boady in his dreamlike state.

"I don't know." Said Jon. "I think I shared the Gospel with him. I thought he was going to accept God's forgiveness, but then he fell asleep."

"Forgiveness for what?" Asked Lil.

Jon was taken aback by the question. "We all need forgiveness, Lil." He replied.

"Yes we do." She said.

They both left the room as Boady continued to repeat: "I've got hope in Jesus."

God's ways are not our ways. God works in mysterious ways.

39

The Path to Saint Rumwold

BOADY SLEPT FOR MOST OF the day. Jon was restless, so the first thing he did was make a cross for Carm's grave. He was not a wood worker, so the finished product was crude, but he figured that Jesus had died on a crude cross. He prayed that it was an appropriate marker for her grave; he trusted God that it was.

He then did other chores. He gathered fire wood, weeded the garden, and brushed Thunder. After the mid-day meal with Lil he walked to see Kris and get some bread.

"Sir Jon!" Said Kris as Jon entered his kitchen. "Welcome back. How is Boady? What is 'dragon sickness?'"

"Boady is not well." Said Jon. "He has a madness. He believes that the dragon has damned him."

Kris took the news hard. "Not Boady!" He said. "Boady is such a good soul, a caring soul, so many people depend on him. What can we do my Lord?"

"For one thing, we can stop pretending that I am anything other than your old friend's son." Snapped Jon. "I am the old executioner's son, and though I may become more than that, that is who I will always be. Please Kris, show me the same level of respect and kindness that you gave me the first time we met; you are still that same man to me."

"Of course." Said Kris puzzled. "Are ye hungry lad?"

Jon smiled remembering their first meeting. "I've eaten," he said, "but I think we could use some bread."

"You're your father's son in the best way, lad." Said Kris. "You do well not to forget where you've come from. I'll fill a sack for you."

Jon stayed a while and talked to Kris. It was good to escape thoughts of dragons and duties for a while. Kris was particularly interested about Jon's life at the castle and friendship with the King. Jon found it hard to stay humble as he recounted all that had happened to him recently.

When Jon told about the misery of the Kell lands, Kris was particularly moved. "War is a terrible thing." Said Kris. "I know they're heathens, but I wouldn't wish such suffering on a stray dog much less a child. Our King is doing a fine thing in offering them help."

Jon felt better after this visit. Kris had given him several loaves of bread, but not as many as the first time he and Boady had gone to him for food. The bountiful Summer had lessened the number of people who depended on Boady and Lil to feed them. It was a fairly small burden that Jon carried as he walked back to Boady's house.

Boady was awake and sitting at the table when Jon entered. Jon smiled at the sight.

"There's a welcome sight!" Jon said with a strong feeling of sincerity. "Are you feeling a bit better Boady?"

Lil gave Jon a worried look. Boady looked at him with sad and tired eyes. "I can't just lie there." He said. "I'm so tired, but I can't just lie there."

Jon sat down next to Boady.

"He wants to visit the grave." Said Lil. "I think it's a bad idea. He needs rest, not more tears."

Jon understood why Lil felt that way, but he felt she was wrong. He did not know why, but he felt Boady should see the grave. "I'll take you Boady." He said as Lil gave him the first angry look that he had ever seen from her.

Boady moved to get up, and Jon quickly helped him. They slowly walked outside and approached the grave. At first Boady stood by it just staring. He was struck by how small the hole that had been dug was. He fell to his knees and began to cry.

Lil stood at the house and watched from a distance while Jon knelt down beside him. "Boady, we can't undo what was done," he said, "but you don't have to spend eternity living with it. Accept Christ's forgiveness."

"You speak of salvation after I'm dead." Said Boady angrily through his tears. "I don't need help after I am dead; I need forgiveness now. I don't need the god of the dead; I need the God of the living!"

"Boady, God is not just for the dead." Said Jon quietly. "He conquered death. He lives. God offers you abundant life now; in Christ. Do you think that Lil and I are living just to die? God gives us joy now; His promises are true now. Let God come into your life and be born again into the newness of life."

"Why would God offer me that?" Asked Boady. "I don't deserve it. What can I do for him?"

Jon remembered something else he had read in the Sermon on the Mount:

> "What man is there among you, when his son shall ask him for a loaf, will give him a stone? Or if he asks for a fish he will not give him a snake, will he? If you then, being evil, know how to give good gifts to your children, how much more shall your Father who is in heaven give what is good to those who ask of him?" (Matt 7:9-11)

"It's not because you can do anything for Him." Said Jon. "It's because He loves you. As unlovable as we two murderers and liars are, God still loves us like we are his children. All you have to do is ask, Boady. You can start living for God."

Lil had become concerned and walked up to the two of them. Just when she arrived Boady fell flat across the grave and cried out:

> "Jesus help me! Come into my heart and fix me; make
> me new again! Give me life in You! Let me know that
> You are real and alive!"

Lil fell to her knees and made the sign of the cross. "Thank you Jesus!" She prayed. Then she smiled at Jon.

Boady laid on the grave for a while, but he had stopped crying. Finally, he got up. "I need to leave tomorrow." He said. "I have to visit the shrine of St. Rumwold." He walked back towards the house.

Jon and Lil looked at each other. "Who is St. Rumwold?" Asked Lil. Jon shrugged in reply and they both hurried to catch up to Boady. They walked with him in silence, not knowing what to say. One thing seemed clear: Boady was alive again. Once inside the house he sat down and began to eat with gusto.

The two younger people sat down at the table with him. "Boady, who is St. Rumwold?" Asked Jon.

Boady looked up startled. "He was an infant that died." He said. "The son of King Penda, or something. He was martyred when he was only three months old. Before he died, he managed to preach a sermon to the Bishop, and healed many sick people. It sounds like absolute nonsense to me, but God wants me to go there, and I am going to do what He wants. I am not going to shirk my first duty as His man."

"You don't need St. Rumwold to be in God's family, Boady." Said Lil. "Jesus did it all. You don't need anything but Jesus."

Boady smiled at Lil as if she was crazy. "I know that, my girl." He said kindly. "I am not going there to pray or anything. I just need to go there."

"I'll go with you." Said Jon resolutely.

"Thanks, Jon." Replied Boady. "I have to do this alone. I don't know why, but God has put it on my heart. You showed me the way; I will always be grateful for that, and I know that my hope is not in St. Rumwold, or you, but in Christ alone. I'm not crazy, but I have to go."

Jon and Lil looked at each other. None of this made sense, but there was no room for argument. After he finished eating, Boady decided to go to the stream to wash. Jon went with him and they made small talk.

Boady acted as if nothing had happened, except on their way back, as he walked by the grave, he paused. "She deserves a better cross." He said. "You did well, Jon, but when I get back I'm going to make her a better one. She'll always be a saint to me."

Boady ate well again at the evening meal, and afterwards Jon once again struggled through a reading of the Sermon on the Mount.

As Jon ended, Boady commented on the final words that Jesus had said in the Sermon. "I am building my house on the rock." He said. "The winds and the flood may come, but Jesus has saved me once; He won't let me perish."

The two younger people were amazed. Boady was certainly a changed man. Afterwards, they all went to bed and slept soundly. They all thanked God in their prayers. For this brief moment, their worries were cast aside; the world seemed a peaceful and hopeful place.

When Jon awoke the next morning, the first thing he noticed was that Boady was not in his bed. He jumped up and quickly woke Lil. "Boady's gone!" He exclaimed. "He must have left without saying good bye."

Both of them hurried into the other room feeling panic, but there they found Boady kneeling by Lil's cross. Good morning, you two." He said. "You're up early; would you like to join me in prayers?"

This was a very different Boady. While Boady had participated in their prayers before, he had never said any himself; at least not that they could remember. Previously, while he had not been hostile to their faith, he had given a sense that he had not shared it either. He was a helpful person in the community, he cared for the sick and the hungry, but he had not seemed to do that as a matter of faith; he was just a decent guy who did his duty. Of course, only Jon and the Duke knew that he was also a cold blooded killer.

Lil knelt down beside Boady and Jon soon joined them. They all made the sign of the cross in wonderment. "Father, you are our hope and salvation." Prayed Boady. "You are the real and firm foundation of our lives. Guide us, Lord Jesus, guide my steps on the journey to St. Rumwold. Help us to know how we are to kill this dragon, and the many dragons that trouble our lives. Protect Lil and Jon while I am gone; thank you for bringing them into my life. Have mercy on the soul of little Carm. She called on You as I am calling on You; let us both know that you are there for us, even in the dark moments. Thank you Lord Jesus, thank you. Amen."

"Amen." Repeated Jon and Lil.

"Shall we go wash up?" Asked Boady. "I've already stoked the fire."

"I'll fix breakfast." Said Lil distractedly. "Please bring me some eggs and some water on your way back."

Jon grabbed a pot and the two men made their way to the stream. On the way, Boady stopped at the grave and said: "I'll get you a new cross, don't you worry my sweet little saint."

Jon was bewildered by his behavior. Was Boady sane? Jon had his doubts.

They began to wash. "The Duke stopped by yesterday to check on you." Said Jon. "He wanted to pay you some money he said he owed you."

Boady looked up with a suddenly serious look on his face. "I don't want his blood money." He said. After a pause he seemed to change his mind. "Tell him I will collect it when I return." He added mysteriously.

Jon filled the pot with water and Boady went and collected some eggs. Lil had heated a pan and began to scramble the eggs. The table was set with bread and cheese. After she had cooked the eggs, she used the water to wash herself.

They all sat down and Boady began to make the sign of the cross. "Let me." Said Lil. "Father, You give and You take away. Blessed be

Your name. We thank you for this food, and we thank you for saving Boady; guide him Lord. While we may not understand Your ways, bless the journey that he is about to take. May Your will be done; we pray in Jesus' name, Amen."

Boady smiled at her. "You pray in such a lovely way, my girl." He said. "I am so glad that God brought you into my life."

The meal progressed mostly in an awkward silence. Boady smiled the whole time; he smiled so much that Jon firmly came to suspect that he was still suffering madness. When they finished Boady got up and began to arm himself with his daggers. He noticed that one was still bloody. He stared at it a moment and then thought: "I can wash it." He took his canteen and went to the stream.

"Do we let him go?" Asked Lil as she and Jon watched him fill his canteen and clean his daggers.

"I don't know how to stop him." Replied Jon. "He seems determined; we will just have to trust in the Lord."

Boady stopped at the grave on his way back and appeared to say a quick prayer. Then he stood before them. "I should be back in four or five days." He said. "It is a two-day journey to the Saint's shrine, and I don't get the sense that I will need to stay long."

"Why are you going?" Asked Jon.

"I don't know." Came the reply. "Somehow I think that God intends to show me how to kill the dragon. I don't know what the infant Saint has to do with it, but I must go."

Lil wrapped her arms around Boady and held him so tight he thought she might not let go. "You'll be alright my dear little girl." He said softly. "I'll be alright as well. You take care of Jon and the others while I am gone. I will see you soon."

"Are you sure you don't want me to go with you?" Called Jon.

"I have to do this alone." Replied Boady. "But I am not alone. Jesus is with me; don't worry."

Nevertheless, they did worry. They watched as he walked away. They did not go back inside until he was completely out of sight.

About an hour later they heard the heavy hoofs of Beast who was carrying Duke Heimsteady. Jon went outside to meet him.

"Good morning, Sir Jon." He said as he began to dismount. "How is Boady today?"

"He is much better." Replied Jon. "He is changed, but he is better."

"Good!" Replied the Duke. "I'd like to go in and visit with him. I have his money."

Jon gave the Duke a wry smile. "I told him you wanted to pay him, and he said that he would get the money later." He said. "Meanwhile he has left on a pilgrimage to St. Rumwold."

"Who in blazes is St. Rumwold?" Asked the Duke in surprise. Jon merely shrugged. "You let him go off by himself in his state? Are YOU mad?!"

"Boady has a new strength." Said Jon. "I don't understand why he is doing it, and it does not seem that even he understands, but he feels that he has to go. He feels he will learn how to kill the dragon there."

"And you let him go." Declared a clearly flabbergasted Duke. "This is the craziest thing I have ever heard. You better hope he doesn't say something that will hurt us all."

"I have faith." Replied Jon calmly.

"We'll soon find out what that's worth." Said the angry Duke remounting his horse. He glared at Jon who stood before him with a calm confidence. Finally, he rode off. "I should have killed him while I had the chance." He thought as he left.

At first Boady walked with a confident spring in his step, but as the miles passed he began to doubt what he was doing. He had no faith in St. Rumwold, so why would he go there. As he began to doubt his mission, he began to doubt Jesus. Why would God forgive him? Why did God love him? None of this made sense.

Then he saw some flowers growing on the side of the path that he was on. They reminded him of the flowers on Carm's grave. He had only one hope: Jesus. Either God was real or he wasn't. It wasn't Boady's faith that would create God, God had created him. If God was real, then Boady was saved. If God was not real, well, then it really didn't matter what he did. Boady carried on in hope as much as in faith.

He had not seen a single person all day. Apparently the path to Saint Rumwold was not well traveled. As it got dark he set up camp next to the path. He lit a small fire and began to eat. While he had been walking, Boady felt like he had purpose. Now that he was sitting alone eating, he felt utterly alone. He prayed, but he could only pray so long. He considered moving onwards in the dark, but he knew that he needed rest. He leaned up against a tree and waited for sleep to come.

Soon, he sensed the approach of someone. Reflexively he pulled a dagger out of his belt and hid behind the tree.

"Hello?" Someone called in a heavily accented voice. "Is anyone there? I come in peace."

"Who are you?" Growled Boady. "What do you want?"

"I am a weary traveler from afar." Said the man stepping near the fire. "I mean you no harm. I simply seek company for the night. This is a lonely path that we tread."

The man was oddly dressed and was of different appearance than anyone Boady had ever seen before. He carried a large pack, but whatever was in it must not have been very heavy, for he handled it with ease. On his head he wore a sort of wrapping; clearly this was not a Saxon, nor a Kell, nor a Norseman, nor any type of a man Boady had ever seen.

The man set down his pack. He had a sword on his belt with a curved blade, and a spear on his back. He looked dangerous, but somehow Boady did not feel threatened.

"I have my own food." Said the man. "I will share it with you if you like."

Boady stepped out from behind the tree. "Who are you?" He asked.

"My name is Sami." He replied. "I come from the land of Sham, beyond the River Jordan, near what you call the Holy Land. So many of your people come to our land, I thought I would visit yours. My intentions are more peaceful than those you send to us."

Despite the fact that he looked very much the part of a warrior, Boady felt a sense of comfort with this man. "Forgive my rudeness." He said. "You are welcome to share my camp and my fire." Boady put the dagger back into his belt.

"I am Sami." Said the man. "What is your name?"

"My name is Boady." Came the reply. "I have only basic supplies, but I can offer you some bread and some water."

"Very nice, Boady." Said Sami. "If you have enough water I have some tea that we could share."

"What is tea?" Asked Boady.

Let us boil some water and I will show you." Came the friendly reply.

Boady emptied his canteen into a little pot that he had brought knowing that there was a stream nearby. As the water heated, the two men talked.

"I am a dragon hunter by profession." Said Sami. "I have heard that there is a dragon loose in the Kingdom of Mersya."

"That is very interesting." Said Boady. "I am seeking a way to kill a dragon."

"Perhaps I can help." Said the strange man, in the strange clothes, with the strange profession.

Boady smiled to himself. He finally understood why God had set him on the path to St. Rumwold.

40

Are You the Dragon

WHILE BOADY HEATED WATER ON the fire, the dragon hunter, Sami, produced a bag filled with dried leaves. He sprinkled these leaves into the pot and smiled. "Even on a fine warm evening, a cup of tea can be relaxing and aid in the conversation." He said.

"You are traveling a lonely road." Said Boady. "Why would you come to Mersya by this way?"

"I have visited the holy sights of your people all along my journey." Replied the man from Sham. "When I heard of St. Rumwold I was most intrigued. I am coming from there."

"And what did you think of St. Rumwold?" Asked Boady. "I have never been there myself, but I know something of his story."

"The people of this land have a curious faith." Replied Sami. "The story is difficult to believe. Nevertheless, I saw desperate people giving their last coins in the hopes that the infant saint would heal them."

"Not all of us put our faith in the bones of a long dead infant." Replied Boady. "Some of us worship a living God; a God who daily reassures us of His existence. A God who came to earth to save mankind and to dwell among us so that we could relate with Him."

"I worship the God of the prophet Mohammed: Allah." Replied Sami. "I believe that you try to worship Him as well, but you have confused Him with His prophet Jesus. There is only one God."

"We also only worship one God." Replied Boady. "I do not know this Allah that you speak of, but our God came to us in the form of His son, Jesus. He died for our sins and conquered death by rising from the dead."

Sami looked like he wanted to say something, but changed his mind. "Tell me about this dragon you wish to slay." He said changing the subject. "Have you seen it? What has it done?"

"You ask more difficult questions than they may seem." Replied Boady. "In one sense, yes, I have seen him; I am very close to him. In another sense… The dragon has killed the innocent and continues to do so. His legend grows and I fear he may never stop killing. It is time I rid myself of him."

Sami took a small cup from his supplies and poured some tea into it. He then added some honey to the tea. Producing a second cup, he repeated the process and handed the first cup to Boady. "I think you will enjoy this." He said. "Mr. Boady, this dragon seems very personal to you. Did it kill someone you love?"

Boady took a sip of the tea. Its warmth was soothing and the sweetness of the honey gave it a flavor that made it a special treat. He savored it while thinking of how to respond. "The dragon is killing me." He said at last. "Perhaps it has already killed me. I am not the man that I once was."

The man looked at Boady while deep in thought. "I have killed two dragons on my journey thus far." He said. "Your dragon seems a bit more mystical than the others. I will tell you a secret: although I have killed two dragons, I have never actually seen one."

"I don't understand." Said Boady.

"Ah, but I think you do." Said Sami. "Twice, in Gaul, on my way here, I met people who were under the oppression of a dragon.

378

In both cases the dragon was not a physical beast; it was a story that took on a life of its own. Once the story was ended, the people were able to live in peace. Mr. Boady, is that the sort of dragon you need me to slay? This dragon seems so personal to you; are you its claws and its breath and its maw? Are you the dragon?"

At first, Boady was shocked and afraid, but then a sort of peace came over him. While he did not see himself as the dragon, he had been its breath, and especially its claw. Perhaps it was because of his weak emotional state, or perhaps it was the tea, but he came to a determination that, for once, he would tell the secret whose keeping was killing him.

"I am not the dragon." He said. "I am under its power. Yes, this is the same sort of dragon that you killed in Gaul."

"This is an amazing land." Replied Sami. "You believe in infants that preach sermons and you believe in dragons. The world has enough real wonders; why do you have to create more? Let me show you something."

The strange man retrieved something from his pack. When he unwrapped it Boady was confronted by the head of a hideous beast. It had a long snout and large, very sharp teeth. Boady was awestruck by what he saw.

"I thought you had never seen a dragon!" He exclaimed. "And yet, you carry a dragon's head in your pack? How does it breathe fire?"

"It does not." Replied Sami. "These beasts are called crocodiles. They inhabit the waters in the south of Sham, and are plentiful in the Nile river in Egypt. They are long, lizard like animals; this one was probably two or three paces long. I have found that in these superstitious lands, they are thought to resemble a dragon's head."

"It does indeed." Said Boady in wonder. "I need to have it. Can I buy it from you?"

"Mr. Boady, it is very expensive, and you need more than just a dragon's head." Replied Sami. "How would you kill it? How can you escape the fire of a beast like this? What will you do with the rest of its body? Convincingly slaying a dragon is not so easy as showing up with its head."

Boady realized that he was right. There needed to be more than a dragon's head to convince people that the beast had been killed. Belief dies hard. If the tale was not convincing, the Duke could easily bring the dragon back to life.

"Put some more wood on the fire." Said Sami cryptically. "Make it hot enough that it is difficult to stand nearby."

Boady did not ask why, he simply began to gather wood. While he fed the fire Sami began to put on a sort of armor that comprised most of the pack that he had been carrying. The armor did not seem heavy or thick enough to stop a weapon; Boady was sure that he could easily pierce it with a dagger. Meanwhile, the fire became so hot that Boady had difficulty standing near it.

"Behold." Said Sami. The strange man, now clad in even stranger armor, walked up to the fire, circled it closely twice, and then walked right through it. Boady was mystified. He should have been burnt up, but he came to stand in front of Boady unhurt. Was this magic armor? Boady poked the armor and it gave way to his touch. It was warm, but not burnt; he could see Sami smiling inside of his helmet.

"That is amazing." Said Boady with awe.

Sami removed the helmet. "Don't you want to ask me if it is magic?" He said.

"It certainly seems magical." Said Boady. "Still, you do not strike me as a magician."

"No, I am not." Replied Sami. "War is a terrible thing. When we attack a city we throw fire at it until it is a raging inferno. Then some of us, those who have this armor, charge through the flames and slaughter the stunned and bewildered inhabitants that still survive. It is how we fight."

"Yes," said Boady in a quiet voice, "war is a terrible thing. Is that why you are here?"

"I do not understand what you are asking." Said Sami in reply.

"You have traveled across the known world to this path; why?" Asked Boady. "Did you grow tired of war? Are you also sick of the killing? Were you asked to kill one too many innocents?"

"The land I come from is a land of constant fighting." Said Sami. "I did my duty since I was old enough to ride and hold a

380

sword. I am taking a break from my duty. We are all born to our duty; although it is not always pleasant."

"Although we are men from worlds apart, I think I understand what you are saying." Said Boady solemnly. "I also seek to escape unpleasant duty. Let us be brothers in arms; I wish you to be my friend."

Sami looked at Boady with a very serious expression. "In all of my journey in these Christian lands, you are the first to offer me friendship." He said. "I would value knowing that I at least made one friend in my travels." The two clasped hands, and then gave each other an awkward hug.

"Tomorrow I will take you to my home." Said Boady. "My girl Lil will make us a fine meal and you will meet my friend Sir Jon, who has been quested to slay the dragon. He is a good man, and he knows the secret of it. Let us rest, my friend."

Sami took off the rest of the armor with Boady's help and the two laid down to get some sleep. As the fire burned lower and lower they could see the stars looking down on them. Boady felt a sense of release; he no longer craved sleep. He thanked God for sending him Sami. He would have thought that God would send him a Christian, but he was not going to try to tell Him how to answer his prayer. He had a peaceful night's sleep; as did Sami.

When they awoke the next morning, Boady found himself in a good mood. He did not feel entirely himself, but the difference was stark. Perhaps it was just that he had felt so badly ever since he had last been the dragon, but Boady attributed it to the fact that he now had hope; hope for forgiveness in Christ, and hope that he and Sami could finally rid this land, and himself, of the dragon.

The two shared their food and so, had a hearty breakfast. Sami made some more tea, and Boady found that the drink seemed to energize him. He had no idea how rare tea was at this time, or the distance that the leaves had traveled in order for him to drink it. Sami was a generous guest.

"Did you sleep well, Mr. Boady?" Asked Sami.

"I did." Replied Boady. "And you?"

I was surprised at how well I slept." Said Sami. "You give me comfort in our friendship. I sense that you are trustworthy. Many men might have tried to kill me in the night in order to steal the dragon's head and the fireproof armor."

Boady was glad that that thought had not occurred to him, but he was also a little puzzled why? He knew that he would have at least considered it beforehand, but now he was changed. "This dragon has killed too many already." He replied seriously. "I have pledged my friendship to you. You have no reason to fear me, and I do not think I have a reason to fear you."

"I trust you, Mr. Boady." Said Sami. "I am not sure why, but I sense that I can."

Boady smiled. "Since we are friends," he said, "You can drop the 'Mister' in my name. I am a common man; you can call me Boady."

"Ok Boady." Replied Sami with a smile.

The two packed up their belongings, filled their canteens at the stream, and began to walk the way that Boady had just come. Boady spent the time pointing out different types of trees and flowers on the way and made comments about the habits of different animals and insects that they encountered as they walked. Sami listened with enthusiastic interest. It had indeed been a lonely road that he had traveled, and it felt good to experience some companionship.

Neither spoke of God during their journey, but Sami stopped several times and prostrated himself towards the southeast when he prayed. While Boady did not join in, he also prayed during this time. Boady was impressed by the devotion that Sami showed to Allah; he hoped that he would develop equally devout habits towards his God and Savior. Still, he understood that his salvation was not dependent on what he did, nothing he could do would atone for his sin, forgiveness relied on the work of Christ. He prayed in gratitude, not in obligation. He prayed thanks for the gift he had already received, not in order to earn that which he knew he could not deserve.

They ate their mid-day meal as they walked, both in a hurry to arrive at their destination. It was late in the afternoon when they came into Duke Heimsteady's estate and very shortly thereafter they were approaching Boady's house.

Jon was brushing Thunder after having taken Lil for a ride in an attempt to brighten her day. When he saw Boady and another, oddly dressed man approaching he ran inside to tell Lil that there would be two more for the evening meal. Lil ran outside to insure herself that it was really Boady, back already from his pilgrimage to St. Rumwold's. The sight of him cheered her far more than the ride had.

Jon took Thunder to his stall while Lil added some more food to the stew that she was cooking. They both came back just as Boady and Sami approached the house.

Lil could not contain herself; she rushed upon Boady and gave him a big hug. "I'm so glad you're back." She said through tears of joy. "Did you find what you were looking for?"

Boady smiled but did not answer the question directly. "Sir Jon, Lil, this is my new friend Sami." He said. "I believe he is the answer to my prayer."

"Welcome Sami." Said Lil. "If you are Boady's friend, then I am sure you are my friend as well."

"Likewise," said Jon shaking Sami's hand, "any friend of Boady's is a friend of mine. Please call me Jon while we are in friendly company."

Sami was struck by the genuine friendliness of the two young people that he was meeting. For most of his journey in the Christian lands he had been met with suspicion and outright hostility. There was something different about this group of people.

"It is indeed an honor to meet you both." He said with his heavy accent. "Boady tells me I will enjoy your company and that Lil is certain to have a special meal for we two hungry travelers."

"I just put some more food into the stew." Said Lil blushing. "It should be ready soon. Perhaps you three men should wash up and the food will be ready when you return."

As they walked to the stream Jon felt it might be necessary to give Sami the usual speech about Lil's meal time habits. "Lil insists that we wash before every meal." He said. "It is a pleasant enough habit, and it is easier than displeasing the lady of the house."

"It is the custom where I come from." Replied Sami. "It seems that you may be the most civilized people that I have encountered thus far!"

Jon decided to spare him the rest of the standard warning; he was confident that Sami would be polite in his eating habits.

"Jon, Sami has a way for us to kill the dragon." Said Boady in excitement. "We can discuss it after we eat; I told him the truth."

Jon was shocked by what he heard. Had the Duke been right? Had Boady already betrayed them all? He became a bit more guarded. "I look forward to hearing what you have to say." He said stiffly. "Lil does not know the truth about the dragon, so it is best we do not discuss it around her."

Sami noticed the change in his demeanor and said nothing. The men washed and returned to the house. The table was set for four with Sami's seat being next to Jon on the newer bench. There was a large pot of stew in the center of the table as well as a fresh loaf of bread. It had been a long time since Sami had had this plentiful a meal.

"I'll say grace." Volunteered Boady before anyone else had a chance. While he made the sign of the cross, Sami bowed his head. "Father, you are an awesome God! You are gracious to us when we do not deserve it. Bless this meal, and guide us all in everything that we do. In Jesus name I pray, amen."

The 'amen' was repeated by Jon and Lil, but Sami clearly said something else: "Bismillah."

"Does that mean amen in your language?" Asked Lil.

"In a sense." Replied Sami. "It means 'In the name of God.' It is an expression of thanks for the blessing that we are about to receive. What does 'amen' mean?"

The three Christians looked around the table at each other. None of them knew the answer to Sami's question; it was simply what they said at the end of their prayers. Jon determined to ask Father Leonis or Brother Johan if he got the chance.

Seeing their difficulty, Sami changed the subject. "Lil, the stew looks delicious." He said. "May I ask what sort of meat is in it?"

"It is deer meat." She replied. "It is the last we have from a deer that Boady hunted. Have you eaten deer before?"

"Indeed I have." Said Sami smiling with what seemed to be an attitude of relief. "I did not recognize it because it smells so deliciously. I am sure this will be the best I have ever eaten."

"Amen means 'So be it, truly.'" Said Jon suddenly remembering some long lost lesson. "We also feel that it means we are in agreement on what was prayed. It is not a Latin word, although I do not know what language it is from."

"You are remarkable people indeed." Said Sami in response. "It is Hebrew, the language of the Jews. You are the first non-priestly Christians I have met that know what they pray."

"So you are not a Christian?" Asked Lil. "You do not know Jesus?"

"My people know of Jesus." Replied Sami. "We revere Jesus as a prophet, but we mostly follow the prophet Mohammed. We do not think that either Mohammed or Jesus were gods, there is but one God: Allah."

"But Jesus is so much more than just a prophet!" Interjected Lil.

"Lil, we both feel that we have found the truth in our relationship with God." Said Sami. "I do not think that we can both be right, but I would be a fool to follow your teachings, and perhaps you would be a fool to follow mine. I pray that the true God reveals Himself to both of us and that we follow His teaching. If He uses my life to influence yours, or your life to influence mine we will both be blessed. Meanwhile, let us eat in peace."

Jon liked what Sami had said. He did not want to follow any man's teaching; he wanted to follow the teaching of the God who lived in his heart. Silently he prayed that God would enter Sami's heart, but he did not think that he could argue Sami into believing in Jesus. He would have to show him the way if God gave him the chance.

"Yes!" Said Boady in a loud and resolute voice. "Let us have peace around the table. We have enough strife without creating more."

The rest of the meal passed in pleasant conversation. Sami told of the land of Sham beyond the River Jordan. He mentioned that he rode horses and this led to a discussion of the various advantages between the large horses that people in this part of the world rode, and the smaller, faster, and more hardy horses that Arabic people rode. Jon offered to let Sami try to ride Thunder, but warned him that the horse could be very temperamental.

When the meal was finished, Jon helped Lil clear the table.

"Lil, we three men need to take a walk." Said Boady. "We will come back shortly."

Lil's curiosity was piqued by this pronouncement, but she understood that she was to be excluded from the conversation that they were about to have. She hoped that Jon and Boady would tell Sami about Jesus, and she prayed for that while they were gone.

41

How to Kill a Dragon

T HE THREE MEN WALKED OUTSIDE and wandered away from the house as the sun began to set. They passed near the grave and Boady stopped to stare.

"Who is it?" Asked Sami.

"She is the dragon's latest victim." Said Boady. "A little girl who was in the wrong place at the wrong time. It turns out that Jon knew her; her name was Carm. I need to make her a better cross."

"Let us hope that she is its last victim." Said Sami putting a hand on Boady's shoulder. "Death is so often found where it has no proper place."

"So, you two have a plan to kill it?" Asked Jon seriously.

Boady shook off his melancholy and became animated. "Sami has something that looks like a dragon's head." He said. "He also has armor that allows him to walk through fire. We show the King how we will kill the dragon, and then go off for a couple of days to hunt it. We set a huge fire where we fought it, and come back with its head. Problem solved."

Jon thought the idea had possibilities, but he wanted to see the dragon's head. He also wondered why Sami would do this for them; a dragon's head would be of great worth. "It could work, God willing." He said, wondering whether God was willing to substitute one lie for another. "Why would you do this for people you only just met, Sami?"

"Well, Boady is the first man I have met on this journey who is willing to call me a friend." Replied Sami. "But this is not the first time that I have run into this situation either. I am not sure why Allah put me in possession of three crocodile heads, but I have used two of them to slay dragons in Gaul. Perhaps this is my duty on this trip. I do expect to be paid. In Gaul they promised to pay me but tried to kill me instead. I need enough money to return home."

"How much money are we talking about?" Asked Jon.

"It is difficult to say," replied Sami, "but you will agree that the dragon's head is worth a lot of itself, and ridding yourself of the dragon is priceless. I am hoping for ten gold pieces."

Every time he looked, Jon realized that there was more money in the world than he had ever imagined. He had assumed that he would need to ask for the money from somewhere, but this was a large sum to be asking for indeed.

"Sami, let me speak to Jon for a moment." Said Boady pulling Jon aside.

"Of course." Said Sami. "I will go and look at Jon's horse." He wandered towards the stall.

"Jon, this means everything to us." Said Boady. "I have money saved, including the half a silver of yours, and the Duke owes me another silver. Altogether it is about four gold pieces' worth. Do you have any money?"

Jon had just spent a good bit of money on the scriptures that he had bought. Most of that was Johan's, but Johan had not actually wanted it. He felt he had been silly. "I have one silver and five coppers." He said. "I will get another silver in a few weeks. There's no way we can get ten gold by ourselves."

"We will have to ask the Duke." Said Boady. "I am not sure that he wants the dragon dead as much as we do."

The two walked towards Sami, who saw their approach. "It is a fine horse, Sir Jon." Said Sami. "It is large, but seems like he would be very fast."

"Sami, we can come up with a little more than four gold pieces ourselves, but we will have to get the rest from the Duke." Said Jon bluntly.

"Or perhaps your King?" Replied Sami. "My friends, it pains me to ask you for such a large sum. Friendship includes a duty to help one another, but I need this money. We will be helping each other."

"The three of us will see the Duke tomorrow." Said Jon. "If I had the money I would pay you twice as much, Sami, but I do not have the money. Can you show me the head?"

"It is with my belongings in the sleeping chamber." Replied the dragon slayer. "Perhaps Boady could keep Lil occupied while I show it to you."

It was agreed and the three men went back into the house. Boady made small talk with Lil while Jon and Sami went into the other room.

Without speaking, Sami retrieved and unwrapped the crocodile head. Jon was shocked by what he saw. The maw looked vicious with its sharp and fanglike teeth. "There are beasts like that living where you come from?" He whispered. "No wonder you left."

Sami smiled and put the head away. "I have learned that it will take more to convince people." He replied. "We cannot merely burn wood as people will see through the deception. We need to make a different kind of fire. A fire that will burn hot and quick without leaving wood ash behind."

"How does one make such a fire?" Asked Jon.

"I can show you." Said Sami, still whispering. "We need Sulphur, pitch, charcoal, and tow."

Jon nodded in response. "We can get pitch and charcoal from the Duke, perhaps tow as well. There is Sulphur in the Kell lands to the West. We should be able to get some. How much?"

"The more the better, but we have to carry it with us as well." Replied Sami. "Perhaps a large sack or a small barrel. The dragon only needs to breathe once."

Jon nodded again, and the men returned to the main room. Jon did not read the scriptures that night since he did not want to offend Sami. Instead the four spent an hour or so listening to tales of Sami's travels. Soon enough it was time to sleep. They all slept soundly, but Jon felt a sense of nervous excitement. The end of his quest was near, but there were still obstacles to be overcome; the Duke was the first challenge that he would face.

Jon woke earlier than the others the next morning. He left the sleeping room and knelt by Lil's cross. "Father, guide me." He prayed. "I feel hope in ridding us of the dragon, but I also feel misgivings; one lie is being replaced by another. Help me to know what to do." He paused but felt nothing. "Please, Lord, don't be silent...Amen." He rose from his knees and went outside. Walking past the garden, he thoughtlessly picked a carrot to give to Thunder. "You're a good friend." He said as he fed the horse the carrot and stroked it between its ears. Jon was restless, he wished this day was already over.

Walking towards the creek, he stopped by Carm's grave. He stood for a moment looking at the cross, but nothing came to his mind. He continued on and washed. When he had finished he walked back up to the house.

Lil had just finished praying when he entered. "Good morning Jon." She said. "Did you sleep well?"

"Thanks. Lil, I did." He replied. "How about you?"

"I slept very well." She said with a smile. "I am so thankful that Boady seems to be getting over his dragon sickness. I take it that Sami can help you kill the dragon?"

"I think he can." Said Jon evasively. He did not want to lie to Lil. "He has killed dragons before; he gives us hope."

"Praise God!" Replied Lil. "I have been praying that He would show us the way!"

Boady and Sami came into the room. "Good morning my friends." Said Sami as Boady walked to the cross to pray.

"Good morning." Said Lil. "Jon says that you have killed dragons and can help us! I am so glad that God brought you to us!"

Sami gave a tense smile. "I have dealt with these situations in Gaul." He replied seriously. "It is not easy."

"You are an answer to prayers, Sami." She said. "I know that you are a part of God's plan for us all. Any ways, breakfast will be ready shortly if Jon would set the table. Perhaps you can go outside and wash up."

Boady finished his prayers and he and Sami went to wash up. On the way to the stream Boady urged Sami to go on alone as he paused to pray by the grave. He joined Sami at the stream and the two were soon on their way back to the house. Sami asked for privacy in the back room as he went in to say his prayers as well. When he was done, they all sat down to a hearty breakfast of eggs, cheese, and bread. At its conclusion the men looked at each other seriously.

"I guess we need to go and see the Duke." Said Jon. "Are you ready?"

The men nodded their assent and they left.

"Jon, I think you should do most of the talking." Said Boady on the walk to the manor. "You seem to have a way of saying the perfect thing."

Jon was not enthused by this, but truth be told it was an accurate statement. The rest of the walk he prayed fervently that God would guide his words. They walked up to the front door.

"Please tell the Duke that Boady and I are here to see him with a guest." Jon informed a servant.

The man returned shortly. "The Duke bids you wait in the court room." He said. "He is just finishing his breakfast and will be with you shortly." The three men were shown to the room where they waited in impatient silence.

The Duke arrived with a burst of enthusiasm. "Boady! It is good to see you recovered!" He said. "How are you feeling?"

"Better, my Lord." Replied Boady in a calm and quiet voice. "We come with a plan to rid us of the source of my sickness forever."

"And who is our guest?" Asked the Duke looking at Jon.

"My Lord, this is Sami." Replied Jon. "He is a dragon slayer that Boady met on his recent journey."

"Indeed?" Said the Duke walking up to Sami and apprising him like he might examine a new horse. "Have you slain dragons before?"

"I have slain two dragons of the same type you have in Gaul." Replied Sami in his heavily accented voice. "I am confident that this one may also be slain, my Lord."

"So you have discussed our dragon with him?" The Duke asked Jon and Boady in a stern voice. "Why would you do that? How has he earned your trust?"

Boady and Jon looked at each other. The fact was that Jon had no idea why Boady had shared the secret; it had merely been presented to him as something already done. Nevertheless, Boady gave Jon a look that relayed his expectation that Jon should respond.

"Sami has a dragon's head, and has described a plausible way for us to fight and kill it." Replied Jon. "He can demonstrate his ability to withstand fire, and has a way we can make a special kind of fire."

"Do you?" Said the Duke pacing. "Perhaps you can share the plan with me Sami."

"Of course, my Lord." Said Sami. "I will wear some special armor that I have and demonstrate to the King and anyone else that while wearing it I can withstand the dragon's breath. The plan would be for me to distract the dragon and draw its breath while Sir Jon pierces it with a spear. This will cause the dragon to erupt into a ball of flame, and an explosion leaving little remaining except for its damaged head."

"And this head is convincing, Sir Jon?" Asked the Duke.

"It is my Lord." Replied Jon. "If you care to see it you can visit Boady's house and we can show it to you."

"That is quite alright." Said the Duke still pacing and in thought. "I trust you; we need to trust each other. I think that the less I know, the better. The plan seems easy enough, why do you need me?"

"We need supplies and money." Said Jon in a matter of fact manner.

"What supplies and how much money?" Asked the Duke.

"We need pitch, charcoal, tow and Sulphur." Said Jon who then paused.

The Duke was looking at him expectantly. "I can give you all of that." He said. "We have some Sulphur left from the Spring fertilization. How much money?"

Jon was not sure how to ask the Duke. "The cost will be ten gold pieces." He said bluntly.

"That is a great deal of money." Said the Duke calmly and taking his seat. "Why do you need so much, and why should I pay the entire cost?"

Again, Jon did not know what to say. "It is the agreed upon price." He stated fl .tly. "Boady and I will pay a share. We can pay about four gold pieces worth, so we need six more from you."

"You have four gold pieces already, Sir Jon?" Said the Duke sarcastically. "The King must be quite generous to his favorite knight. Why don't you ask him for it? I am sure he would give it to you."

Jon was developing a strong dislike for the Duke. He did not at all like the tone with which he was being spoken to. "If you would like me to discuss it with him I will." He replied boldly. "I was not there at the King's death."

The Duke glared at him. After several moments of silence Jon continued: "I suspect the King will reward us for killing the dragon." He said. "I will share the reward with you. I will give you six parts to our four."

"Sami, I wish to speak with my men alone." Said the Duke. "Please wait in the adjoining room until I call you back."

Sami nodded and Boady showed him to the waiting room. The Duke sat silently, obviously deep in thought. "Why did you share the secret?" He finally asked.

This time Jon clearly indicated that Boady should answer. "He explained to me the circumstances behind the other dragons that he had slain." Said Boady sheepishly. "Apparently, what happened in Gaul was not so different from what has been happening here. He gains nothing from betraying us."

The Duke glared at Jon as if he were hoping that the confession would be his and was disappointed that it was not. "And why can't we pay him after the fact?" He said.

"That did not work well for him in Gaul." Replied Jon. "We need him to get this done."

The Duke got up and began to pace again. "Boady, kill him when the job is done." He said. "Let him be the dragon's last victim. Bring me back the money."

Boady looked shocked and hurt. Jon recognized a bit of the look Boady had when he was suffering from dragon sickness. Jon decided to answer: "He is not a fool." He said. "He would seem to be an experienced warrior. What if we can't?"

"Duty is not always pleasant, Sir Jon." Replied the Duke forcefully. "You must. Failure is not an option. Either I can trust you or I can't. Will you and Boady do your duty?"

The relationship between the Duke and Jon had deteriorated rapidly. Neither had much trust left in the other. In one sense it really did not matter how Jon answered.

"We will do what we can." Said the young knight eliciting a pained look from Boady. "As I said, he is not a fool."

The Duke gave Jon a hard and distrustful look. "Take the supplies and I will get you six gold pieces before you leave." He said. "Arrange a demonstration with the King, and then return here before you depart. You may leave through the waiting room."

The Duke left abruptly before either of the others could respond. Boady looked to Jon. "Don't worry, Boady." He said. "It is not our duty to steal justly earned money. Sami will get away."

The two went into the waiting room where Sami had become an interesting curiosity to the few children who were waiting, and a potential threat to those same children as far as their parents were concerned. Jon motioned for him to follow, and the three men went outside.

"Let me guess," said Sami, "he'll give you the money but you need to have the dragon kill me in a last valiant battle."

"It's like you were in the room with us." Replied Jon. "We won't do it, Sami. The Duke has more to lose than six gold pieces. You'll make it out alive."

"I wouldn't betray you, my friend." Said Boady looking him in the eye with a serious expression.

"I believe both of your intentions," said Sami, "but we must be on guard. Shall we gather some supplies?"

It took several trips to gather the needed supplies, and when they were gathered it was very clear that it was more than the three men could carry. "I'm not sure Thunder has ever been a pack horse." Said Jon. "He will be this time."

Sami showed them how to mix the ingredients and insisted that they be stored away from the house. Jon determined that he and Sami would make a trip to see the King the next day. When they had finished preparing, Jon let Sami try to ride Thunder, expecting the horse to shy away from him.

Sami approached the horse and spoke to him in his native language. Thunder responded well and he mounted without help or difficulty. He rode the horse gently around the house. "He is a fine horse." He said. "I should like to run him."

Jon gave his ascent and Thunder took off at a gallop. Truly Sami was a fine horseman; Jon had never seen Thunder so fast or so in control. They returned at a full gallop before Sami pulled him up at the last second and easily slid out of the saddle. "A very fine horse, Sir Jon." Said Sami. "You are a lucky man indeed."

Sami went to the garden and picked a carrot which he fed to the horse. Jon had not seen Thunder so comfortable with anyone but himself. He almost felt jealous. After the ride, the two put the horse in the stall after allowing him a long drink at the stream.

In the meantime, Boady had been carving the cross Jon had made for Carm into a far more ornate marker. "It's not done," he said, "but it is a bit more appropriate." The cross itself was much smoother than Jon had left it, but Jon detected the beginnings of a sculpture running up from the bottom of it. It clearly was not being made into a crucifix, but Jon decided not to ask.

The rest of the evening passed in pleasant camaraderie and uneventful peace. A message arrived advising them that the Duke would accompany them to the castle the next morning. The news did not seem significant. It had been a good day and the four occupants of the house slept well.

42

The Dragon Still has Life

THE DUKE WAS NOT PLEASED with developments. He felt that there was power in the dragon: the power to control Sir Jon and Boady. Now they had a plan to eliminate the dragon and he was powerless to stop it. In fact, he was expected to pay for their effort. More and more he felt that he should have killed Jon when he had the chance. Although the Duke did not consider himself an evil man, his heart had become as hard as stone.

"Fine, the dragon is to be slain," he thought to himself, "but I'll not lose money over it. And I will get Boady back to do my bidding."

As he was walking, he saw Aethelstan approaching. "Stan, I have a job for you." He said. "You may need Bif to help you. Let's talk about it."

The two of them sat down in the empty dining room. Aethelstan waited expectantly.

"Boady and Sir Jon have found a dragon slayer." Said the Duke. "The man dresses peculiarly and supposedly he has fire proof armor. He is in all likelihood a Moorish heathen and it seems unjust that he should take ten pieces of Christian gold as a reward for ridding us of a scourge that is no worse than he. I think you can do something about it."

"What can I do about it?" Asked Stan with interest. "Do you want me to take his armor and kill the dragon myself?"

"No, son, the dragon is a cruel and vicious beast and I do not want to expose you to it." Replied the Duke. "The way that they plan to kill the dragon is to make him explode. They will puncture his side with a spear while he is breathing fire. Apparently they believe that the dragon will ignite himself. When the dragon explodes, I want you to stop the foreigner and take the money. Sir Jon and Boady will be with him, so you need to stay covered, but the explosion will tell you where they are and you can set on them while they are still stunned from it. While I am not telling you to harm Sir Jon, if he or Boady were killed, we can blame it on the dragon. Don't let them stop you. Do you think you can do it?"

This was a big job, and Aethelstan relished the opportunity to prove himself capable and worthy of his father's trust. "I can get it done." He said. "I'm not sure how much help Bif will be. He is a good target archer, but I am not sure he could kill a man; he didn't loose a single arrow when we met the Kells. He might be more of a hindrance that a help."

"Stan, I've seen you fight, and you're very good." Said the Duke. "But I don't think you can take three men by yourself."

"I don't think I could take them with Bif either." He said. "I thought I only needed to kill one man. Boady is pretty good with those daggers."

The Duke was starting to have doubts about the plan. "I strongly suspect that Sir Jon and Boady will defend the heathen." He said. "The moor could be taken with a good arrow shot, but Sir Jon and Boady would fight for the gold. Let's let it be; it's too dangerous. Your life is worth more than ten gold pieces. Never mind, son. If I think of something else, I'll let you know."

Aethelstan was disappointed. He felt that this was the glorious and dangerous job for which he had been preparing all of his life. And his father had practically given him permission to kill his nemesis, Sir Jon. There had to be a way. The fact that the mission was dangerous was what made it worthy of his talents. He would figure something out.

Aethelstan spent much of the day wandering around pondering the task at hand. At one point he saw Thunder being ridden by a man in strange clothing. He assumed that he was the heathen that his father had told him about. It was hard to deny the quality of the rider or the horse as he watched them at a full gallop. "Godless scum." He thought. "Look at him riding what should be my horse!" He began to think of this as an opportunity to right all of the wrongs that he had recently suffered. He determined to find a way to make himself master of the situation.

"If only Boady wasn't there." He thought. That was it! Boady was his father's man. The Duke could order Boady not to go. He decided to bring this up as soon as he could.

That evening, the Duchess excused herself from dinner, so Aethelstan and his father ate alone. When the meal was over, Aethelstan dismissed the servants and told them to clean up later. The Duke was intrigued.

"Father, I have been giving the matter we discussed this morning more thought." Said Aethelstan. "I can do this alone if you simply remove Boady from the situation."

"Stan, I appreciate your eagerness," replied the Duke, "but I think it is best you put this out of your mind. I was wrong to bring it up. Besides, I don't have a good reason to insist Boady not join in the hunt."

"Come father," replied Athelstan, "now is not a time to be timid. Boady is your man. You are sworn to protect him as much as he is sworn to protect you. Should he really be exposed to the dragon again when he got dragon sickness the last time? You would be remiss to let him go. He could endanger their mission; who knows how he will react when he sees the dragon again. Why do they need him along anyway?"

Nobody had ever called the Duke timid. It hurt him to hear his son, of all people, do it. Then again, could Aethelstan handle the two remaining men? "What makes you think you can handle the other two?" He asked.

"I'll take the moor with an arrow before the fight has even begun." Replied the son. "The other does not even deserve the title of knight; he's never fought a battle. I can take him easily, and I will enjoy it. Sir Jon has stood against me every chance he could; it is only right that I remove this obstacle."

"Son, I would remind you that you have never been in battle either." Replied the Duke. "How has Sir Jon stood against you?"

"I'd have my knightly spurs now if not for him." Said the angry young man. "He first took my knighthood at the coronation, then stopped me from earning it against the Kells in the preserve, and now stands between me and the friendship of the King. Then, I was humiliated by having to serve as page to him, my inferior! He even took my horse! God only knows what filth he tells the King about me. He is jealous of my skill, and I aim to show him he has good reason to be jealous."

The Duke knew that most, if not all, of this was nonsense, but he understood how his son felt. Sir Jon was a natural rival and had bested Stan in every way that they could be compared. Perhaps his son deserved a chance to prove himself the better man. "I will consider it." He said at last. "Meanwhile, why don't you accompany me to the castle tomorrow to see the demonstration they plan for the King."

Aethelstan was gratified by the invitation. While his father had not agreed to his plan, he felt that things were going his way. In any case, it was rare for his father to include him in the Kingdom's business; perhaps he was finally gaining his confidence. Stan slept with dreams of glory that night.

Before going to bed, the Duke sent a messenger to tell Sir Jon that he and Aethelstan would be accompanying them to see the King. They were to meet at the stable the next morning. He then put Aethestan's plan out of his mind and slept.

The following morning the Duke had horses saddled for Boady and Sami. When they and Sir Jon arrived the party mounted and began the ride to the castle. Sami's horse was the smallest and poorest of the lot, and on it he seemed small in comparison to the Christian riders. Nevertheless, it beat walking. There was banter on the ride, but there was also a tension in the air. The party arrived before noon and were taken into the castle after the horses had been stabled.

The King and Father Leonis met them in the council chamber which had already been set for the mid-day meal. When the King entered, a large smile broke out on his face.

"Boady! It is good to see you!" He said. "How are you feeling? Lil and I were quite worried about you."

"I am feeling much better, your Majesty." Replied Boady. "The Lord has healed me and sent an answer to my prayers; that is why we are here to see you."

"Oh?" said the King looking to the Duke. "Tell me Uncle, what brings you here, although we are always pleased to see you."

"Apparently, Boady and Sir Jon have found a dragon slayer." Said the Duke. "They are here to explain what they intend to do."

"Good news, Sir Jon!" Exclaimed the King. "Tell me about it."

"Your Majesty, I would like to introduce you to Sami from a land called Sham that lies beyond the River Jordan in the Holy Land." Replied Jon. "Sami has some armor that can withstand fire and has slain dragons in Gaul. He has explained how to do it."

"We are pleased to meet you Sami." Said the King. "It is a shame that Brother Johan is not here as he has been to the Holy Land. Tell us, how can one kill this dragon?"

At the mention of Brother Johan's name there was a flash of recognition on Sami's face. He collected himself to reply. "Your Highness," he began, "the dragon's main weapon is its fiery breath, but it is also its main weakness. As Sir Jon said, I have armor that can withstand the fire. I will distract the dragon and get him to breath fire; when he does, Sir Jon will puncture his side with a spear, and the dragon's own breath will ignite him into a ball of flame. That, my Lord, is how you kill a dragon."

The King looked at Sami with a dubious expression. "You will burn the dragon in his own fire?" He asked. "What happens to Sir Jon when the dragon erupts?"

Sami and Jon looked at each other. They did not think that they would be questioned to this detail. "Slaying a dragon is not a safe thing to do, your Highness." Said Jon. "Once I puncture the dragon I will run, and hopefully I can get away with only a few burns."

The King looked concerned, but Father Leonis looked impatient. "Your Majesty, we must get on with our meeting." He said. "Sir Jon, the plan sounds rather sensational. You have armor that can resist fire? I have never heard of such a thing!"

"Yes, Father," replied Jon, "we can demonstrate it for you. If you would have a large fire built, Sami is prepared to don his armor and walk through it. I am quested to slay this dragon, and God has shown a way. Your Majesty, surely you can give us some time later this afternoon."

"See to it that a fire is built, and schedule our viewing, Father Leonis." Said the King. "Sir Jon must be given the chance to fulfill his quest."

"Yes, your Highness." Replied the priest. "Meanwhile, gentlemen, we must get on with our schedule. I will send someone to get you when it is time. We should be able to see it in two or three hours; I will have the fire started immediately. In the meantime, Sir Jon you have a suite of rooms to eat in and the kitchen is at all of your disposal. Please excuse us."

The five men were shown out while others were ushered in to meet with the King while they ate their mid-day meal.

The fact was that neither Jon nor the Duke wanted to spend time together. On Jon's part this was especially true since Aethelstan was around, so the party split. The Duke and Aethelstan insisted on taking Boady with them to eat, while Jon and Sami got some food in the kitchen and went to his room.

Sami laid out his armor and explained each part that he would wear.

"What is it made of?" Asked Jon.

"It is made of what the Greeks call Asbestos." Said Sami. "The fiber is mined from the earth and woven into cloth or even something thicker like this suit."

Jon noted that the suit was not all that thick, and was probably worthless against more conventional weapons. In that sense it was not armor at all.

Meanwhile, Aethelstan did his best to ingratiate himself with Boady. He asked him questions about the dragon and the sickness that he had experienced because of it, but Boady was reluctant to answer. Finally, the Duke asked Aethestan to stop.

"Stan," he said, "clearly Boady has been through a lot and does not want to discuss it. Let's give him some time to recover."

"Agreed." Said Aethelstan. "I am merely concerned for him. I am not sure he should go up against the dragon so soon after his last encounter."

The Duke grunted in response and Boady lowered his head, which gave Aethelstan the impression that he agreed with what had been said.

The fire was built in the main square, where criminals were generally executed. At first the town's people thought that a witch would be burned and discussion centered on who the witch was. When the fire was lit without a victim the town got into a fervor of excited speculation and a crowd began to gather.

The fire continued to burn and be fed more fuel until it was so hot that it was hard to get close enough to feed it further. After about two or three hours the word was sent that the demonstration would begin. The spectators stood reasonably far back from it since the heat was quite intense. The King, of course, was given a prime viewing spot along with the Duke and his party. Sir Jon escorted Sami into the square.

There was little preamble or drama associated with the demonstration. Sami walked up to the fire and circled it closely a couple of times. Despite the armor that he wore, the heat was uncomfortable. At last he went into the flames and kicked at a few of the burning embers. The crowd was in awe of what they saw, and many made the sign of the cross to ward off any of the devil's work that might be helping in the proceedings.

Sami emerged from the flames and bowed to the King. Aerdwulf was impressed and began to clap. The rest of the crowd imitated him and soon Sami was the beneficiary of a raucous round of applause.

"We would see you in our council chamber as soon as you can." Said the King to Sami and Jon. With that he turned to leave, and the crowd began to disperse. The Duke, Boady, and Aethelstan followed the King back into the castle, while Jon took Sami back to his chamber to remove the armor.

While they waited for Jon's and Sami's arrival, the King spoke to Boady. "How is Mistress Lil?" He asked. "I trust she is much relieved by your recovery?"

"She is her usual bright self, Majesty." Replied Boady. "Her ministrations of joy no doubt greatly aided my recovery. Of course, she sends along her greetings and good wishes to you."

The King blushed. "Thank you Boady." He said almost absent-mindedly. "She is a joy. To what do you attribute your recovery?"

"I now know God's grace as I never knew it before." Boady replied with great sincerity and seriousness. "Jesus has rescued me from my greatest tribulation. My hope is now fully in Him."

The others noted that Boady had not said any of this in the way one would usually address a King. He merely stated it as a matter of fact. For his part, Aerdwulf was intrigued and pleased by what he heard. It was good to know that one worshiped a God who can rescue us from our deepest sorrows.

Jon and Sami entered the room.

"Very impressive, Sami!" Said the King as they entered. "The fire was quite hot, surely it must have hurt."

"It was very hot, your Majesty." Sami replied. "It is not comfortable to walk through fire, and the heat alone can make it difficult to breathe, but as you can see, I survived."

"You did indeed!" Replied the King. "Sir Jon, when will you go and kill the beast?"

"Boady, Sami, and I plan to leave tomorrow." Said Sir Jon. "Hopefully we will find the beast quickly."

"Excellent!" Said the King. "You will be suitably rewarded on your return."

At this point Aethelstan interjected himself into the conversation. The King had been pleased that the Duke's son had been quiet up until then, but he barely controlled the urge to roll his eyes.

"Your Majesty," said Athelstan, "it concerns me that Boady should go along. He is just recovered from his last encounter with the dragon, it would be terrible for all of us and Mistress Lil if he was injured again in this battle. While Sir Jon is quested, it seems a needless risk to send Boady into harm's way again."

Aerdwulf was shocked; Aethelstan had made a good point! He was loath to risk someone so important to Lil if it could be done without him. It was bad enough that Jon would be going; did he need to risk her whole family? "Sir Jon, do you need Boady?" He asked. "It does seem like an unnecessary risk for someone who only recently was nearly destroyed by the dragon. Can Wil or someone else assist you?"

Jon was caught off guard and suspicious. It was very unlike Aethelstan to care for the wellbeing of someone else. What could he say? Strictly speaking Boady was not necessary, but Jon wanted him along.

"We may be able to do this without Boady." Said Jon. "His usefulness is in tracking the beast. We could use his help with that."

The King paused to think. Boady did seem to have a penchant for finding the dragon or its recent kills. Nevertheless, he had seen the shape Boady was in the last time he had found the dragon. He could not put Lil through that again. "We urge you to try to find the beast without Boady." The King said. "If you cannot, we can consider sending him back out a bit later. Boady is a most valuable part of our realm, and we do not wish to risk him unnecessarily."

Jon was stuck. "Of course, your Majesty." He replied while Boady looked on in shock.

"Good." Said the King. "Father Leonis, please make sure that Sir Jon has everything that he needs. Gentlemen, avenge my father. As much as we would like to visit, we greatly desire the dragon's demise."

The King turned to leave and Father Leonis came up to Jon. "Is there anything you need?" He asked quietly.

"No, Father." Said Jon distractedly. "I think we have matters under control." As he said this it occurred to him that for the first time since the plan had been concocted, things did not seem totally in control. Nevertheless, as desirable as Boady was, Sami and Jon could still get the job done.

While most of the party was grim and determined on the ride back, Aethelstan was ebullient. He felt that things were going his way, and that God was with him. Before long, the heathen and Jon would likely be dead, either killed by the dragon or by himself. He would be rich and vindicated.

The Duke kept his thoughts to himself, but he was worried. How could he regain control of his son? Did he even want to stop him?

43

The Measure of One's Worth

EVERYONE WAS TIRED WHEN THEY arrived back at the manor, but the Duke asked them to wait when he dismounted. He was gone a good bit of time, but when he returned he handed Sami six pieces of gold. "End this." He said bluntly and then turned to leave. He had determined to allow matters to take their course.

Having returned the extra horses, the three men walked back to Boady's house with Jon leading Thunder.

"Why would Aethelstan suddenly show such an interest in my wellbeing?" Asked Boady.

"I don't know." Replied Jon. "He must be up to something. Watch him Boady; make sure he doesn't try to interfere in some way. I doubt that the Duke would let him in on the secret, but Aethelstan will surely seek to share in what he sees as glory."

The three men and Lil had a late supper when they returned. They were grateful for the chance to wash up after a long day. Afterwards Boady went outside by himself. They assumed that he was going to visit Carm's grave, but when he came back he had a sack of money.

"There's a few silvers and a lot of copper, but it should be close to four gold's worth." He said looking at Jon and handing Sami a fairly large sack of coins.

"My friend," said Sami, "I take this with reluctance. I have no wish to take all of your money, but I need it as well. Thank you."

"Here is another silver and five coppers." Said Jon. "The King said he would reward us, and you deserve your pay. We will be alright; our faith is not in the money that we hold."

Suddenly, Lil came forward with two coppers. "If you need it Sami, here is the money that I have." She said. "I have everything I need right here."

Sami was genuinely touched. In Gaul, as in much of the world, money was never forthcoming; people did everything that they could to hold on to it. These people, however, seemed to have a treasure greater than gold. "Lil, I have enough money now." He said putting it away without counting. "You keep your coppers and try to get more so you may have a fine dowry when you get married."

"Are you sure?" Asked Lil sincerely. "This is all the money that I have, but it is not my treasure; my treasure lives in my heart. I don't even know what a dowry is. Is it something you wear when you get married? What does it look like?"

The men all chuckled when they heard this, and Boady reached out to gather Lil into his arms. "You're a treasure, my girl. You are worth far more than gold!" He said. "Keep your money, Sami has enough with what we gave him."

The men went outside to relieve themselves before going to bed. As they walked towards the woods Jon suddenly stopped. "That's what he wants!" He said.

"What are you talking about Jon?" Asked Boady.

"Aethelstan." Said Jon. "He wants the money. Sami said that in Gaul they tried to take his money after the dragons had been slain.

I bet that spoiled runt of the Duke's wants to take this money. Then he can say we died when the dragon exploded. Boady, you need to stop him."

It was a sensible explanation, and it also had the advantage of being basically true. But Aethelstan did not just want the money. He mostly wanted Jon dead.

"He got me out of the way so he could rob you." Said Boady. "He knew that I would hear his approach and probably kill him if he attacked. Don't worry, I'll keep a close watch on him. Until you return I plan to spend a lot of time with my new friend and benefactor."

Jon slept restlessly that night. It was not dreams that kept him awake, it was the excitement of fulfilling his quest. He had been through a lot of change recently, and this chapter of his life was about to end. What would be next? He also wondered if the dragon that never existed would ever die. Would the lie continue to live on?

After prayers the next morning, breakfast was a somber affair. Jon was tired, but also full of nervous energy. "We'll probably be gone a couple of days." He told Lil and Boady.

"I hope not." Said Boady in return. "I mean; I hope you find the dragon quickly. I will be watching and waiting here."

Jon understood that Boady had a tough job in keeping an eye on Aethelstan. It probably was better to just get this over with. The three men went outside to load supplies on Thunder. Jon saddled the horse and then loaded their belongings around it.

"Perhaps we should slay it tonight." Said Sami. "The Duke's boy may spend all day looking, but he will likely return after dark."

They agreed that this made a lot of sense. With grim determination Jon and Sami headed off to locate a suitable place to find and slay a dragon. Boady excused himself from Lil and went to visit the manor.

When he arrived, he found the grooms saddling Aethelstan's horse. "I'm going to saddle the horse I rode yesterday." He told them taking liberties. "The Duke wants me to check on some things." The grooms knew and trusted Boady so they let him proceed.

Aethelstan appeared fully armed and carrying a bow. He did not notice Boady until the forester was next to him on the horse he had saddled.

"Boady!?" Said Aethelstan. "What are you doing here so early?"

"I thought I would ride around a bit and check the grounds." Replied the surprisingly serious Boady.

"I was not aware that my father had given you liberties in the stables." Said the startled Duke's son. "Does he know about this?"

Boady was about to answer when the Duke came outside "Where are you going Stan?" He asked authoritatively.

Aethelstan looked at him a moment before answering. "Hunting father." He said pointedly.

The Duke noticed Boady sitting on a horse. "Boady, you go with him." He said. "Keep him out of trouble."

Boady nodded while Aethelstan scowled. He turned his horse and began to ride off. He determined that he would lose Boady somehow.

The usually quiet and serious forester was uncharacteristically glib on the ride. He asked Aethelstan about his studies and training at arms. He suggested that they go hunt away from the preserve as the game might be less wary. Finally, the young man had had enough.

"Why are you suddenly so interested in me?" He asked.

"I was quite taken by the compassion you showed me before the King." Said Boady. "I had never known that you cared so much about me. I relish this opportunity to get to know you better."

"You are a valuable part of this demesne." Replied Stan. "My father relies on you. I protected you the same way I would protect a valuable horse or cow."

Boady refused to take the bait. "You do treat your horses well." He said with a smile. "I appreciate knowing how much you value me."

When they stopped for a mid-day meal, Aethelstan refused to share his food. Boady picked some apples and offered to catch a rabbit to cook, but the young man refused. Boady then suggested that they try fishing for a while. The Duke's son became quite frustrated.

As the afternoon wore on he determined that they should go back to the manor.

"I don't know how you ever hunt successfully the way you prattle on." Said the exasperated Duke's son. "If you sought to gain my favor, you have failed miserably."

Boady smiled as they returned and made certain that the horses were unsaddled. Aethelstan went inside. Afterwards, Boady made a point of informing the Duke that his son had returned.

"I'll watch him." Said the Duke grumpily.

Aethelstan was glad that they had not heard an explosion. He hoped that the dragon would not be found that day and that he could escape after supper.

Meanwhile, Sami and Jon found that the preserve was hardly deserted. Apparently the Kells were desperate enough that they would risk a dragon to find food. As the day grew later less people were noticed and they found a spot to prepare for the killing. Their meanderings through the preserve had gotten Jon disoriented and he was unsure of where they were. Had he known, he would have been surprised at how close to the Duke's demesne they were.

As they laid out the mixture that Sami had prepared, they debated whether the fire proof armor needed to be worn. They decided against it. A fuse was laid and the dragon's head was placed close, but not too close, to the main collection of chemicals. The idea was for it to get burned, but not to lose it by having it destroyed or thrown into the brush by the blast. They then moved some distance away from the site to wait for dark and eat supper.

Back at the manor, the Duke and his family had begun to eat their evening meal. After supper, Aethelstan excused himself and returned to his room. The Duke decided to check on him shortly thereafter.

"Stan, I want to make it clear to you that I want you to forget the conversation that we had the other day." He said. "It's not worth it. Money is important, but there are many things that are more important: you being one of them."

The young man remembered what he had said to Boady and took his father's expression of love as a comparison to money. Was

411

he just another thing that the Duke owned? "Of course, father." He replied. "Your wishes are of the highest importance to me."

The Duke placed his hands on his son's shoulders. "I am proud of you my boy." He said. "You will be a fine knight and a great Duke someday. Be patient; your day will come."

Aethelstan gave him a smile in return. "Good night, father." He said. "Sleep well and I will see you in the morning."

The Duke uncharacteristically hugged his son and left. As he walked away he reflected on how negligent he had been in spending time with his boy. He determined to include him in more of his day to day activities.

Stan waited until the household had settled down and then began to arm himself. Quietly he slipped off into the stable and began to saddle his horse. Wren heard something and came to see what was happening.

"Good evening, Sir." He said cautiously. "Are you planning a night time ride?"

"That's none of your business." Snapped the irritated Duke's son. "Get this saddle on, will you?"

Wren finished saddling the horse. He was about to tell his master that he was done, when he was hit by the hilt of Aethelstan's sword. Wren was stunned, but unfortunately he did not fall unconscious. He was hit again and again until he finally lay unconscious on the floor of the stall. He was a bloody mess.

Aethelstan looked down on him and smirked. "You're not even worth a chicken." He thought to himself. He then got on the horse and rode off into the evening. He sensed that a world of opportunity lay before him.

It was finally dark, and the moment to kill the dragon had come. "The explosion will be loud and bright in this dark." Said Sami in warning. "We need to find someplace to hide when it erupts. Also, cover your ears tightly, and do not look at it. Make sure that Thunder is turned away from the blast and covered as well as he can be. Tie him tight, poor boy, he'll have it worse than us."

Jon nodded in assent. Sami lit the fuse and they ran for cover. Jon hid behind a tree, his back to the blast site, while Sami lay flat in a shallow depression covering his head and ears with his hands. The fuse did not burn quickly and Jon began to suspect that it may have burned out, but suddenly there was a tremendous blast and a blinding flash of light. Even though Jon had his back to it, the brightness momentarily blinded him, and the concussion of the explosion immobilized him and left him feeling battered when he regained some of his senses. Both had suffered minor burns from the heat, and had an intense ringing in their ears.

Aethelstan was also stunned by the large boom and bright light that erupted before him. His horse reared up and he only barely managed to stay in the saddle. He recovered quickly and as soon as he calmed his horse headed towards the glow that he saw not too far away. He hoped he would not arrive too late.

Boady and Lil heard the explosion as it shook their house. They immediately began to pray that Jon and Sami were alright. After a while they went outside and saw the glow of a fire burning. Boady considered heading off to check on them, and after a while he left on foot.

The Duke immediately ran to check on his son, and was mortified when he did not find him. As he was leaving for the stable some of the other stable hands brought the bloody and beaten Wren into the house.

"What happened?" Asked the Duke.

Wren was weak and disoriented, but he made a simple reply: "Aethelstan."

"One of you come with me to saddle Beast." Said the Duke in a hurried way. "The rest of you see to it that Wren is taken care of." He then hurried off to the stable expecting that someone would follow.

The Duke assisted as Beast was hurriedly saddled by him and one of the stable hands. He mounted and headed off into the night not knowing what he would do, but hoping that he would not be too late.

It took Jon and Sami a while before they became mostly functional again. The explosion had left a small crater and there were fires burning all around them. The first thing they did was check on Thunder. He was alright, but very stressed. Next, they went to retrieve the dragon's head; but it was not where they had left it. They split up to search for it, aided by the small fires that burned all around them.

Neither could hear particularly well, but they determined to split up and search the area. Both prayed that it was still intact. They hoped that it had not gone too far.

The search was neither quick nor easy, but it certainly had desperation. While being able to hear would not have allowed Jon to see any better, being largely deaf was disorienting. Perhaps he also would have noticed when Aethelstan rode up.

The Duke's son spotted Jon alone and intent on his search. Calmly he dismounted and took his bow. He was so consumed by his desire for murder that he did not notice how the fires were spooking his horse. The horse bolted as soon as it was free from its rider.

Aethelstan hardly noticed and cared less. He put an arrow to the string and aimed. He was tense, but determined not to miss, so he waited for a clear shot. Jon suddenly turned away and presented an easy target. Just as the unseen arrow flew he bent down to pick up the dragon's head. The arrow missed and lodged in a nearby tree.

Jon saw the arrow and dropped the skull to draw his sword. Aethelstan charged to close the distance with his own sword in hand. Jon parried the first stroke but was surprised by its strength; clearly Aethelstan knew how to handle a sword. Silently he prayed.

All Jon could do was block the sword that was repeatedly thrust and swung at him. His opponent had a calm look of intense hatred on his face. Jon dodged rather than met a stroke and swung wildly while Aethelstan was off balance; a large cut opened on the Duke's son's cheek. Jon had managed to draw first blood and that changed the dynamic of the fight. Aethelstan was now less confident, and Jon began to feel he had a chance.

The young knight pressed his attack slashing fiercely and forcing his opponent to give ground. Soon, however, Jon's arm began to weaken, and the ringing in his ears made it hard to maintain focus. A smile formed on Aethelstan's bloody face. He began to drive Jon backwards. The knight took side steps to help maintain his balance, but the Duke's son was striding arrogantly. He sensed that the kill was near.

As Jon backed up he kicked something out of his way. Athelstan did not see it and tripped. Jon pounced with all of his weight driving his opponent to the ground face first. He hammered his opponent's back and head with the hilt of his sword. Soon, Aethelstan ceased to struggle; he was unconscious.

Jon looked to see what had caused Aethelstan to trip; it was the dragon's skull. He realized how lucky he had been; by all rights he should have lost the fight. Still, it did not seem right to praise God at that moment. Instead, he used his sword to cut strips of cloth from Aethelstan's shirt and securely bound his unconscious foe. He then took the skull and went in search of Sami.

Sami had not been far away, but his hearing was also still suffering from the effects of the explosion. Jon motioned for Sami to follow him and they returned to where Aethelstan was just regaining consciousness. Sami was puzzled by what he saw, but as a soldier, he immediately checked the bonds that Jon had put on the prisoner. He cut more strips of cloth and made them more secure.

They took Aethelstan and the skull back to their camp where Thunder waited. Perhaps if their hearing had been better they may have managed to have a discussion on what to do next, but while they shouted as loudly as they could, they could not understand each other well enough to make a plan. Aethelstan was now awake and was also shouting at them, but he was easy to ignore in their current condition.

The shouting continued for some time, and eventually the Duke came near enough to hear it. He rode into their camp and took in the situation. "Sir Jon, have mercy on my son." He said calmly, but Jon could not hear him.

The two dragon slayers stared at the Duke mounted on his huge horse. They saw his mouth move, but they heard no sound. Jon drew his short sword and immediately held it to Aethelstan's throat. The Duke held out his hands to indicate that he meant them no harm, but Jon had already been attacked once that night and was not in a trusting mood.

He motioned at Sami who came near. He then shouted as loudly as he could: "Take Thunder and go!" Sami was not sure that he understood, but he brought the horse to Jon. The young man shook his head. He mimed that Sami should ride away.

Sami finally understood. Jon was giving him his horse to insure that he got away. A tear came to his eye, but he mounted and left. Before he was out of sight he returned and handed Jon a gold piece to pay for the horse. They both wished that they could say goodbye.

Jon was now alone with the Duke and his son, but he held a sword to Aethelstan's throat. Not being able to hear, it seemed like the three of them would be in for a long night.

44

The Executioner's Son

A S Boady hurriedly walked towards the preserve it occurred to him that he had no idea of why he was going. He supposed that he mainly wanted to make sure that his friends were alright, but what could he do if they were not? Nevertheless, he felt compelled to get there as soon as possible.

As he neared the edge of the preserve he came upon a tired and upset horse. As he came closer he recognized that it was Aethelstan's, and a sense of panic arose. He managed to catch it, and was aided in calming it by an apple that he found in his pocket, left over from lunch. When he mounted, it took a bit before the rider and horse began to work together. Clearly the horse did not want to reenter the preserve.

Fires were still burning, but they were starting to burn themselves out. As he progressed deeper he heard what he thought were voices shouting at each other and headed in that direction. Getting closer he thought he recognized the Duke's voice, but there were two other voices that he could not recognize.

He rode into the camp and everyone became still. He saw the Duke, still mounted on Beast, and Jon holding his short sword to the throat of a tightly bound Aethelstan. His initial reaction was joy that Jon was still alive, but then he wondered what had happened to Sami.

Ignoring the Duke, he addressed Jon. "What's going on, Jon," he said, "are you alright?"

Jon did not respond, but pointed to his ears.

Boady turned to the Duke. "My Lord?" He said. "Did the dragon try to kill again?"

"Aethelstan snuck off after supper." Said the Duke. "He beat Wren in the stable, and must have done something to Jon as well. Jon can't hear and seems intent on murdering my son. You have to calm him down."

Boady was surprised at how calm he felt. He got off of the horse and tied its reigns to a tree. "What happened to Sami?" He asked.

"Jon gave him his horse and he took off." Replied the Duke. "I think he thinks I came to kill him."

Boady had been subservient to the Duke for his entire life. It was not that they lacked a bond of friendship, but behind their mutual affection was always a sense of their place in society. This night, Boady understood that he served a higher Lord.

"And why did you come?" He asked.

"When I found out that Aethelstan had gone, I went in search of him." Said the Duke. "He is my son. Although I have not always been a good father, he is my son."

Boady was struck by the emotion that the Duke conveyed in what he said. There was humility in it; it was not the arrogant pronouncement of a man born to greatness.

Aethelstan was puzzled by what he heard. His father had always been demanding and in charge, but at this moment he seemed helpless and weak. What the son did not realize was that this apparent weakness had its source in the father's love for his child.

Boady walked up to Jon and looked at him. He noticed a small trickle of blood coming from his right ear. He smiled and reached out to take the sword from his hand. Jon was about to speak, but Boady put a finger to his lip. Jon gave him the sword.

"Now untie me!" Demanded Aethelstan.

Boady gave him a bemused look. "Horses do not untie their masters." He said.

"I'll have you flogged or executed for this!" Shouted the Duke's son.

Boady held the sword up to the boy's throat. "Perhaps." He said. "But only if you survive to see the morning."

Aethelstan looked stunned. The Duke knew how easily killing had come to Boady in the past and took the threat seriously. "He's my son, Boady." He said. "Don't kill my son."

Boady turned to look at the Duke. "Yes, he is your son." He said. "But what if he were my son? What if he were Kris' son, or Wren's? What if someone else's son had done the things that he has done? You uphold justice, do you not? What is justice in this case, my Lord?"

The Duke did not immediately answer; he looked down for a long moment. "I would ask for mercy, not justice." He said at last. "My son has done wrong, but I ask you for mercy."

"And if someone asked you for mercy, would you give it?" Asked Boady. "I have watched you render 'justice' out of impatience. Men always want justice until it is them on trial; then they want mercy. In any case, it is not my forgiveness that he needs; it is Sir Jon who was wronged. It is Sir Jon's mercy that you need. But he cannot hear you. It seems we will have to wait until he can. You may as well dismount, but keep your distance."

The Duke had no answer for this. While Boady had the power to free his son, it was not Boady's decision to make. The Duke also realized that were he in Jon's position he would not show mercy; justice seemed so much easier than mercy. Order was maintained through justice, but this was his son.

Before dismounting, he considered fighting for his son, but in his rush to find him he had come unarmed and unarmored; he was not sure he could defeat Boady alone, much less Boady and Sir Jon. He got down from the horse and took a seat on the ground.

Aethelstan despised the helplessness his father was displaying but held his tongue. If he were the Duke, he would have come with men and administered justice himself. Might made right; there was no room for sentimentality in this world. It did not occur to him that his father's weakness was rooted in his love for his son. He tried again to loosen his bonds.

Boady noticed this and rechecked them. He was impressed; the bonds were quite secure. "You won't get loose from them." He said to Aethelstan. "You'll probably make them tighter by trying."

Jon had been watching but could not hear what was said. He could tell that Boady seemed to have the situation in control, but he was frustrated that he could not participate in it. How could this be resolved? Aethelstan deserved to die for his crimes.

Boady got Jon's attention and signaled that he should try to sleep. The young knight was very tired, and he felt the fatigue of a body that needed healing as well. Nevertheless, the ringing in his ears and the others around him made sleep hard. He decided to pray.

He recited the 'Our Father' as he had read it in the Sermon on the Mount. When he prayed "forgive us our sins as we also have forgiven those who sin against us" he paused to think. Finishing the prayer, he remembered what came after it in the scripture that he owned: "For if you forgive men their transgressions, your heavenly Father will also forgive you. But if you do not forgive men, then your Father will not forgive your transgressions." (Matt. 6:14-15)

Jon knew that he had committed murder; perhaps he had only been following his duty, but he had murdered someone all the same. Had Aethelstan? He had tried to commit murder, but he had failed. Jon believed in God and His Word; did he believe enough to put belief into action? If he forgave Aethelstan, wouldn't he simply try to kill him again? Was the Duke's son worth saving? Jon prayed some more.

He began to drift towards sleep. But his mind and heart would not be still. He remembered things that he had heard while sitting bored in church: "Vengeance is mine, I will repay, says the Lord." (Rom 12:19) Did Jon want God to take vengeance for Wulf Schumacher? And then, a stunning verse came forth from his heart:

"But God demonstrates His own love towards us, in that while we were yet sinners, Christ died for us." (Rom 5:8) Jesus had not died for the good people; he died for sinners like Aethelstan, Boady, Duke Heimsteady, and Jon himself.

What was Aethelstan worth? He was worth the sacrifice of God's only son. Jon's heart tugged at him. He did not want to forgive Aethelstan, but if he had more than mere belief, if he had faith, he knew that he must. But what if he did not?

Jon's father had been the King's executioner; the son was in a position to carry on his father's work. Was he not his father's son? Jon had loved his father, but he did not want to carry on the family business. His earthly father was dead; Jon was now an adopted son in God's family. While he would never forget or regret where he had come from, he now had a new identity. He did not want to return to the past. "Jesus, give me the strength to forgive as you forgive." He prayed. Jon decided that he was no longer the executioner's son. He fell asleep while the other three remained awake awaiting to hear what he would say.

Jon slept deeply and late. The three other men became hungry. "There's food in my saddle bags." Said Aethelstan. "Get me some."

Boady looked disdainfully at the bound young man. "My Lord, would you mind getting us all some food?" He said.

The Duke went to the saddle bags and pulled out some cheese and bread. He broke off a piece of each and tossed the rest to Boady. Boady ate slowly wondering if he should feed his prisoner.

Aethelstan was seething. "Well, what about me?" He said.

"I suppose that the condemned deserve a final meal." Said Boady calmly. He then stuffed a large piece of bread into the bound man's mouth.

"Boady, please." Said the Duke plaintively.

Boady got up and held his sword before him. "You can feed him, but I will be watching." He said. "You know that I will kill you both if I feel that I must. It would be my duty, and I always do my duty; pleasant or not."

The Duke began to feed his son smaller morsels of food being careful to not make any questionable moves.

"Father, attack him." Whispered Aethelstan. "You are a Duke. You're bigger and tougher. He won't dare to raise a hand against you."

The Duke did not whisper his response; he spoke loudly and clearly: "Stan, you don't seem to realize what you have done." He said. "I have sent Boady to kill countless people and he has done it, not for justice, but for me. If I were armed I might stand a chance, but probably not a good one. Your life, our lives, are in his and Sir Jon's hands and yet you feel no remorse! I have failed you as a father."

"Then just leave." Said Aethelstan. "What good is a Duke if he cannot exercise power?"

The Duke looked crestfallen. "I can't leave." He said. "My only son is in mortal danger. While I don't know what I can do, I have to try to save him. I may have failed you in so many ways, but I cannot desert you now."

Aethelstan was stunned by what he heard. He had always had a sense of destiny; a sense that he could do no wrong since he had been born to greatness. He found it difficult to grasp that his fate was in the hands of an executioner's son and a peasant who served his father's demesne. "How can you be so weak?" He asked.

"You are my weakness." The Duke responded. "If you had not gotten involved; if I had not involved you, we would all be fine. I tried to be strong of my own will. I tried to take control of the world and bend it to my ways, but I am not a god. Even a Duke cannot create reality. I sense that the only thing that can save you now is if I humble myself and beg for your life."

"They can't get away with killing me." Said Aethelstan. "If they do you will surely avenge me."

"They could kill us both and blame it on the dragon." Said the Duke. "Who's word would stand against a Knight of the Realm and the King's best friend? Who would even speak for us? Wren?"

The seriousness of the situation began to sink in to Aethelstan. His birth would not save him. He vowed to himself that if he got out of this he would have his vengeance. Fortunately, Sir Jon was known for being kind hearted. Aethelstan was confident that his destiny would be fulfilled.

As Jon awoke, he heard the muffled sound of conversation. The ringing in his ears had diminished, although it was still there. "I think I can hear a little." He announced more loudly than was necessary.

Boady rushed over to him. "Jon, can you hear me?" He said loudly and slowly.

"Yes, Boady, I can!" Responded Jon in an equally loud voice.

"What happened?" Asked the elated forester.

"Aethelstan tried to kill me." Jon shouted. "He missed with an arrow and then came after me with his sword; but he failed."

"Where was Sami?" Asked Boady.

"We were separated and neither of us could hear." Came the reply.

The Duke stepped up to Jon. "Sir Jon." He said. "Have mercy on my son. You have been wronged by him and by me, but be a greater man than we are; spare his life as I once spared yours."

Jon was struck by the humility that the Duke was showing. It helped him in his determination to forgive as he had been forgiven. He took the sword from Boady and walked over to Aethelstan. "And what do you have to say for yourself?" He said.

Finally, Aethelstan came to grips with the fact that he was a condemned man without defense. He faced the executioner's son holding a sword in his hand. He became afraid, stammered, and suddenly wet himself.

"Have you nothing to say?" Asked Jon loudly.

The Duke came over to him. "Don't let the dragon take another life." He said. "It is dead; you killed it. Forgive him."

Jon turned to look at the Duke. "He will only try to kill me again." He said. "I have a new identity; I am no longer the executioner's son, but what if he lives? What will he do with his life?"

"I don't know." Said the Duke honestly. "I suppose I can send him away. Keep the money, take his horse, but spare his life. I will be responsible for him."

"I don't want or need your money, or his horse." Said Jon. "There is nothing you can give me for his life. How can you be responsible for him? If you send him away he will come back. He needs to ask forgiveness."

"I won't grovel before you!" Shouted the accused. "I will die like a man if I must." Generally speaking, brave men do not sit in their own piss while making such statements, but Aethelstan still could not understand his guilt.

"Boady, see if there is a rope in Aethelstan's belongings." Said Jon. "An executioner's son learns how to hang an unrepentant criminal. I've never done it myself, but I am told that death can come slowly or quickly. We'll see which it is to be today."

The Duke became panicked. "Stan! Ask for forgiveness!" He pleaded with his son. His boy seemed at a loss for words.

Boady brought some rope and Jon began to fashion a noose.

"Stan, all you have to do is ask forgiveness!" Pleaded the Duke. "How can you let a false sense of pride condemn you?"

"I will not humble myself before him." Shouted the proud condemned man.

Jon paused what he was doing. "Then don't." He said. "I am not a greater man than you. Confess to God. Ask Him for forgiveness. I will not judge where God has forgiven."

This elicited no response from the bound man. Jon walked over to him and gave him a long look. He put the noose around his neck and tightened it. Aethelstan looked at him with wide eyes. Jon slung the rope over a nearby branch. It took several tries, but it was finally looped.

"Help him to his feet, Boady." Said Jon. "I'm afraid we're going to have to hoist him up, so I suspect it will be a slow death. My Lord, you may leave if you wish; there is no need for you to witness this."

"Please Sir Jon!" Shouted the Duke. "Spare him for my sake!"

Jon ignored him and began to tighten the rope.

Boady noticed that it was highly unlikely that Jon would have the strength to pull him up himself. "Shall we tie the rope to his horse?" He asked.

"No." Said the executioner's son. "I can do it."

The rope was tightened and Aethelstan began to gag. Tears came to his eyes. He emptied his bowels. It did not seem that he was dying like a man. "Forgive me!" He rasped in a voice too quiet for Jon to hear.

"I think he is trying to speak, Sir Jon!" Said Boady in a loud voice.

Jon gave the rope some slack and handed it to Boady.

He walked over to the condemned and weeping man. "Did you say something?" He asked.

"Forgive me!" Cried Aethelstan loudly.

"What should I forgive you for?" Asked Jon.

"I tried to kill you. I have lived as if the world and everything in it belonged to me. I have mistreated so many people, not just you. I have disrespected my father and my King. I am guilty and deserve to die, but I beg forgiveness." Came the sobbing response.

"And who am I?" Asked the executioner's son.

"You are Sir Jon, a Knight of the Realm." Cried a confused Aethelstan. "The man who holds my fate in his hands."

Jon motioned for Boady to make the rope slacker. "I am that," He said, "but I am also the executioner's son, and a guilty and condemned man like you. I cannot judge you because I only live by God's grace. Foremost, I am the least in the adopted family of God. Accept His mercy if you want true forgiveness. You have mine."

The Duke and Boady were stunned by what Jon had said. Aethelstan continued to cry.

"Let him go, Boady." Said Jon. "We need to go and see the King."

Jon went to pick up his belongings, the dragon's head, and a bit of left over bread. Boady joined him and the two walked away leaving the Duke with his son.

45

God Helps Those
Who Need Him

I T WAS A BEAUTIFUL LATE Summer's day as Boady and Jon walked towards town and the castle. The birds were singing, but Jon could not hear them. Although he could understand Boady if he spoke loudly and slowly, the sound was muffled; still, it was an improvement over the immediate aftermath of the explosion.

"I'm not sure you will be welcome back at the Duke's estate." Said Jon loudly to Boady.

Boady put a finger to his lips to indicate that he could hear just fine. "We shall see." He replied. "Lil is a favorite of the King, and the Duke and I have been a team for a long time; perhaps it will work out. At least you didn't kill his son."

"I couldn't have done it." Said Jon trying to speak more softly. "How can I judge him? Both of us have committed terrible sins and can only live with ourselves because of God's grace and forgiveness.

426

Could I deny that to someone else? Still, there was a part of me that wanted him dead."

"I wonder if you won't get the chance." Boady replied. "Sometimes facing death will change a man, but I have my doubts about him. I suspect that he hates you even more now."

"You know," said Jon, "there is no way I should have been able to beat him in our fight. I couldn't hear even as well as I can now, and he is a good swordsman while I barely know how to hold a sword. I was either very lucky, or someone greater than me fought for me."

"You mean like a guardian angel?" Asked Boady. "I think you're better than you think."

"Maybe an angel or something," said Jon, "but I'll give the glory to God. We have free will, but God also guides our steps. Think of what has happened to me these past weeks; did I earn any of it? Everything I am is because of God. Even if I do have a skill or talent, it is only because God gave it to me. I think I am less than you think."

"That's a good way to look at life." Said Boady. "I think you better get trained in fighting, though, remember that God helps those who help themselves."

"You know, Boady," Replied Jon stopping to look at him, "you have that all backwards. God helps those who need Him, and we all need Him. I think I should get better with a sword as well, but Aethelstan's skill did not win him the fight. Ultimately, it is better that I rely on God. I can't earn Him, and I can't buy Him; I have to accept His love and my place in His family as an undeserved gift."

The two walked on in silence for a few minutes. Jon broke the silence with a proposition: "Boady, I need someone to train me in fighting, and you are the best I know." He said. "I doubt you will be alright staying at the Duke's demesne and I could use a page. Why don't you and Lil move in with me at the castle."

Boady smiled. "I'm a little old to be your page, aren't I?" He said. "Lil and I are important where we are; some people wouldn't make it through the Winter without us. Beyond that, the King and Lil look forward to seeing each other because they are not seeing each other all of the time. That relationship is odd enough as is; I don't want to set her up for a broken heart. Sir Bendris and Wil can train you."

Jon did not know what to say as everything Boady had said was true. "I guess it's all in God's hands any ways." He said as they approached the outskirts of town. "I guess it has been all along."

As people saw Jon and Boady entering the town they came out to stare. Jon held up the dragon's head and their walk became a procession with people cheering on all sides as they came to the castle. The head had become somewhat mangled in the explosion with some of it charred by fire and other skin blown away, but this only made it appear more authentic.

Jon heard the cheering and applause as muffled noise that made it impossible for him to make out any particular sound. One might say that it totally deafened him once again. The King met them before the castle and spoke, but Jon heard none of it. He stood silently as everyone looked at him. After a short pause, Boady stepped forward to explain the situation and they were shown inside and taken to the relative quiet of the council chamber.

There was little ceremony in this meeting as the King came to stand before Jon and shouted: "You did it Jon! You avenged my father!"

The young knight did not know what to say. He knew that he had not in fact done that. While he hoped that the dragon had been slain, it had been created by Wulf's father's death; it was not the cause of it. He smiled and handed the head to the King.

The King marveled at what he now held. "What a fierce looking beast!" He exclaimed. He then looked at Boady as a thought occurred to him. "Why are you here Boady? I thought you were instructed not to go? Where is Sami?"

"I did not go, your Majesty." Said Boady. "When I heard the explosion I could not contain myself and went to check on Sir Jon. It was good that I did. He was entirely deaf when I found him although he has some hearing now. Jon gave Sami his horse and he fled some difficulty that they encountered."

The King turned back to Jon. "What sort of difficulty caused Sami to flee?" He shouted.

"Bandits, my Lord." Said Jon. "We were in no condition to fight so I told Sami to flee. I think he is OK. Boady arrived to rescue me."

"Sami fled not even wanting his reward?" Asked the King loudly.

Boady and Jon looked at each other before the young knight answered. "The Duke, Boady, and I paid him before the mission." He said. "Sami had been denied his reward in Gaul. I believe he is heading back to his home in Sham."

The King's response was too quiet for Jon to hear, but Father Leonis, Sir Bendris, and Boady heard it clearly enough: "You did that for me?" He took a step back and sat down in a chair deep in thought. Getting back up he walked up to Jon and shouted: "How much did you pay him?"

Jon thought the King was angry with him, so he hesitated to answer. "Ten gold." He said shyly at last.

"You shall have your ten gold back, and five more." Declared the King. "Also, Sir Bendris, see to it that Sir Jon is given the finest horse in our stable; but not Mayflower."

Father Leonis looked shocked. Fifteen gold pieces was a huge sum of money! Sir Bendris merely stifled a laugh as he knew that Mayflower was nowhere near the finest horse that the King owned.

"Thank you, your Majesty." Replied Jon. "While I honestly would appreciate being able to pay Boady and Duke Heimsteady the ten gold pieces that they mostly paid, no further reward is required for me completing my quest."

Father Leonis leaned over and whispered something in the King's ear. The King looked up at him annoyed. "Very well, Sir Jon, but you shall have the horse as well. Is there anything else you desire?" He shouted.

"I should like to train with the guard, you Majesty." Replied the Knight. "I need to learn how to fight better."

The King turned to look at Sir Bendris.

"That can be easily arranged after you have recovered." Shouted the Captain of the Guard.

There was a moment of silence as nobody knew exactly what else to say. "Have the dragon's head displayed for the people." Commanded the King. He then walked closer to Jon and said loudly enough for him to hear: "Welcome home, Sir Jon. I look forward to seeing you at evening prayers."

CPSIA information can be obtained
at www.ICGtesting.com
Printed in the USA
FSOW02n1413131216
28309FS